SARA A. NOË

Happy Reading!

A
Fallen
Hero

Sara A. [signature]
07.02.22

CHRONICLES OF AVILÉSOR
- WAR OF THE REALMS -
BOOK I

Text Copyright © 2017 by Sara A. Noë
Library of Congress Control Number: 2018910180
All rights reserved.

Printed in the United States of America

First edition, 2018

"You Are My Sunshine" by Jimmie Davis
Copyright © 1940 by Peer International Corporation
Copyright Renewed. Used by Permission.
All Rights Reserved.

Cover font: Black Asylum by Kevin Christopher // KC Fonts
Used by Permission.

Hardcover ISBN 978-1-7325998-0-2
Paperback ISBN 978-1-7325998-3-3
E-book ISBN 978-1-7325998-4-0

Cover design and print layout by Sara A. Noë
E-book layout by Polgarus Studio

"Noë's excellent plotting and highly engrossing narrative grab hold of readers' interest from the first page and keep them engrossed. The characterization shines as Noë skillfully takes readers into the intriguing supernatural world as Cato and his lab family make their harrowing escape. A superb debut!"

- The Prairies Book Review

"So many elements to love . . . the layered world building, the distinct and compelling POVs (villains included!), the harrowing conflicts Cato must battle through—and, of course, the found-family bond between him and his lab-siblings, which is such a powerful presence throughout the story. Don't be surprised if you say 'one more chapter before bed' and find yourself closing the cover at dawn."

- NAM Editorial

". . . *A Fallen Hero* blurs the line between science-fiction and fantasy, adding paranormal elements and beings into a war-torn world . . . Noë's tactful narrative and deeply layered plotting offer a unique world that readers can fully immerse themselves in to walk alongside heroes and villains. Page by page, this debut novel will hold readers' attention until the very end, presenting just enough resolution to leave them satisfied while unanswered questions will have them pining for more."

- Chronicle Focus Editorial

Dedicated to the teachers who awakened my passion for writing
and guided me down this cobblestone road:

LeahRae Harris
Martha Snyder
Lorraine Tighe
Greg Fruth
Sharon Solwitz
Jo Pilecki
Roger J. Kuhns

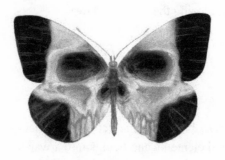

with a special dedication to a dear friend
who was always a lighthouse in the dark:

Sue Spitler

SARA A. NOË

A
Fallen
Hero

CHRONICLES OF AVILÉSOR
- WAR OF THE REALMS -
BOOK I

— Prologue —

Voices.

They rolled together like waves crashing on a rocky shore. White waves of white noise. If I squinted at a woman's lips, I could make out the word *Phantom*. It was repeated so often I could believe it was the only one spoken, an unceasing, eerie murmur of "Phantom, Phantom, Phantom . . ."

My gaze passed over the sea of faces saying *Phantom* in rushing whispers that made the air hiss like wind tearing through wild grasses. Eyes bored through me while I stood still, blinded by quick, bright flashes from cameras. Dizziness created fuzzy edges; that last blow to the head had rattled my brain. Time was a curious clash of too slow and too fast—people trailing by at a crawling speed but appearing as nothing more than a blurred streak of motion in my vision.

Behind me, the stark white spire of City Hall's clock tower stabbed the cobalt sky. The building was set at the back of an open cobblestone plaza flanked on either side by a covered walkway along the fronts of shops and cafés. Cables stretched across the plaza, suspending lights above our heads; at night you'd swear they were floating. The far side of town square was penned in by a row of trees separating the central fountain from Main Street.

The plaza was large enough to host several thousand, and City Hall's portico formed a perfect stage for a speaker to stand atop the steps and address a crowd. Today, though no event was scheduled, the square was packed.

I was the one standing on the portico.

The people watched me warily, as if I'd suddenly transformed into an unrecognizable animal that might attack at any moment. Today, I was, whether I wanted to be or not, the center of attention.

A sleek black vehicle had been parked near the portico steps. It was

1

an armored truck, the back completely enclosed from the cab to keep anyone or any*thing* secure. The back doors had been thrown open, waiting to swallow a victim. On either side of me stood a man dressed in white. My two guards were bigger than me in every aspect—height, bulk, strength. But to be fair, I'd never been the strongest or tallest in my grade: an average-sized teenager, lean and lanky while my coordination caught up to my growth spurt, and I noticed this now more than ever in the shadows of these sturdy, broad-chested men.

They'd taken one person away. I didn't know her name, probably never would. She'd already killed at least five innocent people by the time I realized I couldn't stay in hiding and let anyone else die. I'd known it was a bad idea to act with Agent Kovak in town, but there had been no choice.

I'd lain low for as long as possible. I was just a few feet away from her when I donned my mask and uncapped the warm power in my core that made my eyes glow—one green, one blue. By the time she sensed me in her range, I'd already thrown the first punch.

In retrospect, I suppose I should have handled it differently. I should have ended the fight quicker, but I'd managed all these months without killing anyone. I didn't want to start today. Would it have been so wrong to kill a killer? Surely God would have forgiven me.

But I didn't. I held back. I gave her a chance to return to her home Realm, and she seized that opportunity to slam my head into the wall hard enough to blacken the edges of my vision. I didn't actually see the shot that downed her, but it must have come from Agent Kovak's ecto-gun. His men were on us like a swarm.

She spat, cursed, and kicked when they dragged her into the back of another black vehicle. Nobody stopped them. I wasn't sorry when the men closed the doors on her blood-splattered face and drove away. The only reason I was still here right now and not on my way to God-only-knew-where was I had loved ones fighting for me.

The cords cut into my skin, restricting the circulation to leave my hands cold and tingling. I curled and straightened my fingers. *Focus on the numbness. Don't focus on the crowd, the voices, the cameras. Focus*

2

on the little details. That was all I could do to keep my head from spinning.

I felt . . . strange. Empty. Like every bit of warmth and substance in my core had been scooped out and all that was left of me was a hollow shell since the Agents secured this metal band around my upper arm. When they'd found me lying on the ground, they had yanked my right arm back so hard I was sure the socket would pop. I was still reeling from the pain when they jammed the neutralizer over my biceps and twisted it into place before hauling me to my feet.

Now, I couldn't concentrate. My thoughts were scrambled. My body was drained.

I shifted my weight, and the men tensed. Where did they think I was going to run? I doubted I could even walk in a straight line. I glanced up at them, but they resolutely stared ahead and refused to meet my gaze.

I'd like to say I'd been in worse situations, but at the moment none came to mind. That was okay, though. This was just a huge misunderstanding. I couldn't be in trouble; I hadn't done anything wrong. Technically. Yes, I made mistakes, but it wasn't like I ever broke the law—just told a few lies. Okay, *big* lies, but last time I checked, that wasn't illegal.

The girl standing at the front of the crowd made my heart skip a beat. She was the only still person in this motion-sickness blur of forms. Her emerald eyes were trained on my face, looking at someone she thought she knew and now realized was a total stranger. I had the sudden, ridiculous, and—given the current circumstances—inappropriate thought that I'd never kissed her. Now I'd probably never have the chance.

People continued to murmur droning waves of nonsense while they snapped pictures of me, their unmasked hero, the freak who had been hiding among them pretending to be normal. A few angry, desperate voices rose above the rest, perfectly clear over the white noise because I'd known them since birth. "He was born human!" Mom cried, her voice cracking with strain. "He should be protected by human rights!"

3

Agent Kovak shook his head while adjusting the shades on his nose. "Humans can't do the things your son can. And ghosts, as you well know, have no rights in this Realm."

"But he's half! That should count for something!"

Kovak bared his teeth in what might pass as a cruel smile. "It doesn't."

"But I can prove he's human! I have his birth certificate!"

"Doesn't matter," he said with a casual shrug. "Last time I checked, humans couldn't turn invisible and walk through walls. He's not human anymore."

I caught my breath. *No.* No, he was wrong. I'd lived my human life in the Human Realm. I kept my jaw clenched so tightly it hurt to ensure no words could escape, though all I wanted to do was scream.

Screaming is bad.

Don't scream.

Oh, my head hurt. "I have to take him . . ." Kovak was saying.

I swayed, and the men on either side grabbed me with rough hands to hold me up. Mom cursed—something I'd rarely heard in the fifteen years of my life—and shot back a vile retort at Kovak. As they argued, my eyes followed my sister sneaking behind my guards. She slid something into my pocket.

"Don't forget," she whispered.

The Agents noticed her and yanked her away from me with enough force to make her yelp. "Hey!" I took a hostile step.

They turned in on me, and then wordlessly, each grabbed an arm and hoisted me up. The blurry, slow-motion time frame snapped back into real-time the moment my soles left the concrete. They were carrying me toward the armored vehicle. The doors were still open. Waiting.

"No!" I kicked and squirmed, just as desperate to avoid that vehicle as the woman before me. I'd rather be in handcuffs in a police cruiser; at least I'd know what to expect in a normal human prison, and I'd know I have rights. "Wait! *Wait*! Mom! What's happening?"

"Shut up," the one on my left growled. They threw me inside.

4

"Cato!" Mom called.

"What will you do to him?" my sister asked as she backed out of their way.

Agent Kovak turned his back on Mom. One of his men pushed her to her knees, twisting her arms behind her. Kovak strolled to the truck to gaze greedily down upon me, as though I were a rare treasure he'd unearthed. He smiled. "Whatever we want." He lowered his voice, his next words meant for me alone. "You, my young friend, are going to make my career."

I rolled over and pushed myself onto my elbows just in time to see Mom twist free and shove Agent Kovak away. "I'll come get you, Cato! Be strong. I'll get this mess straightened out."

I trusted her. I was scared, but soon, I hoped, this ordeal would be over. I'd have to face a flood of consequences, but I'd rather do that than endure an interrogation and likely dissection under Agent Kovak's steely watch.

The doors were closing. A surge of panic shot through me, a petrifying fear that this would be the last time I saw their faces. "Wait!" I yelled again.

"I love you!" my sister called out. "Don't ever forget!"

With a slam, the outside world vanished, and I was sealed away in absolute darkness.

Two years later

— Chapter One —

Wind

The truck jolted, sending the cages sliding into each other. I gritted my teeth and squeezed my eyes shut, as if that might somehow quell the pain that ripped my head apart.

It didn't. Nothing could, and *They* never gave me any drugs to numb the never-ending headaches. I'd swear I could still feel the thick needles of the neural monitoring system penetrating the ports in my skull. The NMS was *Their* favorite experiment. It was my nightmare— my freedom and manacle, the price that must be paid to be allowed in the Arena.

What I wouldn't give to be standing in the Arena now with Jay, RC, and Ash. My joints ached, muscles stiff, and my body tingled with a numbness brought on by limited blood circulation in this cruelly small cage. I rubbed the round ports spanning across my forehead and tried to focus my thoughts on something—*anything*—other than my current predicament. I could pray, but I'd lost my faith in God a long time ago.

The truck lurched, drawing a grunt from my throat. The motion exacerbated the throbbing in my head. *Lucky Axel for being sedated through this nightmare.* I exhaled, curling my fingers through locks of hair, twisting, pulling until the tiny pinpricks of pain that sparked across my scalp lessened the deeper pounding ache. I needed to focus on something, but I had nothing, not even memories. Trying just frustrated me; my recollection of my old life had been ripped slowly from my consciousness over time by the NMS. All that remained were murky, fragmented glimpses.

I opened my eyes and studied the dim interior. The last time I was in a truck, I was alone, my hands tied in front of me while I cowered in the dark. This time, I was not bound, just caged. And I wasn't alone.

The others were dozing, except the twins. They blinked at me in the darkness, their blue eyes aglow. Axel, who was locked in the metal container next to me, had been so heavily dosed with tranquilizers that he'd be out for hours. Next to him, a muzzled black-and-white kitten was crammed into the tiniest cage. Her fragile body rose and fell with the quick, shallow breaths of a nightmare as she flexed her claws.

I could hear wind. The Outside was just on the other side of the truck's wall. I'd never been so close to it, and the dismal reality that I couldn't smell the fresh air made me feel cheated. One breath, that was all I wanted. Air that wasn't sterilized and stale.

I wasn't cold, but I shivered anyway and wrapped my arms around my bare torso, trying to remember the comfort of an embrace. Unless I was in the Arena, all I was allowed to wear were black sweatpants and the neutralizer band around my right biceps. Sometimes I couldn't even wear sweatpants.

They weren't watching us, and I trusted the twins not to tell *Them*, so now was one of the few times I could uncover my whisper.

I pondered that word before I moved. *Whisper.* Proof that I'd been fully assimilated. It was RC's word, now embedded into my vernacular as well. A whisper was a secret confined to a small group of trusted people. A true secret never passed through the keeper's lips. We didn't have many secrets in Project Alpha, mostly whispers. Secrets weren't safe in eroding minds.

Squirming in my confinement, I shifted my body enough to extract a folded photograph from the small hole inside my waistband. It was a miracle I'd managed to keep it hidden for so long. Without the help of Finn and Reese, it would have been taken from me and destroyed.

It had aged since the day my blood-sister slipped it into my pocket. The surface was crinkled and permanently creased, the edges bent, a corner torn. The ink had faded after a few cycles through the wash, but the twins always managed to find it and return it to me. I ran my thumb across the bleached surface.

My counterpart was laughing in the picture. Strange, that I once knew how to laugh. My laugh might be broken now; I hadn't had a reason to try to revive it. I wondered if I still resembled this version of myself. I hadn't looked at my reflection in a mirror since . . . Before. How long ago was that?

My fingers drifted up to trace the edge of my sunken eye socket and trail down my sallow cheek. If I ever had the opportunity to look at my own face again, I guaranteed it wouldn't match the full, healthy, sun-touched face in the picture I held before me.

My blood-sister's eyes sparkled as she beamed at the camera. I had the image imprinted into my mind, so whatever *They* did to me, however many times the NMS penetrated my brain, I would not forget her face.

Saying her name hurt too much, so I didn't. I tried to recall what her voice sounded like, but how could I possibly remember? I didn't even know how long I'd been a captive where the only possible escape was death, and *They* wouldn't allow that until *They* decided you were no longer valuable enough to live. Then you'd be sent to Project Omega. Prisoners who went into that Project never came back out. Someday I'd make that journey, and I dreaded it because everyone knew *They* dissected ghosts alive on that terrible floor of death. Finn and Reese confirmed that rumor. They didn't know how to lie.

I refocused on the photograph to take my mind away from my inevitable future. We did look like a family back then. Dark hair, same noses, same eyes. Three people occupied the snapshot of my old life, and yet rather than focus on the third, I noticed who wasn't there. I didn't know what to call him. *Father, Dad*—those words had drastically different meanings. Father, the man who sired me, or Dad, the man who raised and loved me? I didn't know why he wasn't in this picture. I remembered absolutely nothing about him, so I supposed I must call him Father.

My mother was standing behind my blood-sister and me in the picture, her smile reserved but genuine. She loved me when she thought I was human.

"I'll come get you, Cato!"

9

But she didn't. She never came. Never visited. I never heard from her again after Lastday. I hated her with such deep passion that I could feel my destructive Divinity stir.

Backstabber. Traitor. Liar.

Heat. I felt the change strongly enough to know that my eyes, normally one blue and one green, both flared green in the darkness just for a moment as my power peaked in rage. And then the neutralizer contained it deep in my core again.

I'd suffered plenty of time in my prison to nurture the festering hatred. She loved her money and her career more than she did the monster that was me. So, here I was, on the way to more torture. *They* would have brand-new, expensive equipment to use on us. New pain.

I closed my eyes again as the truck heaved.

My days of waiting to be rescued were long over. I'd finally given up, and the resulting depression nearly killed me. Slowly, I'd clawed my way out of despair to endure my new life of captivity. Of white walls and linoleum floors, sterilized rooms, sharp instruments and needles, the cold metal bars of my cage, the taste of blood, the heat of electricity, and a man's voice saying, "Begin."

The roar in the background was maddening. I closed my eyes to listen. Wind. The sound reminded me of a fan, but it was more exhilarating because I knew it had to be real. We must be flying over the asphalt.

My chest ached. The steady beat against my rib cage accelerated.

Outside. I was supposed to believe it was a myth, but I knew that wasn't true because I came from there.

Now, I tempted myself with the dangerous and forbidden thought of escape, which *was* a myth. That fact had been beaten into me. There was only one way in and out. A single guarded door led to the extensive maze of tunnels that, if you knew the right course, could take you aboveground to the Outside. But the only prisoners who ever made it *out* that door had already been cremated in Project Omega. No exception. Not a single one had ever walked out alive—only ashes scattered unceremoniously across the prairie.

Each Project occupied one level, and each level could be individually sealed to contain disasters or—though to my knowledge it happened only once and before my time there—to keep an escaped prisoner from advancing to another floor. As if that weren't discouraging enough, my Project, Alpha, was one of the classifieds, which meant it was even deeper underground than the unrestricted ones. How many levels down, I had no idea.

I never saw the prairie above the subterranean fortress with my own eyes, but I knew it existed, its horizon knowing no bounds. If by some miracle a prisoner did make it out of the tunnels, *They* could easily do an aerial sweep and locate the fugitive in the middle of the flat land. To escape, I would have had to break free of my cage, traverse the heavily monitored hallway of Alpha, make my way up through several classified Projects above me with equally tight security, and find a way to open the double-reinforced doors, navigate the tunnel maze, then trek across the endless prairie to find civilization. That escape plan wasn't even factoring in the retinal scanners to access the other levels.

But now, I wasn't underground. I didn't have to pass through all those barriers. Just a cage, a truck door, and two handlers, so easy in comparison. The myth of escape might actually be feasible.

I opened my eyes and curled my fingers through the bars to feel the lock. The illusion of escape evaporated. My cage lock required a key with an electronic chip in it, so I couldn't pick it even if I did have a tool. The Outside air never touched us and never would. I would not breathe fresh air ever again.

Escape was a dangerous thought. But I could hear wind for the first time in years, and I tried to recall what it felt like, what it tasted like. I was sick for it. I wanted to scream. One scream to channel the pain, misery, frustration, and hatred and release them into a force powerful enough to break the bars and cleave open the truck so I could stand unimpeded in the middle of the wrecked metal.

I caught my breath. Just imagining such a potent scream drew the heat inside my core, just for a moment before the green power was smothered once more. I pressed my throbbing forehead against the cold bars. If only escape were that easy. If only . . .

It could be.

My head turned to find the two pairs of blue eyes glowing faintly in the dark. Wild, dangerous hope choked me. "Hey," I whispered to my lab-brothers. Their eyes blinked at the sound of my voice. Nearly half my age, Finn and Reese were identical right down to their personalities. In fact, the only way I could tell them apart was Finn's hat worn backward so his unkempt brown hair stuck out the front. Reese didn't wear a hat.

I gripped the bars and called out to them softly so as not to disturb the others: "You can get out. All you have to do is use your power, and we could escape."

It would be so easy for them. All ghosts had a set of basic powers, one of which was intangibility—the power to move through solid objects. Every one of us locked in the back of this truck had that ability, but Finn and Reese, confirmed by the telltale glow of their irises, were the only two right now with access to their power reserves. They were born and raised in that place; they didn't have to wear neutralizers, because they wouldn't dare use their supernatural abilities to defy their masters.

Unless I could convince them, just this one time.

Their gazes were cold and despondent. Finn narrowed his eyes at me and then hung his head. Disgruntled, I turned my attention to Reese, not that it made a difference because I couldn't appeal to one without also convincing the other. "Don't you want to see the Outside?" I asked, desperation cracking my words. "It's real. It's just on the other side of this wall."

Reese wrapped his arms around his legs, hugging his knees to his chest as though afraid the Outside was going to crush him if he dared to leave the refuge of his cage. Finn squeezed his eyes shut. Too bad *He* wasn't as much of a fool as I'd hoped; *He*'d spent years brainwashing the twins to fear the Outside.

"You're wasting your breath." Jay, awoken by my quiet pleas, was watching me with one half-opened eye.

I loosened my fingers from the thin bars and drew my hand into my lap. I stroked the edge of my photograph. "I know. But it's so close. Can't you hear the wind?"

He didn't answer, just sighed and closed his eyes again, exasperated by my delusional talk of escape. I couldn't tell if he was asleep, but he clearly didn't want to be bothered by my hope.

Now that I'd refocused on the wind, it sounded louder, relentless, a wailing roar in my ears. Finn and Reese couldn't crave what they'd never experienced, and Jay, he'd been there too long to remember the Outside.

I squinted at my picture in the dimness again, trying to tune out the wind. *Focus.* My blood-family. *Focus on them.* I wanted to forget them, and at the same time, I clutched at their memories because I was afraid I'd lose myself if I allowed the wounds to scar.

"Don't forget."

But I had. I was Cato to the Outside world and my lab-family, but I was A7-5292 to *Them*. The numbers were tattooed on my inner forearms, branding me with the moniker *They*'d assigned me.

Don't forget . . . don't forget, I replayed, trying to remember how my blood-sister's voice sounded when she said those words. But I couldn't. I was lucky to still have her face in the photograph. The realization that her voice had been erased from my memory was a familiar panic always triggered in the instant I was aware another piece was gone. I should have been used to it by now, but I wasn't, and I didn't think I ever would be until my mind was blank. Someday, I may very well end up like Finn and Reese, completely compliant, brainwashed into believing only what *They* deemed fit. And then—

An ear-shattering screech rudely interrupted my trepidations. Before I could make sense of it, I was thrown face-first into the metal bars. Our cages crashed together. Those who had been dozing were wide awake now.

The wild, animal-like squeal of rending metal nearly burst my eardrums, drowning my own screams. The truck whipped to the side, and then the whole vehicle was off balance, rolling and pitching us about as our cages banged into each other in a thunderous orchestra of chaos.

I was upside down. Ash's shrill scream crescendoed and faded in my ear as our cages were smashed together and then thrown apart. The truck flipped. I couldn't tell which way was up anymore. Everything whirled and blurred together, crashing and crumpling and banging and squealing, burning rubber, gasoline, asphalt, screams . . .

And then the truck shuddered to a stop.

Silence.

— Chapter Two —

Wreckage

The sudden quiet slammed into me, just as deafening as the cacophony moments before.

Ringing.

An acrid smell filled my nose. As I focused beyond the high, irritating frequency buzzing between my ears, I realized the silence wasn't really silent at all. A punctured radiator hissed above the gurgle of spilling fluid. There was a quiet *tick-tick-tick*ing of heated metal cooling.

I couldn't see. I blinked a few times. Was I blind?

I squirmed. Torn metal bit my skin. I sucked in deep breaths to stave off claustrophobia. I couldn't hear Ash anymore. I couldn't hear anybody. Only my own breathing. What happened? Where were the others? Were they hurt? Or worse . . . what if they didn't survive?

That thought nearly pushed me over the edge of a panic attack. It didn't matter that I was trapped in what may be my final tomb. What terrified me was the thought of being alone.

"Jay!" I shouted, wincing at the sound of my own voice. "Ash? RC, are you there?" My head throbbed. *Out. Have to get out.* I closed my eyes and focused inward, into my core where there should have been a light. *Find my center. Find my center . . .*

If I could trigger that elusive light, bring the warmth tingling through my blood—if I could override my neutralizer just for a second to make myself intangible . . .

The neutralizer didn't even allow my Origin to flicker this time. *Damn it.* I'd felt the power stir briefly in rage before, but now, when I needed it most, it was just out of reach.

I opened my eyes again and pressed against the twisted mess of metal encasing me. It wouldn't budge. *Can't move.*

Breathe.

Can't!

Inhale.

I'm going to die.

A *thump* distracted the panic in my head. I held my breath. Another *thump*, another, like open palms striking something—rhythmic, strong. Urgent. Then the clinking and scraping of metal shifting as a body scrambled out of the wreckage. I strained to listen. A cough.

Someone else survived.

A man's voice ordered, "Stop! Move, and I shoot! On the ground, *now*! You hear me, rat? Get down! I said, *get down!*"

My lungs ached, but I held my breath and prayed the next sound wouldn't be a gunshot. A moment passed, then a *thump* with a metallic ring followed by the dull *thud* of a body hitting the ground. A simultaneous *click-ping!* Another *thud.*

Silence again.

Not knowing what was happening threaded insanity into me. A frustrated scream clawed at my throat, silenced by a girl's timid voice drifting through the wreckage.

"Are *They* dead?"

Ash's voice trembled with terror. I melted with relief.

I thought I heard RC answer her, but his voice was quiet, muffled, and I couldn't make out the words. Jay's voice came next: "Get me out of here." I couldn't hear the reply, but then he said, "There has to be a key somewhere. Check *Their* pockets."

Ash whimpered, "I can't."

"Yes, you can. I know you can. Please try."

I could envision her shaking her head and backing away from the limp bodies of our handlers. "No, Jay, I-I'm sorry. I can't do it."

RC said, "Here."

The faint *pop* of a lock preceded the grind of metal as bent hinges rotated over Ash's meek second apology.

16

"It's okay," said Jay. "Really."

Ash laughed nervously. "We're Outside. I don't believe it. We're really Outside." She laughed again.

My relief at their survival was overshadowed by the burning desperation to see the Outside for myself. "Ash!" I shouted, pounding on the twisted cage of metal surrounding me. "Can you hear me? Help! Help me—I'm trapped! Ash! Jay! RC!"

"Wait," said Jay on the other side of debris. "Did you hear that?" He paused. "Where's Cato? And Axel?"

I closed my eyes and cried, "I'm under here! Jay, can you hear me? Help! I'm here!"

"Cato?" His voice was closer, right above me.

"Yeah, I'm trapped! I-I can't move!"

Calm and collected, as if nothing were out of the ordinary, Jay commanded, "Help me."

I fell silent and stopped pounding as my metal tomb began to tremble like a—like—What was it? An earthquake. That was the word.

The debris settled again, and I was still trapped.

RC said, "I can't."

Fresh panic choked me. "What do you mean you can't? Can't *what*?"

Jay soothed, "Don't worry. We're going to get you out, Cay. I promise." Hands dug at the shrapnel. I stilled myself to listen to metal scraping against metal, hinges grinding, pieces being thrown.

"I think I found Axel," Ash called in the distance.

Jay asked, "Is he okay?"

"I don't know."

"See if you can pull him out. RC and I will get Cato."

The first slice of a dark ceiling with tiny specks of light opened above me. I blinked a few times and inhaled, dizzy. My eyes couldn't focus on the ceiling. Why? And I expected to see a silhouette above me, but no one was there.

The ceiling twinkled. I lay perfectly still, marveling at its apparent height. A tiny yellow light blinked to life, there and gone, and then another at the edge of my vision. My eyes rolled to follow a tailpipe drifting past of its own accord. *I must be hallucinating.* Was that a symptom of blood loss?

Now I could see the silhouette of a shirtless teenager on his hands and knees at the edge of my vision. Jay's strong arms lifted and tossed the debris. "Don't move, Cay," he advised. "We've almost got you out."

A breeze tickled my bare toes when he shoved a tire off my shins. I had associated the tightness in my chest with panic, but now I comprehended a heavy panel was pinning my body.

Jay didn't try to remove it. He just sat there on his knees, watching me. I opened my mouth to beg him for help, but before the first word, the wreckage shifted on my rib cage, knocking the air out of my lungs. I couldn't even grunt. Nobody was touching it, and yet it shifted again, then began to rise. I filled my lungs with a deep breath of air—fresh air. Outside air.

Jay and I watched the panel levitate, tilting, leaning until it was vertical. The edge touched the ground, and whatever force had been holding it was released so gravity could reclaim the debris and send it toppling away from me.

I sucked in another full breath. It tasted good. I didn't know air *could* taste good, but it did. It was an elixir. I inhaled hungrily, my head clearing beneath the strange and stunning ceiling. Slowly, I realized . . . that ceiling might not be a ceiling at all. Was it . . . ? Could it really be . . . the actual night sky?

A figure stood a short distance away. He gazed down at me, one eye glowing a brilliant violet in the darkness, and I understood. A glance at his right arm confirmed my suspicion—the neutralizer was now a shredded piece of metal and wires. Our resident Telekinetic ghost had most of his powers back under control. I realized RC had tried to lift all the wreckage from my body at once but had been unable to move more than a few small pieces at a time. He held his arm stiffly at his side. Dark liquid dripped from his fingertips.

Jay rose to stand behind him, his ribs and lean muscles shadowed in the faint light. "You okay?" Jay asked me.

Was I okay? I sat up and gazed around in bewildered awe. I was within the remnants of my cage, which saved me from what otherwise would have been a terrible, crushing death when the armored panels caved in. I never would have thought I'd be grateful for the cage.

The truck was a barely recognizable crumpled mass lying upside down next to us in the ditch, and farther down the road, the mangled remains of another vehicle bled a dark pool of spreading gasoline on the asphalt. Debris from both vehicles was strewn everywhere. Ash was hauling a metal container from the wreckage.

Beyond her, the Outside was endless. Thousands of eerie and hauntingly beautiful yellow lights winked in the darkness. The flat horizon stretched unbroken, inhabited only by neat rows of plants. *Plants!* I almost crawled to one so I could touch its leaves and dig my fingers into the soil, so desperately did I want to smell it so I could remember what the earth smelled like. But I was still too stunned to move.

I drew in another deep breath and savored nature's aroma, separating its rich scent from the acrid taint of the wrecked truck. I was small in this huge place. There was an infinite sky above me where a ceiling used to be, soil beneath my feet, and fresh, clean, natural air. The wind, to my disappointment, had abated, or it never actually existed. Perhaps it was only the roar of the moving truck I'd heard.

One of the yellow lights glowed to life right above me. RC held up two fingers, then rotated them toward his face, drawing the blinking light closer so he could study it. "Oh. It's an insect," he said in surprise as he watched the tiny creature's wings beat against his invisible telekinetic tether, its light flickering.

Another drifted in front of me, and I reached out in wonder to cup my hands around it. The little body crawling up my index finger pulsed with a yellow glow from beneath its black wings. I opened my hands, extending my finger and turning my hand as I lifted it up so I could watch the insect. Its legs tickled my skin. It raised its black top wings to open a second pair underneath, and then it was hovering in front of my eyes. Its abdomen blazed as it flew away.

A high-pitched, muffled *mew* broke my trance. I turned toward the sound, and the black-and-white kitten blinked at me from her perch on a tire. She pawed at the muzzle and made another pitiful noise of complaint. "Hold still, Kit," I said, reaching for her. The kitten's ears flicked back when my fingers fumbled with the strap. "Let me get that off you."

I unclasped the muzzle and let it fall. Kit pricked her ears forward and mewed again, rubbing her face against my hand in thanks. I slid one finger beneath the wire tied around her neck and untwisted it. As it fell away, the kitten's body turned to black smoke, then reformed into the body of an almost-humanlike little girl balancing lightly on the balls of her feet. She sported a pair of sharp fangs and feline ears, and her golden irises glowed in the darkness.

When she joined our family, she had said she was six years old. Now, she must be seven or eight. Kit was an Amínyte ghost with the ability to shift into one of two forms, which she referred to as "fur" and "skin."

She curled her bare toes over the rubber. Unlike Ash's sports bra-sweatpants attire, Kit's usual uniform was a simple gray knee-length dress. Her long black hair fell down over her shoulder, and she directed one soft, velvety cat ear toward me and the other back toward the sounds of Ash dragging the container. She grinned, flashing her fangs. I hadn't seen her smile in forever. *They* had taken her most prized possession, and she'd been spiraling into a depression ever since. But this smile was genuine, lighting her eyes in a way that forced my own to crinkle.

Kit blinked and tilted her head back as her eyes rolled upward. I followed her gaze, and for a minute we both stared at the tiny points of light speckling the sky. I knew they had a name, and I thought it started with an *S* . . .

Kit might know. She'd been exposed to the NMS only a few times, so her memory was sharper than the rest of ours. "What are they?" I asked her.

She turned to look at me again with her big eyes, the irises glinting gold in the night. Both of her black furry ears pricked forward at the sound of my voice. "Stars," she said, her answer soft with wonder.

"Stars," I repeated, letting the rediscovered word roll off my tongue.

I was far away on a rooftop with my hands folded behind my head. My blood-sister was lying next to me. We kept silent, content to enjoy each other's company beneath the endless night sky. "Look, Cay," she said, pointing. "A shooting star. Make a wish . . ."

Kit's glowing eyes were trained on me in concern. I blinked, patted her cheek in absent-minded reassurance, and looked around. My hands closed around dirt and gravel, which spilled through my fingers. My heart stopped. My hand flew to my hip, and I shoved my fingers into the hole in my waistband. *Where is it?*

I fell to my knees and shoved debris aside. *No! I need that picture!* I grabbed a mangled cage and threw it away, discovering the corner of my treasure. The rest of it was buried beneath the truck bed. I pinched it and tried to pry it free. It wouldn't budge. Fearing it might rip, I changed tactics, throwing my shoulder against the metal frame and pushing with my entire body. My bare feet slid in the gravel.

I hung my head, glaring at the photograph right in front of me. A small body crawled under my arm. Kit peered up at me and smiled sweetly, then stuck her hand through the metal. Intangible, she seized the photograph and pulled it out as though the truck weren't even there. She held it up to gaze at the image, head tilted, and then she offered it to me.

"Thank you," I said, accepting it.

Pleased that she'd been able to help, she beamed, then turned to smoke as she transformed back into a kitten. She scampered off. I folded the photograph and tucked it safely in my waistband again. My gaze crossed the scene—Ash pulling Axel's sealed container from the mangled underbelly of the truck, Jay examining an opening into the heart of what was almost our tomb, Kit darting through the smoking wreckage in search of something, RC standing frozen like a living statue staring at two bodies lying a few yards away.

My heart dropped again. Finn and Reese?

Upon closer inspection, the bodies were those of adults, not the kid brothers. But then, where were they?

"Are *They* dead?" I asked, recalling the sounds of a scuffle.

RC swallowed hard. I waited for him to gather his thoughts, but after a minute, I thought he'd forgotten. I opened my mouth to remind him, but RC finally said, "Cato, we're Outside. I mean, bloody Scout, I never thought I'd see the Outside again." He shook his head. "It happened so fast. I was thrown from the truck. When it was over, it was just me and Ash, and Jay was still locked in his cage, and then *They* crawled out."

He dragged his fingers through his mop of messy brown hair. "*They* startled me. I didn't know my neutralizer was busted. I didn't even think; I just turned away and threw my arms over my head. A piece of the truck hit the guy in the head. I didn't even mean to. The other shot a tranq at me, and . . . and I didn't realize I did it, but there was a metal plate, just floating there in front of me. The dart hit it and bounced off. So . . . I threw out my hand. The plate hit him in the head, and *They* haven't moved since. I don't know if I killed *Them*."

I studied the bodies. "I think *They*'re breathing."

I was on RC's right side where a thin scar trailed over his milky, blind eye. He turned his head so he could fix me with his glowing left eye. "Should I kill *Them*?" He vacantly surveyed all the sharp debris available.

"No," said Jay from behind. We both turned to face him.

"But *They*'ll wake up," Ash said, her fingers slipping on the sealed container she was trying to open. She paused to wipe blood out of her eye. Kit scampered past her and squeezed into the wreck, her tail slithering out of sight.

Ash was right. If we let *Them* live, we'd pay for it when *They* woke up. But if we killed *Them*, our punishment would be a thousand times worse.

Jay didn't answer. He turned back to continue sifting through the debris. Kit was scouring farther away, her tiny body able to wriggle into tight places. She could cover more ground in her feline form, although it cost her all the other powers when she wore her fur. What they were seeking, I had no idea. Ash looked at RC and me, arching her eyebrow questioningly. I shrugged.

RC left the unconscious bodies to help Ash open the container. I finally spotted the twins huddled in their cages near the engine. Other than a few cuts and bruises, they appeared physically unharmed, but their faces were deathly white.

I rose to comfort them. The Spasm hit me without any warning. It started at the ports ringing my cranium—twelve, to be exact—igniting to white-hot pain. The agony spread in a microsecond. Even if I had a foreshadowing of its coming, there was no way to brace myself. It was as if my head were made of glass that just shattered into a million pieces, obliterating time and space, pulling me into anguish with no beginning, no end. I clapped my hands over my head and squeezed my eyes tight. My mouth opened, and I clutched my hair again, but nothing I did would ease the pain until the Spasm passed.

Gravel pressed into my cheek when I opened my eyes. My throat was sore and raw; I must have been screaming. Each breath seared the inside of my esophagus. My knees stung from the impact.

Still queasy, I hauled myself into a sitting position. I glanced down to see the injuries I'd sustained. My skin was blemished by blood and fresh bruises that contrasted against my light skin. Shrapnel had ripped up my feet, and gravel had been plastered into my kneecaps when I collapsed. Once the adrenaline wore off, I was going to hurt, and yet all of those visible wounds paled in comparison to the pain of the Spasm.

A hand appeared in front of my face. I gratefully accepted Jay's help up. "Finn and Reese," I choked out, my tongue thick in my cotton mouth.

Jay glanced over at them. "Yeah, they aren't handling the Outside well. They're in shock." He tossed a bundle at me. I caught it and stared down at the fabric in my hands, confused. When I peered up at Jay again, he was pulling a long-sleeved shirt over his head. I looked over my shoulder once more to make sure Finn and Reese were all right. I wanted to go to them, but I was barefoot, and a sea of glass and metal lay between us, so I knelt and unfolded the bundle to find my Arena uniform wrapped within a black cloak.

I slipped out of my black sweatpants, unconcerned by the presence of my lab-siblings. We had no privacy in that place, so we had nothing to hide from each other.

I picked metal bits and stones out of my knees before pulling up the black pants, and then I eyed the calf-high boots. My bloody feet were already throbbing at the thought of sliding inside. I seized the cloak instead and worked it against the sharpened edge of a broken pipe until a rip formed and I could tear away a strip to wrap around each foot. I'd hoped the extra padding would provide some comfort, but my nerves screamed when I pulled the boots on.

The sleeveless shirt—solid black with a white Alpha symbol on the chest—was next. Every inch of my body protested the contortion necessary to push my head and arms through the holes. The weight of the fabric awakened each new bruise.

I concealed my hands with fingerless gloves, which were tailored for a fighter. My knuckles were protected by padding, on top of which were metal studs beneath the outer layer of fabric. I donned a set of thin elbow pads and knee pads. Finally, I laced the gauntlets tightly around my forearms to complete the wardrobe and cover the tattoos I despised so much. This simple change of clothes made me feel slightly less vulnerable.

Jay was pulling his gloves on. He made a fist and gazed at it in satisfaction, watching his fingers strain the fabric. Our uniforms were almost identical except that his and RC's gloves were full-fingered and their shirts were long-sleeved, thicker too, with padded ribs to protect the torso. I'd always preferred my lighter-weight shirt, but now, practically human, I picked at the breathable fabric and wished for just a little more protection.

I slid my photograph inside my gauntlet and frowned at the salvaged objects by Jay's feet—one pair of gloves, a small computer with no screen or keyboard, eight silver disks, a solid metal staff, and a harness. Noticing the source of my puzzlement, Jay explained, "It's all we have. We might as well take it with us." He seized a backpack and dumped out dozens of vials, then shoved the computer and gloves inside.

"Take it with us?"

He fixed me with a serious stare. "You weren't planning to wait around for *Them* to come take us back, were you?"

"I, um . . ." To be honest, I'd been so overwhelmed by the Outside I hadn't thought that far ahead. *They* would never let us go. "Where?"

Jay shrugged and gathered the staff and harness. "Away from here."

With a grunt, RC pushed the lid of the sealed container off. I took a few tentative steps closer to stand beside Ash and peer inside where Axel continued his drugged sleep, unharmed and oblivious to the recent events. His chest rose and fell with deep, even breaths. A metal collar holstered vials filled with anesthetizing drugs. His coal-black hair covered his eyes, a muzzle clasped over his face by three straps. *They* had good reason to take such precaution because his fangs, unlike Kit's, were venomous. Without his fangs and glowing eyes, Axel could pass for human. He didn't look like the most dangerous ghost to ever walk either Realm, but that was exactly what he was. He was a half-breed, like me, but very different. Ghosts called him half-nydæa. Humans had another name for such a creature, but I couldn't remember.

Months in the Arena had tuned my muscles and made me lethal. I would have been in fantastic physical condition had I not been starved during most of my captivity. But Axel . . . I couldn't even compare myself to him. His paper-white skin was flawless, every muscle sculpted to perfection. Even while he was unconscious, I felt insignificant beside him. We were, to the best of our knowledge, the only two hybrids in existence.

Jay set the harness, the staff, and a bundle of clothing at Ash's feet. He seized the eight silver disks and handed them to RC with another bundle. Using his good arm, RC exchanged his pants and slipped on his boots, then tossed a leg pouch back at Jay. "Help me?"

Jay knelt and started to buckle the strap around RC's leg so it rested on the outside of his right thigh. "Other side," RC requested. Although he'd always worn it on his dominant right side, Jay glanced at RC's wounded arm and wordlessly secured the pouch to his other leg.

RC inspected his silver disks. Four were solid, and the other four had a hole through the center. RC carelessly tossed the solid disks back into the wreckage. He studied the four with holes, then dropped one and placed the other three in the pouch.

Jay knelt to pick up the disk RC had dropped. "Take all four," he advised, offering it back to him.

RC glared at it as if repulsed, even though it looked exactly the same as the other three. "I don't want it."

Jay didn't argue, but he kept the fourth disk. Kit plodded over to us, her tail drooping, and when she changed back to her skin and stood, her ears were flat, her face downtrodden. "Jay, I can't find it," she whined. Her eyes were about to overflow with tears glittering in the starlight. Her lower lip quivered.

"What, this?" he said with a smile, tossing something at her. She caught it, and immediately her face lit with joy.

"You found my Name! Thank you, thank you!" she chimed, throwing herself at Jay. I observed the embrace as *They* might an experiment. None of us had ever hugged each other. Jay acted equally surprised; he didn't know how to respond to the little girl with her arms around his waist. He awkwardly patted her back, but instead of letting go, she squeezed tighter until he returned the hug. Satisfied, she stepped back, beaming as she proudly hung a long loop of cord over her head. Attached was a smooth, round pendant.

I was told she'd been born with the ivory clenched in her tiny hand. All Amínytes were. The bone was marked with their three-sided symbol. On the other side, her name had been carved. The pendant changed to a collar when she was in her feline form, and it was her most prized possession. If she had to choose between me and that pendant, she would choose her Name. Amínytes associated their pendants with their very identities. *They* had taken it from her upon arrival, just as I knew *They* would have taken my photograph. Had it not been such a source of mystery to *Them*, her Name likely would have been destroyed, and Kit's sanity along with it.

She held the pendant up to eye level and tilted it toward the light, scrutinizing the ivory for any damage *Their* tests might have done to it. Serious again, Jay said, "We don't have much time. It won't take long for *Them* to realize what happened and come after us . . . if *They* aren't on *Their* way already."

I gazed down the long, straight road in one direction, then the other. No lights. No inkling as to which direction we'd even come from. We were in the middle of nowhere.

Ash fastened the cloak over her padded black sports bra with the white Alpha symbol on the front. Her Arena outfit was different from ours. Like my gloves, hers were also fingerless. Her capri leggings stopped just below her knees, leaving a gap to the tops of her calf-high boots. Each pant leg had a slit up the side, exposing a marquise of open skin on the outer part of her thigh to help keep her cool. Compared to RC's and Jay's full-length uniforms, she and I had less padding and coverage due to our Divinities.

RC started to tug his shirt over his head, but he paused to try to pull the neutralizer free first. Even though it had been damaged, the device tightened automatically, cutting into his arm. He hissed in pain. "How am I supposed to get it off?" he asked in response to our solemn stares. "It hurts."

Jay shook his head. "You don't. I'm sorry, but you're going to have to deal with the pain and access to only part of your power."

RC sighed. Ash strapped on the harness and sheathed her metal staff so it rested diagonally across her back. "Give me a blade." She held out her hand.

RC turned so his pouch faced Ash. She reached inside and removed the disk. It was a seemingly harmless circular piece of metal with a slit around the perimeter and a hole through the center, useless to any of us and any human. But in RC's hands, it was deadly. There was no switch to activate the blades inside. His left eye glowed, and tele-kinesis made the blades eject from the slit with a sharp *chink!*

Ash carefully hooked one of the curved blades into the fabric of RC's shirt. She sawed at the threads until the whole right sleeve was free, then set the bladed disk on the ground before helping RC pull his shirt over his scarred back. He struggled to contort his left arm into the sleeve. Although he'd never favored that arm, he had an old wound there, a mysterious pair of round scars with blackened dendritic-patterned veins marking his forearm. I was sure *They* were responsible for those scars because beneath my right elbow pad, I also had dark-ened veins spreading like a black tree from the crook of my arm, and I couldn't remember how it happened.

He pushed his hand through the sleeve, concealing the marks on his body. He gritted his teeth when Ash tied the cut sleeve tightly over the damaged neutralizer.

I asked, "Do you know what you're doing?"

She shook her head. "I'm just trying to stop the bleeding. That's what Dr. Anders would do first . . . I think."

RC gritted his teeth. "You should have used it for yourself," he grumbled.

Ash lifted her quaking fingers to touch the gash above her right eyebrow that was still oozing blood. "I'm okay," she insisted.

A hand landed on my shoulder, and I turned to look at Jay. "Cato, I'm going to talk to Finn and Reese. You should come with me. I might need help."

"Help with what?"

"You're half-human. You might have better luck convincing them."

Jay was wrong; I knew the twins would listen to him over me. Besides, they didn't view me as a human. If they did, they would refuse to speak in my presence. Just as well—I'd rather they accept me as a ghost than fear me as a human. "You do the talking. If you need me, I'll chime in."

He inclined his head.

We navigated through the wreckage, giving *Their* bodies a wide

28

berth, but as we passed, Jay paused. "What?" I asked.

He narrowed his eyes, staring at *Them*. "Jay?"

He eased cautiously toward the bodies but hesitated a few feet away, checking for any sign of movement. He crouched down low until he was on his hands and the balls of his feet. He reached for the nearest man's neck.

I held my breath, terrified the human would seize Jay. Already, my overactive brain was anticipating how to react. Attack? Wait to see if Jay could handle himself? Run? Surrender? I didn't know, and that frightened me.

Jay's fingers found what they were searching for, and despite my fears, the man didn't move when Jay slipped a cord over his head and retreated with his prize. He gazed at the silver whistle in his open palm, then put the cord over his own head. The whistle dangled on his chest as though it had always belonged there. "Just in case," he explained in answer to my unspoken question, turning his attention back to Finn and Reese.

The twins peered up as we approached. "Hey," Jay greeted warmly, smiling as he knelt. I remained standing just behind him. Jay offered his hand. "Why don't you guys come out?"

They shook their heads resolutely. Jay sat down in front of them. "Don't you want to look around?"

Again, they shook their heads. Their cages were bent and twisted from the accident. Finn was still locked inside, even though he could have become intangible and escaped if he wanted to. Then again, he'd always had that freedom. Reese's door had broken open. He must have been thrown, but he had crawled back inside. In fact, he'd crudely put the panels of his cage back together and was holding them in place to keep the cage from collapsing.

Finn hugged himself, shivering. They didn't know the texture of gravel or pavement or grass, or how good fresh air could taste, or the sound of insects. Their cages were their sanctuaries.

Jay said, "We're leaving now. You need to come with us."

The twins' blue eyes flashed. "Leaving?" Reese whispered in horror.

"We can't leave," his blood-brother said. "We have to wait for *Them*."

Jay exhaled slowly. We made brief eye contact before his gaze returned to our lab-brothers. "Listen, I know you're scared. But we escaped. We're free. You don't really want to go back, do you?"

"We have to," the twins answered simultaneously.

"No, you don't. We can run away."

Their eyes grew wide. "Run away?" Finn repeated, horrified at the suggestion. He recoiled, pressing his body farther into the cage away from Jay.

"*They'*ll send us to Project Omega for that," said Reese.

"No, *They* won't," Jay said with absolute certainty.

Finn muttered, "We'll be punished."

"Severely punished," his twin added.

"*They* won't let us eat for days."

"We have to stay."

"*They'*ll come back for us."

When I first met Finn and Reese, I'd had a hard time following their speech pattern, but now I was well accustomed to it. I found my head swaying side to side as I made eye contact with whichever twin was speaking.

Jay studied them both in consideration. The twins' eyes glowed brighter for a second, and then they shook their heads and braced themselves. Finn said, "Jay, we can't. It's against the Rules."

"*They* own us," Reese said.

I snapped, "*They* do not."

Finn responded by raising his fist to show the dark number 2296 tattooed in his skin, beneath that the Greek letter gamma written as γ. "We've all been branded."

"We all belong to *Them*," they chanted in unison, like a perverse nursery rhyme that didn't even rhyme. My forearms itched as I thought about my own tattoos under the gauntlets. Finn and Reese had never been Pure; they'd been Marked since the day they were born.

I told them, "I promise there's a better world out there."

Still, they shook their heads. "We don't have a choice," said Reese.

"The door is locked," Finn added.

The naivety of that statement was enough to make me hang my head and sigh. Jay patiently said, "Those cages have never trapped you like the rest of us. You can walk out anytime you want."

"The door is locked," Reese repeated.

His twin said, "Humans locked the door."

"We can't leave until a human unlocks the door."

"We must obey the Rules."

Jay said, "You don't have to live by *Their* rules. *They* can't hurt us anymore."

They looked at him as if in pity that he could be so delusional.

"Do you trust me?" Jay asked.

Finn and Reese stared at him as if trapped in an impossible conundrum.

"Listen," Jay said, finally losing his patience, "we're wasting time, and we need to move. You're our lab-brothers, and we're not leaving you behind. Cay, grab Finn. I got Reese." He slipped something small out of his gauntlet and tossed it to me.

Jay reached into Reese's cage and seized his wrist, but the boy tightened his grip on the bars of his cage and shook his head again. With a sigh, Jay gave a jerk, yanking Reese out. The kid fell in the gravel and scrambled back, startled at the feel of loose rocks. The cage collapsed as soon as Reese's hands weren't there to hold it together. That didn't stop Reese from twisting around and trying to crawl back inside. Jay easily grabbed the boy and hoisted him into the air.

I examined the key I'd caught. All of our cages were calibrated with the same microchipped locks. I wondered if Jay gave me the key hoping Finn would accept a half-human unlocking his cage as a satisfactory substitution.

Not likely.

The lock was damaged, so I had to jam and wiggle the key into the hole, then turn it with a little extra force. The locking mechanism was stiff, but it finally opened with a quiet *pop*. I swung the door open and extended my hand into Finn's cage. He shrank away from me. Fingers mere inches away from him, I hesitated. I'd never touched Finn before. Not Finn, Reese, or Axel. I reached farther, and we made contact for the first time.

I pulled a resisting Finn from his cage. "No, Cato!" he pleaded. I scooped him into my arms. He struggled silently, but I held on with little effort as he whimpered in frustration and tried to push away from me to get back to his safe place.

I followed Jay to the rest of the group. He handed Reese to Ash, then stooped to retrieve the backpack containing the computer and gloves. "We can't waste any more time," he said, shouldering the bag.

Ash set Reese down but kept a firm hold on his arm so he wouldn't run, although he squirmed and twisted in a desperate attempt to pull free. He suddenly yanked out of her grip by becoming intangible. He spun, but the moment he solidified, Ash grabbed his T-shirt and pulled him back.

Finn was just as determined to escape from me, but I kept him pinned against my chest and whispered, "Don't even think about using your power." He glared at me in frustration.

"What about Axel?" Ash asked, glancing at the sleeping teenager at our feet.

Jay paused. "If he's unstable when he wakes up . . ." He glanced at Kit and decided not to complete that thought, instead opting to finish, "He's too dangerous."

RC's lips pressed into a tight line. He looked away, but he didn't dispute Jay's statement.

Kit's ears fell once she realized they were talking about abandoning Axel. She cried, "No, we can't leave him! *They*'ll take him back!"

"Kit," Jay murmured.

"No! Jay, he's our lab-brother!" She squared off against him, fists clenched, ears pinned, her whole body trembling. Then her eyes filled with tears, and she collapsed on top of Axel's chest, sobbing.

Jay gazed down at the pair. Kit was right—Axel was our lab-brother. Jay was also right—Axel was dangerous. In that place, confined within his cage, he was under control. Out here, Axel would be as unpredictable as he would be unstoppable. And yet, I couldn't help but think how harmless he looked when he was sleeping . . .

Jay still hadn't reached a decision. He fiddled with the whistle around his neck and asked the twins, "How long will he sleep?"

Reese frowned, temporarily ceasing in his struggles to escape Ash's grip. "How many doses are left?"

Jay set the backpack down on the ground. "Kit," he said firmly, "get up. C'mon, let's go." He pulled her away. Kit stepped back, sniffing and rubbing her bloodshot eyes. Jay knelt beside Axel to study the collar around the hybrid's neck. It was ringed with small vials embedded into Axel's skin. Gently, Jay shifted Axel's head so he could count the vials. I watched Axel's face for any sign of consciousness. The movement shifted his stringy black hair away from his forehead. Unlike the rest of us, Axel had neither ports in his skull nor scars marking their past presence.

"Fifteen," Jay counted. "Six are empty."

The words were barely out of his mouth when Axel's eyebrows twitched. A red light on the collar flicked on with a quiet *beep*, and the liquid in another vial drained into his veins. Axel's expression went placid again even as Jay's tightened. "Seven," he corrected.

Finn muttered, "About twenty minutes per dose, give or take."

Jay gazed at Axel sleeping. Eight doses left. That was . . . Well, I wasn't sure how long it was. Too long to leave Axel here defenseless, not long enough for us to travel very far.

Reese did the mental equation for me: "One hundred and sixty minutes."

"Approximately two-point-six hours," said Finn.

"And that's a generous estimation," Reese added.

Jay rose. We watched him, waiting for his verdict—try to cut the collar off and leave Axel in the hope that he'd awaken in twenty minutes with enough time to escape, or take him with us and pray he didn't wake up in a bloodlust and kill us all—but Jay turned back to the wreck without even looking at us. "Would you say Axel is closest to RC in height?"

I exchanged looks with RC and Ash, who both shrugged. "Guess so," I said. "Why?"

Jay didn't answer aloud, but he selected another bundle of clothes and stuffed it into the backpack. Axel, Kit, Finn, and Reese didn't have sets because they didn't participate in the Arena. Jay, RC, Ash, and I were the fighters, so the four of us each had a set of combat uniforms, plus a spare for each.

On a whim, I said, "Question. Can I have RC's spare pouch?"

Jay tossed it at me without a word. I loosened the straps and fixed the buckles around my thigh, then tucked my precious photograph safely inside.

Jay held up RC's fourth disk and said, "Blade, please."

RC flicked his hand at Jay as if dismissing him; the blades ejected with a quiet *snick*. Jay crouched down and cut at the threads of one of the remaining cloaks until he could tear away the bottom section. He rose and held up the disk, silently requesting the blades to be sheathed. RC obliged.

Jay handed me RC's fourth disk. Understanding his wordless request, I slipped it into the pouch with the photograph. Jay shoved one of the remaining three cloaks into the backpack and handed me the second to replace the one I'd crudely tailored for my feet. He turned to Ash next. She closed her eyes and let him tie the long strip of black cloth just below her line of ports to cover the gash above her eye.

Jay leaned down, seized Axel's arms, and hauled the limp body over his back, then stood. Axel's head lolled on Jay's shoulder, his arms dangling in front. My gaze found Axel's single imperfection—he was missing the last joint of the little finger on his right hand. Kit wiped the back of her arm across her nose, watching Jay. Even though Axel was unconscious, the proximity of his venomous fangs so close to Jay's exposed neck made my skin prickle.

"He can't stay with us, but we won't leave him behind in this state for *Them* to capture. We'll take him away from here and leave him somewhere safe before he wakes up. He'll be on his own from there," Jay announced.

RC shook his head in a way that was more downhearted than defiant. He didn't have to say the words we were all thinking: *Axel was never meant to leave that place.*

Jay must have had the same thought because he reinforced, "I wouldn't be able to live with myself knowing he's still a prisoner while we're free. Now, we've already wasted too much time. *They*'re probably on *Their* way."

Finn and Reese looked around in search of their masters, as if they expected *Them* to appear any second.

Ash turned a slow circle. "Where do we go?" she asked.

I searched for a landmark. Nothing but the empty horizon, which was far vaster than I remembered from Before. Ash, RC, and I scanned our surroundings, then magnetically turned back to face Jay, my elder by only a couple of years, the soothing voice when I had wavered on the edge of despair in my cage, the one who had assessed our medley of skills in the Arena and organized us into a team to survive whatever type of Scout *They* released in there with us—a *Sacrificial Creature Originating Under Theta.*

Jay was staring at the bright orb suspended in the sky, eyes wide, taking in the white glow. He stared at it as if spellbound. "That way is as good as any."

He broke his intense gaze and started walking along the road in the direction of the . . . orb, but not orb. *Damn it, I know this.* Not a star. Hopefully the name would return to me.

Kit's body, dress and all, turned to smoke as she shifted into her fur and trotted at Jay's feet. Ash pulled Reese after them, but he locked his knees, his soles skidding in the gravel. "No!" he cried, beating Ash's arm with his fist.

She hardly batted an eye as she hoisted him up into her arms again and continued walking. Reese stared over her shoulder with wide eyes at the wreckage and the ruined cages. I followed with Finn. RC grabbed the backpack and brought up the rear.

Outside. It was much more fantastic than my faded memories. The fresh air had given all my senses a much-needed jolt. I felt as if I'd been sleeping all this time, and I'd finally woken from a nightmare. We were really escaping.

But danger lurked in this deceivingly peaceful alien world. *They* would be on our trail in a matter of hours, not to mention that except for Kit and the twins, who all had passive Divinities, and RC, who had access to only a fraction of his, none of us had our powers to defend ourselves. We were ill-equipped to handle a world we knew little about, and soon, we'd be hunted.

I held Finn firmly in my arms, though he continued to squirm. He was so light, his body so frail I was afraid I might break him if I squeezed too hard. Within a few minutes, he realized he couldn't wiggle free and shrank into my arms. Even I found the monstrous change in scale overwhelming; I could only imagine Finn's perception. He was so helpless in my arms, so defenseless.

I promise I'll protect you.

That was what families were supposed to do for each other. Together we were fugitives, dark shadows following the ribbon of road into the night full of mysteries ahead of us, dangers at our backs.

— Chapter Three —

Fugitives

Agent Kovak stood in the middle of the road, a metal disk clenched in his hand. Fury and frustration twisted his face into a scowl as he swept his gaze over the skid marks on the asphalt, the contorted mass of armored panels and two undercarriages on the side of the road, the open metal container, the black vehicles parked nearby, the frantic beams of flashlights, the men sifting through the wreckage, and the team of whining dogs with their noses pressed to the ground.

Agent Byrn, his shoulders hunched even more than usual so his short, thick neck disappeared, shuffled forward to stand next to Kovak. "No bodies so far," he reported dryly.

"Where's the helicopter?"

"On its way."

Dr. Anders, still dressed in his white lab coat, pushed his wire-rimmed glasses farther up on the bridge of his nose as he consulted a clipboard. He ground a piece of gum between his teeth before pushing the wad against his cheek and announcing, "We're missing A6. The container is here, but he isn't in it. And ECANI is gone." He flicked a lightning bug that had landed on the clipboard.

Kovak could feel the vein pulsing in his temple. "Goddamn it. A6 was sedated. Where the hell is he? And where the *hell* are the twin runts?" He chucked the disk with all his might at the container. It ricocheted off the side, rolled a few yards, and spun in place until settling in the gravel. It was just a practice disk; the lethal bladed ones were nowhere to be found.

Anders resumed his quiet chewing and shook his head. Byrn took a few hesitant steps and peered into the container to confirm that it was indeed empty. "Not good," he said, turning a shade paler. "Doc? How long do we have?"

Anders glanced at his wristwatch. "A couple hours tops. When A6 wakes up . . ."

He didn't have to finish. Kovak squeezed his eyes shut in a grimace and turned away to draw a bottle of medication from his pocket and pop a small white pill into his mouth. He swallowed and rubbed his temples. A6 had been a mistake. Byrn had always said as much, but Kovak had managed to talk him into transferring the monster from Delta to Alpha instead of destroying him. Losing the other seven was bad enough . . . If A6 awakened before they had a chance to secure him, he would slaughter innocent people by the dozens at a time.

Kovak returned the pill bottle to his pocket. A6 may look like a fourteen-year-old kid, but he wasn't. He couldn't even talk. The growls and snarls from the mutt's throat had sent chills down Agent Kovak's spine every time he stepped foot in the Alpha containment room. If Anders had underestimated the time for the drugs to wear off, they were already too late. If the other Alpha subjects had been stupid enough to take the sleeping demon with them, they were going to be the first ones to die by A6's fangs if the half-breed woke up in a bloodlust.

Kovak rubbed his hand down his face. "How could this have happened?"

Anders backed away to continue inventory, the scent of peppermint left in his wake. Byrn turned to look at the red streak smearing the road farther back. In a daze, he said, "Our transport hit a deer." He nodded at the rusted red body of a mangled pickup truck in the field of debris. "Our driver slammed the brakes and swerved into this poor guy turning at the intersection. D-O-A."

"I don't care about *him*," Kovak said.

As though he hadn't interrupted, Byrn muttered more to himself, "They were driving so fast they didn't stand a chance of braking in time. The truck went off the shoulder and flipped several times."

Kovak kicked a taillight. It skipped over the asphalt and landed somewhere in the soybeans. "A *deer*! I'm planning for the war of the century and *that's* what caused this? Son of a *bitch . . .*"

Byrn wearily rubbed at the wrinkles in his forehead, and Kovak rounded on him. "I told you we should have sent a convoy!"

"What," Byrn retorted, "to broadcast to every kálos that we're opening a new lab? The whole point of sending the truck alone in the countryside in the middle of the night was so it wouldn't draw any attention."

"And how much attention do you think we're going to get when people learn that we let a monster loose?"

"You're worried about A6? Seriously? Do you have any idea what the backlash is going to be when A7's face is all over the news? The media is going to go berserk."

Kovak opened his mouth, but Byrn cut him off: "Just listen. *You* can hide in your office and go off on hunting trips under the radar, but *I'm* the one who has to deal with the reporters and the investors and every entitled, pompous ass above us. I've been trying to rally human-kind against a single enemy, and A7 blurs that line. If that half-breed wanders into the public's eye again . . ."

Kovak rubbed his temples to ward off the headache building like a thunderhead. "This has to be contained. Immediately." He and Byrn flinched and turned when the dogs began baying and straining against their leashes.

"They caught a scent," said Byrn.

Agents followed the howling canines west into the night, flashlights and tranquilizer guns in hand. Kovak shook his head and reached for the medication again. "Shit. They're heading toward the Rip. How could they possibly have known?"

"I don't think they did. Coincidence."

Kovak narrowed his eyes. "I don't believe in coincidences."

***

We followed the fading orb in the sky. The bioluminescence of the insects was gone now. To our right, a field of eerie red lights blinked on for five seconds, off for five seconds—not a city, we were pretty sure, but still a mystery in the darkness. I watched the lights for any abnormality in their five-second loop. They were consistent, but not quite synchronized when they turned off and on, a handful coming to life a second before the others and winking off while the rest were still glowing. Unlike the lights from the insects, these lights didn't move. We'd been in their midst for a while now, and they didn't seem to be harmful. Human machinery, I suspected, but what was their purpose? I didn't trust them.

Behind us, the clouds were lightening in a mesmerizing transition from blue-black to pink and orange. I broke my suspicious gaze away from the light field to tip my head back and observe the sky. To my disappointment, the stars were disappearing as the morning light spread, but as the day arrived, the Outside expanded before our eyes.

Colors were fresh pastels brightening with the soft light, so different from the harsh fluorescent lights we knew that cast a sharp edge and cold pallor. Even my lab-family looked different. RC's skin glowed as if tanned from rays he hadn't seen in years. And Kit's fair complexion looked less sickly and more porcelain, as if the Outside was already curing her.

We were all being cured. Jay's hair, ashen gray despite his youth, had adopted a warmer hue, and the tangled waves of Ash's deep-red locks were enriched. Her long hair and Kit's parted around their faces, revealing their foreheads and the procession of ports. Now crusted, Ash's head wound had stained half her face. She had the bizarre appearance of wearing a half-mask of dark war paint that was flaking off every time her fingernails raked the itchy skin.

Most of my lab-family could pass as nearly human. Axel with his fangs and Kit with her fangs and ears stood apart. Otherwise, our glowing eyes were the only trait that revealed what we were, although right now with our powers neutralized, Jay, Ash, and I could pull off being human.

I kept a firm grip on Finn's wrist. He didn't fight me anymore. He walked willingly at my side, his body pressed so tightly against mine that we'd stumbled over the other's foot on more than one occasion. To think, until a few hours ago we'd never had any physical contact, and now he was practically attached to my hip as his head rolled to gawk in every direction of the Outside with wide-eyed wonder.

Ahead of us, Ash was holding Reese's hand. She gripped her staff loosely in her other hand, more for security, I thought, than out of necessity.

She halted.

I stopped short, barely avoiding a collision. I scowled and opened my mouth to chastise her, but I stopped when she turned her head. Her hand let go of Reese to fly to her mouth, and I backed up in surprise when she turned, dropped her staff, and fell to her knees.

Still holding Finn's hand, I slowly turned to look behind me.

A blinding light rising from the horizon cast golden rays through the veil-thin clouds hovering just above the ground. Ash was so choked up she could barely force out the words: "I never thought I'd see the sun again."

Jay and RC stood there, dumbstruck. Kit closed her eyes to cherish the sunshine on her face, then transformed into her feline form to let it warm her fur. The twins studied the colored sky, but their expressions were impartial.

We didn't speak, didn't move until the sun broke the horizon and the soft colors transitioned to blue. Jay shifted Axel's deadweight on his shoulders, and our walk continued. I pitied Axel for missing such a soul-reviving experience. I couldn't think of a better sight for his new eyes to see for the first time Outside, but hopefully he'd see many more sunrises.

"Who turns on the light?" Finn asked.

His question broke the lingering spell. I frowned and exchanged confused looks with the others. "What light? Are you talking about the sun?"

"That light in the blue ceiling," Reese answered.

"Yes, the sun," I repeated, then explained, "Nobody turns the sun on."

The twins shook their heads. "No," said Reese.

His brother said, "*They* turn the lights off when it's time to sleep and turn them on when it's time to wake up."

"Lights don't turn on and off by themselves."

"So, who controls the big one?"

I replied, "It's not a light. There's no switch. It's . . . nature, it's planets, the Earth revolving . . ."

I trailed off at their blank looks. They'd been in shock just at the vastness of the Outside; they might have a total psychological breakdown if they tried to wrap their heads around how small we really were in the grand scheme of the universe. I deferred, "It's hard to explain."

The twins frowned in discontentment at my failure to answer their seemingly simple question. Reese pointed. "What are those?"

I looked out across what in the darkness had appeared to be the field of blinking red lights. As I'd suspected, the morning had revealed them to be machines. Hundreds of white towers were erected from the ground. Each structure had three blades rotating slowly in the lazy breeze. The nearest towers were colossal, appearing to shrink as they spanned away toward the flat horizon. Usually machines meant humans, and yet this place seemed to be absent of life other than the insects and birds. Our nighttime trek had brought us more than halfway through the field of spinning white towers, which would stop at the tree line ahead.

"I have no idea," I said. If I'd ever seen one of those towers before and known its name, my broken memory couldn't pull the word from the murky depths. Wind . . . something. Wind fan? That didn't sound right.

A quiet *beep* made us all stiffen. It was a reminder that tranquilizer dose number fourteen had just been administered into Axel's bloodstream. One left. Less than an hour.

Jay gazed at the closest machine. "Do you think it's hollow?" he asked.

None of us had an answer. Jay halted in the middle of the road. He knelt to lower Axel to the ground and then rifled through RC's backpack until he pulled out the bundle of clothes. "Reese, come with me," he said as he heaved Axel over his back again and headed for the nearest spinning wind tower. The boy followed him without a word of inquiry.

I shot a confused look at RC and Ash. "What's he doing?" I asked Finn.

"Jay wants to leave Axel inside the tower."

Sorrow condensed in my chest when I realized it was time to part ways with one of my lab-brothers, probably for good. I wished I had the chance to say a proper goodbye. I couldn't imagine crossing paths again in this vast place, not unless *They* caught us all again.

Finn sat down to wait, which wasn't a bad idea, so I joined him. Ash gracefully seated herself beside me and laid her staff across her lap. RC stood resolutely a few feet away, arms folded, jaw clenched, brow wrinkled.

I lifted my hand to shield my eyes from the sun and squint at Jay and Reese when they finally reached the base of the white machine. Reese walked through the wall, then returned. Jay nodded and spoke to him, and then Reese set his hand on Jay's elbow. The three passed through the wall and out of sight.

Kit shifted into her skin again in a billow of black smoke. She remained crouched on all fours, eyes trained at the place where they'd disappeared. Her lower lip started to quiver. "I don't wanna leave Axel," she whimpered.

Ash turned away, rationalizing, "He's still free."

"But it's not the same. He won't be with us."

Jay and Reese emerged from the tower without Axel. Kit started to cry again, her shoulders shaking with quiet sobs.

"Are you sure we should leave him?" I asked solemnly.

RC wouldn't look at me or anyone else when he said, "While he's asleep, he'll slow us down. And when he's awake, he's too dangerous. He might . . ." Kit gazed up at him, and he trailed off.

Kill us, I finished silently. Aloud, I assured Kit, "Axel can take care of himself." Fat tears continued to roll down her cheeks, her hiccupping sobs unbroken. Nothing I could think to say would be able to soothe her.

I clambered to my feet with a quiet moan as my bruises reminded me they were still fresh. Ash stood before I could offer my hand, but Finn remained sitting until our lab-brothers rejoined the group.

Jay seemed fine, but Reese was ashen with dark circles shadowing his half-closed eyes. Becoming intangible was a taxing endeavor, and phasing another person, let alone two, through a wall would have drained most of his power supply, which wasn't strong to begin with due to his passive Divinity. The glint of his cobalt eyes had dulled a bit from the depletion.

"Let's keep moving," said Jay, his gaze on the trees ahead.

Kit swiped at her tears and changed to fur again. Her tail drooped on the ground, and her silky black ears were pinned in silent mourning. I couldn't bear to see her so miserable, so I watched the field of rotating machine towers. Without the cover of darkness, the open land made my skin prickle. I hurried to match Jay's pace, which had quickened with a sense of urgency.

Agent Kovak sulked in the passenger seat with his arms crossed while he scanned the sweeping landscape. Byrn had both hands on the wheel, but his gaze also roved the horizon, occasionally flicking up to the rearview mirror to ensure the two identical vehicles were still following.

Kovak leaned forward to glance at the speedometer—137 miles per hour. He settled back in his seat and started tapping his fingers against his arm. *Not fast enough.*

A helicopter circled overhead. On the right side of the road, windmills dotted the fields, their white blades slowly rotating against the azure sky. The only other sign of movement was the lazy circling of turkey vultures above.

"I don't see them yet," Kovak grumbled.

"They're on foot. We'll overtake them."

Kovak simmered in silence, his acid reflux burning a larger and larger hole in his stomach with each passing minute while his blood pressure boiled. He dug his medication bottle out of his pocket and popped a pill into his mouth.

Byrn asked, "Is it safe to keep taking those?"

"Since when did you become a doctor? Just focus on the road."

Byrn eyed him sidelong, then redirected his glare through the windshield again. The line of trees ahead marked the end of the windmills and a break in the farmland . . .

And an ideal hiding place, Kovak thought, unfolding his arms and gripping the door handle on his right, his left hand still curled around the pill bottle.

As the helicopter flew ahead, Byrn eased the brake until the vehicle slowed to a stop at the edge of the woods. He shifted into park. "I'll bet every cent to my name they're in there," he said.

Agent Kovak stepped out. He slammed the door shut and gazed into the trees, arms folded. A hawk screeched somewhere in the woods. "They wouldn't have stayed on the road," he said over the thunderous roar of the passing helicopter. "They're smarter than that."

The driver's door slammed, and Agent Byrn circled the vehicle to stop at Kovak's side. "I hope our rats have enjoyed their freedom."

Agent Kovak nodded. "It's over."

— Chapter Four —

In the Ashes

She'd heard that in death, a man looked as though he were sleeping.

Not this man. His mouth was agape as if frozen mid-scream, his glassy eyes open wide, staring into nothing until Doc respectfully closed them.

"Raiders, to me!" called the clear voice of a woman.

Shannon Jennings tore her gaze away from the dead man. She'd been so entranced she hadn't noticed the townspeople gathering to watch the procession march down the aisle of City Hall.

How much City Hall had changed over the last couple of years. The great wooden doors were barred shut. The benches that had lined the colossal room for town meetings had been removed and dismantled, then used to board up the windows. In place of the benches were blankets, mattresses, and cots where displaced people slept. At the front of the room, three terraces rose up to a short stage where the leaders could address the town, and mounted on that wall was a large white-board, the remnants of a quickly sketched raid plan still drawn in blue marker.

City Hall harbored a fraction of the fifteen thousand residents who had once lived in Phantom Heights during its prime. People didn't come here anymore; the major highway that used to flow into Main Street had been rerouted to bypass the town. City Hall had transformed from a meeting place to a sanctuary, although Shannon thought of it more as a prison. Many times a day, she found herself lamenting her decision to remain in Phantom Heights with her mom, who had tried to persuade her to leave and live with her grandparents.

"I'm not leaving without you," Shannon had asserted.

"I can't go. People still need me here," her mom told her.

"But *I* still need you too. If you're staying, I'm staying."

Nothing her mom could say would change Shannon's mind once it was set. And now she was stuck here. She hadn't graduated from high school, was unlikely to attend college now even with her 4.0 GPA, and could only imagine what her future might have been beyond the conflict zone.

The raid team was gathering around their leader in front of the barred double doors that opened to town square. Despite Madison Tarrow's role in fracturing Shannon's family beyond repair, Shannon still held the ghost hunter in high respect. The past, as far as Shannon was concerned, was behind them. Now all that mattered was survival, and without Madison, they all would have been dead a long time ago.

"We meet Cooper in ten," Madison announced as she consulted a clipboard. "All right, listen up. I've got a roster change from this morning's raid. Behr, Parish, Blumenthal, Shepherd, Izard, you're blue with Emerton this round. Wright, Bell, LeFevre, Schumaker, you're with me. If I didn't call your last name, your team doesn't change. Final weapon check."

All attention was on the raid team; nobody was even looking at Shannon. People were too busy watching the raiders pass, reaching out to touch them, whispering kind words beneath Madison's authoritative roll call. This could be the last walk for some of them.

Shannon tied back her long hair and knelt by the deceased man's body. "I need to borrow this, Danny," she whispered as she unfastened the weapon belt from his waist. "Hope you don't mind." The belt was heavier than she had expected when she pulled it free; it was laden with pouches and loops to hold his Glock, ectogun, knives, Taser, ropes, and various other weapons.

Shannon slipped through the crowd with her head down so her mom wouldn't see her smoothly tuck in with the last of the raiders. As she fumbled to cinch the belt over her hips, she listened to the men muttering ahead of her.

"Two in one day? I don't know if I have another in me. This morning was brutal."

"Yeah, you can say that again. Bad drop."

"They could've aimed a *little* closer to City Hall."

"Pilot must've been taking fire. As much as I don't want to admit it, we should have better luck with Wes this time . . . if anything's left by now."

The other man scoffed. "I'm willing to admit it. I just hate hearing the arrogant prick brag about it."

From behind, a girl's voice seethed, "What are you doing?"

Shannon nearly jumped out of her skin when a hand seized her wrist and yanked her back. Instinctively, she snatched the ectogun out of the holster. She recognized that voice before she even turned to face her assailant. "Back off, Tarrow," Shannon hissed. She jerked her hand free.

"You back off, Jennings. You aren't a raider."

Three grades would have separated Shannon Jennings and Vivian Tarrow if they'd still been in school. The ghost hunter's daughter had inherited her mom's pretty green eyes, slim frame, and fiery spirit. Although Vivian had always claimed she was never interested in following her family's footsteps and becoming a ghost hunter, she handled her weapons with enough skill to convince Shannon otherwise.

Shannon shot her a sour look. "I just want some fresh air."

"Where'd you get the weapons?"

Shannon bit her lower lip and glanced guiltily over her shoulder to where Danny's body lay. Vivian lunged for the ectogun, but Shannon was just as quick to twist away. "I'll stay right behind you, okay?"

"No, it's *not* okay! Have you even fired one of those before? You'll shoot someone in the back before you help the team."

Shannon opened her mouth to fire back a retort, but a lean body pressed between the two girls, and she found herself staring through a pair of lenses into the cool gray eyes of Trey Selman. "I'll keep an eye on her," he assured.

Vivian huffed. She shouldered past them and snarled, "If anyone on the team gets hurt because of her, I will never forgive you."

Shannon tilted her chin down as she watched Vivian pass. She almost didn't hear Trey ask, "Okay, so how much shooting time you got under your belt?"

"Huh?"

He stared at her through his sleek prescription goggles, which had replaced his impractical contacts a while ago. "Shooting time. Have you had any target practice?" Shannon peered at him through her dark lashes, heat burning her cheeks. Trey shoved an unsolved Rubik's cube into his pocket as he drew an ectogun from his belt. "All you have to do is flick this safety switch right here. Just aim and pull the trigger. Easy, right?"

"Yeah, sure," Shannon said weakly.

"The core recharges itself, so you'll never run out of ammo. You can hit a ghost with ectoplasm even if it's intangible."

Trey reached toward her. She opened her fingers, thinking her hand was his objective, but to her embarrassment, he instead unholstered another gun from her belt. "Bullets are in short supply; don't waste them." He tapped the ectogun in her hand. "Down it with this." He held the Glock in front of her face. "Save this gun for when you're sure you won't miss the kill shot. Okay?"

Shannon opened her mouth, but her voice was gone. *It.* Down a living person—an *it*.

Trey gave her a crooked grin to reassure her when he reholstered the gun. The blond scruffy beard he'd sprouted gave him a bizarre aura of juvenile maturity, like a kid forced into an adult's role too quickly for his own body to keep up with the sudden responsibility. In Shannon's humble opinion, he was cuter clean-shaven. He gestured to her belt. "May I?"

Though unsure what he was asking permission for, she nodded. Trey reached into a pouch on her hip. "Sweet, Danny still had a couple left," he said, drawing something out in his fist.

"A couple what?"

"E-zaps. We're running low, but don't worry about them; only good for close combat. I don't think that's something you're planning to attempt today, am I right?"

"Right," Shannon squeaked.

Trey smiled at her and pocketed the small gadgets. "Just stay by me."

She nodded. She'd known Cato's best friend for a long time, ever since elementary school, but Trey, like City Hall, had changed. He wasn't the same goofy kid he'd been two years ago. None of them were. Although he still sometimes had the mannerisms of a puppy trying to play wolf, Trey had grown in this time of crisis more than any of their peers. He was Madison Tarrow's only true apprentice.

Shannon had always known he was smart; he had a talent for computer hacking, which occasionally used to get him into trouble even though his misdemeanors were caused by curiosity rather than a desire for wrongdoing. But he was maturing into a fine ghost hunter, a true protégé. Cato would have been proud.

As the raiders converged around their leader by the doors, Shannon withered under Vivian's brutal glares while Trey buoyed her with a wink. She kept her head down, skimming the crowd until she spotted her mom standing next to Mayor Correll. Shannon turned her back and subtly inched forward to put a few raiders between her and her mom. She checked the latch on the gun holster at her hip.

"Save this one for when you're sure you won't miss the kill shot."

Yeah, right. No way was she planning to unsheathe that Glock if she could help it.

Madison drew her ectogun, and the other raiders followed suit. "Blue team, give us fifteen before you start."

"Blue team?" Shannon whispered.

Trey explained, "Emerton leads the blue team. Madison and I head the green team with Wes. We find the best places to raid and send coordinates so the blue team can meet us with the truck."

"What truck?"

Trey gave her a sidelong look. No doubt he was regretting his decision to babysit her on the mission. "How did you think we transported supplies from the drop zones to City Hall?"

No time to answer. With a nod, Madison pulled out the horizontal bar and pushed the doors open. Shannon's heart leapt into her throat. This was it. She was really doing it. She was going outside.

The raiders moved forward. Now that Shannon was aware of the team's division, she noticed that Police Chief Emerton and a small band of raiders held back. The green team advanced, and she timidly trailed at the back of the group.

She caught her breath the moment her boot crossed the door's threshold. Her view outside was distorted, the scene of the ruined town bathed in a green tint. The doors slammed shut at her back with the finality of a death sentence. From inside, the bar slid into place. No going back now.

The raiders clustered together on the portico, sheltered behind the four columns at the top of the stairs. City Hall was shrouded in a transparent green barrier arching down from the tip of the clock tower in a protective dome. Shannon inhaled. The air carried a dank heaviness of smoke and decay. Her fingers tightened around the ectogun. As soon as the raid team stepped through the shield, it would be the only thing to protect her.

Shannon gazed out upon the open cobblestone plaza flanked on either side by a covered walkway along the boarded windowfronts of abandoned shops and cafés. Cables stretched across the plaza, suspending broken lights above their heads. Shannon could remember summer night festivals when she'd swear the lights were floating in the air like will-o'-the-wisps. The far side of town square was penned in by a pathetic row of half-dead trees separating the central fountain from Main Street.

Shannon shuddered. She'd heard rumors that the fountain wasn't dry anymore, and from here, she could see the contorted bodies filling the basin, almost inhuman in their death poses, the stench of decomposition carried on the breeze. Ghosts had rigged the fountain to put on a hell of a show. Even from across the plaza, Shannon could see the weak jets of blood spurting upward from the basin.

She flinched from a shadow darting on the other side of the transparent shield. The sky far in the distance glowed in bursts of green, blue, and violet to the sounds of faint screams and booming explosions.

A man's chilling voice said, "Well, I see the vermin have crawled out of their hidey-hole."

Madison raised her ectogun. The rest of the group mirrored her, taking aim at three ghosts on the other side of the shield. Shannon studied the creatures with wary curiosity while the other raiders looked down upon them with disdain. The leader was shirtless, and his burgundy cloak fell open to reveal his knotted muscles. White tattoos covered every inch of his burnt-umber skin in lines that stemmed from a circular flame motif on his upper arm. The irises of his eyes glowed crimson. Half a step behind him lingered a smaller man covered in a partial exoskeleton with bony spikes. The third ghost looked human—only her glowing blue eyes revealed her true bloodlines.

Madison said, "We don't want unnecessary bloodshed. Let us pass."

Shannon swallowed; she wouldn't have been able to speak so bravely. It was all she could do to hold the ectogun steady. She glanced at Trey, surprised to notice even his hand shaking. The whole raid team shifted with restlessness in the unnerving limbo of tension between peace and violence, mind reigning in instinct with fingers curled over triggers.

Shannon took a deep breath and tried to mimic Trey's braced stance, but she didn't dare release the safety on her ectogun. Not yet. She didn't trust her finger on the trigger. Her mind advised to stay still, but her body was in fight-or-flight mode.

The ghost woman's lips peeled apart into a gleeful smile, and the leader laughed. "That's no fun," he said.

Madison aimed her ectogun at his broad chest. "This is our town, and you will let us pass, or we will send you to the Realm Beyond."

The bone ghost snickered. "*Their* town? Did you hear that?"

The woman replied silkily, "I think they're delusional."

Shannon released the safety, just like Trey showed her. Although twenty humans outnumbered three ghosts, odds were not in their favor.

The ghosts here weren't *really* ghosts, at least not by true definition. They were mortal. Her mom preferred to call them demons, but Shannon wasn't sure that was accurate either. When humans first encountered the creatures with glowing eyes who could turn invisible, walk through walls, and manipulate ectoplasm in their hands, they were mistaken to be ghosts. The misnomer stuck, but these "ghosts" still had beating hearts.

The conflicts between the races escalated when ghosts started kidnapping humans for the slave trade and rumors leaked that Agent Kovak had been experimenting on ghosts and other creatures from the Ghost Realm. The town of Phantom Heights, aptly named, had always been a hotspot for brief Tears in the barrier that separated the Realms. Then came the Tear that didn't vanish like the others, and it was named the Rip.

With no way to seal the Rip, Phantom Heights found itself right in the warpath. The ghosts lashed back at humankind by damaging property, capturing and torturing humans, and often killing the prisoners who weren't dragged back through the Rip to be sold as slaves.

Madison Tarrow, who not only hunted ghosts but also studied them and developed weapons to combat them, had completed her late husband's prototype shield that repelled ectoplasm. She called the new energy source entoplasm. Ghosts, with a natural source of ectoplasm in their bodies, couldn't pass through, so within the border of the transparent green dome that surrounded City Hall, the humans were almost safe.

The ghost woman wrapped her arm around the leader's and rested her head against his shoulder. "I'm bored. Make them come out and play with us."

"If that'll make you happy, darling."

Heat waves radiated off his body as smoke curled up from his cloak. Shannon blinked, certain her eyes were playing tricks when the white tattoos on the man's body turned to glowing crimson to match his blazing eyes.

The raider standing next to Madison burst into flames. He screamed and started flailing as the fire engulfed his body and licked at the air, snapping warningly at the nearest raiders.

"Get out!" Madison yelled. "Now! Everybody out! Open fire!"

Shannon stood still, transfixed by the man ablaze. A couple of raiders had shoved him to the ground and were trying to smother the flames with their jackets while he rolled and thrashed. "Get out!" Madison was still calling.

Get out.

Shannon understood the words but couldn't make herself move.

"Come on!" said a boy's voice in her ear.

Get out.

A hand latched onto her jacket and yanked her forward.

Get out.

"Why?" she asked dazedly. Heat scorched her back. Stunned, she turned to see a wall of fire behind her, moving forward, driving her away from City Hall. Trey was pulling her down the steps. "We're supposed to be safe inside the shield."

"From ectoplasm, not fire. Come on, we have to move!"

The ghost woman's manic cackling was what finally snapped Shannon out of her stupor. "Look at them scatter! The building next! I want to watch them *all* burn!"

Shannon stumbled away from City Hall as the leader replied, "That would be a waste, my love. There's still good merchandise in there."

Slaves, Shannon thought. *Fodder. Playthings. That's all we are.*

Her feet landed on the cobblestones. Trey led her toward the shield's edge. The transparent green wall loomed in front of them. Shannon hesitated. What would it would feel like to pass through? Would it slow them down?

Will it hurt?

She squeezed her eyes shut and took a deep breath as though about to dive into a pool of water in the instant before her fingertips met the entoplasm.

Nothing. She felt nothing, not even heat, not the slightest resistance. She opened her eyes and looked over her shoulder to confirm the

4 | In the Ashes   - A Fallen Hero -   Sara A. Noë

shield was indeed behind her, and then she faced the city, no longer green-tinted but alive now with its true colors as if a filter had been cast off. Trey and the raiders in front of her knelt to take aim, and Shannon suddenly found herself an open target. She fell to her knees. On either side of her, shots of green ectoplasm exploded from the barrels, aimed directly at the three ghosts. Shannon had expected the sharp *cracks* of gun reports, but the ectoguns were quieter than she'd expected, a charging whine followed by a *shoom* when the energy was released. A transparent red dome of condensed ectoplasm swirled around the leader and the woman still laughing at his side. The bone-man had erected a smaller red disk. The blasts from the raiders' ectoguns collided harmlessly against the shields in a volley of light bursts.

Shannon's finger curled over the trigger.

"Just aim and pull the trigger," Trey had told her. Easy. *Right.*

Her weapon was pointed at the ground, her wits still unrecovered from the surprise attack. How naïve to let herself be lulled into a false sense of security inside City Hall's shield. All that time locked inside, she'd convinced herself she was safe there. Now, realizing how easy it would be for a ghost to burn City Hall to the ground with a snap of his fingers, her stomach turned. And pyrokinesis was just one of many devastating powers.

Ectoplasm was not the attack to fear when confronting a ghost; it was the Divinity. Almost every ghost had one divine power, and each Divinity ranged from passive abilities, like self-healing, to active powers, like telepathy. Identifying a ghost's Divinity as quickly as possible and devising a counterattack was crucial to survival. The seasoned raiders probably recognized the physical markers of the man with bony protrusions, but Shannon hadn't a clue what his Divinity might be. The leader was definitely a Pyro. The woman was an unknown, which made her even more dangerous.

Madison ordered, "Don't let up! Keep them occupied at that distance!"

The ghost woman stepped away from her tattooed lover. As her eyes glowed, electric-blue ectoplasm gathered in her palm. "I want to play. Let me take a few shots before you burn them all to a crisp." The energy crackled like sapphire lightning converging into a single mass in her hand.

Lift the gun, Shannon told herself. All around her, the raiders were firing in succession. *Shoot! Damn it, do something!*

She couldn't move. The ectogun was too heavy to raise. The leader let his domed barrier dissipate so he could replace it with a round shield of red ectoplasm instead. The woman had room to return fire.

At first, Shannon thought the female ghost must be a Telekinetic because her ectogun was finally rising. It had been so heavy, and now it didn't weigh an ounce, as if her body suddenly knew how to wield it. Up, level, parallel to the ground, aimed at the woman's head. *Fire*, she instructed herself. The leader's shield was partially disintegrating again so the woman could unleash her ectoplasm at the raid team. *Pull the trigger.*

Her finger tightened around it.

Pull. Now, do it now. Pull the trigger!

She couldn't.

Shannon's lips parted as if in preparation to gasp or scream—she wasn't sure which. The red shield had opened. Before Shannon could make a sound—before the woman could release her power—a hulking, four-legged creature charged across town square, its glowing yellow eyes fixed on the leader. He turned, too slow to react, too slow to reform his shield in time. Shock contorted his face as fangs sank deep into his shoulder and jaws locked into place.

In a petrified trance, Shannon lowered her ectogun until it pointed at the ground again.

"Lunos!" cried the ghost woman. She fired her ectoplasm at the massive wolf-beast instead of the humans. The energy struck the creature in the shoulder to no effect; she might as well have tossed a pebble at it.

The embattled leader became intangible to free himself, and the wolf's teeth clicked together on air. The moment the ghost solidified, the beast was on him again, long white fangs bared to tear into the neck flesh.

The bone-man rushed forward, fingers outstretched. "Don't let him touch you!" Madison screamed.

The wolf didn't react quickly enough. Fingertips met fur. At the ghost's touch, the wolf convulsed with a sound like sticks snapping, or in this case, rib bones. The animal whipped its head to the side, knocking away the bone-man with the flailing body of the Pyro still pinned in its massive jaws. The wolf jerked its head violently back and forth like a dog with a chew toy until there was a sickening *snap!*

The leader's limp body fell in a heap on the cobblestones.

Shannon flinched at the jarring *crack* of a gunshot's report that echoed down the streets. The blue-eyed woman collapsed, her blood misting in the air, Madison's Glock still leveled at where she'd been standing just a moment before.

Hackles raised, the wolf turned to face its final attacker, vengeance in its yellow eyes. A deep growl rumbled in its throat. The bone-ghost pivoted to flee, only to be downed with another *crack* from Madison's gun. The impact knocked him to the ground, but his exoskeleton had protected him from the bullet. He started to rise.

The wolf pounced. Shannon had to turn away. She heard the screams, the snarls, the *crunch* of bones yielding to the monster's strong teeth and crushing jaw, and then all went quiet. Shivering, she lifted her head to meet the wolf. It gazed intelligently at the humans, blood dripping from its muzzle.

Madison scowled. "You're late, Cooper," she snapped as she holstered her gun.

The raiders straightened. Shannon stayed on her knees for a few more seconds before she realized it was safe enough to stand. The lunos metamorphosed, the fur receding into skin. Bones popped into new placement as the beast rose onto its hind legs.

A new creature stood before the raid team, wiping the blood from his face and licking it from his hands with a coarse tongue. He was in limbo form, more wolf still than man, hunched over on two legs bent into furry haunches, his feet monstrous paws, a layer of fur covering most of his skin, his bushy tail whisking back and forth, teeth razor sharp. Ghosts called him a *lunos*, subclass of the weir. Humans preferred werewolf.

"I was delayed," he answered in a gravelly voice. His features were contorted in manageable pain. Gray fur grew and receded, bones creaking, his body trying to resume the form of the wolf even as he forced it to maintain limbo.

Trey, still gazing at the mutilated bodies and the crimson rivulets trickling between the cobblestones, said, "Was that really necessary?"

The werewolf narrowed his eyes. "He would have done the same to you." A growl deep in his chest followed the words and rattled Shannon's bones.

She swallowed and set her palm over her racing heart. She'd seen Wesly Cooper in his wolf form before, but never like that. He was always docile, more like a giant dog. *That . . .* that would haunt her dreams forever. She'd never be able to look at him the same in either form ever again.

"We missed the last supply drop," said Madison in a rush. "And our raid this morning brought back a poor yield. We needed you."

"I'm sorry. I still don't think it's a good idea to risk me being here near the full moon."

"And now you've gone and gotten yourself hurt already."

The wolf-man poked the ribs on his left side and winced, then forced a toothy smile. "I'll be all healed up by morning, and in the meantime, my nose still works just fine."

Madison waved her hand impatiently. "We need to move, and you're no good to us in limbo."

He nodded, visibly relieved, and sank into a crouch as he allowed the transformation to resume. Thick gray fur rippled in waves over his skin. He bent down onto all fours, his face lengthening into a snout with a groan and the grinding of bones, his hands curling back into paws. His wolf form was massive, closer to the size of a bear than a real wolf, his shoulders broader, a short mane of dark fur erected between his shoulder blades and up his neck. This body was prehistoric, a distant and much larger cousin to the extinct dire wolf, or so he liked to claim.

Wesly Cooper left a sour taste in Shannon's mouth, and not because she'd just witnessed his bloodlust. He was the wealthiest man in Phantom Heights, claiming he'd maximized his assets by making wise investments in the stock market. Perhaps in part that was true. Shannon had once found a folder on her mom's desk that contained police reports of mysterious bank robberies all over the country. In every instance, the police were baffled because the security cameras had detected nothing. The money was just gone . . . as if taken by a ghost. Shannon didn't know how Wesly Cooper was involved, but she suspected that stolen money had somehow ended up in the werewolf's pockets.

Cato had been a hero. Wes was a thief. It wasn't fair that Cato was gone and Wes was the one they had no choice but to trust. The only reason Wes had even stayed in Phantom Heights was Madison's threat to report him to the Agency of Ghost Control if he tried to move anywhere in the Human Realm. With his cover blown, he'd be forced to either live in hiding or retreat into the Ghost Realm.

The AGC was a small branch of the government that had been assembled to study and manage ghosts in this Realm. At the Rip's first appearance with its unwelcome visitors, the country's leaders turned to the "specialists" at the AGC for guidance. Agent Kovak assured them the situation would be managed.

He passed that responsibility on to Madison Tarrow, the local ghost hunter. Agents appeared every so often to study the major Tear, but they left the homeland security of Phantom Heights to Madison and any apprentices she chose to teach. Eventually another hero joined the effort—a masked ghost with bicolor eyes. Where he came from, no one knew at the time. He was a camera-shy, tantalizing mystery in the news until Agent Kovak ripped off the mask.

On the day of Cato's arrest, Shannon had been the one to pick up his bloody neoprene mask off the cobblestones. She could never forget the terror in his eyes the instant before the doors closed over his face. That moment was the beginning of the end.

Many humans were killed in the weeks following Cato's arrest. Shannon still remembered setting a penny on the gravestone of Vivian's brother because she had no flower to give. Even though Trey stepped up in his apprenticeship, Madison was distraught by her loss, and Phantom Heights descended into bloody chaos.

Shannon's mom had begged Kovak to send aid, but her pleas fell on deaf ears. "I can't afford to waste any manpower," he said. "We're researchers; we're not an army."

"Then send the army!" Shannon remembered her mom shouting into the phone.

"It's not that simple. Attacks from the Ghost Realm have been sporadic. Right now, we're dealing with individuals and gangs. If we send in our military, it's going to trigger a military response from their end. We aren't prepared for a full-scale invasion."

"How could he say that?" Shannon had asked her mom at the dinner table. "What are we supposed to do?"

Her mom had dabbed a napkin to the corner of her mouth, as composed as if they were discussing the weather. "He says he's working on a new weapon. Unfortunately, it isn't operational yet." She had set her napkin down and leveled her piercing gaze across the table at Shannon. "Mayor Correll is planning to issue evacuation orders tomorrow. I want you to go live with your grandparents."

But Shannon had refused to leave without her mom. The next day, she sat at the front window and watched Mr. and Mrs. Kollar cram their belongings into their van across the street while little Kathleen waited in her car seat. The Cheswicks pulled out of their driveway minutes later, followed by the MacLennans. One by one, the neighbors all left.

When the President of the United States declared a state of emergency for Phantom Heights and sought the AGC's counsel, Agent Kovak again advised against military involvement at the Rip. Soldiers and ghost hunters were deployed to neighboring towns for protection, but too many ghosts had already established a foothold in Phantom Heights for Madison to regain control.

And so, when Phantom Heights was clinging to the brink, Agent

Kovak deemed it a lost cause "until humankind is equipped to wage war against these supernatural terrorists."

And Phantom Heights fell.

Wes was no hero as Cato had been, but Madison's threat kept him in check . . . for now. He was an irreplaceable asset during raids, and sometimes he left Phantom Heights to buy supplies that couldn't be scavenged in the ruined town.

The raiders were regrouping. Shannon cast a look back at City Hall. How surreal, seeing it from the other side of the shield. The transparent green dome encompassing the white bell tower reminded her of the little church in the snow globe that sat on the mantle every Christmas. The fire on the portico had died out when the Pyro was attacked; it had been sustained by his power and couldn't burn on marble without it. The only traces of the blaze were faint tendrils of smoke rising from the scorch marks and a blackened body charred beyond recognition.

The wolf looked up at the swollen moon low in the west. He tilted his head back and howled, announcing to enemies that he was on the hunt.

Goose bumps erupted on Shannon's skin. She shivered.

Last chance to go back.

— Chapter Five —

Hunted

Howls echoed through the trees in the dawn.

I tripped over a root and stumbled, catching myself one-handed with barely a break in stride.

My body ran on with a mechanical rhythm, adrenaline forcing my muscles to keep moving despite the fatigue. I was not going back. I would rather die free in the Outside than return to that place.

Helicopter blades beat above the trees, blowing swirling storms of leaves around us in the man-made tempest. Ahead of me, the kitten collapsed, convulsing on the ground as she turned to smoke and re-assumed her skin. I skidded to a stop and seized the girl in my arms, pressing my hand over her mouth to muffle her screams.

The group paused while I held her body against my own, her heart-breaking squeals muted behind my palm while she thrashed. Finn and Reese, who had been lagging behind, doubled over with their hands on their knees, drawing deep, ragged breaths. I closed my eyes and wished the Spasm would pass quickly. Finally, Kit went limp in my arms.

I looked up in time to see the twins running back the way we'd come, toward the dogs and searchlights. "Jay!" I cried.

He cursed softly and sprinted after them. With a few long strides, he overtook them and tackled the boys to the ground.

"Let go!" shouted Finn.

RC marched over and hoisted Reese to his feet with one hand. Finn made a noise of frustration when Jay pressed his face into the dirt and said, "Not a chance. You don't get it, do you? It's too late! *They* think you ran away!" He heaved Finn up and shook him. "*They* will punish you!"

Finn's face crumpled in terror and defeat. Jay knelt to eye level, keeping firm hands on Finn's shoulders. "The only way to escape punishment is to keep running. I need you to trust me. It's the *only* way. Understand?"

Finn sniffed and nodded. Through the trees, beams from flashlights cast strange rays and shadows in the early morning mist wafting between the tree stalks. *Trunks.* Not stalks.

The dogs' howls chilled my blood and raised droves of goose bumps along my bare arms. "We have to move," I said.

Jay released Finn. "Let's go." He gave the boy a gentle shove.

We resumed our mad dash, Jay running behind Finn and Reese to keep them from doubling back. The twins were panting, struggling to keep pace with the rest of us. Reese tripped. He rolled onto his side, clutching his abdomen.

"Get up," Jay ordered, pausing to look down on him.

Finn collapsed to his knees beside his blood-brother. "Can't," Reese rasped. "Can't . . . run . . . any . . . more . . ."

"Please . . . let us . . . rest," Finn begged.

The baying was louder, more frantic, *closer.* I shifted my weight in the leaves, too anxious to hold still for even a few seconds. Had to keep moving, had to get out of there. We didn't even have a few minutes to catch our breath. "There's no time!" I said.

Jay threw the backpack at RC, who caught it in his left hand. Jay crouched down. "Get on my back." Finn obeyed. I knelt too so Reese could clamber onto my back.

Ash and Kit took off again as RC shouldered the backpack and followed. As soon as the twins had clasped their hands around our necks and hooked their legs around our waists, Jay and I rose and dashed after the others.

Again, I was amazed by how light the twins were; Reese barely burdened me at all. He set his chin on my shoulder, too drained to even raise his head. I had more than enough adrenaline to carry us both forward.

The morning shadows shortened as we sprinted on, led by the tiny but fast kitten scampering through the dead leaves. I ducked my head as the helicopter flew above us, swirling the leaves in a gale. "This way!" Jay called.

Kit, who had been in the lead, slid to a stop and changed direction. I'd hoped the thick canopy would hide us from the pilot, but we just couldn't get away. *They* must be using infrared to track us.

I voiced this concern to Jay, who glanced up to glimpse the underbelly of the helicopter flying over a gap in the canopy. There, mounted on the front end, was a rotating globe that looked suspiciously like a camera lens. Jay must have seen it too because he called, "RC? Can you take out that sensor?"

The Telekinetic cast a skeptical look up. "It's far away," he said as he ducked under a low limb. "I'm not sure I can get that high."

"Try," I pleaded. "Or we'll never make it."

He shoved his hand into the pouch on his thigh and drew a single silver disk. His good eye flared, and the curved blades ejected with a quiet *snick* lost in the roar of the copter.

He stared skyward as he ran, his gaze fixed on the churning tree tops. He was patient. His eyes narrowed, searching while he waited for the opportune moment. Finally, the trees opened up for a few critical strides, leaving a gap where the blue sky was visible for a moment before the black machine blocked it.

RC had only seconds to act before we were under the canopy again. With a grunt, he flung the disk up with all his might. We slowed to watch. I tilted my head back to follow the bladed weapon spinning toward the lens on the bottom of the helicopter. Dead-on! The blades collided with the sensor, but the disk clashed and bounced off, leaving barely a scratch.

"Try again!" Jay shouted.

RC grimaced in pain but held up his wounded arm, one hand outstretched to control the disk, the other controlling . . . I didn't know what. Nothing seemed to be happening.

The helicopter veered at an angle so the man in the open cabin had a clear line of sight when he raised a rifle to his eye. He was aiming at me. The sight of the rifle made me stop dead in my tracks.

The globe on the helicopter's belly detached and fell somewhere in the trees, but it didn't matter because a dart was flying toward me, and all I could do was watch it come. In my peripheral, RC threw his hand out in desperation, but my gaze was fixed on the dart.

I swallowed, cross-eyed, staring at the tranquilizer dart frozen in the air an inch from my nose. My heart beat once, twice, thrice—the longest second of my life.

The dart spun around, and when RC's intense gaze danced back up to the helicopter, the dart followed, rocketing back toward the shooter. The man's own tranquilizer struck him in the neck. He pulled it out, stared at the dart sitting in his palm, and fell to his knees, then collapsed on his side.

That would've been me.

The helicopter swerved out of RC's range. Whatever spell I was under broke when Ash seized my cloak and yanked me forward. We were under the trees again. "How'd you do it?" I choked out, looking at RC over my shoulder.

He swiped at the blood gathering in one corner of his mouth and then held up a long, thick industrial screw. He pocketed it, then held out his open hand as we sprinted on. From somewhere in the trees, his silver disk whisked through the air, returning to its master. RC retracted the blades and sheathed it in his pouch, his work done.

The helicopter stayed above us, but its pursuit had changed. It drifted farther away, first off to the right, then passing over us and falling behind and to the left, then roaming back to our right. It was doing unfocused sweeps until finally, it retreated. Its roar faded into the distance, leaving only barking in the wake of the loud rotors.

I'd swear we'd been running for hours. Whether or not that was true, I couldn't say. We leapt over fallen logs, wove between tree trunks, pushed our way through wicked brambles, and paused only when one of us suffered a Spasm. Closer and closer, *They* came. As fast as we ran, the dogs were always gaining. I could hear the rustle of dead leaves beneath their paws.

Movement from the corner of my eye made me gasp; I knew what the blur was before it even registered in my vision. I turned my head to see a bloodhound vault over a fallen tree. Teeth snapping, globs of foamy saliva dripping from its jowls, it ran low to the ground, gathering itself to leap at the nearest person—Jay, who still had Finn on his back.

RC's hand disappeared into his pouch, but by the time he could pull his disk out, it would be too late. As the dog leapt, Ash stepped in front of Jay, her staff in both hands. She let loose a battle cry and swung with all her might, cracking the beast in the head to down it. The canine snarled and crashed to the ground, but it scrambled to its feet with jerky, disjointed movements, teeth still bared.

Ash readied her staff again, but it was RC who made the next move. He threw his disk, blades out. It clipped the dog in the shoulder. Not a fatal wound, but critical enough to down the animal, which yelped and fell in the leaves, whining and licking at the bloody gash.

"What is that thing?" Reese whispered in my ear. He was staring over my shoulder with wide eyes. I frowned. Hadn't he seen a dog before?

The rest of the pack was moving in fast, *Them* right behind. We turned and ran. The adrenaline was good; it drove me onward. The panic setting in was bad; it made me jittery and dysfunctional.

We weren't going to make it. Part of me accepted that and wanted to give up, lie in the leaves, and imprint my last memories of the Outside to hold onto for as long as I could, even though clutching memories was like trying to hold water. Surrender with dignity.

Another part—an animal of desperation that clawed at me from the inside—rejected that premise. It would fight to the last breath. The adrenaline fed that side of me, kept me going even when I couldn't feel my legs and every breath was like inhaling needles.

The afternoon was waning. Ahead, the ground was a shimmering surface through the trees. It was strange, surreal, out of place even in this foreign world, but within a few more strides, I realized what it was.

Water.

A creek blocked our path. Kit halted at the edge, her paws inches away from the sparkling surface. "Should we cross?" I asked when I reached her.

"No," Jay answered, sloshing into the water. It swirled around his calves. He stopped and turned to us. "We'll follow it. The water will hide our trail."

I splashed in after Jay, who started trudging down the creek. Kit pinned her ears back, mewing softly. RC scooped her up in one hand and set her on his left shoulder where she dug her claws into his cloak to hold on. He followed us while Ash lingered on the bank, staring at the water. She hopped from foot to foot in indecision, but the sounds of the approaching dogs compelled her to splash in after us.

— Chapter Six —

Tomb

For a moment, all was quiet. I tried to steady my ragged gasps, straining to listen while imagining the dogs with their noses to the ground, sniffing the bank where we'd entered the water. *Did we lose them?*

Howls broke out with renewed frenzy.

I whirled. Reese's grip around my neck tightened. High on panic, we hurried faster, certain our hunters would burst from the trees any second. The water hadn't fooled the dogs. *They* were still coming.

My skin crawled in expectation of the sting of a dart finding its mark. The water felt thick, the mud sucking at my feet to keep me from moving forward.

We had decided that we'd rather die than go back. RC had his lethal silver disks; all he had to do was slit our throats. It would be quick, much preferable to dying in Project Omega. As much as I feared death, I'd decided this was the way I wanted to go. I would die free in the sunlight.

Even though I was resolved to the decision, my throat clenched when RC grimly drew a disk in preparation.

And then, the baying ceased.

The sudden quiet was disconcerting. I looked left, right, left again, straining to hear over the sounds of our splashing.

I was almost relieved when the first howl broke the unnatural lull again, followed by a chorus of barks and whines punctuated with yelps. A woman's voice called, "There! I see him!"

I turned toward the sound of the voice. That was it; we were done. *They*'d spotted us. *They* . . . were nowhere to be seen. And maybe my imagination was skewing my perception, but . . . the dogs didn't sound as loud. Despite their renewed howls, they seemed to be moving in the wrong direction. Distance was growing between us and *Them*.

Ash tripped and landed on her hands and knees in the water, sobbing. "I can't run anymore!"

Jay splashed to a stop. The rest of us slowed, knee-deep in the creek. I twisted around to see Ash angrily push her long auburn hair behind her ear. She sat up and swiped the tears and mud from her cheek with the back of her glove.

"Shh," said Jay, holding up his hand.

We held our breaths to listen. Kit, still perched on RC's shoulder, flicked her ears back and forth. I heard—or at least I convinced myself that I did—the dog pack far away, their howls off in the distance. I turned, my cloak fanning out in the murky water as I scanned the tree line on either side of the creek.

"What happened?" I whispered, still too petrified to speak at a normal volume in case this was a trick.

Nobody had an answer.

Ash trudged toward the bank. "Not yet," said Jay, grabbing her bare arm. "We should keep going to make sure they don't come back and pick up our trail again." Ash closed her eyes and sighed, hanging her head.

The adrenaline leaked out of my body so fast the exhaustion nearly downed me. Reese's weight quadrupled on my back. My knees gave out when I knelt, the cool water rising up to my waist. "Reese, do you think you can walk on your own for a while?"

My passenger slid off. Jay let Finn down in the water next to me. "We should keep moving," Jay advised.

Kit twitched her tail, blinking blearily. RC reached his left hand up to his shoulder and patted her on the head. Still alert and on the lookout for danger, Jay trudged downstream again at a slow pace. I followed, Reese by my side as the others trailed after us. Ash hesitated, casting a longing look at dry ground before traipsing at the rear.

We walked in silence. I observed the woods as we traveled—the slender trees, the bright green leaves, the shifting patterns of shadows.

A small, furry animal skittered up a tree, waving its bushy tail. The howls of the dogs were gone. New sounds I hadn't noticed before filled the void. Twitters and chirps, and leaves rustling, and a deep croaking *burrup* of a water creature hidden on the bank.

The water swirled around my knees. Small shadows darted around the rocks, scattering when I came too near. Jay gasped in front of me and stopped dead in his tracks. I turned forward at the sound of a splash to find him on his back, screaming and clutching his head. He choked as water entered his airway.

I rushed to him and lifted his head above the water. He probably didn't know I was holding him. The others watched in numbed exhaustion. Jay's movements became less violent as his cries softened to moans and he finally relaxed. It took every ounce of my strength to haul him to his feet. He staggered, as if his legs couldn't hold his weight, and I held onto him for a few extra seconds until he found his balance. I let go of Jay but froze, looking around in alarm. "Where are Finn and Reese?"

The others turned in circles, scanning the trees for our lab-brothers. My fear was they'd slipped away again to try and return to their masters, but no, I found them nearby. Finn was on the bank with both hands on the trunk of a tree, his nose inches from the bark. Reese stood farther back in the water, his head tilted up. Although he never turned around, he knew we were watching him and asked, "What is it?"

"A tree," said Ash.

"Tree," Reese echoed, committing the word to memory.

We'd been running through the woods for a full day, and they were just now asking what trees were? Then again, they'd been following us blindly. There was no time for curiosity earlier.

Finn's fingertips drifted across the rough bark. "This is such a strange object. What cause did humans have for building it?"

"They didn't build it," I said in surprise.

The twins directed their uncomprehending stares at me. "You're wrong," Finn whispered. I stared at him, startled to realize how shaken he was by my response.

Reese said, "Humans built the world. You were born human, Cato. You should know that."

I shook my head. "Humans built that place. Outside is a completely different world. Those trees are alive, and they grew here by themselves. Humans didn't build them."

"Wrong," said Finn.

His brother said, "If they were alive, we'd be able to hear their thoughts."

"Therefore, they can't be alive."

I opened my mouth, but nothing came out. Although they were incorrect, their logic was sound. I attempted to explain, "Trees might not have thoughts, but you know they're alive because they grow. That big tree started out small enough to fit on your thumb."

"Not possible," Reese insisted.

I snorted. "Seriously? You're fluent in multiple languages, you programmed the NMS, and you invented a super-computer, but you can't accept that a tree is alive?"

Finn tilted his head, his vibrant blue eyes fixed on my face. "How are our linguistic and computer-interface aptitudes relevant to our ability to classify biotic and abiotic components of the environment?"

The string of words spilled from his mouth all at once, and I had to ponder his response for a moment before I even understood what he'd said. Why couldn't they speak like normal kids their age? I silently scoffed at myself. Finn and Reese normal . . . *right*.

Rather than try to explain, I said, "You know what, never mind."

Jay urged, "Come on. We shouldn't linger too long."

The twins, their heads still craned back to look up at the canopy, splashed over to us. Not more than a few minutes later, Finn halted, peering at something in the water. He bent down and dove his hands into the creek to snatch something from the bottom. He straightened and approached me with the object in both hands. "Cato, what is this?"

I glanced at it. "A rock."

Mesmerized despite my dismissive reply, he held it closer to scrutinize it. "Is it alive?"

"No."

"Oh. Then it's dead?"

"No. It was never alive."

Finn's brows drew together. "But how can a tree be alive and not a rock? Neither moves nor thinks."

I exhaled and rubbed the back of my neck. *How the heck should I explain this?* Before I could even try, Reese approached holding another object in one hand. "Cato, what is this?"

"A leaf."

He held it up in front of his face. "Is it alive?"

Frustration started to gnaw on my patience, but I really couldn't blame the twins. It was only natural for them to have questions. I tried to see the world through their eyes. Every object at that place was made by humans. The ceiling, the floor, the walls, the lights, the cages, the computers . . . *everything.* Even the air seemed to be synthesized with chemicals. It made sense that Finn and Reese reached the conclusion early in their lives that everything in the world was created by humankind. The concepts of night falling without a person turning off the light or trees growing by themselves without being built by humans were so foreign they couldn't accept them.

Reese was still staring at his leaf, waiting for my answer. I cleared my throat and attempted to explain, "Right now it isn't alive, but it used to be. It's like . . . like your finger. Okay?" Both twins stared at me, waiting for me to clarify my analogy. "Pretend *They* cut off one of your fingers. You'd still be alive, but your finger wouldn't be anymore. So, this leaf was alive when it was attached to the tree, but now it isn't. Does that make sense?"

They considered, then bobbed their heads in understanding. Finn asked, "Do trees bleed when they lose their leaves?"

"No."

Reese asked, "Does it hurt?"

"I don't think so."

Finn looked at the setting sun and noticed, "The light moves."

"Yes." By now he knew better than to ask me why.

Twilight fell, and then night washed over the land. We were guided by the light of the glowing white orb in the sky. No, not orb. *Moon.* That was it. I knew it had a name.

Finn kicked at the water as we walked. "Who put all this water here?"

"Nobody," I said.

"Then why is it here?"

I rubbed my eyes with my thumb and forefinger. "I don't know."

I expected the twins to keep rambling questions, but they must have comprehended my frustration, and by now they were too tired. For the moment, they were content just to observe this new world as we followed the winding creek through the woods. They trudged after us, trailing behind and moving slower and slower.

"Hey," said Ash, her exhausted voice so soft I barely heard her. I turned to find her pointing at an old tree rooted by the bank. The water, when the creek was higher than it was now, had washed away much of the dirt from its massive roots, exposing deep crevices. "Couldn't we rest there for a little while?"

Jay surveyed us—how Ash swayed on her feet, how the twins were falling asleep standing up, how Kit was drained from clinging to RC's cloak, how RC held his injured arm with his head down. "We'll be hidden from view," I persuaded. "And we'll be right by the water."

"All right," he relented.

The mud sucked at our boots as we slipped and scrambled out of the creek. Ash paused to remove the staff from her harness so she could squeeze between thick clusters of roots. She settled in and closed her eyes, gripping the staff diagonally across her chest like a child might snuggle with a teddy bear.

Finn and Reese swayed in place, blinking lethargically and looking lost. Jay and I watched them, waiting for them to act.

They didn't. Jay sighed and stepped forward, gently scooping Reese into his arms. He laid Reese down in a fissure, then turned and picked up Finn. He was tender as he set Finn down next to Reese. The twins huddled together in their crevice, asleep immediately. I suspected the small, dark, confined space reminded them of their cages, and as twisted as that was, it comforted them. Their world was scaled down so they were protected from the Outside, at least for tonight.

RC watched Jay lovingly tuck the twins into the roots. His pained expression transformed to uneasy suspicion as he surveyed our beds for the night. He studied the intricate threads of a spider web catching the moonlight in the branch above us, then eyed the roots as if he were afraid a Scout was hiding there waiting to jump out and attack. "I'll keep watch," he announced.

I sat down on a root's bulging knot. Jay said, "You sure?"

"Yeah." RC drew one of his silver disks.

Jay lingered near him. "I can keep watch. You need to sleep."

"So do you. I'll wake you if I need you."

I was too tired to partake in the argument and secretly relieved I didn't have to volunteer to stay awake first. My tongue felt swollen when I slurred, "I'll take watch after you, Jay." Fatigue had numbed me. I eased my weak, wet body inside the crevice and stopped fighting the pull on my eyelids.

Darkness. The roots encompassed me—*like a tomb*, I made the mistake of thinking. I inhaled the earthy scents of creek mud, moss, and rotted wood. All I could hear was the rush of water and the quiet rustling of leaves in the breeze. With a muffled groan, Jay settled into the roots nearby. The dogs were nowhere to be heard, and the knowledge that RC was watching over me was a blanket of comfort.

"Cato?" came a soft whisper. I barely discerned the form of a hand settling on the roots beside me. I lifted my leaden arm to grasp the bare fingers. "No bars between us this time," Ash murmured, interlocking her hot fingers between my cold ones.

"No bars," I mumbled back.

The weight of four petite paws settled on my chest. Kit crept forward to touch her nose to mine as if to say goodnight and express her shared pleasure at not being separated in cages. She kneaded my chest for a full minute before she curled up into a tiny ball and draped her tail over her face. Her eyes closed as she settled in with a weary sigh. Faint purring vibrated my rib cage.

I stroked the top of her head with one finger, my consciousness drifting away, my hold on Ash's limp fingers slackening. Like I did every Lightsout, I whispered, "My name is Cato," so I wouldn't forget.

And then I was in a sleep so deep I was dead to the world.

— Chapter Seven —
Shadow's Stirrings

Azar stood at the window, legs braced, arms crossed, staring out at the desolate cityscape. The sky was a deep indigo with striations of cyan in the low rain clouds. Although the ever-present cloud cover never ruptured to allow sunlight to reach the surface, Avilésor was not a gray, dull world. Atmospheric winds and gas concentrations were constantly redesigning the clouds in form and color. Yesterday, the sky had been a solid jade; the previous day, the clouds had been churning and swirling, beautiful warm hues of red and orange and pink with highlights of yellow; the day before that, it had been a bicolor sky, violet to the east fading into pink in the west.

Today, the heavy moisture promised an afternoon thunderstorm. Fog was beginning to rise and curl in the streets, dampening stone and metal and glass as it drifted between the broken dwellings of what had been, many centuries ago, one of the great Five Cities. Solaris ruled the North, Delkoa the South, Vel the West, and Thordain the East. Szion occupied the heart of the Realm.

The remains outside Azar's window were what was left of Szion. Azar sighed, troubled by the bleak cityscape before him. The kálos race was not peaceful. It had brought about its own destruction with feuds and battles in an endless struggle for power. Szion's infrastructure was failing. It had been an architectural wonder in its prime when King claimed it as his stronghold. Now, more than four thousand years later, the foggy streets had the air of a graveyard. No wonder kálos were so eager to escape.

But that was unacceptable for two reasons. One, the thought of kálos escaping the lawful grip of the Shadow Guard sent Azar into a foul mood. And two, humans in Cröendor were preparing for war while kálos continued their immature squabbling amongst themselves. Azar's impossible task was to unite káloskind, something that hadn't been done in history since the great King had seized control of Avilésor at the start of the last Dynasty. The human government was building a weapon, and time was against Azar. The lowly slave race might actually pose a real threat. What a sickening thought.

A timid rap of knuckles on the door jolted him from his reverie. "Enter," he said, still facing the window.

A raven with a white-tipped wing rested on a perch in the corner. It ruffled its feathers and squawked at their visitor.

Azar watched the Captain of the Guard emerge in the window's reflection. "Close the door." Hassing hesitated, then obeyed before he turned nervously to face Azar, who didn't waste time with the usual *ehlai* greeting and asked, "What did you find?"

The captain shifted. "Nothing new concerning the weapon, sir."

Azar's red eyes flashed in the reflection. Shadows gathered around his figure like a cloak that trailed across the floor.

Hassing backed up, gulping, his eyes wide in alarm. "*But*, I did hear some interesting information, sir, a new development that could help us, if . . . if you would hear me out."

"It better be good," Azar grumbled, never once turning to look at his subordinate.

Hassing's reflection nodded eagerly. "It is. I promise. The Agents have been developing their weapon in Project Alpha."

Azar scowled. "Hmph. You're telling me what I already know." The room darkened, and the bird squawked again.

"Yes, sir, I know, but you see, we have a rare opportunity to get inside information."

Azar narrowed his eyes, cautiously curious. "Oh?"

"There were eight kálos incarcerated in Project Alpha. They escaped last night. Sir, they're loose in Cröendor."

Azar finally turned. "You're telling me the very kálos who know everything there is to know about the weapon escaped from the AGC?"

Hassing nodded. Azar's heart flew as his mind turned over this new development. He dropped his gaze to mask his excitement. "Interesting. If we can get our hands on them . . ."

"Unfortunately, that's easier said than done. The Agents are hunting them down."

Azar waved his hand dismissively. "We'll just have to find them first."

Hassing reached behind his head to tighten his short ponytail. "Are you thinking the fugitives will ally with us?"

"Possibly. We do share a common enemy. If they won't, I'll just take the information I want by force. Either way, I need them."

"I heard they're supposed to be extraordinarily powerful. That's why they were chosen for Project Alpha."

"Even better. I want you to find them and bring them to me. Take whoever you need from the Shadow Guard to get the job done. If they don't come willingly, bring them by whatever means possible. But don't hurt them too badly. I want them alive and intact, do you understand?"

"I do. I'll just fetch Titon and—"

"No. Leave Titon here."

Hassing froze. "Sir?"

"This is a delicate matter, and I want a quiet extraction. Titon will draw too much attention in Cröendor."

The captain inclined his head and muttered, "As you wish."

"It's not a wish—it's an order. I want those fugitives, Hassing."

"Yes, sir." Hassing bowed deeply as he backed away.

"Good. You're dismissed."

The captain, in his haste to escape Azar's office, turned and nearly ran face-first into the closed door. With a nervous chuckle, he became intangible and walked through the wood.

Azar returned his gaze to the window. His reflection gazed back at him—ebony skin as dark as a moonless Cröendorian night, the irises of his ruby eyes glowing. His black hair was sheared short with swirling patterns shaved away, a closely-trimmed beard tracing his jawline.

"Rayven," he murmured.

The bird blinked at him, and its obsidian feathers shifted to smoke as the animal's form expanded and fell from the perch. Bare feet landed on the floor, a man in the raven's place. He immediately fell to his knees, bowing his head. A single griffin feather was tied in a lock of his long, straight, black hair. He wore no shirt and baggy, loose-fitting pants that cut off just below his knees. Around his neck was a round ivory tag that gleamed against his tan skin.

"Yes, Master?" Rayven asked while keeping his gaze trained on the floor.

Far below Azar's office window, Hassing was striding into the stone courtyard with two Shadow Guards at his heels. "I have a job for you as well. I want you to tail the Agents."

Rayven gulped and raised his head to stare at Azar in horror. "The Agents?" he squeaked.

Azar turned enough to glance over his shoulder at the slave still bowed on the floor. "No need to worry. Keep your distance and remain in your animal form, and they won't catch you. I need you to alert me if they know where their fugitives are, or if they've captured them." At Rayven's insistent hesitation, Azar snarled, "Unless you dare to refuse my order and take my punishment instead?"

"N-no, Master!" Rayven leaned forward until his forehead rested on the floor. "But . . . there are many Agents. Um . . . w-which one should I follow?"

Azar turned back to the window. "Come here, Rayven."

Rayven jerked his head up and started trembling, but he remained on his hands and knees. "I said, come *here.*" His slave stumbled to his feet and meekly approached, already braced. Azar watched him draw near in the reflection of the window, and when Rayven was within reach, he seized the man by the back of the neck and pulled him closer.

Rayven grimaced when Azar hissed in his ear, "You are to go into Cröendor and follow whoever is in charge of the search. Any significant news of the fugitives I'm looking for, and you return to me with a report. Use whatever spies you can find in Cröendor to assist you. Understand?"

Rayven nodded quickly. Azar tightened his grip, evoking a weak groan of pain. He whispered, "And if you don't return, I will hunt you down and strip you of your Name, and then you will live in a cage in the dark for so long you'll forget the light. Am I clear?"

The slave nodded again. "Good." Without loosening his hold on Rayven's neck, Azar reached out and pushed the window open. He shifted his hand from the slave's neck to his shoulder and dug his thumb into a pressure point. Rayven grimaced, and his body turned to smoke as he was forced to resume his other form.

Azar smiled as he watched the raven with the white-tipped wing fly under an arched sky bridge toward the outskirts where the Rip connected the Realms. Wrapped around the bird's leg was a cord with an ivory tag.

Azar didn't move until the bird vanished from sight. His smile widened; he finally had a rare opportunity to forge an alliance with powerful kálos who could give him the information he so desperately needed to begin planning his counterattack, maybe even give him enough of an edge to lead the first strike before his enemies had the chance to make their play. Everything was lining up in his favor.

All he needed now were the fugitives from Project Alpha.

— Chapter Eight —
Half-Blood

"Please don't do this. Please, I swear I'll do whatever you want, please no . . ."

Reese didn't even blink at my plea. He hit ENTER. White-hot pain lanced through my head with a rush of metal as the thick needles shot inward through the ports in my skull.

He grabbed a fistful of my hair and forced my head back. I stared up at Him through a film of burning tears. "There, see? The worst is over. That wasn't so bad, was it?"

He released my hair and seized the back of my neck, compressing with his strong hand to keep me compliant. He steered me out of the room into the long hallway again. My head throbbed, the thin spikes deeply embedded to inject the fibrous sensors into my brain like spider webs—if only I'd known then how they caught memories instead of insects.

"All right, we're going to play a little game now . . ."

My eyelids peeled apart, snapping the invisible sutures of sleep. Instead of bright fluorescent lights, sunlight streamed through the leaves of the great tree. Winged . . . things—the word was on the tip of my tongue—*birds* twittered in the late morning. Tears were still wet on my cheeks. I was drenched in a cold sweat, my heart thumping hard.

Where am I? Did They *drug me again?*

Was I even awake?

Pain. Even my hair follicles were screaming. Twitching my fingers, marginally tilting my head, swallowing . . . it all hurt. I touched my forehead, expecting my fingertips to meet metal, but the ports were exposed. No NMS.

My muscles were so stiff I was sure I'd become part of the tree. With a groan, I hauled myself upright. *Ouch.* I felt as if I'd been pulverized in the Arena. I rubbed my eyes. Slowly, the memories of the last day seeped back into my consciousness. I was . . . Outside? I was. I was Outside. Why hadn't Jay woken me for my shift to keep watch?

He probably never took his turn. RC's head was bowed as he snored. Kit must have left me for a drink of water sometime in the night, and she'd nuzzled in with the nearest person—Jay, whose mouth hung open, head tipped back against the trunk as if he'd fallen asleep watching the moon through the branches. All of my lab-siblings were sleeping, their chests rising and sinking with light, shallow breaths.

My stomach voiced its complaints and then twisted into a knot to punish me for not feeding it. Eating was a necessity, not a pleasure. The "food" at that place was tasteless gruel, but at least it eased the hunger pangs that now tortured me.

I flicked my dry tongue over my cracked lips. The sound of gurgling water tempted me to crawl to the edge of the bank, where I removed my gloves and gauntlets and cupped my hands to fill them with the cool water. I raised it to my lips and drank deeply. The water alleviated the pain in my stomach but didn't satisfy it.

Once I'd quenched my thirst, I raised a handful of water to my face. I froze, staring at the tattoos in the soft, pale skin on my forearms. The number on my left arm identified me as the five thousandth, two hundredth and ninety-second subject to be admitted to that place. The number on my right arm identified me as the seventh subject in Project Alpha. When I was there, those were my names. A7-5292. I hated those tattoos, those names . . . I wished I could rid myself of those reminders, but all I could do was conceal them beneath my gauntlets so at least I didn't have to look at them.

I splashed water on my face, then scrubbed at the dirt and blood crusted on my skin. I settled back and pried off the boots. Unwinding the cloth made my new blisters scream. Tears pricked my eyes when the last layer ripped off the dried scabs of blood and pus.

I submerged my sore, swollen feet in the cold creek water. Gently, I cleansed them, then patted them dry with my cloak before redressing them. Eager to cover the tattoos branded into my skin, I laced up the gauntlets and tugged the fingerless gloves back on. I rose, hesitating at the edge of the bank. A warm breeze sighed through the woods, making the branches sway and the leaves rustle with a soothing whisper over the babbling creek. I couldn't hear even the faintest sound of a dog barking. I closed my eyes and inhaled deeply, enjoying the feel of sunshine on my face and peace for the first time in a long time.

I lifted my arms to stretch my tight muscles. Pressure in my lower abdomen made me turn away from the creek and venture past the crooked old tree where we'd taken refuge. As I passed, a figure emerged from the roots, and Ash groggily called my name. I paused.

"Cato?" she repeated as she rubbed sleep from one eye. "Where're you going?"

"I have to pee."

"Don't go too far, okay?"

"I won't," I promised. True to my word, I stayed closed to our campsite when I relieved myself behind a shrub. As I finished, I frowned and turned my head slightly. I'd heard nothing but the usual sounds of the woods, and yet I thought I saw a shadow dart in my peripheral.

My heart fluttered, eyes flitting in search of the dark shape. Unease condensed into a pit in my stomach. My skin crawled. I felt like something was watching me. And . . . something else. There was a charge in the air, like electricity but not. It was a pulse, like a second heartbeat that was out of rhythm from mine. I spun a slow circle, searching, but all I found were tree trunks and underbrush.

I exhaled and reluctantly faced the creek, glancing over my shoulder one more time. Must have been a bird gliding by—that was why I hadn't heard anything. Still, I couldn't shake that sense of foreboding that made my hair stand on end.

The sun had vanished behind a cloud bank. The pleasant breeze had a chilly nip to it when I returned to the tree and discovered the others awake and sitting by the water's edge. My conversation with Ash must have roused them. The kitten greeted me by rubbing her face against my boots, circling my feet, and purring. I bent down to scratch her chin before approaching the others.

Kit trotted after me, turning to smoke and reforming into her skin when we joined the group. The twins were seated with their knees drawn up to their chests, staring at the water. They didn't even raise their heads. The dark circles under their eyes made me wonder how much time they spent sleeping and how long they lay awake shivering in their damp root bed while imagining the punishment their masters would concoct for their disobedience. RC twirled a silver disk between his fingers, his injured arm resting limply in his lap. Jay inclined his head in a silent acknowledgment of my presence.

"So, what's the plan?" I asked.

"Keep moving," he answered vaguely, his eyes unfocused while he stared at the water, lost in thought.

The atmosphere now felt alarmingly wrong. The charge in the air had intensified. I sensed that a predator had me locked in its sights. Again, I didn't hear anything out of the ordinary. Water trickling over rocks, leaves rustling, birds . . . *No.* The birds, I suddenly realized, were all gone.

I felt a pair of eyes watching me.

I turned my head slowly, afraid I'd see a passing shadow again that would disappear as soon as I became aware of its presence. A figure cloaked in black was standing in the dappled shadows of the trees, watching us.

He took a few hesitant steps forward, then paused again. I froze in place. Ash gasped and leapt to her feet with RC and Jay. The twins didn't react at all. Kit stood slowly, more wonderstruck than afraid.

RC had dropped his disk when he stood, and now it was lying by his boot. He could have drawn another, or used his telekinesis to move the one on the ground, but he just stood there, staring. Ash gripped her staff in front of her body. It wouldn't protect her, and she knew this.

We were about to die. My brain accepted that fact without even bothering to conjure an alternative scenario. And yet, for some strange reason, the only thought that registered was, *I've never seen Axel standing before.*

Axel had never been in the Arena with RC, Jay, Ash, and me. He was never conscious when he was taken from his cage. The only positions I'd ever seen him in were sitting, lying down, squatting on all fours, or pacing in a stooped crouch.

Now he stood erect, his shoulders back, his head held high, his posture perfect. Of course his posture was perfect—to match his perfect body. To my surprise, I realized I was taller. Why that surprised me, I wasn't sure; Axel was several years younger than me. And yet, I'd always imagined that if we stood side by side, he would tower over me. Maybe it was because his demeanor was so intimidating. Even though I had a solid four inches on him, I still felt small and vulnerable in his presence.

When you looked at Axel, you tried very hard to make yourself believe he was a kid. Thirteen, maybe fourteen. But somehow, despite his appearance, you knew he wasn't. There was something about him, something otherworldly and feral. His youthful, humanlike appearance was deceptive. He was an animal. He had tracked us even though we'd put so much distance between us and him. He was the most efficient hunter in the world.

And now he was likely going to kill us.

I had a nanosecond to sift through these thoughts. Stupid thoughts. If I was about to die, I should have been thinking something more meaningful. But all I could do was stand there with my mouth open and stare at Axel and note how strange it was to see him clothed in RC's full uniform since I had never seen him wear anything except black sweatpants.

Jay lifted the silver whistle around his neck and set the end in his teeth.

Axel regarded us with wary uncertainty. He eyed the whistle, then took a step back. "Jay, wait," he pleaded. As soon as he opened his mouth, I glimpsed his venomous fangs. Unlike Kit, who had one set of pointed canines, Axel had two sets of fangs—the lateral incisors as well as his canines, making a total of eight razor-sharp teeth designed to pierce flesh. They weren't very long, but that didn't make them any less lethal, and I knew they extended deep into his gums to lengthen when he was on the hunt.

"Please don't." He tossed his hood back in an attempt to demonstrate sincerity. Axel's hair, like Jay's, was too long and drifted over his eyes. But while Jay brushed his gray bangs off to the side so he could see clearly, Axel let his stringy jet-black hair hang over his face without any attempts to tame it. His clairvoyant red eyes glanced at each of us in turn.

I went completely stiff when they fell on me. In that one second, he'd analyzed everything about me—my breathing, my heart rate, the dilation of my pupils, the tension in my muscles. He could smell every hormone in my blood. He could see every single pore in my skin, every salty bead of perspiration welling up to be chilled by the air. He saw beyond the visible light spectrum to observe the heat of my body. He knew every pressure point, every artery, every weakness, every possible way to kill me. I could hide as much from him as from the mind-reading twins. He didn't need to read my mind when he could read my body.

I was pretty sure Axel had more than six senses. That charge I'd felt in the air before was emanating from him in low pulses, as if he were sending out energy that let him *feel* the environment. I hadn't noticed it when he was sleeping, and I'd been so well-adjusted to it at that place that it was only after Axel's absence I noticed it again. I still couldn't find the right words to describe it because it was like nothing I'd ever felt before. Like . . . like a sudden drop in air pressure right before a lightning strike. I didn't know if it was electromagnetism or something more like echolocation. I wouldn't have been surprised if it was a source of energy that didn't even have a name yet because it had never been properly studied. This extra sense or combination of senses let Axel tune into every tiny detail of his surroundings. He was created to be the perfect mesh of animal and power, even without a true Divinity.

One second dragged on forever while he held me petrified in the grips of his chilling, all-seeing red eyes. I couldn't breathe, couldn't blink, couldn't move. *Hypnotic* was the word that came to mind.

And then he released me. With a single flick of his eyes, Axel's gaze fell on the whistle again. He backed up another step. "Please, Jay. I didn't come here to hurt you."

Although Axel hadn't made an offensive move yet, Jay kept the whistle in place. I didn't need to look at my other lab-siblings to sense the tension in their coiled, distrustful bodies. Axel could snap in a second. At that place, we were protected from his episodes by electrified bars. Out here, there was nothing between us—only Axel's self-control.

He seemed to be more affected by our terror than by the whistle in Jay's mouth. He couldn't meet our petrified gazes anymore. His fell to the forest floor, and he mumbled, "I . . . sorta followed your scent. I've been, well . . . I've been tailing you since yesterday. I understand why you left me behind. You'll never have to see me again. I just . . . After everything we went through together, I . . ." He awkwardly cleared his throat. "I wanted to say goodbye."

I exhaled, the release of the pent-up breath relaxing my muscles just a little. Despite my initial alarm, Axel was speaking coherently. For now, at least, he was stable. But who knew how long until the monster inside him had to kill? It was inevitable. He was designed to be a perfect mesh, but he wasn't.

I was finally able to glance at Jay, who remained stoic.

"Axel?" Ash asked. She gripped her staff tighter. "Where will you go?"

"Dunno," he said with a deceptively careless shrug. "Maybe the Ghost Realm."

I swallowed, an ache carving a hole in my chest. Axel couldn't live with humans. He didn't fit in with ghosts. And he didn't belong with nydæa. The thought of him alone wandering the desolate parts of the Ghost Realm made my heart clench.

Jay ran the tip of his tongue over the hole of the whistle, debating.

He studied Axel with calculating intensity. Our lab-brother was still waiting for Jay's verdict. He kept his head down like a dog admitting fealty, as if he already knew Jay would reject him.

Axel turned away. "Follow the creek."

"Why?" I asked.

"Because I said so. If you don't want your stupid asses locked up in cages, stay in the damn water."

Well, apparently freedom hasn't dampened his legendary short fuse.

"How many times have I told you to watch your mouth?" Jay chastised. "I don't want Kit picking up on your foul language."

Axel let out a long breath. "Just keep to the water," he repeated. "It'll lead you out of the woods. Good luck with your new life. I'll never forget you."

He jerked the hood over his head and strode away. I stared at his back, surprisingly melancholy at the thought of never seeing him again. Again. Ash wrung her staff and bit her lower lip, as if she wanted to call Axel back but had lost her voice. Kit's ears, which had been pricked forward hopefully, fell. RC had turned his back; he wouldn't look at anyone. The twins gazed up at Jay, who stared at Axel's cloak. He sighed and called, "Wait."

The half-breed paused and glanced hopefully over his shoulder. Jay hesitated, giving himself a few more seconds to think his decision through. He let the whistle fall between his fingers and dangle around his neck again. "You can stay with us."

Axel turned back to face us. "Really?"

We all looked at Jay. He nodded. "We're a family, right? But just a fair warning—if you go into a bloodlust . . ." He held up the whistle as a warning.

Axel nodded in acceptance of the conditions. Kit beamed and bounced gleefully on the balls of her feet, barely curbing her desire to run to Axel. I stared blankly at the newest addition to our group of fugitives. "How did you find us?"

Axel pushed his hood back again and leaned against a tree with his arms crossed. The collar, I noticed, was gone. He probably yanked the needles out of his neck as soon as he was conscious, though there weren't any residual wounds. "Wasn't hard. Your scent carries far." He glared at RC in particular, who plopped down again, cradling his arm. He either didn't notice or purposely ignored the way Axel eyed his wound.

"Question," I said. "Are you the reason *They* stopped chasing us?"

He just smirked at me, radiating pride, his expression answer enough. Jay, Ash, and I seated ourselves by RC, Kit, and the twins, but Axel hesitated where he was, unsure about joining the group despite Jay's acceptance. He shifted uneasily before sitting down near us but not with us.

I studied him. Just as I'd never witnessed him stand before today, I'd never spoken to him in such close proximity, either. His cage was separated from the rest of ours, so our communication at that place happened across the room. For the longest time, I didn't even know Axel was capable of talking. He put a lot of effort into his monster act to trick *Them*, and he couldn't risk me revealing his secret. It wasn't until I was officially a lab-brother that he deemed me trustworthy and spoke his first words in my presence.

RC's uniform was a good match in size, although the corner of his cloak had been torn away. With the glove covering Axel's hand, I couldn't even tell he was missing part of a finger. He'd told me once before—and I didn't know if it was true or if he was just trying to scare me—that *They* had cut off his finger for the sole purpose of seeing if Axel could regenerate a new one. He was a fast healer, but he couldn't grow new body parts.

Dark circles were just beginning to form shadows beneath his eyes, and his hair was bedraggled. He looked thinner than I remembered when we pulled him from the metal container. The sunshine and fresh air had not warmed his pale, sallow cheeks. I knew he'd only deteriorate more in the next few days. He watched RC from the corner of his eye with a hungry, wild gleam I didn't trust, like a carnivore that had locked onto the scent of a wounded animal.

Axel must have sensed my suspicion because he blinked, glanced at me, and then looked away. "I'm fine," he mumbled, glaring into the trees.

"Okay. I'm glad you're here, Ax." I was sincere about that. Axel would sense *Them* coming long before the rest of us, and his extra protection was welcome. Despite the risk he posed, our lab-family would have been incomplete without him. Kit couldn't take her adoring eyes off Axel, nor could she smother her giddy smile.

Jay leaned forward. "All right, we need to decide our next move. Axel bought us some time, but we can't live in the woods forever."

Ash said, "I know you think the water is safe, Axel, but we might as well be on the road; it's too obvious. I think we should go in a different direction."

Before Axel could respond, I disputed, "But what if we can't find our way back to the water? We need to drink."

Axel prophesized, "It's gonna rain."

"Yep," Kit chimed moodily, setting her chin in her hand.

"Rain?" Finn asked in confusion.

"Water falls from the sky," said Kit in a dreamy voice as she glanced up at the rolling clouds. The twins stared at her as though she'd just proclaimed the most ridiculous statement of all time.

Ash muttered, "Great."

"My point was," Axel said irritably, "water won't be an issue. And we're being watched."

We rolled our heads in different directions, spying nothing out of the ordinary before we had the sense to look at Axel, whose head was tilted up. Gazing back at him from the branches was a big black crow. Two more alighted a few branches up and studied us.

"Axel is right," said Finn. Both twins' eyes were glowing.

Jay inquired, "Do they mean us harm?"

"No," said Reese.

"They're just watching," his twin said.

"Rain will make the ground soft," Axel said, rerouting the group's focus back to the issue at hand. "You're gonna leave footprints. That's why I told you to stay in the water. No trail for humans to follow."

"What about dogs?" I challenged.

"I took care of the dogs."

"How?"

Axel stared me down, and then his lips parted in a toothy smile. "You think I killed them?"

"Did you?" I fired back.

He held me in his hypnotic stare for a few seconds, but I refused to back down. "Unrelevant," he finally said.

"*Ir*relevant," Finn corrected.

Axel rolled his eyes. "Whatever. Not relevant. You get what I mean. I didn't have to kill them. Dogs're smarter than humans. My plan was to cross my trail over yours and lead them away deeper into the woods, but the dogs freaked when they smelled me. They bolted. They know when to run away from a predator that's higher up on the food chain."

I held the stare-down for two more seconds before I relented and broke my gaze. Jay tightened the gauntlet around his wrist. "Anyway, the creek has to lead somewhere, so at least we won't be wandering around in circles. I say we follow it."

Ash hung her head, displeased but unable to dispute Jay's rationale. Kit stretched and yawned, then casually crawled into Axel's lap.

I gaped at her. She was much braver than the rest of us, who were still keeping a safe distance from the half-breed. Kit snuggled into a little ball, closed her eyes, and sighed in contentment with her cheek against Axel's muscular chest.

My attention shifted from Kit to Axel to see how he was reacting to this unexpected display of affection. He stared down at her in surprise with his arms held away, and then his startled expression hardened into an annoyed scowl. He rose, never touching her with his hands, and Kit was left kneeling on the ground. Axel turned his back on her.

Although we'd all witnessed his cold rejection, no one said a word. Jay set his hands on his knees and stood stiffly with a glance up at the cloudy sky. "We better move. We've wasted a lot of time already."

We staggered to our feet, except Finn and Reese. They remained sitting with their chins on their knees, staring sullenly at the water. Jay gazed down at them for a moment, then held out his hand. "Come on."

Reese swiveled his head to study Jay's open hand. His face was blank. I worried the twins might have finally snapped. Jay waited patiently for Reese to raise his gaze and meet his eyes. The boy looked at Jay's proffered hand again, and then he placed his hand inside Jay's.

Jay pulled Reese to his feet, then his twin. He clapped Finn on the shoulder. "Let's go," he said, gently guiding the twins forward. They reluctantly stepped into the creek again.

Kit spun to me, holding her hands up, and I scooped her into my arms. Her body shifted into smoke, and the girl I'd been holding was a kitten that scampered onto my shoulder. She rubbed her face against my cheek, her whiskers tickling, a rumbling purr vibrating deep in her throat. I scratched her chin and followed Jay and the twins into the cool water with RC and Ash on either side of me. The crows watched us from their perches.

We stayed a few feet from the bank, just far enough in the water to conceal our trail but close enough that the water didn't rise any higher than my calves. Axel kept to the trees, moving alongside us. I watched him leap effortlessly from branch to branch, his hood thrown over his head again. It was eerie how he flitted as fast and silent as a living shadow. If I hadn't known he was there, I never would have detected him.

As we trudged along the creek, the wind strengthened. Even my weak, human sense of smell could now detect the moisture in the air. The trees were stirring as if sentient and angry.

"What is that?" Finn asked. He balked and took a step back, his eyes wide as they danced suspiciously over the moving trees.

"It's just the wind," I assured. "It won't hurt you."

"What is wind?" Reese asked.

The others exchanged looks. I tried to explain, "It's the air moving. Like at that place when *They* turn on the fans."

Apparently my explanation was inadequate because Finn and Reese shook their heads. Reese said, "The moving blades of the fans disrupted the air particles."

Finn stated, "There's nothing disrupting the particles right now. How can air move by itself Outside?"

I shook my head. "It's complicated."

"Then explain," they demanded in unison.

"I can't. I'm sorry."

We resumed walking, Finn and Reese pressed close to us for safety. They skittishly eyed the swaying branches. Before long, the first droplet of water landed on my cheek. Surprised by its cool contact, I brought my hand to my face to wipe it away.

A steady rain began to fall. My first reaction was to brace myself for pain, and I halted. I knew rain wasn't supposed to hurt, but I was so used to being sprayed with the hose in Detox that when I felt liquid falling on me, I expected the sting of chemicals to burn my skin while the stink filled my nose. I counted to five.

No pain. The rain smelled good, and the water drummed my skin, pure and painless. The tension washed out of my muscles. I raised my face to the sky, smiled, and closed my eyes. The storm moved in, mixing falling leaves with raindrops, which peppered the creek's surface.

The others had slowed to a stop in front of me. Finn and Reese cowered from the rain and threw their arms up to protect themselves from it. I at least knew logically, even if my body needed to be reminded, that rain was just water, not chemicals. They had no idea. Slowly, they came to realize the rain was harmless, and their arms fell. They were absolutely mystified as they gazed around, eyes round at what to them was an impossible phenomenon.

Ash scowled, using one hand to throw the hood of her cloak over her head while gripping her staff tighter in the other as if ready to beat the rain with it. RC and Jay turned their faces up in wonder, grinning faintly as they felt rain for the first time in many years.

I glanced to the right where Axel was crouching on all fours on a lower limb, a dark, cloaked figure watching us through the curtain of falling water.

Kit made a displeased noise in her throat. I smiled at the melancholy kitten hunkered down, ears pinned, eyes closed, and I gently plucked her from my shoulder. I held her in the crook of my arm, pulling the edge of my cloak over her to shelter her from the rain. She nuzzled against me.

I started and nearly crushed her when a splintering rumble shook the sky. Finn and Reese splashed to Jay and clutched him in terror. Ash flinched, glancing up fearfully at the clouds while RC backed up a few steps, his eyes dancing in search of the sound's source.

His voice cracking on the verge of panic, Reese asked, "What was that?"

Jay remained completely still as the rain fell around us. Axel leapt from the tree branch and landed in the water several yards away from his perch with barely a ripple. "Relax, Bot. It's just noise, and it's far away in the sky," he said over the rain. "We should keep moving."

Despite his assurance, none of us stirred. I heard the sound again, but this time it wasn't as loud. Water dripped from my nose and the hair plastered to my face. Kit peered out from the edge of my cloak.

Jay started moving again with the twins on either side, clutching his cloak for security. The rest of us followed. Axel walked alongside us, somehow not splashing a drop of water.

One of the twin's voices rose above the storm: "Rain comes from the clouds?"

"Yes," Jay told them.

"So . . . are there pipes inside clouds?"

Finn held out his palm to catch raindrops. Rather than wait for an answer, he inquired, "Is this called water, or rain?"

I couldn't help but smile at their innocent questions. Finn and Reese tipped their heads back to squint at the bruised sky. Light flickered in the clouds, and the sound crashed again, making us flinch. The rain fell harder. The only sound was the orchestra of the downpour showering the creek and rustling the leaves. For now, everything was strangely and wonderfully peaceful.

— Chapter Nine —

Broken

Vivian Tarrow hit the ground on her stomach, cowering as glass exploded above and rained down in glittering shards. She raised her head. Her ectogun was lying a few feet away. When she reached for it, the twinkling glass bit her skin, drawing blood.

Her adrenaline high prevented the pain from registering. She seized the ectogun, released the safety as she rolled onto her side, and then squeezed the trigger.

A blast of green ectoplasm erupted from the barrel of the gun, which recoiled in her hand with a charging whine followed by a *shoom*. Her shot struck a ghost in the side of the head. He went down, stunned enough to buy her maybe ten seconds if she was lucky.

Trey crawled to her. "Viv!" he cried, ducking when an explosion above their heads sent splinters flying. "We gotta get outta here!"

She glared at the group of ghosts who had separated the two of them from the raid team. One was holding her backpack, which was filled with boxes of uncooked pasta and a couple of dented cans of ravioli. "Not without my bag."

"Are you insane? We have to get back to the team! Just leave it!"

"Every little bit counts," she insisted, turning to fix her mom's apprentice with a determined scowl. "Cover me."

"*Viv!*" Trey shouted, but she'd already scrambled to her feet and was running toward the ghosts. One noticed her approaching and raised his hand, palm toward her, tendrils of green energy condensing into an orb. Vivian leapt sideways, narrowly avoiding the ectoplasm. Behind her, Trey covered his head with his hands when the energy hit the window pane, raining more wooden splinters down on him.

"Just like dodge ball in gym class," Vivian muttered as she leapt to clear an overturned garbage can. "Except this will hurt a lot more."

The rest of the gang was becoming aware of her reckless approach. They turned, eyes glinting at her. "C'mon, Trey," Vivian whispered in frustration, diving to the ground to avoid three more blasts of ecto-plasm.

A cloaked man loomed over her. His violet eyes glowed, and his fingers closed around a sword that appeared in his hand. *Great, an Arsenal,* Vivian identified. A ghost with the ability to summon objects stored in a metarealm.

He raised the sword above his head to skewer her. As his gleaming blade came down, she rolled to the side. The concrete scraped her knuckles when her weight shifted on top of the ectogun she refused to release.

The sword rang when it met the sidewalk. Its wielder was already moving with the momentum for a second attempt, but a blast of green ectoplasm smashed into the Arsenal's chest, sending him reeling back several steps with a grunt. The sword clattered at Vivian's feet.

She turned to see Trey on his knees, ectogun leveled. His shot had been true, but the Arsenal was already lurching forward again. Vivian shoved her hand into the pouch on her right hip. Her fingers found the last e-zap. As the ghost reached for her throat, she palmed the little gadget her mom had invented and slapped it on his forearm.

The effect was immediate; crackling tendrils of neon-violet ecto-plasm coursed around his body, highly concentrated around the e-zap. He fell to his knees, screaming, drawing the attention of the others. E-zaps were effective but short-lived and good for only one attack. When in direct contact with a ghost, they disrupted the ghost's internal ecto-plasm reserves. The Arsenal's own degraded energy was being drawn out of his body to attack him.

Vivian had less than fifteen seconds before the e-zap shorted out. She took advantage of the distraction to leap up, seize the strap of her backpack, and yank it off a woman's shoulder. The ghost hissed and swiped at her. Vivian leaned back to avoid the slap, surprised when a razor-sharp talon sliced her cheek instead of a hand. A little lower, and the tip would have severed her larynx.

She stumbled backward as the ghost lunged at her again. Both hands had transformed into vicious talons. Vivian swung the backpack to bat away the claws. Another swipe, and as she leaned back, she tripped over her own heel. Falling on her butt was all that spared her throat from the talon that *whoosh*ed through the air above her. A familiar charging whine preceded a barrage of green ectoplasm blasts that knocked Vivian's attacker backward into the angry gang. The ghosts raised shields in defense.

Vivian was staggering to her feet when a hand seized her wrist and jerked her up. "*Move*," Trey growled, towing her behind him as he ran. He fired off a few more shots.

"You took your sweet time," she teased.

"You were in my line of fire."

"Well, thanks. I owe you one," she said with a glance over her shoulder. The ghosts were in pursuit.

"Yeah, well, we aren't out of trouble yet." They rounded a corner. "We have to find the rest of the team, and your mom is going to kill me if anything happens to you."

Footsteps and shouts followed. Trey seized a doorknob. He yanked, but the door didn't budge. The apprentice swore softly and threw his shoulder against the wood.

"Trey, they're coming," Vivian warned, peering around the corner.

He stepped back. "I *know!*" he said, kicking hard at the wood as he punctuated the final word. The door flew inward. "Let's go!" He dashed inside.

Vivian fired at the first ghost, causing him to duck out of sight around the corner again. She hurried after Trey, but she was held fast. "Wait, I'm stuck!" she called. Her bracelet had snagged on the jagged edge of the doorframe.

Trey doubled back, grabbed her wrist, and pulled. The bracelet, made of blue and bronze cords woven together, snapped, and she fell into his arms.

The talon ghost appeared in the doorway, her yellow eyes blazing in fury. Trey pulled Vivian away. "Wait!" she cried, reaching for the broken bracelet on the dusty floor.

Trey jerked her away just in time to avoid an explosion of ectoplasm inches from their heads. They ducked, then took off running. Vivian cast a longing look back at the colored cords as her bracelet was trampled beneath the feet of their pursuers.

Trey steered her through the maze of rooms in the abandoned building. "In here!" He yanked her around a corner into a dark room.

Vivian cried out as her feet went out from under her. The floor collapsed, and there was nothing but air beneath her; she was falling, tumbling in wood and plaster with Trey flailing beside her.

She hit the floor hard. Her legs buckled. Pain shot up from her ankles and knees. She lay on her back in the debris, perfectly still, too afraid to move and find out if her legs were broken. Her chest heaved as she stared up at the hole in the ceiling. She heard a cough beside her, a body shifting.

Trey hauled himself up into a dazed sitting position. "Hey." He reached over to touch her arm. "You okay?"

Vivian groaned and pulled herself up. "I think so." She looked up to see how far they had fallen. "Trey, my bracelet. We have to go back and get it."

"We can't." He fumbled for his ectogun in the debris and holstered it as he staggered to his feet. "We have to get out of here." He offered his hand, but she didn't take it.

"My brother gave it to me."

Trey sighed. He knelt and placed both of his hands firmly on her shoulders. "I know it has sentimental value to you, but what do you think he'd say if he knew you almost killed yourself over a piece of jewelry?" He tapped one finger to her forehead in a light scolding.

Vivian swallowed hard. *It's all I have left.*

Trey rose and offered his hand again. "We have to get back to City Hall."

She stared at his hand. Finally, she sighed and set hers in his, allowing him to pull her to her feet. She took a step and stumbled when she put weight down on her right foot. Trey's arms immediately caught her, and he asked if her ankle was sprained. Dizzy, she frowned and shook her head, and after a few more steps, the pain ebbed enough that she could limp without help even though he tried to grip her elbow and convince her to lean against him. She pulled away. Exhausted and battered, they trudged across the room and pulled open a door that led to a rickety staircase.

Vivian stared up at the rectangle of dim light at the top. She felt lost down here, wandering this wild place that used to be her home. Everything was lost. She was wearing a pair of men's boots found in a closet, just a little too big but better than her sneakers so worn that she'd used cardboard to cover the holes in the bottoms. The jacket wasn't hers, either. She had taken it from a boutique mannequin three raids ago on a chilly night. The jeans did belong to her, and they were crusted with blood, most of which was her own, and the holes revealed her hairy knees, but shaving wasn't important anymore.

Lost. Her house was dark, windows boarded, abandoned in a neighborhood of abandoned houses. Her room. Her bed. Her clothes. Her school. Her future. Her life. All she had were the clothes on her back, the weapons in her belt, and her mom. Her dad and brother were dead. She hadn't seen her grandparents, aunt, uncle, or cousin in years. No pictures. Just a bracelet to remind her of a happy Christmas a long time ago, and now that was gone, too.

Trey led the way up the steps. Vivian hung her head as she trailed behind. Her wrist felt naked. It was stupid, she knew, that she was so attached to a physical object. But that bracelet wasn't just a piece of jewelry—it was a reminder of the past.

Something everyone else seemed to have forgotten.

Trey hesitated at the top of the stairs and pressed his finger to his lips. Vivian froze. Floorboards creaked over the murmur of low voices in the next room. Trey waved his hand, indicating for now the way was clear and she should follow right behind him. He hurried up the remaining few steps and sprinted for the door that led outside. Vivian dashed after him, casting a longing look back at the far room where her bracelet was forsaken in the doorway.

The two emerged in the street. The last they'd seen of the raid team, the truck had taken heavy damage and was belching smoke from under the hood. Wes, though he'd sulked and grumbled about being a werewolf, not a bilocorn, had grudgingly agreed to wear a makeshift harness and haul the truck back to City Hall, but it had to have been slow going with the raid team walking alongside to guard him and the truck.

Trey skimmed the rooftops in search of a column of smoke, but there were too many. "We'll wait at City Hall," he decided. "Come on. We can cut through the Fruth building." He took off at a quick pace toward the arc of the green dome visible above the rooftops.

Vivian remained where she was. Her eyes followed the delicate path of a white butterfly that fluttered past and alighted on the window-sill. It fanned its wings, showing off black tips, dark spots, and gray lines that looked familiar somehow, like a Rorschach test tickling her memory.

It's a skull.

Vivian realized this the instant before the butterfly took flight again. She watched it climb the breeze above the buildings, inexplicably certain it wasn't of this Realm. She'd never been superstitious, but she doubted it was a good omen.

"You coming?" Trey asked.

Vivian finally followed. He respected her silence as the blocks passed, and for that she was grateful. When they reached the tallest office building in Phantom Heights, Trey held open the door with a playful bow. "M'lady," he said, sweeping his arm across his body to gesture inside.

She couldn't force herself to return his smile. Cold wetness hit the top of her head, and she paused to look up at the cloudy sky. A steady drizzle was starting to fall on Phantom Heights.

— Chapter Ten —

Burnout

Dusk bled the last bit of color from the landscape when the rain finally ceased. The creek we'd been following opened into a pond at the edge of the woods. We lingered at the mouth, gazing out across the wide open land beyond the water. Lights glittered in the distance. In the twilight, RC's left eye was glowing violet, the twins' eyes bright blue.

Axel sniffed at the air, staring intently at the lights on the horizon. Even though they were miles away, he reported, "Humans. I'ma guess about eight hundred."

Kit climbed onto my shoulder, her claws pricking my skin through the wet cloak. "What should we do, Jay?" I asked. The hole inside of me that used to be my stomach growled like a monster that wouldn't let me forget it was hungry.

The poor twins were trembling so hard their teeth chattered. "W-why are w-e sh-sha-king?" Reese stammered.

"You're cold," Ash told them.

"Cold?" Finn repeated, as if he understood the meaning of the word but had never experienced it before. He probably hadn't, now that I thought about it. Not in the meticulously regulated environment at that place. The initial shock of being strapped down to a metal table was a different degree of cold than this body-numbing dampness that seeped deep into the bones.

Axel rolled his eyes and snatched the backpack. "Here."

Reese caught the two extra cloaks, but he and his blood-brother stared at the garments in confusion. Ash took one and draped it over Finn's shoulders, then took the other from Reese and did the same.

Jay hadn't said a word yet. He was watching the lights. "We need food, or we won't make it much farther," he finally stated.

True enough, Finn and Reese could barely stand. The dry cloaks they were wrapped in were way too big, and they were still shivering in their sopping clothes. I quietly reminded, "Humans will turn us over to *Them*."

"I know it's risky," Jay admitted. "We'll have to be careful." He nodded at the lights on the other side of the open fields. "There won't be many places to hide, so I think we should travel as far as we can while it's dark. It's the only cover we'll get."

He was thinking logically, and yet the thought of walking all night was dismal enough to zap what dwindling strength I had left. In the open landscape, a spotlight from a helicopter could lock onto us, and there'd be no escape. We could be surrounded.

I wasn't the only one to realize this. Nobody moved. Even Jay was hesitant. He advised, "Take some time to rest. We have a long night ahead." He splashed to the bank, and we followed without a word.

Kit hopped off my shoulder as soon as my boot settled on the muddy shore. Finn and Reese fell onto their hands and knees in the silt, crawled to dry ground, and collapsed, their eyes already closed.

I glanced over my shoulder. Axel was the only one who hadn't followed. He was standing exactly where we'd left him in the middle of the creek, his fists clenched, head down, scowling at his reflection. Ash called, "Aren't you coming?"

Our lab-brother remained motionless. "Ax?" Jay queried. His fingers drifted up to the whistle.

Axel heaved a sigh and returned to us. "Are you all right?" I asked as he strode past me. He didn't grace me with a glance.

Jay's suspicious eyes followed Axel, but he let his hand fall. He seated himself near the twins, facing the faraway lights. RC scrutinized a tree trunk before he leaned against it, his glowing eye disappearing.

Ash sat cross-legged with the staff across her lap. I wandered a little farther so I could settle in between the roots of a massive tree. I poured creek water out of my boots and unwrapped my feet so they could dry. As soon as I leaned back against the tree, the weight on my eyelids became too heavy to resist. I didn't want to sleep. Jay would probably make us move as soon as darkness fell, and *They* were still looking for us, and it wasn't a good idea to fall asleep, but maybe . . . just for a few minutes . . .

When I jerked awake, the light had barely changed. Axel was crouched on the root next to me. His head was turned toward RC, who was dozing. "There's a spider on your shoulder," Axel announced.

RC's eyes snapped open. He leapt up as if the tree had electrocuted him. "Get it off!" he cried, hopping up and down. He flung out his arms. A telekinetic wave erupted outward like a sudden gale that snapped his cloak and pounded the rest of us, shaking loose leaves from the trees and making the boughs quake.

Axel clutched his midriff and leaned back until he rolled off the root and lay on the ground, laughing like a maniac. "You should have seen the look on your face!"

"Jackass," RC seethed. Axel sat up, still chuckling.

Jay wearily called, "Knock it off."

Axel grinned mischievously at him, but he sobered in an instant and gazed into the trees. I stiffened, afraid *They*'d found us, but he was alert, not alarmed. A moment later, Kit triumphantly marched out of the woods. "I got us something to eat!"

She beamed with pride, but Jay, Ash, and I all recoiled from her offering while RC just stared at it with absolute repulsion. Clenched in her hand was the bushy tail of a furry woodland creature. She held it out to Jay, who leaned back when the carcass swung close to his face. "Kit, we can't eat that," he told her gently.

Her ears fell. "Why not?"

"Yeah," Axel chimed in, "why not? It ain't diseased, and she made a clean kill."

Jay looked sick. "I'm sorry. We just . . . can't," he barely finished. He had to turn his head away.

Kit turned to Axel and held up the corpse. "We can share."

"No."

Again, her ears, which had risen with hope, fell.

She moodily walked away from the group and sat down near the water. Unfortunately, she wasn't far enough away for the *crunch* of bones to be inaudible. My stomach churned.

In the final minutes before night drove away the last of the light from the sky, Jay roused Finn and Reese, then announced, "It's now or never." Without looking back to see if we were following, he started walking.

Kit rinsed the blood off in the water, then transformed in a billow of smoke and darted after Jay. Ash and I exchanged looks. I watched the back of Jay's cloak as he walked away from us, and then I gazed at the distant lights. I rewrapped my feet and shoved them back into my damp boots, then rose with a soft groan. Ash muttered under her breath, "At least we can walk on dry land."

We followed Jay with RC at our heels. Finn and Reese hesitated, then reluctantly trailed after us, too terrified to be left alone in the dark woods even though they didn't want to keep going. Axel sullenly brought up the rear.

I cast one more look back before we left the safety of the woods. Five crows were roosting in the trees, their gleaming black eyes watching, but soon they were lost in shadows and we were trudging through the darkness, our way lit only by the moon.

The glow-bugs reemerged in all their mystical splendor, a field of pulsing yellow lights surrounding us in every direction. Kit sprang up to bat at the insects with her little white paws when they drifted too close, and then she pounced on the poor creature if she was lucky enough to knock one out of the air.

But the night dragged on, and after a while even her energy expired and she plodded along beside us, paws dragging, tail drooping. When Finn and Reese began to stumble, Ash and I carried them on our backs. The lights on the horizon didn't seem to be getting any closer no matter how long we walked. Above us, the clearing sky opened holes to the stars, and I observed with my head tilted back until my neck ached. The night sky left me wonderstruck, but all the while my ears strained for the sound of a helicopter. I loved the stars but missed the cover and protection of the trees. We were exposed out here.

Despite my perpetual fear, the night kept quiet, just the constant hum of insects. Mosquitoes whined around my ears, but with Finn on my back, I couldn't swat at them. Ash and I eventually became weary under the weight of our passengers. Ash handed Reese off to Jay, Finn walked, and we rotated.

Our journey was slow, but eventually I could see individual lights instead of a mass glowing on the horizon. The blisters on my aching feet rubbed raw with every step until I'd developed a solid limp, but I didn't take my gaze from those lights. They promised food and shelter, if I could only reach them.

We didn't speak. Only once did Axel's voice break the quiet: "Huh, look at that."

"What?" I whispered hoarsely.

"*That*, up ahead."

His annoyance only fueled my own. "Ax, it's dark. I can't see anything."

He stopped dead in his tracks. "You can't see in the dark?"

"No. Why, can you?"

I sensed him staring at me. Rather than answer, he said, "I thought everybody could see in the dark. Is it . . . normal, to *not* be able to?"

"Well, yeah. I mean, Kit can probably see pretty well in the dark, but the rest of us can't. What do you see?"

Disturbed by my answer, he continued ahead with no response.

Within the hour, the sky began to lighten, and broad strokes of pink and orange blossomed above us. Reese was on Jay's back again. He coughed and said, "Jay, we're hungry."

"And thirsty," his twin croaked from Ash's back, rubbing his eye with his fist.

"I know," Jay acknowledged wearily.

I raised my head to look at our destination. The lights were gone, but I could see tiny buildings. Somehow, they looked farther away than ever despite our progress.

The black-and-white kitten turned to smoke and rose onto two legs in her skin. "Jay?" Kit inquired softly, her velvety cat ears flicking back. "I'm sleepy. Can't we rest?"

"No. I'm sorry, but we can't stop. We have to keep going."

I'd noticed that Axel had been steadily placing a good distance between himself and the rest of us as we walked. He kept his head down, a scowl seemingly permanently etched into his brow.

"You okay?" I asked him.

He glared at me through locks of hair and snarled. The feral sound made me stiffen. Only now, in dawn's light, did I notice just how sickly he looked. He'd definitely lost weight since the accident, and the way his lackluster hair hung over his dilated eyes and pale face made him appear ill. In response to my query, he put another few steps between himself and the group.

The sun emerged from the unbroken horizon. I inhaled deeply and watched my second sunrise, and this time Axel got to see it, too. I cast a glance in his direction to see if he appreciated it. Apparently not; he was squinting, and he massaged his temples as if the light had given him an instant migraine. That shouldn't have surprised me, considering how sharp his night vision was. His eyes were still adapting to the Outside lighting. When he did lower his hands, he turned away from the sunrise with total disgust and flung the hood over his head. *Whatever.* His sour attitude couldn't ruin the gorgeous view. This must be a sign that a new beginning was unfolding for us.

I'd barely finished the thought when Axel turned to stare at the distant tree line behind us. He said the words all of us had been dreading and yet secretly expecting: "*They're* coming."

Panic knocked me breathless like a physical blow. We were in the middle of nowhere, an open field with low rows of knee-high plants. Even if we sprinted with the last bit of our remaining strength, the town was too far away for us to even hope to reach it in time.

"The dogs?" Jay asked quietly, his voice forcibly calm.

"Helicopter."

Axel might as well have told us to sit down and surrender. We'd be spotted in seconds. I was so exhausted that defeat doused me in cold hopelessness. The panic was already gone; giving up somehow felt right. Why keep fighting? I was done. Every muscle ached, and lazy clouds fogged my brain. It was over. My adrenaline expired a long time ago. At least I was able to see two sunrises. And the moon, and the stars. I felt rain on my skin.

In my peripheral, RC drew one of his silver disks. I wouldn't have to be tired and sore anymore. I had no regrets about dying like this. Dying *free*.

Jay was gazing at the distant woods where the black specks of cawing crows rose up from the trees. "How long?" he asked.

"A few minutes," Axel answered, his eyes narrow, as if he were actually watching *Them* come, even though I couldn't hear the helicopter yet.

A few minutes. Knowing that was how long I had to live was a terror I'd never imagined. Renewed panic drove the wispy clouds from my mind, fear not just at the thought of dying, but also the need to make every moment count. I felt as if I needed to *do* something, and I was running out of time. I couldn't waste what was left of my life just standing there waiting to die, but I was *so* tired.

A few minutes. Then it would all be over. I could rest forever.

"Did *They* replace the sensors?" Jay asked. "Axel, can you tell if *They*'re using infrared?"

"*They* aren't," Axel replied, his answer slow with curious puzzlement. "It's probably just a perimeter sweep around the woods now that it's light."

RC mumbled, "What's it matter?" He gestured at the horizon. "*They* don't need infrared to see us. There's nowhere to hide."

"Come here," Jay said urgently. Certain he must have something to say before RC slit our throats, we crowded together. Only Axel remained, staring at the sky. Now I could hear the faintest roar of the helicopter coming closer.

Jay said, "Four of us have power. If we all hold onto one another, can you make us all invisible?"

I straightened. Ghosts could pass the basic powers of intangibility and invisibility to others, even humans, animals, and objects if in direct contact. That was how ghosts could become completely invisible, clothes and all. But passing power on to another living being was a lot harder than affecting the clothes on your own back.

RC scratched his head and studied his damaged neutralizer. "Invisibility costs so much power . . . I don't know. I'm not sure I have the reserves to make myself invisible with this thing active, let alone the rest of you."

The twins glanced at each other uncertainly. "It won't be easy," said Reese.

"But maybe for a minute or two," Finn finished thoughtfully.

"We have to try," Jay said with conviction. "I don't know about the rest of you, but I'm not ready to give up yet."

I clasped Ash's warm hand firmly in mine, then set my other hand on Kit's shoulder. The helicopter was coming into range. The twins held hands, and then Finn seized RC and Reese grasped Jay, who held onto Kit. The leader turned to the last person. "Ax, come on!" Jay called.

The helicopter cleared the treetops. The sight of the black machine in the early blue sky stopped my heart. Axel stared at it, still as a statue, and then he slowly turned to face us with an eerily calm expression.

"Axel!" Ash called as the distant roar intensified. She extended her hand toward him. "You have to be touching us!"

Axel shook his head.

My throat tightened as my stomach sank. "What are you doing?"

He lifted his chin resolutely, and then he was gone in a streak and the stir of a breeze. "*Axel!*" Kit screamed. She twisted around, trying to spot him, and I tightened my grip on her shoulder.

Jay glanced up at the approaching helicopter. "He'll be okay. But now would be a good time to not be seen."

Finn and Reese bowed their heads and closed their eyes. RC's unscarred eye flared with power. Kit sucked in a deep breath as though she were about to plunge underwater. I gazed around the group, hoping with every fiber of my being this wouldn't be our last stand. "Please," I whispered to no one.

And then, I felt a familiar tingle rush through the hand on Kit. It washed over my body with the warmth of a painless electrical current. One moment I was looking across the circle at Jay, and the next, I saw only the horizon.

I blinked several times and looked down at where my feet should have been, but I saw nothing except plants smashed into the soil with broken stems. I squeezed Ash's hand to ensure she was still there. She squeezed back.

The helicopter approached low overhead, whipping the plants around in a frenzy as the deafening sound of the rotating blades pummeled me to the bone. Even though I was invisible, I felt naked. Vulnerable. I wanted to hide. There was nothing between the humans in the helicopter and me on the ground.

RC groaned and cried out in strain; his power must be failing. For a moment, I saw the others flicker into sight. RC was lying on the ground, unconscious, a line of blood running from his nose. He'd burned out. Finn was on one knee so he could keep his hand on RC.

In that instant, I realized the price of our gamble. It was all or nothing. Without RC, death was not an option anymore. We would either be free or be taken back to that place.

Invisibility shielded us from sight again, but we were relying on the three youngest with passive Divinities. Kit and the twins wouldn't last long. None of them were higher than Level 2.

The blades beat at the air above me now, pounding me with the force of the wind. Dust clouded the air, forcing me to close my eyes. I tasted dirt. It clogged my nose, scratched my throat, stung my face.

Please hold on, I silently begged. *Just a little longer. Hold on.*

Kit let out a sighing whimper and went limp. I had to crouch to keep my grip on her. Her power, too, had burned out, which meant our invisibility was supported by only Finn and Reese now.

The helicopter banked, its tail facing us as it retreated to continue its wide sweep around the edge of the woods. The twins collapsed.

We were exposed.

No one moved a muscle. Those of us still conscious had our eyes trained on the helicopter, watching, waiting for it to loop back. It was too close; *They* had to have spotted us.

But the machine never deterred from its path. The noise faded as it continued away.

I swayed on my feet, light-headed, and I realized I'd been holding my breath. I released my hold on Ash and Kit as I rose and stepped back, refilling my lungs. Ash tried to sit, but her legs buckled and she collapsed gracelessly on her butt, trembling. "That was so close," she whispered.

Even Jay was pale and shaken. He wiped his brow with the back of his gloved hand. A breeze swept past me, and then hooded Axel was standing a little ways from the group, his arms crossed over his chest, as nonchalant as if nothing had happened.

Jay knelt beside the twins and swept the chestnut hair away from Reese's closed eyes. Reese stirred at his touch. Blood had gathered in the corner of Finn's mouth, and Reese had a bloody nose. Ash nudged RC's shoulder, but he didn't move. I bent over to scoop Kit into my arms. Crimson tears had stained her cheeks. I held her close and wiped the blood away with my thumb. "You were so strong, Kit," I whispered, even though she couldn't hear me.

Jay lifted the twins. "If the helicopter comes back, we'll be defenseless. We have to reach that town." Ash bobbed her head in understanding and pulled RC over her back, taking extra care with his injured arm. Jay started walking again, and we fell into step on either side. Axel trailed behind.

We had paid a steep price to avoid being seen. The four with access to their powers were now not only powerless, but also deadweight slowing us down. It would take at least a day, maybe longer, for RC, Kit, and the twins to fully recuperate from their burnouts. Axel could alert us to more danger, but every time I glanced at him, I swore he looked worse. Jay, Ash, Axel, and I would be on our own to scavenge for food and water in a human town we knew absolutely nothing about.

My stomach sank. A steep price indeed.

— Chapter Eleven —

Parting Ways

We passed the day carrying our comrades and constantly glancing over our shoulders at the distant tree line. The sun was hot on my back, roasting me inside my black cloak. Water trickled through every thought. RC, Jay, and Axel must have been even hotter with their long sleeves.

Kit finally stirred in my arms and opened her dull eyes. She was too weak to carry on a conversation, and I was too tired and too thirsty.

The sky was strange. It was clear as water, except for a few narrow bands of clouds. Three of them were not quite parallel but oriented in the same direction, as if a giant hand had swept a fine paintbrush over a blue canvas. And what was even stranger, a fourth line was being drawn now from a tiny point I couldn't identify. Maybe Finn and Reese were right. Maybe humans did make clouds.

As we drew nearer to the town, Axel lagged farther and farther behind. I glanced back at him to find he had his fingers twisted in his hair and his eyes squeezed shut. I also noticed a change in the air. The subtle pulses of energy from the half-breed were now more frantic—a low, wild charge. I wondered if it was tied to his heartbeat. Was his heart beating so fast it was no longer a recognizable pulse?

We were so close when Axel stopped. We didn't notice his absence at first until Ash chanced a look back and realized he was far behind, standing with his head down. We doubled back to him.

"Jay," Axel muttered, raising his head to look at the leader as soon as we halted in front of him. His appearance was haunted and sickly— the dark circles were deeper, his hair disheveled, beads of sweat on his forehead, face gaunt and pale. He shifted. "I'm . . . not feeling well, and

111

you're all hurt, and RC . . . My teeth are starting to ache. I think we should part ways for a while."

Jay studied him. He set the twins down in the grass and ordered, "Hold your breath and let me look at your eyes."

Axel tensed. "No."

Jay glared at him, and Axel glared back until with an irritated snarl, he folded his arms and made a point to inhale and hold it in. Jay stepped directly in front of him, closer than I'd dare to be right now. He stared into Axel's eyes. "Your pupils are dilated," Jay reported ominously, backing away.

Axel exhaled. "I know."

"You don't have much time left."

"I *know*."

"You're not going to do anything stupid, are you?"

Axel raked his fingers through his hair. "Not if I leave now, I hope."

Jay was silent, solemn. I rubbed the back of my neck while Ash shifted RC's weight. "Where are you going to go?" Jay inquired.

"Dunno," Axel said with a shrug. "But I don't want to hurt any of you, so . . . I can't stay with you until I'm—" he grimaced "—better."

"Okay," said Jay, finally relenting. Axel nodded, and then he was gone.

I asked, "Are you sure it's a good idea to let him go?"

"Was there much choice?" Jay replied in a tired monotone as we pressed on. "Besides, none of us could stop him from leaving, and it wouldn't be wise to try."

"People will die with Axel on the hunt," I muttered gravely.

Jay's silver eyes flashed in frustration for the briefest second before his power was neutralized again. "I know that, Cato, all right? I know! We knew when we decided not to leave him behind. It doesn't matter if Axel travels with us or if he's on his own; he will probably kill people. That was the consequence of letting him escape."

Ash looked down at her boots in discomfort, letting her dark red hair fall in a curtain to hide her from our quarrel. I swallowed, taken aback by Jay's outburst. He glanced at me and noticed the startled look on my face, and then his expression softened. "I'm sorry. I'm just . . . I'm tired and stressed and hungry and thirsty and . . . I didn't mean to snap at you."

"You don't have to apologize."

He nodded. "Come on. We're almost there."

I sighed, my mind still on Axel. We were mistakes, he and I. Half-breeds weren't supposed to exist. The fact that we did was one common bond Axel and I shared. Axel's pure blood was tainted in the lab, mine in the Flash. To an extent, although our non-ghost halves were drastically different, we understood each other. And yet, Axel despised humankind with every fiber of his being. We had, I decided, a complicated relationship.

Kit, noticing my troubled expression, cuddled closer. I forced a weary smile for her sake. We were near the outskirts of the town, which made me wonder if perhaps that was why Axel had been so insistent on leaving. He couldn't stand being in close proximity to so many humans when in such an impulsive, unbalanced state of mind. But without him, we were even more vulnerable.

"Cato," Kit croaked, her voice so soft I had to lean down to hear her, "I'm thirsty."

"I know, Kit-Kat," I murmured sympathetically. "We'll find some water soon."

"And . . . Axel will come back, won't he?"

I was afraid of making a promise I wasn't sure could be kept. But her dull golden eyes were gazing up hopefully at me, so I reassured, "Of course he will." Content with my answer, she sighed and leaned against my chest again to doze.

Jay paused, staring at the town. He glanced up at the sun and then back to the faraway line of trees behind us, his brow furrowed in consideration. "What are you thinking?" I asked.

"We should take shelter and rest until dark."

"Take shelter where?" asked Ash. Jay nodded to the right, and I followed his gaze across the field to a big red building with a white house. A herd of odd black-and-white creatures grazed in the distance. "Oh," Ash mumbled.

I winced as hunger pangs twisted my stomach. Jay started for the red barn with Ash on his heels. I remained where I was, torn between my yearning to reach the town and find food, and my desire to lie down and sleep. As hungry and thirsty as I was, Jay was right; we didn't want to be caught in the open again. I stumbled after them.

The crops gave way to a gravel drive. I craned my neck to look up. Now that I was close, the barn was bigger than I'd thought. The red walls soared up above me, a sharp contrast to the azure sky. Jay set the twins down and heaved open the sliding doors, which rumbled like the noise the clouds made during the rainstorm.

We lingered in the doorway and peered into the gloom. Dust particles swirled in thin rays of sunlight. The ground level was separated into sections, and at the end of the main aisle was a ladder leading up to a loft where hay bales were stacked.

This was where Jay headed with the twins. I gazed into each stall as I passed, but they were all empty despite the lingering musty odor of animals and manure. Jay paused at the foot of the ladder and set Finn and Reese down in the dirt. "I'll go up first, and then you hand them up to me." He seized the rails of the ladder and ascended.

Exhausted, I tilted my head back and watched him climb, his black cloak swaying behind him. The dust made Ash cough.

"Okay," he called, leaning over the edge of the loft. He was high above us, and I had to climb halfway up the ladder to hand Kit to him. Ash lifted up one twin, whom I grabbed and passed up to Jay, then the other. Maneuvering RC proved to be an awkward challenge. He was some help, but not much, too weak to pull his body up the ladder and unable to use his injured right arm. Ash followed right behind him with her hand on his butt; I seized his cloak, pulling him after me. All three of us were panting when we tumbled over the top of the tall ladder.

Jay had laid Kit and the twins down in the hay. Ash and I flopped down while RC crawled away from the edge. "Rest while we can," Jay advised as he settled into the straw.

RC managed to pull himself up into a sitting position. He stared at the round window across the barn where the sky had painted a blue circle. His eyes were vacant and dull, leaving me to wonder if he was really even seeing.

"You should sleep," said Ash without even opening her eyes. "You must be weak."

"Just tired." His voice was so heavy with exhaustion it was a miracle he could even keep his eyes open. I had used all my power once. Not a fun experience, and definitely not something I wanted to do ever again. I'd passed out in an alley behind a store and awoken a while later, disoriented and weak, but I was able to return home where I slept for fourteen hours straight, much to my blood-family's worry.

Ash was already breathing deeply, asleep before RC even finished his sentence. I made a nest in the hay and burrowed in, curling into a tight ball and trying to ignore the straw that tickled my nose. I scooped Kit into my arms and held her close to me, and she snuggled against my body with a sigh. My fingers searched through the hay until they found Ash's. My brain was shutting my body down before I'd fully settled in.

"Cato," Kit whispered.

"Hmm?" I mumbled, slipping away fast.

"I'm still thirsty."

I sighed, wishing I could end her thirst, but all I could do was sympathize. "I know, Kit."

She whined softly. My eyelids were so heavy I couldn't keep them open anymore, but I murmured, "Hey, Kit-Kat, you were very brave today."

I felt her shift to look up at me. "Really?"

"Mm-hmm." I forced my eyes open to meet her gaze. "I'm so proud of you."

Kit nestled into my arms and stuck her thumb in her mouth. She was quiet for a moment, then said, "Cato? Families protect each other, right?"

"That's right," I agreed drowsily.

"Then I was a good sister?"

I gave her a gentle squeeze. "I couldn't ask for a better one."

She wriggled with pleasure. "Really?"

"Yep. Arena's Honor."

Satisfied, Kit closed her eyes and started sucking contentedly on her thumb. I stroked her long black hair, humming the broken pieces of a song I couldn't quite remember but found soothing nonetheless. I made it through a few bars, then softly sang, "You make me happy when skies are gray," and then I hummed a little more in the absence of the lyrics, my mind turning even as sleep pulled me under. I meant what I'd said, but the heartache still hurt.

My half-forgotten song trailed to silence. I closed my eyes and rested my cheek on top of Kit's head. "My name is Kit," she whispered so softly around her thumb I almost didn't hear her. She nuzzled against my ribs and resumed suckling.

They wanted me to believe I was A7-5292. Every Lightsout before we dozed off, Jay made sure we remembered to say our names aloud so we would never forget. Before I fell asleep in the hay with my youngest lab-sister in my arms, I mouthed the words: *My name is Cato.*

— Chapter Twelve —

Tea Party

Dying sunlight streamed through the canopy. A woman bent a wet branch as she stepped over a rock, picking her way carefully along the uneven forest floor. The branch flew back when she released it, slapping Agent Kovak in the face and showering him with raindrops.

He let out a frustrated growl and shoved the branch aside as he stormed forward. "Sorry," the guide muttered.

"We've been all over these godforsaken woods," Kovak seethed. "We should have caught them by now! Are you sure we're still on the right track?"

"Well . . . we thought so, but—" she pointed "—see those two fallen trees that cross each other like an X? We passed them yesterday."

He stared at her. "What?"

Agent Byrn stumbled into view, battling a branch that had snagged his sleeve. With a loud *rip*, he freed himself but surrendered part of his jacket to the limb. "We're walking in circles," he realized when he finally caught up. Even his super-duty hair gel was no match for the brambles, which had pulled strands loose until his hair looked like dry hay glued on top of his sweaty red head.

"Circles," Kovak repeated in disbelief.

"So it would seem," concurred the guide. "But I don't see how—"

"It doesn't matter how." Kovak smashed his fist against the rough bark of the nearest trunk. "Son of a *bitch*!"

"Where's the closest town from here?" Byrn demanded.

"About ten miles northwes—"

Agent Kovak marched away before she could finish. "We need to expand the perimeter," he said over his shoulder at Byrn, who was already following.

"But the pilot confirmed they haven't left the woods."

Kovak turned his head to give his business partner a frigid glare. "Are you willing to stake your career on an aerial sweep? If we miss our window of opportunity, the trail will go cold."

"It's already cold," Byrn muttered under his breath. "This makes no sense! We were on the right track even without the dogs." He shoved his hand into his damp pocket and removed a scrap of fabric as evidence. "How do you explain this? They broke branches in the underbrush. We've seen footprints, size ten, confirmed to be from A4's boots, and paw prints, too. How could they—?"

"I don't have the slightest idea," said Kovak. "As soon as we get our hands on them, I'll be sure to beat the answer out of one of the runts."

Jay was shaking my shoulder and calling my name. I frowned and rolled away, but he persisted until I finally grumbled, "What?"

"The sun is setting."

I opened my eyes in the dim light. Kit was still nestled in my arms, fast asleep, her thumb loosely in her mouth. "Axel?" I asked.

"No sign of him."

I nodded, trying to clear my head of the sleepy fog. That was the deepest slumber I'd enjoyed in a long time, so deep not a single nightmare had plagued me. I was by no means refreshed, but I had more strength. Yet, when I raised my hand to rub my eyes, it was trembling. I couldn't remember the last time I'd eaten.

"Wake up, Kit," I whispered hoarsely, nudging her. She inhaled, sighed, and burrowed in deeper, nuzzling into my chest. "We're going to find food now. Come on, you gotta get up." Kit groaned, and her eyelids fluttered open. She stretched with a wide yawn.

Jay had already started down the ladder. Ash crouched at the edge of the loft, the twins and RC sitting nearby. I rose and knelt to pick up Kit, whom I cradled in one arm as I carefully descended the ladder. When I touched the floor, I handed her off to Jay and looked up to receive Finn from Ash above. The sound of a latch made me gasp.

I whirled when one of the large doors slid open, throwing waning sunlight into the barn. Ash froze, Finn still in her arms.

I was standing in the middle of the aisle, completely exposed. Jay and I split and ducked into the empty stalls, but Kit was too surprised to react, and she sat where Jay left her, blinking in stupefied puzzlement at the unexpected visitor. It didn't matter; I knew Jay and I had been seen.

A long shadow stretching down the length of the barn aisle loomed over Kit. It grew as it walked forward. For a moment, I almost deluded myself with the possibility it was Axel.

But I heard footsteps. Axel was so quiet he never made footsteps.

I made eye contact with Jay crouching in the stall across the aisle. He nodded once, and I returned the gesture, readying myself for a fight. Based on the stranger's shadow, our opponent must be tall. Jay and I weren't exactly in peak fighting condition right now, but with two against one, we might stand a chance . . . if the human was unarmed.

I took a steadying breath. Kit was eclipsed by the shadow now. Jay made a hand signal, and there was no time to think, no time to plan. Just act and hope for the best. We lunged out of hiding to confront . . .

A little girl in a sundress. "Hi," she greeted.

I stared, dumbfounded, at her. She was no older than the twins, her bare feet dirty, her short brown hair pulled back into pigtails. Her dress was burnt orange with red flowers lining the bottom, and it astounded me. I guess I assumed all humans Outside dressed in white. *They* always wore white lab coats, and the handlers wore white shirts, and at some point during my captivity, my mind latched onto the concept that humans wore white and ghosts wore black or gray, and that was just how it was. In retrospect, I remembered that was a misconception.

Realizing this human girl was waiting patiently for me to respond, I straightened and echoed, "Um . . . hi."

She tilted her head. "What are you doing in Daddy's barn?"

I looked at Jay again, unsure how to proceed. He shrugged, just as flustered. This human wasn't afraid of us. She just stood there, awaiting an answer. When we didn't give her one, she asked, "Were you playing hide-and-seek?" She beamed. "That's my favorite game."

I had no idea what this girl was talking about, and from the look on Jay's face, he didn't either. Ash was peering down from the loft. She silently lowered herself over the edge, descended the ladder, and grimly drew her staff over her shoulder the moment her feet touched the ground.

When the girl turned and spotted Ash, she gasped and said, "Oh, wow, you're prettier than any of my dolls! I like your hair."

Ash hesitated. She rose from her fighting position and held the staff in front of her with both hands, more like she wanted to hide behind it than fight with it. A small, forced smile formed, followed by a hollow, "Thanks."

Jay seized my cloak and pulled me after him as he strode away from the girl toward Ash. We huddled close. "What are we going to do?" he hissed.

"She's human," Ash whispered back. "Humans are enemies, and she's no exception."

"She's a little kid," I argued. "She isn't going to hurt us."

"No, but she'll lead *Them* right to us. We can't let her leave."

"What are you suggesting?" asked Jay. "Kill her?"

"Of course not. Are you thinking of taking her with us?" Ash shot back.

I said, "She'll slow us down."

"And if she goes missing, we'll have every human in the area looking for her," Jay added. He turned around and approached the girl, then knelt on one knee to look her in the eye. "Hi there."

She asked, "What's your name?"

"Jay."

"I'm Kara." She lifted her chin and announced, "My daddy owns this *whole* farm, all the way to Mr. Hendrick's field on the other side of the trees."

"Wow. Your father sounds like an important man."

"He is. And I'm his helper, so I'm pretty important too."

Jay battled an amused grin. "I can see that. I was wondering, is someone as important as you any good at keeping secrets?"

She answered coyly, "*Maybe.*"

"Okay," he said, leaning back on his heels. "Well, see, you can't tell anybody we're here. It's a secret. A really *big* secret."

Kara gave Jay a dubious look as she set her hands on her hips and cocked her weight to one side. Jay exhaled and glanced around. His eyes settled on Kit. "Kara," he said slowly, "if you don't tell anybody we're here, I'll show you a magic trick. Do you like magic?"

She gasped and bobbed her head. Jay motioned, and Kit nervously crawled over to him, her ears back. "Kit, why don't you show Kara your fur?"

"Jay," Ash whispered, "she burned out a few hours ago. You can't expect her to change forms."

"Just try for me, Kit. Please?"

The Amínyte hesitated, glancing between Jay and Kara. She complained, "But Jay, it's too hard to change into my fur. I wanna stay in my skin."

"I know you're tired, but if you can change just for one teeny tiny minute, then you can wear your skin again."

Kit squeezed her eyes shut in concentration, her body stiffening with unnatural strain, and it took longer than usual for her to become smoky and translucent. Kara's eyes grew wide as she watched Kit transmute into a kitten. The feline plopped down on her haunches and gazed up at the human girl.

Kara's lips formed a silent *ooh*. "Can I pet her?" she whispered.

Kit's ears flattened. She leaned away, hissing, hackles raised along her back.

Kara, who had already started to extend her arm, yanked it back in alarm. At first I feared she'd be angry and fetch her father, but once the surprise faded, she smiled, leaning forward on her hands and knees to gaze lovingly at Kit. Jay enticed, "She'll change back if you promise to keep us a secret. You can't tell anybody, okay? Especially not your mommy and daddy."

Kara nodded and fixed her eyes on Kit, watching expectantly. The kitten's body was engulfed in black smoke as she transformed again, and Kara applauded as the smoke faded.

Jay stood. Kara leapt up and spun toward the open door. "Don't worry! I promise not to tell anybody about my imaginary friends in the barn!"

She skipped down the aisle. Her whole weight was needed to shove the door shut behind her. For a full minute after the last echoes had faded, we still didn't move, our ears straining for her return. Jay finally said, "We're leaving. *Move*, before she comes back."

Kit leaned her heavy head on Ash's shoulder, completely drained. Ash sheathed her staff, then wrapped one arm around Kit while she fondled the girl's velvety ears and stroked her hair. Jay ordered, "Kit, hide in there. Cato, Ash, you and I will get the others."

We responded immediately. Ash carried Kit to one of the empty stalls and set her down, then scaled the ladder after Jay. I scrambled over the edge and onto the loft, but we didn't even have a chance to start carrying our lab-brothers down before the doors down below slid open again.

I ducked behind a hay bale, silently cursing Kara for her loud mouth and us for letting her go. Surely she was leading *Them* to us, or her father. Ash and Jay threw themselves down in the hay.

The red sunlight filtered down the aisle. Kara's long shadow trotted in and paused in the middle of the barn. "Jay?" she called. "Are you still here?"

Jay peered over the top of the bale, then straightened. Surprised by his lack of caution, I raised myself up and peered into the aisle below, where Kara was standing with a bucket clutched in both hands. She grinned when she spotted us. "Are you thirsty?" she asked, raising the bucket. "I got some water, but we can pretend it's tea."

And so we all ended up sitting in a circle on the floor of the barn. Kara's "tea" bucket was passed around. Once I started drinking, I didn't want to stop. It took every ounce of willpower to pull the bucket away from my lips and pass it on to RC, who struggled to tilt it up with his good arm.

"Kara," Jay said, immediately capturing her attention. "Our friend is hurt. Do you have anything to make him feel better?"

"Daddy's got a first-aid kit in the tack room," she answered cheerily, standing and skipping to a closed door near the ladder. She disappeared inside.

RC passed the bucket back to Jay, who returned it to me. "There's a little left. You can finish it."

I pushed it back toward him. "I don't need—"

"Yes, you do. We can't afford to let you get dehydrated."

My mouth was already watering, and I accepted the bucket. A muffled crash in the other room preceded an "Oops!" just before Kara reemerged, a white box with a red cross tucked under her arm. "I cut myself last week, and Daddy used the stuff in here." She plopped down next to RC, opened the box, and pulled out a tube of ointment and a box of bandages. "Just squeeze this stuff on your cut and then stick the bandage on, and it'll be all better." She added a bit of advice: "It helps if someone kisses it, too."

RC glared at her, silently warning, *Don't even think about it, kid.*

"Kara!" a woman's voice called in the distance.

Her face fell. "Oh, it's suppertime." She cast a longing look back at us. "I'll be back in the morning, 'kay?"

"Okay," Jay assured as she shouted, "Coming!" and sprinted down the aisle, pigtails flying. We remained seated, watching her close the sliding doors behind her to seal us in the barn. Jay muttered, "Too bad we won't be here. Let's go."

He seized the tube of ointment but left the box of bandages, as they wouldn't do much good on RC's deep wound. I downed the rest of the water while Jay scooped up Finn and crouched so Reese could mount his back. Ash took Kit, who was awake but too weak to stand. RC was stiff in following, but at least he was able to walk. I let him put his good arm around my shoulders and use me as a support even though he didn't ask for help.

Jay pulled the door open a crack, peering out into the dusk. Lights glowed in the house to our left, but the yard was empty except for some brown birds pecking at the ground. We stayed low as we crept across the yard, though our escape wasn't silent when a murder of crows on the barn roof was startled into flight. They cawed above the dry rustle of feathers and wings flapping.

The lights of the town in the distance guided us forward, a beacon and a warning. They promised food, but only if we were resourceful enough to steal it without getting caught. The water I drank wasn't enough. Kara had reminded my stomach how empty it was, and now it roared, demanding more.

Agent Kovak leaned against the SUV to survey the map his partner had flattened out on the hood. "I just don't get it," Byrn was saying. "We've been over every inch of these woods—nothing. We've been circling the perimeter—nothing. They just vanished."

Agent Kovak drummed his fingers against the vehicle. Byrn leaned closer to the map, as if the answer were hidden somewhere in it and he could find it if he just concentrated hard enough. Any closer, and his sweaty nose was going to leave a grease mark.

"We lost them," Kovak growled. "I don't know how, but we did." He pressed his knuckles into his chest where the sharp pain was starting to prickle again, his stomach tightening. All this stress was going to put him in an early grave.

"The public has to be alerted," said Byrn. Kovak reached into his inside jacket pocket as he heaved a sigh of reluctant agreement. He uncapped the bottle and popped a pill into his mouth. "We have no choice. How do you want to do this?"

Kovak swallowed. "Minimally." He returned the pill bottle to his pocket. "No specifics, no interviews. This stays as quiet as possible. I don't want anyone to know they're kids, and I *especially* don't want news to leak that one of them is half-human."

— Chapter Thirteen —

Scavengers

By the time the horizon swallowed the sun, we were close enough to see windows gleaming in the fading light. *Windows!* These buildings actually had windows so people could look Outside whenever they wanted!

The town seemed small. This was the first one we'd encountered, so I wasn't sure how it scaled in comparison to other human towns. Houses were scattered around a general store, a few family-owned shops, and a large, open structure where vehicles connected to hoses. The nearest house had a shed in the backyard, which we took shelter behind. Although I'd been fascinated by the windows at first, I now saw the danger of them. They were like eyes in the walls.

Jay set the twins down and rose to peer around the corner of our hiding place. He tossed the tube of ointment at me and ordered, "Stay here," and then he dashed away.

I asked, "Where's he going?"

Ash shook her head, then closed her eyes and leaned back against the wall. I gripped the tube and stared at the corner where Jay had disappeared. He was alone without his powers in a human town with *Them* looking for us. Not that I would have been much help to him, but worry formed a cold pit in my stomach. What if he had a Spasm and attracted the attention of the locals?

I crawled to the corner and craned my neck around the edge. Jay wasn't in sight. I halfway considered leaving the others and trying to find him, but what good would that do? I could be wandering around lost looking for him while he was back here.

I inspected the tube. I wasn't sure what to do with it, but after a few minutes, I discovered the tip turned until it twisted completely off. Ash untied the sleeve from RC's arm so I could dab the ointment around the edges of the damaged neutralizer. He drew a sharp breath and squeezed his eyes shut at the touch of my fingers.

I did as much as I could, but I was frustratingly limited because the deepest part of the wound was concealed beneath the metal band, which was so tight on his arm I couldn't work my fingers inside.

RC seized my wrist and snarled, "That's enough. You're hurting me."

I drew back. "It's going to get infected." My lab-brother just scowled at me, so I turned to Ash. "Your turn."

"I'm fine," she said, but I'd already squeezed a dollop onto my thumb and offered my hand. She sighed and held still, though she winced when I peeled back the strip of cloth and smeared the ointment on the scabbed gash above her eyebrow. I started to reach for a minor cut on her cheek, but she leaned away. "We should save the rest for RC."

My skin crawled, as though I was being watched. Unnerved, I glanced around, even checking the nearest windows. Finding nobody, I looked up straight into the intelligent eyes of a crow perched on the gutter. It blinked at me and tilted its head. Two more were on a nearby roof, one on the tall pole strung with wires, three alighting in the nearby tree . . . I couldn't count all of them.

I jumped when a voice whispered into my ear, "I found a place for us to hide."

Jay was crouching beside me. I exhaled and set my hand on my racing heart, so relieved I thought I might melt. I capped the tube and shoved it inside my pouch with the disk and photograph.

Jay was meticulous about staying out of sight during the journey. He led us under hedges and along fences before stopping beside a low building's half-open window. "It's empty except for some vehicles and tools." And with no further explanation, he let go of RC and hopped over the windowsill. He leaned out and extended his arms, into which I placed Reese. Jay pulled him inside, then reappeared for Finn and Kit.

Ash and I worked together to guide RC through the window. The two of us were the last ones inside.

I dropped to the floor and gazed around with a critical eye. Three vehicles partially stripped of their parts were parked in the spacious garage. A long counter mounted on the far wall displayed a mess of tools and oily rags. The windows were so grimy I could barely see out of them, which, I supposed, was good if humans had just as little visibility inside.

Kit's ears were back. "How will Axel find us here?" she whimpered.

I assured, "He can find us anywhere."

Jay picked up a metal tool with a long handle and a crescent-shaped end. "I know it's not the best place, but it'll work for now."

"Let's go find some food," said Ash. She turned back toward the window.

"No!" Jay dropped the tool and seized her by the arm.

Ash stared at him in bewilderment. "Why not?"

He released her and peered out the window. "We should wait until it's completely dark."

I groaned and glanced at the burning sky, which indicated at least an hour before night truly fell. "Jay, we haven't eaten in three days. I feel like I'm going to pass out."

He fixed me with a serious stare. "I think waiting a few more hours to eat is worth not being captured, don't you?"

He was being rational, but I was so hungry my survival instincts pushed reason aside. All that kept me from dashing outside right now was my deep fear of *Them*. Hunger was no stranger to me after all. I'd tried to starve myself to death at that place once. A day in Quarantine with a tube down my throat was good incentive not to try that again.

I leaned my back against the wall and slid down to the floor, drawing my legs up to my chest and wrapping my arms around my shins. All there was to do now was wait.

I closed my eyes and started to doze, and I'd swear only a few minutes passed before a hand gripped my shoulder. I started, jerking my head up to darkness. Beyond the window, lights on tall poles had sprung to life. Ash was kneeling in front of me.

I didn't want to get up. I wanted to lie here on the sticky floor and sleep forever without a single dream. That was a terrible wish to have now that I was finally Outside with an entire world waiting to be explored. *Fine, I take it back.* I just wanted to sleep uninterrupted for a few days, that was all.

I yawned and forced my aching muscles to move. My joints creaked when I stood, premature arthritis adding stiffness to a body that shouldn't feel this old for many more years. Once on my feet, I stretched my arms above my head and let a groan morph into another yawn. My stomach was so empty it had passed the threshold of pain. It must have shriveled to the size of a grate. *Grape.* Damn, I was tired.

RC, Kit, and the twins were still sleeping. Their strength was returning so slowly. If *They* found us here, we wouldn't stand a chance.

"Ready?" I asked.

Ash nodded, staff in hand, and took a step toward the window, but Jay stopped her again. "You're the only one of us who's armed. I think you should stay here and protect the others. Cato and I will go find food and bring it back."

Ash scowled. "But you'll be in more danger. I should go with you."

"We can defend ourselves. They can't."

Ash glanced down at our sleeping lab-siblings. She gripped her staff in both hands with a mortified look on her face, silently panicking about the responsibility placed upon her. I touched her arm to give her encouragement, but she flinched.

I asked, "What about Kit? She knows her way around the streets better than any of us."

"She needs to rest after changing for Kara," Jay replied. "It's just you and me for this one." He squeezed Ash's shoulder and said, "Keep them safe. We'll be back as soon as we can."

"Be careful," Ash said, her voice feeble. "And hurry back."

Jay inclined his head and climbed through the window. I hauled my protesting body after him and fell gracelessly onto the sidewalk outside.

Jay pulled me up without a word, and we stayed low while we dashed to take shelter behind a large shrub where the streetlights didn't reach us.

No sooner had we ducked down into our hiding place than a vehicle roared past in a whir of flashing red-and-blue lights and the wails of a siren. Jay and I shrank into the foliage. An instinct from Before made me afraid of the sirens. They symbolized cages and restraints.

Jay whispered, "Do you think they're looking for us?"

"Don't know," I whispered back.

He peered through the leaves of our hiding place. "All right, Cato. You're the human. Where do we get food and water?"

"I don't know."

"Stop and think. If you're hungry, where do you go for food?"

I closed my eyes, sifting through the fragments of memories. My stomach growled, and I focused on that feeling, trying to recollect how I satisfied it. I remembered being in my house, in a sunlit room with a tiled floor, opening a small wooden door—a cubby, no, *cupboard*—and reaching inside to find food. I couldn't remember what the food looked, tasted, or felt like, so my damaged memory used the only type of food I did remember—a small plastic cup of tasteless ground paste.

I opened my eyes. "Inside their homes. In the kitchen."

"We have to break in? Isn't there another way?"

"Probably, but none that I remember."

He clutched his stomach. "Fine. Then we'll find a building that looks empty."

I skimmed the windows, pausing on the silhouettes of a man and woman arguing. "There," Jay announced, pointing through the branches at the perfect place to break in—an open ground-level window, the view within completely dark. I nodded and rose.

The Spasm slammed me back down.

I writhed and screamed as my head felt like it split open. This time was different; not only was I absorbed in the pain, but I was suffocating too. My screams were muffled. Something was blocking my airway. I thrashed, kicking like a wild animal while I clutched my head. I wasn't aware of my outside environment, but my body was desperate to survive, and it struggled to draw in oxygen between the screams.

When the pain ebbed, I opened my eyes to find Jay kneeling over me, his gloved hand clasped firmly over my mouth. I sucked in a ragged breath when his palm left, refilling my lungs with the cool night air. "You good?"

I scrambled up, swiping away tears. "Yeah."

"Are you sure? You have to be completely focused if we're going to do this without getting caught."

To prove I was fine, I stepped brazenly out from behind the shrub, my gaze locked on the open window across the street. Petrified of being in the open and eager to reach the safety of the shadows again, I rushed forward. I'd taken only a few steps when a horn preceded a screech that shattered the stillness.

I whirled. Two blinding lights were bearing down on me. I had only enough time to brace myself before I was struck. Sharp pain resounded through my body as I was knocked off my feet by the force of something heavy smashing into me. I rolled up onto the slanted surface, then fell over the side as my monstrous assailant squealed to a stop. I hit the asphalt with a rough gasp.

"Hey, jackass, why don't you watch where you're going?" a man yelled. I raised my head. A shadow moved behind the lights; he was coming to get me. I scrambled to my feet and took off.

The bright lights and the shock completely disoriented me. I wanted to return to Jay, but I had no idea which direction to go. I stumbled into the blissful darkness and let it conceal me like a safety blanket. The man was still shouting profanities at me from the street. I threw myself down on the other side of a large metal container, shivering.

"Moron!" he called, but he didn't chase me. A door slammed, and then the lights moved away.

I locked my jaw as waves of dull pain rolled across my body in the wake of the assault. What the heck had attacked me? I still couldn't process what just happened. In the light, I might have been able to identify that thing, but in the darkness, I'd seen only those blinding lights.

I peered around the corner of my hiding place to ensure my attacker was gone. A shadow flitted across the street, and then Jay crouched beside me. "Are you all right?"

I was trembling so hard I had to shove my hands into the crook behind my knees to still them. "I don't know," I whispered. I hurt, yes, but I hurt all over. There was no localized pain. That was a good sign, right?

A door in the wall across from us slammed open.

I gasped, squinting at the silhouette of a strange creature backlit in the doorway. Jay clapped a gloved hand over my mouth again and pressed us both into the corner with the metal bin on one side and the wall behind us.

The creature limped toward us. Even if I were prepared to defend myself, fear had me completely paralyzed. I'd never seen a monster like this, not even a Scout in the Arena. From the doorway came a ruckus of clinking, clanging, a faint roar of laughter from deeper within the building, and a man shouting, "I need a runner for Table 3!"

With a grunt, the beast detached half of its body and threw it on the ground, where the unmoving lump lay still. I stared in absolute confusion, but comprehension slowly dawned on me when the rest of the creature straightened and the light illuminated its face. It wasn't a monster; it was a woman.

I breathed in a tantalizing aroma through the open doorway. My mouth began to water. I didn't know what I was smelling, but I knew it was edible and I wanted it. I was practically drooling all over Jay's hand.

The human blew a loose strand of hair away from her face, then leaned toward us. I tensed, waiting for her to notice us peering up at her from the shadows. She set her hand on the metal container and lifted the lid, then heaved the bag inside and closed the lid again. She made a face of disgust and wiped her hands on her apron before she turned away and went back inside, closing the door behind her and sealing the alley in silence and darkness once more.

Jay and I remained frozen for at least a minute, waiting for the door to open again. Finally, Jay released me and stood.

"Did you smell that?" he asked, reaching up to open the lid.

I helped him seize the woman's mysterious bag and haul it out of the bin. Together, we ripped it open and peered inside. I withdrew a used napkin and tossed it aside, then shoved my hand into something cool, stringy, and squishy. I pulled it out, turning my hand toward the light on the tall pole at the end of the alley. It was shiny and red, like blood.

"What is it?" Jay asked, watching over my shoulder.

I lifted it to my nose and sniffed. Not blood. I remembered eating this stuff Before, twirling my fork around it, slurping it into my mouth. "Food," I answered, as I couldn't remember the name of this particular food, but it didn't matter at the moment. I shoved the handful into my mouth.

Ecstasy. Never before had anything tasted so delicious. I closed my eyes, savoring the intense flavor making my taste buds explode. The paste we ate at that place was nothing compared to this, even though we were eating garbage. How could humans throw away perfectly good food? Didn't they realize what a privilege it was?

Jay sifted through the trash bag and pulled out a soggy piece of bread. He tore it in two and handed me a piece, and we shoved our halves into our mouths. Immediately, the combined taste and smell of garlic almost knocked me off my feet. Jay moaned in pleasure, and the two of us attacked the bag with a feverish desire to gorge ourselves. Not even the prizes won from the Arena had so much flavor. It was a feast in a time of famine.

The food was mingled with inedible pieces of garbage, which we threw aside. I wasn't even sure what I was eating; a wide assortment of meals had been dumped into the bag. Too soon, my stomach couldn't hold any more, and I was sorry I couldn't continue to enjoy our dinner. I'd eat forever if I could to sample everything and make up for those years of cruel and unnecessary deprivation. But pain twisted my innards, and I gasped, rolling onto my side.

Jay cried out, curling his limbs into a tight ball. Beads of sweat glistened on his forehead when he turned toward the distant light. "Aargh," he groaned. "Was . . . was the food bad?"

I clenched my teeth to trap a moan. "Don't . . . know . . ." I answered in a strained whisper. It hadn't tasted bad, although I'd been so surprised my taste buds still worked that I might not have been able to recognize bad food if I'd eaten it. Rather, we'd probably filled our empty stomachs too quickly with food that was too rich, and now we were suffering for it.

I groaned on the alley floor, rolling in agony next to Jay. We were useless to travel now, at the mercy of humans if the woman wandered out the door again with more garbage. We dragged ourselves to our safe corner next to the bin and waited for the pain to pass. Spasms ended, so surely this pain, too, would end.

The moon was high when the cramps finally ebbed enough for me to sit up. Jay was on his hands and knees beside me, head bowed, harsh gasps hissing through bared teeth.

Neither of us spoke a word as we returned to our hideout. He took the lead and slunk through the night on high alert, me on his heels with the garbage bag slung over one shoulder. The town was sleeping. Regardless, Jay and I avoided open spaces. We never stepped inside the pools of light; we always skirted around.

My sense of direction failed me, but Jay acted as though he knew where he was going, and before long I spotted the low building we'd made our temporary home, dark in the moonlight. Silent as shadows, we crept through the window and dropped to the floor.

Ash was seated cross-legged, back to the wall and staff lying across her lap, her head bowed. Her chest rose and fell with deep, even breaths. The twins were huddled together; they must have awoken, scooted closer to each other, and fallen asleep again. RC stirred in his slumber. A pair of golden eyes, dimly lit in the darkness, watched us.

"Hey, Kit-Kat," I greeted. She grinned faintly, and her eyes blinked in the gloom, but she didn't move. I knelt and pulled her feeble body into my lap. "We brought food," I told her as I pushed a stick of bread into her hand. She nibbled on it. I chuckled as she closed her eyes and shuddered with pleasure. Even her toes wriggled. "Is it good?" She nodded and took a big bite.

Jay touched Ash's shoulder. She jumped and seized her staff, but then she relaxed when she realized who woke her. "You were gone for a long time," she mumbled groggily.

Jay nudged the garbage bag forward with his foot. "Don't eat too fast," he advised.

A dangerous gleam entered Ash's eyes as her gaze fell on the bag. Her fingers tightened around the staff, her movements fluid like a feline stalking prey when she leaned forward, her eyes no longer on the bag, but on Jay. For too long, we'd had to fight each other for food. We were not animals, but that defensive instinct died hard even though we weren't squaring off in the Arena. Jay yielded a step, and Ash relaxed a little as she tentatively examined the contents of the bag. "I didn't expect you to bring back this much. Won't the humans notice all this is missing?"

"Nope," I said. Kit crawled out of my lap and across the floor to kneel beside Ash, who flinched but then settled down once she realized it was just Kit. "It's garbage. They didn't want it."

Ash had taken her first bite and no longer cared. She was too busy stuffing food into her mouth to worry about where it came from. "Slow down," I cautioned. She paused, glanced at me, and made an effort to chew slower.

Jay roused RC and the twins. Finn and Reese sat up, rubbing their eyes, but RC needed assistance to sit with his injured arm. While Jay helped RC, I handed each twin a roll. They stared at the bread in their hands with blank, bleary eyes. "What is it?" Finn asked, his words slurring. He coughed to clear the grogginess from his throat.

"Food," I said.

They shook their heads. "No, it isn't," said Reese.

They'd expected the cup of paste. I said, "It is. I know it looks different, but I think you'll like it."

They hesitated, watching me with suspicion etched into their brows. Their blue eyes flickered weakly. *Don't waste your reserves*, I silently scolded since they were using their Divinities on me. *I wouldn't lie to you.*

Finally, they raised the rolls in unison and experimentally licked the bread. Everything about it was wrong to them—the smell, texture, weight, consistency, taste. They smacked their lips a few times and stared at me. "It isn't food," they insisted.

"Take a bite."

They did, but with great reluctance. First they bit lightly, testing their teeth against the bread, and then they withdrew to inspect the indents. When they followed with a real bite, I realized they were awkwardly using their teeth for the first time. They swallowed and doubled over, choking.

"You have to chew it." I hadn't thought I'd need to explain how to eat bread, but in retrospect, I should have known after they spent a whole lifetime consuming water and paste for meals. Finn was still coughing, but Reese tentatively began to work the roll between his teeth, becoming more confident in his chewing abilities as he learned how to grind his meal between his molars.

Now that Finn's coughs were settling, he imitated his blood-brother and bit off a piece of bread. He acted as if he already knew what to do since Reese had done it. Soon they were devouring the rolls zealously and admittedly a little creepily. Their movements were synchronized so they took a bite, chewed, swallowed, and repeated in perfect unison. It was odd, but maybe that was just a peculiarity all twins shared.

Behind me, RC groaned, "It's *so* good."

I twisted around to get more for Finn and Reese. Kit was wolfing down some sort of cooked meat while rummaging in the bag for more. She drew out a soggy breadstick, but Jay snatched it. "Not so fast," he said sternly. "It'll make you sick."

Kit pouted. "I want it!" she whined. She stretched her fingers up, but Jay held it higher out of reach. He broke off a piece from the end and handed that to her, forcing her to slow down and wait between each bite.

I rifled through the garbage bag until I fished out a piece of meat. The smell of it was enticing and familiar. Ch . . . it started with ch . . . and then e? N. Chen? No, that wasn't right. I was missing a syllable. Chenik? The elusiveness of its name frustrated me as I turned back to the twins. Copying Jay's method, I ripped away strips of the chenik and handed a piece to each.

"What's that?" they inquired in unison.

"It's food," I said again. "Eat up. You need your strength."

Still, they hesitated. Finn had one bite left of his bread, and he stared at it, confused. "But this is food."

"Yes. So is this." I offered the ch . . . *chicken!* That was it! I offered the chicken again. Each took his share, although they studied the roll, then the chicken, then the roll again, comparing them. I patiently explained, "There are different types of food Outside, and each tastes different. You won't know if you like it or not if you don't try it."

With extreme caution, they raised the new food to their lips for their first taste. They tried to bite down but found the meat much tougher than the bread, and they opened their mouths again, withdrawing without even leaving teeth marks. "Can't we have this kind of food?" Finn inquired. He held up the last of his roll.

"The chicken tastes good too. You just have to bite harder. You'll get the hang of it."

Kit asked, "Can I have some? Please?"

I tore off a piece for her. She gobbled it in two bites, then licked her lips and crawled to the bag again to scavenge for something else. Finn and Reese watched her consume her share, then tried again.

Kit extracted another chunk of chicken and crawled away from the bag. "My friends are hungry too."

"Your friends?" I asked.

She nodded, offering the meat to the shadows. To my surprise, a small, furry form moved in the darkness, a pair of eyes glinting when it caught the faintest ray from the streetlight shining through the grimy window. I stiffened in alarm, then relaxed when I made out the form of a cat. No, more than one. Two for sure, maybe three.

"It's okay," Kit crooned. "It's yummy food." The cats inched close enough to take the food from her hand without venturing too close to the rest of us. Kit fondly explained, "They live under the cabinet in the corner. But they don't mind sharing their home with us."

I didn't understand on what level Kit was able to communicate with cats, if they "talked" in a language or mental concepts. I glanced at Jay, concerned that Kit was giving away our food, but he shrugged one shoulder as if to say, *It's fine. We have enough.*

I closed my eyes and yawned. I hadn't been full—truly, satisfyingly *full*—like this since Before. Now, I could feel my energy fading. I just wanted to sleep.

I retreated from the group and lay down with my back against the wall. With a sigh of contentment, I let my heavy eyelids fall. The voices were just starting to fade into incomprehensible white noise at the blissful shore of sleep when something roused me. I frowned and curled into a tighter ball, trying to tune out the retching sound and return to the calm ocean I'd been floating upon.

Something isn't right.

I peeled my eyes open to find Jay and Ash with the twins, who were hunched over. "What's wrong?" I asked, sitting up on my elbows.

Reese vomited. Finn clutched his stomach and groaned.

Jay answered, "They couldn't handle the rich food." He and Ash helped the boys lie back so they could sleep, their stomachs empty again. I watched in pity. Although my stomach had reacted painfully to the Outside sustenance, at least I'd been able to keep it down and digest it to give me strength. I hoped Finn and Reese would adapt soon. They had to, or they'd starve.

Jay stayed with the twins while Ash, Kit, and RC continued to feast. "My name is Cato," I whispered before I slipped into oblivion to the sound of the bag rustling below their soft voices.

— Chapter Fourteen —

Breaking the Rules

Thin beams of sunlight streaked through the layer of grime coating the window. I would have slept all day if something hadn't disturbed me. Hushed voices were rising into an argument, and I sat up to see Jay set a small black box on the floor in front of Reese.

"I need you to do this," he said.

Reese's thin arms pushed ECANI back at Jay. "No. It's against the Rules."

RC, Ash, and Kit were all awake and watching. I'd never seen Finn or Reese argue about anything, *ever*, let alone with Jay. Trying not to interrupt, I crawled to Ash and whispered, "What's going on?"

Without breaking her gaze on the disagreement, she whispered back, "Jay wants Finn and Reese to hack into *Their* system."

"Whoa."

"Yeah. If you couldn't tell, they aren't very open to the idea."

"Okay, question—why does Jay want them to hack it?"

Ash shrugged, but then she answered, "Jay doesn't want *Them* to find a way to track us when we move again."

"Makes sense," I said, thinking of all the human technology surrounding us now that we weren't in the middle of the wilderness.

"Yeah, well, hacking is easy. The hard part is convincing Finn and Reese to do it."

I directed my attention back to the battle. Finn said, "We'll be sent to Omega. What you're asking is even worse than not waiting for *Them*."

"*They* can't send you to Omega if *They* can't catch you, right? We'll be safe if you do this." Jay shoved the computer back at them.

Reese shook his head and rejected it again. "We can't."

"Yes, you can."

"We *shouldn't*," Reese corrected.

"I need you to."

Finn whined, "But the Rules—"

"You've already broken the Rules! And I don't just mean running away, either. You've broken the Rules before."

"Have not!" they cried indignantly.

"No? You let *Them* believe Axel was a failed experiment." Reese's jaw hung slack, and Finn gaped at Jay with horror and betrayal equal to the reaction he would have had if Jay had slapped him across the face. "Or those times you purposely made *Them* mad enough to punish you by making you stand in The Square all Lightsout?"

Their blue eyes flicked momentarily to Ash before Finn unconvincingly denied, "We would never purposely anger our masters."

"And what about Cato's photo? You broke the Rules every time you snuck it out of the laundry and gave it back to him."

Finn bowed his head. His blood-brother muttered, "That's different."

"Please," Jay begged as he handed ECANI back. "I know it's hard to understand why I'm asking you to break the Rules. If *They* catch us, I'll take all the blame. I'll tell *Them* I forced you. I'll take as much of your punishment as *They* will give me. I promise. I just need you to trust me."

Reese finally accepted ECANI. He stared at the computer for a long time in miserable indecision. Jay seated himself beside them. Softer, gentler, he spoke to Reese. I couldn't hear his words, but Reese was listening intently. Finally, without a word, he accepted the pair of gloves needed to use ECANI.

Alarms blared throughout the AGC.

Dr. Anders strode across the server room to a woman sitting at one of the main computer consoles. He leaned down to observe the screen over Agent Zelkowitz's shoulder. The tech shook her head in frustration. "Oh, they're good," she murmured, her fingers tapping frantically on the keys. "They are *really* good."

"I thought the system was impenetrable."

"It is. Well, it's supposed to be." Agent Zelkowitz scrambled to keep up with the massive code scrolling down the screen. "Not even a black hat can get in. I know of only two people capable of hacking us."

Dr. Anders gnawed on his gum for a moment before he hung his head and muttered the answer in one peppermint-flavored breath: "The creators."

"Bingo. Well, I correct myself. A Technopath could probably breach our security, but I doubt that's who I'm going head-to-head with right now."

"Can you bypass them?"

"I'm trying."

Windows opened and closed while symbols and numbers flashed by, each party trying to out-hack the other. Agent Zelkowitz barely had time to close one connection before another appeared. "They're just too damn fast. It's all I can do to hold them off. They—Oh-ho, here we go. Rookie mistake, kid." She leaned forward in her chair. "I got you now."

⌐⌐⌐⌐⌐⌐⌐⌐⌐⌐⌐⌐⌐⌐⌐⌐⌐⌐⌐⌐⌐⌐⌐⌐⌐⌐⌐⌐⌐⌐⌐⌐⌐⌐⌐⌐⌐

I'd been forgetting this lately because they were so ignorant about the Outside, but watching Finn and Reese operate ECANI reminded me of their true genius. They may not know what a rock or a tree was, but they could hack into the highest-security database in the world if they wanted to.

The twins' invention was a technological masterpiece. *They* had dictated what Finn and Reese learned, and almost every bit of knowledge the blood-brothers had absorbed went into the creation of ECANI, which stood for *Experimental Computer And*—hold on, I knew this— *Experimental Computer And Neural Interface*. That sounded right.

ECANI had to be extraordinary—fast enough to process massive amounts of data, ingenious enough to analyze complex information from the neural monitoring system, and sophisticated enough to handle the programming requirements of the Weapon someday. And it was.

The keyboard and screens projected above ECANI were holograms. If I tried to touch them, my hand would pass right through. Yet Reese's fingers flew effortlessly and silently over the keyboard thanks to the gloves, which had sensors in the fingertips so he could touch the otherwise intangible holograms. Five screens hovered in the air. ECANI tracked his eye movements so all he had to do was lift his hand, and the screens shifted in response so the one he wanted was right in front of his fingertips. He and ECANI were in perfect sync.

Jay stood beside me, watching Reese work. I asked, "You think they can hack *Their* system?"

"I have no doubt. Right?" he asked.

Reese scowled and kept typing. Finn hung his head with a sigh. "Yes," he said. "But *They* know we're trying." He started to chew on a hangnail.

Reese made a noise of frustration. I asked, "What's wrong?"

"*They're* trying to back-hack us to pinpoint our location."

I caught my breath. That was a risk I hadn't considered.

Jay took a step forward. "Can you stop *Them*?" he asked.

***

Agent Zelkowitz proclaimed, "They made a mistake. I found the back door into ECANI's system. Give me ten seconds, and I can tell you exactly where your escaped lab rats are."

She smiled, already imaging the bonus she was sure to get. Anders, the cranky doctor, didn't match her enthusiasm, but that didn't deter her. She made a show of triumphantly raising her hand and bringing her finger down on ENTER, the final stroke needed to take control.

All the windows vanished to be replaced by one message:

GRID FAILURE
ERROR 1 1 1 0 1 – 9 6 0

She stared at the screen, her mouth hanging open. "No."

Anders demanded, "Grid failure? What does that mean?"

The words blinked three times. Then the computer screen went black.

"Shit."

"What? What's happening?" Anders looked up as the lights flickered and went out. The AGC powered down with a low whine, as if it were sighing its final breath. The two sat in total darkness for a few seconds before the backup generators kicked on and the lights, though dimmer than before, sputtered back to life.

Zelkowitz finally had the sense to close her mouth. She pushed the chair away from the computer. "I should have seen that coming."

"*What?*"

"They baited me, and I fell for it." Agent Zelkowitz groaned and dragged her hands through her hair. "Outsmarted by ten-year-olds," she lamented under her breath. Louder, she explained, "I thought I had them. I really did. But that's what they wanted me to think. The lousy runts gave me a decoy opening and then took over the master controls while I was distracted. They beat me. I'm sorry."

Anders slowly started to grind the gum between his molars again. "There has to be something else you can do."

"There isn't." She leaned back and pressed her palms against her closed eyes. "Our entire system has been compromised."

Anders rubbed his chin. Computers were not his forte; his medical degree qualified him to run the experiments, not deal with the complicated software. "Our data's gone?"

"I don't think they deleted it, just cut off our access to the database."

"How much control do they have?"

Agent Zelkowitz massaged her temples. "Everything. Lights, heating, air-conditioning, security cameras, every digital file . . . Hell, they can even hack our cell phones." She looked at him sidelong between her fingers. "They could hack the White House if they wanted to."

Dr. Anders turned away from the dark computer screen. "I have to report this. In the meantime, what can you do?"

Zelkowitz shook her head slowly. "They locked me out. I can do a full system reboot, which should return our basic functions, but as for the data, I don't know if I can recover that. Even if I can regain minimum access, there's nothing stopping them from hacking in again."

Anders paused in the doorway. "They've never disobeyed like this before. They likely did this under duress."

"What gives you that impression?"

The doctor narrowed his eyes. "You don't know A1 and A2 like I do. Whatever they did, it's not permanent. Find a way to get control back."

<hr />

Reese's fingers stilled.

"You did it?" I whispered, too tense to speak at a normal volume.

Reese nodded sullenly, then resumed typing. "What are you doing?" Jay demanded. He took a step forward, no doubt worried Reese might be trying to undo the damage.

Absent with either concentration or guilt, Reese answered, "Making us invisible to technology."

I asked, "What does that mean?"

Rather than answer me, Finn said, "ECANI, voice control on."

A woman's mechanical voice issued forth: "Voice code required."

"Alpha One."

Audio lines appeared when Finn spoke. "Voice code accepted. Welcome, A1-2296."

I said, "You should reprogram it to call you Finn now."

I was sure he heard me, but he didn't respond. He started speaking a language I didn't know. It sounded Asian, maybe Korean or Mandarin. Whatever it was, ECANI understood, because his voice commands were opening new windows and writing code while Reese continued to work manually with the gloves. The screens shifted between Finn and Reese without any hand signals or physical movements beyond almost imperceptible flicks of the eyes, as if the twins were passing the holograms to each other with their minds. It was creepy how in sync Finn, Reese, and ECANI were with each other, as if the three had formed a sentient organism that shared one consciousness.

We watched them work until they were satisfied enough to shut down all the holograms. Without looking at us, Finn quietly explained, "ECANI is jamming frequencies across the spectrum. We shut down all communications in the region."

"Only for twenty-four hours," Reese muttered, wringing his hands. "*They* can't be too angry at us for that, right? It's temporary."

Jay asked, "What about the Grid? Is that shut down too?"

Reese squirmed with guilt. "*They*'ll likely reboot, which will restore all basic functions to the AGC."

"But the files are locked," said Finn.

Reese nodded. "*They* won't have access until we manually unlock the system."

Finn rubbed his eyes and yawned. "We also created a program that will run indefinitely and delete all images matching our facial recognition software within seconds of being uploaded on any hard-lined or wirelessly accessible device with imaging capabilities. We'll be digitally untrackable."

I was too embarrassed to admit that I had no idea what they were talking about, but "digitally untrackable" sounded positive. Jay said, "I don't know much about this sort of thing, but isn't that an awful lot of data to process? I mean, aren't we talking thousands, *millions* of devices all being hacked?"

The twins shot him indignant looks. ECANI was much more than a simple computer, and the fact that he'd even asked such a question was an insult to their invention. "They're all connected," Reese said.

Finn explained, "Within a fifty-mile radius of our location, ECANI will access all electronic devices to monitor for images of us. Anything matching our facial recognition program will be removed."

"Within reason," Reese corrected. "We can't hack into outdated cameras that record on tapes or film, but if those are uploaded to a computer, our program will erase both the source image and all copies."

Although we were far from safe, the odds weren't stacked so impossibly high against us. We might actually stand a chance. "You guys are great," I praised. "I mean it."

Neither twin reacted to my compliment. "We're going to Omega for this," Finn said. "We broke so many Rules . . ."

"No one's going to Omega," said Jay. "I'm not going to let this family fall apart." He sat down between the boys and put his arms over their shoulders. "Trust me. Arena's Honor."

Finn hopelessly shook his head while Reese stared down at the gloves on his hands. I consoled, "I know you guys are scared of *Them*, but *They* can't hurt you if *They* can't find you, and you just cut off a lot of *Their* resources."

Jay pulled the gloves off Reese before he had a chance to undo the havoc he'd wrought. Reese didn't fight to retain the gloves. His hand rose to his mouth, and he started to chew on his fingernails.

Finn fixed his steady blue gaze on me and said, "Cato, we learned a long time ago the pain will always come no matter what. If you fight, it will be worse than whatever *They* had planned to begin with, and then there's extra pain. Angering *Them* hurts only ourselves."

I reminded him, "We're free now."

Finn shook his head. "*They* will find us. There's no such thing as escape."

"You don't believe it because *They* don't want you to."

Now when Finn studied me, it was almost with pity. "You'll see," he told me forlornly.

I turned away, knowing I couldn't win. Their lives revolved around the Rules and the whims of humankind. I feared Finn and Reese would never overcome their bondage mentality, that they'd always adhere to the belief that ghosts existed for the sole purpose of serving humans. It wasn't true. But I'd never convince them of that because the twins had been brainwashed long before I ever met them.

Jay rose with a smile and ruffled Reese's hair as he walked past. Reese cringed at Jay's touch and scowled after him, but then his expression softened as he gazed regretfully at ECANI. All the holograms

145

had vanished. ECANI was deceptively at rest, just a single blinking light on the side panel to prove it wasn't really. This whole town had been hacked, and the humans didn't even know.

───────────────────────────────────

Agent Kovak shifted on the uncomfortable wooden chair and eyed the family sitting across from him. The father looked older than he probably was, his face tan and weather-beaten and his salt-and-pepper hair thinning. The mother was slender and plain, glancing nervously between Kovak and Byrn. But it was the little girl sitting between her parents who had Kovak's attention.

In the corner, the ticking of a grandfather clock marked the passing of uncomfortable silence. Byrn politely sipped at the glass of pink lemonade he'd been given, but Kovak set his on the coffee table without taking a single drink, ice cubes clinking. The mother clenched her long fingers into fists on her knees, her eyes on the beads of condensation rolling down the glass. "There's a coaster right next to you there," she said.

Kovak barely managed to refrain from rolling his eyes. Byrn glared at him. Kovak forced an apologetic smile and moved the glass onto the coaster. "Let's get down to business," he said, keeping his voice even.

The father leaned forward. "We called you because Kara came into the house this morning and asked me if I'd seen her imaginary friends anywhere."

His wife added, "We asked what they looked like, and she drew this." She scooted up to the edge of the musty couch so she could reach across the coffee table and hand a paper to the Agents. Kara scowled and looked away.

Kovak took the paper and studied the drawing, his heart flying. The chair creaked under his shifting weight when he leaned over to show Byrn, who nodded. Kovak folded the paper with the Alpha symbol drawn in red crayon and shoved it into his breast pocket. "Kara," he said patiently, "do you think you could describe your imaginary friends to me?"

She shook her head, causing her pigtails to bounce. "Answer him," her mother ordered.

Kara complained, "But Mom, it's a secret. They won't come back if I tell."

"I'm really good at keeping secrets," Kovak replied, his voice a pitch too high to make it drip with sweetness. "I can find your friends. Tell me, how many friends did you have in the barn?"

"Seven," she replied sullenly under the stern gaze of her father.

The Agents exchanged excited glances. Byrn asked, "Did they hurt you?"

"No. They showed me a magic trick, and we had a tea party."

Agent Kovak almost burst into uproarious laughter at the thought of his test subjects having a tea party with this little girl. Byrn shot him a warning look, and Kovak's chortles turned into unconvincing coughs.

"What kind of magic trick?" asked Byrn.

"She turned into the cutest kitten I ever saw!" Kara exclaimed dreamily.

Pale at the girl's apparent madness, the mother latched a bony hand onto her husband's knee. "Oh, Ed."

"It's okay, Marie. They're gone now." He pried her fingers loose and stroked the veins on her wrist as he faced the Agents again. "We saw the news when we went into town today. Are these the creatures you've been hunting? Were they really here with my daughter?"

Marie's grip tightened around her husband's hand. Agent Kovak ignored Ed's inquiry and addressed Kara again, asking hopefully, "Do you know where they went?" Kara shook her head. "Are you sure?"

"They were gone when I woke up." She heaved a melancholy sigh. "I even brought them a muffin for breakfast. I thought they'd stay if I kept their secret."

"Thank you for talking to us, Kara," said Kovak, donning his sincerest smile.

"You were right to call us, Mr. and Mrs. Spohrer," Byrn told the parents. "May we speak in the other room?"

The four adults left Kara swinging her feet over the edge of the couch, humming to herself. Once they were out of earshot, Agent Kovak murmured, "Kara is lucky to be alive." Marie seized her husband's arm. "Would you mind if we inspected the barn?"

Ed mumbled, "Not at all."

Byrn handed him a business card. "Chances are slim they'll come back this way, but if Kara remembers any more details, please call us." Ed accepted the card with a solemn nod.

The Agents exited through a screen door. "A tea party," Byrn muttered, snickering.

Kovak chuckled. "I would've loved to see that. You do realize the runts would have done anything she said. Kid could've had A1 and A2 playing dress-up and Barbie with her if she wanted."

"The poor bastards wouldn't have had a clue what was going on." They laughed as they crossed the yard and pulled open the sliding door to the barn, inhaling the mustiness of hay, dust, and manure. They strode down the aisle, glancing into the empty stalls as they went.

Agent Byrn commented, "No sign of them."

Kovak raised his head as they neared the end of the aisle. "Let's see what's up there." He grabbed a ladder rung and began to climb. When he reached the top and stepped onto the loft, a slow grin spread across his face. "They were here."

Agent Byrn was just poking his sweaty head over the edge when Kovak pointed to the indentations in the hay. "I see six," said Byrn, already out of breath.

Kovak replied, "A8 was probably in her feline form."

Byrn wiped his brow and descended back down. "All right, we've seen all we need. They can't be far away." He landed gracelessly on the dirt floor, then brushed the dust from his pants. Agent Kovak landed beside him and led the way down the barn aisle.

"Wait, what's that?" said Byrn, halting. Agent Kovak paused and glanced back to find his partner bent over, pulling an object from an empty stall. "Huh. It's a first-aid kit."

Kovak studied it with satisfaction. "They're hurt. Good. That outta slow them down."

They emerged outside and crossed the bristly grass to the SUV parked in the gravel driveway. "So, we know they came this way and they're all alive," Agent Byrn reviewed. "And as we suspected, A6 is on his own. No surprise, but at least we can officially confirm that now."

Agent Kovak nodded. "Get the map," he ordered as he pulled open the driver door.

Byrn sat down in the passenger seat and opened the glove compartment. He unfolded the paper in his lap. "We're about . . . here," he said, pressing his finger to the map. "What are you looking for?"

Kovak peered over his partner's shoulder. "There," he said, jamming his finger on a tiny marked dot. "That's the nearest town. Whatever that girl gave our subjects for their little 'tea party,' it couldn't have been enough to sustain them for long. They'll need to find civilization if they want to eat. Call Anders and tell him to have a tech hack any cameras we can access. I'm not expecting much in such a Podunk little town, but whatever we can get—ATMs, traffic lights, security cameras outside stores. See if we can get access to satellite feed. I want eyes on them."

Kovak turned over the ignition, and the radio erupted in static. He fiddled with the dials as he backed the SUV out of the driveway, but every station was the same, and he turned the volume down in surrender.

Agent Byrn pulled out his phone, but before he'd dialed a single number, it rang. "Byrn. Ah, I was just about to call you. Huh?" In the silence of a long pause, his brows drew together until he was scowling. "All our files were backed up on a separate server, right? Okay, good. No. How long?" He listened again, then wordlessly ended the call.

Kovak said nothing, waiting for his partner to speak.

Byrn glared out the windshield. "We won't be getting that footage."

"Why?"

Agent Byrn shook his head, the vein in his temple pulsing. "Because Anders just called to tell us the entire Grid shut down a few minutes ago."

Kovak took several moments to process this. "The runts?"

"Who else? Stop the car."

Agent Kovak hit the brakes. Byrn, phone already to his ear, threw open the door and hopped out before the vehicle had come to a stand-still. Kovak draped his hands over the steering wheel and watched through the window. Apparently the call wasn't going well; Byrn roared and pitched the phone as far as he could throw, which admittedly wasn't very far. He cursed and kicked at the grass before finally storming back.

He plopped down into the passenger seat again and slammed the door, then leaned back and covered his face with his hands. Kovak stared at the open road ahead. "You planning to go get your phone?" he asked quietly.

"No point," Byrn grumbled behind his hands. "I was on the line with my CIA contact for maybe twelve seconds before the line went dead."

"What?"

"I think the cell towers are down. Every single *one!*" He slammed his fists down on the dash.

Kovak fumbled to pull his own phone out of his pocket. No signal. Not even emergency calls would go through. "Goddamn it." He jammed the useless device into the cup-holder and hit the accelerator so hard the wheels spun in the gravel. "Can't we track them when they're hacking?"

Byrn chuckled darkly and shook his head, and Kovak knew the suggestion was beyond stupid. "I don't understand. They wouldn't do this!"

"They wouldn't have run away, either. I'm telling you, the others kidnapped them, and now those spineless runts are doing whatever they're told."

"But they wouldn't disobey the Rules, even under torture."

Agent Byrn glared out the window. "I want that whole town sur-rounded. Nobody goes in or out. This time, we got them."

— Chapter Fifteen —

Prey

A distant drone made the air vibrate, a sound too obscure to identify, and yet my blood turned cold and the feeling of impending panic squeezed my lungs like a giant invisible hand. Kit peered up at the ceiling as the drone rose to a distinct, memorable roar. A helicopter.

She whimpered, and Jay soothed, "Shh, it's okay. *They* can't see us in here. It's probably just a quick aerial sweep like before. We're safe."

My eyes roamed upward as the roar passed overhead. A petrified gasp parted Kit's lips, and she threw herself at Jay. "What?" he asked, holding her tightly. Trembling, she twisted in his arms and pointed out the window. Jay looked up and instantly turned a shade paler.

I followed their gazes. A few blocks down the street, a familiar black SUV had just rounded the corner. The blood rushed from my head so quickly the room spun.

Jay pried himself out of Kit's death grip to slam the window shut and lock it. "Get down!" he hissed. I obeyed his command instinctively, pressing my back against the wall next to the window. We clustered together on the dirty floor.

On the other side of the glass, a motor rumbled faintly. The vehicle was cruising slowly, its passengers no doubt on the hunt. I held my breath. The SUV passed by our window without stopping, but its departure didn't bring relief.

Jay whispered, "Everybody stay down and stay quiet."

Kit whimpered again, then transformed in a swirl of black smoke and burrowed into the crook of RC's arm. Finn and Reese sat stone still, eyes glowing while dancing vacantly as they searched for the minds of their masters.

151

Seconds felt like minutes, which felt like hours. My muscles were starting to cramp. I shifted, then froze again. I swore I'd heard a man's voice.

My ears strained to catch the words. Somebody was outside.

"I know you're here."

I gulped. The voice was faint, but I was certain I'd heard correctly. It was a familiar voice, one that visited me in almost every nightmare and turned my spine to jelly. It was *Him*.

"Come on out. I know you're here . . ."

The twins lunged for the window. I didn't even think; I grabbed one by the collar of his shirt, yanked him back, and clapped my hand over his mouth, holding him tight. Jay seized the other and pulled him to the floor.

I heard the footsteps now. Many of *Them* were out there, too many to count. Too many to evade. My heart was pounding so loudly I was sure *They* must hear it on the other side of the wall.

"Why make this more difficult than it needs to be? I know you're hurt. You're scared, you're tired, and you have nowhere to go." *He* paused, then ordered, "Give me some water. I'm parched."

"I still say you're wasting your breath," said a voice I recognized as Agent Byrn. "They're not going to come."

I kept Finn secured against my chest, his arms pinned at his sides. He held still, listening to his master call for him. Byrn had no idea how wrong he was.

"You two, start at that house and work your way down the street. Check every garage and shed. And somebody check these doors over here," *He* said, ignoring his partner. *They* were close enough that I could hear the *slosh* of water in a plastic bottle when *He* took a drink. I winced when a flashlight beam cut across our window.

Ash was as tense as a coiled spring next to me. She gripped her staff with white knuckles, tears shining in her eyes. The ball of fur in RC's arm pressed her face into his cloak, suppressing a tiny mew. Reese, who was restrained by Jay, gazed at his blood-brother helplessly. I swallowed hard.

"Okay," *He* sang out again, "I'll make you a deal." *His* shadow drifted across the far wall as the flashlight's beam crossed behind him. The helicopter roared, then faded as it made another pass.

"You come out now and surrender, and there will be no punishment. We'll overlook your little escapade, even that mishap with the Grid. We'll take you back home and pretend this never happened."

Finn started squirming, desperate to obey and escape his crimes without penance. Thank a bloody Scout he'd burned out not too long ago, or he would have become intangible and there would have been nothing I could do to stop him. I tightened my grip, pressing my hand harder over his mouth and making him whimper with frustration. Reese had just as little luck escaping Jay.

He *lies*, I thought at the Mind-Readers. *Don't go to* Him.

We all jumped when the door to our left jerked. "It's locked," a woman announced.

His syrupy voice hardened. "Break it down."

I clutched Finn, squeezing my eyes shut. *He* would have to rip us apart because I wasn't letting go of my lab-brother.

A new voice, one I'd never heard before, demanded, "Hey! You! Yeah, you! Just what the hell do you people think you're doing?"

I opened my eyes, still holding my breath. "Sir," *He* answered in *His* most patient voice, "I—"

"That's *Sheriff* Haller," the man corrected.

A moment of icy silence passed. *He* hated being interrupted. "Sheriff, I'm going to have to ask you to return to your home. This is U.S. Federal business."

"Like hell. I'd like to know what jurisdiction you think you have here."

"We're hunting fugitives spotted in this area. Have you seen anyone dressed in black with this symbol?"

Another pause. "Nope, can't say I have. Then again, I've had my hands full, and I'm gonna guess my headache is thanks to you."

"I'm not sure what you mean," *He* said.

"I've had an angry mob in my station all morning. Internet's down, phones aren't working, cable's off, radios are static, and now you're here, and that seems like an awfully strange coincidence. What in God's name is going on? I demand to know—Hey! What are you doing?"

"We need to search this building," the woman said. "Unless you have a key, this door needs to come down."

"That's Redding's place," said the sheriff. "He's been gone on vacation, and I can personally guarantee that garage has been locked up tight the whole time. No fugitives, and there'll be hell to pay if Redding comes back to find his doors rammed down. Unless you have a warrant, I'm not going to stand here and let you ransack my town."

"Don't make this difficult, Sheriff," *He* warned dangerously. "I told you, this is U.S. Federal business. You'd be wise to look the other way."

"I take serious offense to you trampling all over the Constitution."

The beam of light in the window narrowed as its wielder stepped closer, sweeping it across the garage. Shadows shifted on the walls, and my heart nearly burst out of my chest when the window right above my head rattled. If Jay hadn't had the foresight to lock it . . . I didn't even want to consider that scenario.

Agent Byrn's voice said quietly, "Come on, Kovak. We're wasting time. If the runts were here, they would've come when you called. Let's move on. We still have a lot of ground to cover."

The flashlight paused, the beam lingering hesitantly on the opposite wall. I held my breath, staring at the circle of light. Finally, it retreated.

He said, "Sheriff, we're going to have a problem if you don't stay out of my way."

"We already have a problem. You—"

"*I* am here to find dangerous fugitives who pose a threat to your town. It's in your best interest to help me before innocent lives are lost. I need you to tell your civilians to cooperate. All vehicles leaving will be checked inside and out. We can use any deputies you have to volunteer at the checkpoints. Agent Schaefer will brief you."

Sheriff Haller grumbled in dissent, his complaints receding as he was led away. I listened to the familiar rattle of pills being shaken out of a plastic container. "Give me that water back. And where's that goddamn map?"

"Here," the woman answered. "We're at the intersection of Nowak and Stierna."

"Agent Lynn, I want your unit to cut across to Farmer Street, then split up and work your way down the side streets. Agent Byrn and I are going to finish this block and then take Charapata Avenue downtown. My rats are here somewhere; I can feel it."

Their voices retreated. Fainter, *His* voice turned sugary again as he sang, "Come out, come out, wherever you are! I know you're here. There's no point in hiding from me; I'm going to find you. If you make this easy, I'm willing to make a deal . . ."

We stayed motionless for a minute, then two. Maybe five. The youngest started to squirm with discomfort. I glanced over at Jay, who met my gaze solemnly. His eyes traveled down to Reese. "Are *They* still out there? And don't you dare lie to me, Reese."

The boy's blue eyes flickered. He stared straight ahead. Jay kept his palm pressed against Reese's mouth as a precaution. We watched the Mind-Reader, waiting with bated breath.

Finally, he shook his head.

Jay cautiously removed his hand. "You're sure?"

Reese hung his head. Finn relaxed in my arms as his twin murmured, "We can't hear *Them* anymore."

I pulled my hand away from Finn's mouth. His eyes closed in misery. "That was our one chance not to be punished," he lamented.

"*They* lie," I told him. "*They* would have punished us anyway. You know that."

Every movement stiff and cautious, Ash twisted around, set her bare fingers on the dusty sill, and rose just enough to peer out. "I don't see *Them*."

RC asked, "What do we do, Jay?"

The leader didn't even bother to look out the window to confirm Ash's observation. "I don't know," he admitted.

The hopelessness crushed me. "We're surrounded. If we stay here, we'll starve, and the moment we step outside, *They*'ll catch us."

Ash said, "Maybe Axel can help us. We just have to wait for him to come back."

"No," said Jay, shaking his head. "I don't know where Axel went or when he's coming back."

If, I corrected silently. *If he ever comes back.*

Jay touched the whistle around his neck. "We have to get out of this mess on our own."

"How?" RC asked. His voice, unlike mine, was calm. He trusted Jay and was prepared to do whatever the eldest said. I took a deep breath, mentally resolving myself to Jay's leadership. He'd led us this far, and I would follow him to the very end, no matter how hard my knees trembled or my heart pounded.

We watched him, waiting for his solution. He frowned, staring across the garage in thought, and when he felt our gazes, he glanced at us and then away quickly. "Give me time to think. Just . . . stay down and stay quiet."

The silence was unbearable. We were too afraid to speak, too worried to sleep, too paranoid to even move. I spent the next few hours sitting against the wall, listening to the helicopter. More than once, though never again as clearly as before, I could hear *Him* calling us, so sure was *He* that Finn and Reese would come if they heard. *He* was right; each time, we had to restrain them.

Movement caught my eye, and I glanced down to discover a black-and-white kitten slinking nearby. "Hey, Kit, you doing okay?" I asked, reaching for her.

The cat cringed, pinned its ears back, and hissed at me, hackles raised. Shocked, I yanked my hand back.

"Cato!" Kit's voice chastised. I gawked at the kitten. *Did she just speak to me in her fur?* To further my bewilderment, a girl rushed in and scooped the kitten into her arms. "You scared him!" She cuddled him close.

"Sorry. I thought he was you."

"We don't look anything alike!" She set the stray down, then transformed in a swirl of black smoke. When it cleared, two black-and-white kittens were sitting next to each other. Seeing them side by side, I was able to discern the differences now. Kit's "friend" looked to be a few months older with longer legs. Kit had four white paws, whereas the stray had only two, and he also had more black fur than she.

The Amínyte, still indignant by my honest mistake, padded away with a flick of her tail, the stray trotting after her. Great, as if there wasn't enough tension already—now I'd have to find some way to make amends with her.

Jay was sitting with his back in a corner and his knees drawn to his chest. His eyes followed the two cats, seeing without really seeing. He hadn't said a single word, and I was losing faith. Thus far, his confidence had been what made me believe we actually had a chance. It was becoming painfully clear that he didn't have a plan. We couldn't hide here forever. There was still enough food in the garbage bag to last us a few days if we rationed it, but we needed water. I was already imagining the various scenarios by which my freedom would end, each vision more horrendous than the last.

Across the room, Finn and Reese were sitting by the wall, rocking back and forth. Ash stood guard by them. If they tried to make a break for it again, I'd help her restrain them. Finn had already chewed his fingernails so short that two were bleeding, and Reese had his eyes squeezed shut with his fingers intertwined in his hair, mouthing what I thought were numbers, probably codes. I bet he was regretting his decision to crash the Grid now that his masters were outside waiting to punish him.

Ash and RC had yet to disarm. Except for when she had to drop her staff to hold one of the twins, she'd kept a two-handed vice grip on her staff, and he'd been clenching his silver disk in his left hand even though I didn't think he'd recuperated enough to use telekinesis on it. He might be able to unlock the blades, but I doubted he could make the disk levitate.

The two kittens reached the far corner and started playfully batting at each other. A third with a tawny coat watched them from inside the last cabinet in the row. Its tail twitched, and then it pounced to join in the fun. I watched them play with the melancholy thought that at least Kit was enjoying her last few hours.

Before long, the light was dying. We'd been trapped all day. As the sun set, Jay stood. "We leave tonight," he announced. Less than enthused by his proclamation, we stared at him, but confidence had rekindled in his silver eyes. "We have to time it perfectly, but I think it can work. Ash, I need you as lookout. Cato, take the backpack. Kit, come here."

His new attitude was contagious, and renewed hope charged us into action. Ash took her place at the window while I loaded ECANI and the extra cloaks into the backpack. RC helped me pack food from the garbage bag. My jittery fingers fumbled with the zipper. I had to take a few deep breaths to calm my nerves.

Ash said, "Clear."

There was no time to dwell on the danger; we were already moving. Jay ushered us out the window and guided us through the shadows of the night. Light was our enemy. We had to skirt through backyards and even double back a few times when *Their* flashlight beams appeared. Jay took us as far as the perimeter before we were forced to halt.

My hope shattered. *Their* forces had been directed here: parked vehicles, spotlights, dozens of armed humans marching in organized patrols. There was no way to sneak past.

"Now what?" I whispered, so depressed at the dead end that I was about ready to give up. My eyes followed the tranquilizer rifle in a woman's hands as she passed between posts.

"Okay, Kit," Jay murmured. "Go ahead."

She nodded. She'd carried her stray friend with the black-and-white fur in her arms this whole way, and now she stroked the kitten, then whispered in its ear. She knelt and set the cat on the ground. It peered up at her, mewed, and trotted toward *Them*.

I held my breath, my gaze flickering between the humans and the kitten slinking through the dusk. I didn't know if it was English she'd spoken, but the stray seemed to have understood her. It skirted along the wall of a building, dashing through the beam of a flashlight.

The wielder saw the streak of fur, gasped, and swung his light to locate the feline again. The kitten pinned its ears and darted around the corner.

"There! It's A8!"

"Don't lose it!"

Two men and a woman detached from the patrol and sprinted in pursuit. *They*'d barely turned the corner when a hand shoved me forward. Jay ordered, "Go!"

We had precious few seconds while *Their* attention was still at the corner where the stray and its pursuers had vanished. Instinct rejected the thought of stepping into the open, but even a moment's hesitation could mean missing our window of opportunity. I seized Kit's cloak as I forced my body forward and pulled her with me. Jay pushed Finn and Reese after us, working with Ash and RC to keep them penned in the middle of the group.

Kit was the fastest of us all, so I let her go to take the lead. But she slowed and paused, glancing back at the corner. Her ears fell with guilt. In one move, I scooped her into my arms as I ran past. She entwined her fingers behind my neck and let me carry her as she watched over my shoulder. "I hope *They* don't hurt him."

"He'll be fine," I assured. I didn't say it aloud at the risk of adding another insult on top of my earlier transgression, but the welfare of a stray cat was low on my list of concerns.

Kovak and Byrn marched toward the small circle of men and women with flashlights trained on something in the middle of the street. Kovak shoved his way through to find a black-and-white kitten lying on the pavement, a dart in its shoulder.

He knelt beside it, gently shifting the still body with his free hand. He tilted its head, his thumb brushing against the cat's throat in search of a collar with an ivory pendant. "This isn't A8." He dropped its head unceremoniously on the asphalt.

A woman said, "But . . . the way it looked right at me . . . its eyes, I could have sworn—"

Kovak silenced her with a frigid stare as he rose. The group backed away, watching him warily. The Head Agent glared at his inferiors and snapped, "Get back to your posts." They scattered, beams of light bobbing in the darkness.

Kovak glared down at the tranquilized cat. Byrn shifted and said, "It was an honest mistake."

Kovak nudged the furry body with the toe of his shoe. "I'm getting real tired of playing hide-and-seek."

— Chapter Sixteen —

Black Feathers

Our journey took us through several small farm towns before we felt safe enough to stop in a toolshed. I slept restlessly through nightmares and a brilliant flash of green light that kept reoccurring, followed by the echoes of a woman calling my name.

Dawn was bathing the Outside in newborn light when I woke. I pulled myself up and drew my cloak closer around my body, more for security than to fend off the morning's chill.

Most of the others were still dozing. Kit, thumb in her mouth, was curled comfortably between Finn and Reese, who each had his back against her. Both twins were snoring softly. RC had fallen asleep sitting up with his back against the wall, his hand on Reese's shoe, Ash's head in his lap. Two figures on the other side of the shed were in the middle of an intense conversation.

I rose, stretched my stiff muscles, and joined them, scrutinizing Axel as I approached. As far as I could tell, he was perfectly healthy. The dark circles were gone, and his skin was no longer pallid. Although I was glad to see him well again, dread made me sick. "How many?"

"None," Jay replied, looking up.

Hopeful but doubtful, I said, "Really?"

"Really."

Axel twirled a black feather between his thumb and forefinger. He avoided my gaze. "I'm fine now. At least for a while."

I asked, "So you'll stay with us?"

"As long as you want me."

I'd been about to voice my relief that he'd returned, but his answer made me falter. Instead, I said, "Of course we want you with us. We're lab-brothers." Did he think we'd change our minds and send him away? At his silence, I added, "Right, Jay?"

He nodded. Axel let a long breath escape between his teeth before he said, "Okay then."

"*Okay then?*" I repeated. "Don't you *want* to stay with us?"

He drilled his red eyes into me. When he'd left, the pupils were so dilated the irises were almost black. Now the pupils were much smaller than they should have been in this poor lighting. "You're the only family I got. I don't wanna hurt you, so whether I'm allowed to stay shouldn't be my decision."

Jay said, "The decision's already been made. You're staying."

"As long as you keep your promise." The words spilled from Axel's mouth so quickly they sounded like an extension of Jay's sentence.

I glanced between the two, feeling as though I was missing something vital. Axel had directed his clairvoyant eyes onto Jay, who was determinedly staring at the floor to avoid meeting the hybrid's hypnotic stare.

"What promise?" I asked. Axel didn't move. Jay shifted slightly but wouldn't look up. "What promise?" I repeated louder.

Axel's steady stare applied pressure to Jay until he emptied his lungs in one miserable sigh. He clutched the silver whistle around his neck. "I promised Axel that if he loses control and goes into a bloodlust, we'll stop him before he has a chance to kill anyone. By any means necessary."

I disliked the four words he tacked on the end. They hinted at an ominous future that sounded inevitable. I also hated the word *bloodlust,* even if it was accurate. Harbored inside Axel was an animal that, once it had a taste of blood, clawed its way out and transformed him into a force that must kill until the animal was satisfied. I wished I could pretend Jay's promise would never need to be implemented, but at the back of my mind, I knew there was a strong possibility the day would come when we might have to stand against our lab-brother. I didn't know if I could kill him.

Now, looking at him calm and stable, I couldn't. But if it were my life or his, if I were staring at a nydæa in a bloodlust, could I do it? I didn't know. So I wouldn't think about it.

Axel said nothing. He'd stated his price for freedom. I studied him in search of satisfaction or worry or relief . . . or even disappointment. He was either a master at concealing his emotions, or he didn't have any.

When the others awakened, we moved on, a complete family once again. Everything we did revolved around two goals: survival and evasion. We left that town for another, then another, always moving on before sunrise. Light was our enemy and shadows our ally while technology turned a blind eye to us. We were adapting.

We were learning to survive in the Outside.

Kovak and Byrn sipped at steaming cups of coffee in their parked SUV. It had been another long, sleepless night of chasing down dead-end leads. Byrn had a red pencil in his hand, which he used to draw another X on their map. "Nothing tangible to go on since the bird incident," he noted.

Kovak leaned back against the headrest. The birds were the only anomaly he'd found in the pursuit of his fugitives, and he still couldn't make sense of it. In the outskirts of a small town, the Agents had discovered fifteen dead crows in a field.

"Found 'em like this. Broken bones, every single one," the home-owner reported as Kovak crouched to examine them himself. "Can't imagine it was an animal that done this, but I don't know what did. Never seen anything like it."

Byrn shrugged. "I'll admit it's bizarre, but it couldn't have been our rats. Coincidence."

Kovak rose. The bird at his feet had no blood on its disheveled feathers. Its wings were broken, neck contorted the wrong way, rib bones shattered, but all the damage was internal, as if a strong hand had snatched the poor creature out of the sky and squeezed too hard. "I don't believe in coincidences."

He sipped at his coffee again. Byrn yawned and used the tip of the pencil to count a procession of towns on the map. "Do you think they know where the Rip is?"

"I don't know. Based on sightings, they do seem to be traveling in that direction." Kovak paused to rub his eyes, then added, "Kálos can sense each other when they come into close contact. I think on some level they're also able to sense Tears that will lead them back to their home Realm, and as far as we know, the closest Tear would be the Rip."

"If they escape into the Ghost Realm, we'll never get them back," his partner worried. "Not to mention the catastrophe if kálos knew what we were doing in Project Alpha . . ."

"Is the network updated?"

Byrn hesitated before answering, "To your specifications."

Kovak nodded. For decades, the AGC had paid ghost hunters to deliver kálos. Certain Divinities were more valuable than others. Byrn had wanted to upload a complete file of each Alpha subject to the network and offer the maximum cash reward.

But Kovak had balked. "And release to the public that our fugitives are a bunch of kids between the ages of seven and nineteen?"

"That information isn't going to be a secret if anyone spots them, let alone catches them," Byrn had rationalized.

"But until that happens, I don't want to broadcast it. There's a chance one of our loyal ghost hunters might keep quiet about the transaction. Money talks."

In the end, he'd convinced his partner to post the bare minimum to the network. No ages, no Divinities. He didn't want to risk anyone identifying A7's dual powers. If A7's identity was revealed, the media would swarm like piranhas in a feeding frenzy, and the protests would start again, the petitions, the lawsuits. Just another giant headache that would be even worse than the last time.

But, if Byrn was right and their rats were indeed heading toward the Rip, there was one ghost hunter who didn't have access to the network, not that she would pay attention even if she did. To date, she'd never delivered a ghost alive or dead to the AGC for a reward. As much as Kovak didn't want to admit it, she was unique. She wasn't like the others, who hunted for sport or money. She was smart, inquisitive, a scientist and inventor at heart. If any ghost hunter had a chance of intercepting the fugitives, it was Madison Tarrow.

Kovak turned the key, and the engine purred to life. "I think it's time to give our old friend a visit."

Byrn shot him a severe look. "You sure you want to involve *her*?"

"We just have to play our cards right, that's all."

"We already burned that bridge."

"Bridges can be rebuilt."

"Doubt it," Byrn muttered, slumping lower in his seat and folding his arms like a child having a tantrum.

"Let's see what's been going on in Phantom Heights since our last visit." Kovak put the SUV in drive and lifted his foot from the brake. "I think A7 might be going home."

The SUV pulled out from under the oak tree they'd parked beneath and turned onto the highway. Above them, a raven with a white-tipped wing leapt from the branch where it had been perched, extending its wings to catch the gentle updrafts and glide over the vehicle, its talons tight over an ivory pendant.

— Chapter Seventeen —

Wanted

Shannon was well accustomed to the constant drone of voices. It was almost soothing now, a calming white noise. She'd forgotten what quiet was.

Nearby, Wes was sitting with his back to the wall, picking at his food. He'd been in a dark mood all day, but that was normal at this time in his cycle. Tonight was the night of the new moon, which meant the werewolf was trapped in his human form.

Shannon glanced up when her mom seated herself beside her and offered an opened can with a couple of sliced peaches sloshing in juice at the bottom. "Dessert," she whispered.

Shannon stared at the can in disapproval. "I already had my ration. I wish you wouldn't take extra for me. It's stealing from somebody else."

Holly tucked Shannon's hair behind one ear. "Go on, sweetheart. Take it. Eat." Shannon bowed her head, but she obeyed. Guilt filled her stomach more than the extra food did. Her mom draped one arm over her shoulders and gave her a brief squeeze. "I love you."

Shannon nodded and set the can down, but she struggled to force the last swallow of peach juice down her throat. She leaned into the embrace. Was it wrong, that a secret part of her enjoyed this miserable existence in City Hall if only because it was the first time in her life she was more important than her mom's precious political career? Shannon wished with all her heart that she could believe her mom's sentiments. But deep down, part of her knew that if Holly ever had to choose between her career and her daughter, Shannon would find herself alone.

So, was it wrong? To pretend otherwise?

A commanding knock ceased all conversation. Everyone turned to

166

stare at the heavy oak doors. An eerie quiet blanketed the great hall, augmenting the usually unnoticeable hum of the massive generator in the basement keeping the shield active. Shannon was suddenly glad to be under her mom's safe arm. Nobody ever knocked on those doors unless the raid team was returning . . . which made her wonder who, or *what*, was on the other side. Had an injured raider found his way back? That was the most optimistic scenario.

Shannon was one of the first to look away from the doors and find the leader of the raid team, but she wasn't the only one. People backed away to form a path so Madison Tarrow could stride through the silent crowd, her hand resting on the holster of an ectogun.

Holly stood. The moment her mom's arm left her shoulders, Shannon wished for its return. She almost reached for her mom's hand.

Under the scrutiny of hundreds of eyes, Madison hesitated at the doors, then pulled out the bar and cracked the door open to peer at the visitor.

"Maddie," a man's cold voice acknowledged. "It's been a while."

"Not long enough," Madison snapped, throwing her weight at the door. Strong hands pushed back, overpowering her.

Braced in the doorway were two men in dark suits. A third in a lab coat slouched against one of the stone pillars. Behind them, backs to City Hall with ectoguns and high-powered rifles leveled at town square, were five armored guards with shields.

"That was rude, Madison," one of the suited men chastised as he stepped inside, "not inviting us in. Did you know there are ghosts out there?"

Shannon had seen two of the Agents before, although their names escaped her. The Head Agent was tall, his square jaw clean-shaven. His dark eyes had a piercing quality amplified by his dangerous aura. His partner, in contrast, was shorter and stockier, and he had a weird sort of strut-walk Shannon related to a fat rooster. His straw-colored hair was slicked back with too much hair gel, and his cheeks were always flushed as if he'd been jogging, which was an unlikely event.

The third man she hadn't seen before. He was tall like the Head

Agent but skinnier and much less intimidating. His shoulders were hunched, his hands shoved deep into the pockets of his lab coat. His sandy beard was trimmed close, and a pair of wire-rimmed glasses perched on his nose, lending him an intelligent appearance he probably deserved. He scoped City Hall without a trace of empathy, only impartial observation while he ground a piece of gum like a cow chewing on cud.

The initial stunned silence broke with stirrings and murmurings; those sitting rose, and those closest to the doors backed away. Wes gulped and melted into the crowd. Shannon reached for her mom, but Holly was one of the few drifting forward to meet the visitors, and Shannon's hand closed around air.

Madison seethed, "Get out."

The Head Agent curved an eyebrow as the door closed behind them. His gaze skipped over the squalid living conditions without pause: the filthy people, the boarded windows, the cots and mattresses scattered across the floor, the distrustful glares.

He cleared his throat. "Your shield is impressive." Madison crossed her arms and glowered at him. He pretended not to notice the hostility radiating off her. "But then again, I expect nothing less than impressive from you. It's a shame you've limited your field of study. Biology is much more versatile. If you'd be willing to expand your horizon—"

"Forgive me for not having an interest in dissecting people."

"Oh, I don't dissect people, either." He winked and said, "I don't really consider them *people*."

Shannon's mom reached Madison at the same time as Trey. Madison snapped, "Did you have a point in coming here, or did you feel a sudden urge to make a special trip to berate me?"

"Listen, Maddie—"

"Madison," she corrected. "And you are not welcome here."

"Are you still that upset?" At her simmering glare, he heaved a theatrical sigh and said, "Look, your son's death was a tragic accident, to say the least. But it *was* an accident."

Shannon tiptoed around bodies, inconspicuously inching her way closer. Her mom set a warning hand on Madison's shoulder. "Don't."

Too late; Madison seethed, "It was *your* fault!"

"We do acknowledge some degree of responsibility."

"*Some?*" She rolled her shoulder hard to throw Holly's hand off.

"I tried to save him, you know," he taunted softly. "But I know that makes you miserable—the last face he ever saw was mine, not yours, and you can't stand that."

Before anyone could stop her, Madison rushed forward, swinging. Shannon gasped. The Agent's head whipped to the side, guided by Madison's knuckles. Two of his guards seized her, hauling her back as she swung again, and the other three stepped in front of their superiors in case Trey decided to take the same course of action. Shannon's mom backed up to demonstrate her subservience, but Trey stood his ground.

The Head Agent tenderly touched his jaw, his gaze trained on the floor. "No, no, let her go," he said, still calm. He chuckled. "You've got a mean right hook, Maddie." Reluctantly, the two guards released the ghost hunter, and their boss continued, "But you can't change the past. It's time to move on. The world doesn't stop turning when one person dies."

Holly glared at Madison from the corner of her eye, barely containing her fury that the ghost hunter couldn't keep her temper in check for the sake of diplomacy. Shannon had witnessed many people wither under that look; it was one that had stopped her in her tracks as a child.

The Head Agent looked Madison up and down. "What a pity. You used to be such a great ghost hunter. I'm afraid you've gone soft."

"My skills are just as sharp as they were before."

"I don't think so. Phantom changed you. Do you hesitate before pulling the trigger? Do you doubt yourself now?"

"Get out," Madison repeated.

The man held up his hands. "All right, I apologize. Come on, Maddie, can't we put the past behind us?"

"No! You think I'm the only one you hurt?" She gestured to the townspeople behind her. "Do you see how we're living? You've condemned us all!"

"I'd hardly put it that way."

"Leave, Agent Kovak, and take your friends with you, because un-less you have soldiers or supplies, you're not welcome here."

"Not so hasty, Madison," Holly tried to intervene.

"No. This is on my authority, Holly, not yours, and I want them out of here."

Agent Kovak was stone-faced. "We've been over this before. You didn't hold up your end. It can't be my responsibility to bail you out." He adjusted the cuff of his jacket as he continued, "We're preparing for the first military strike, but we aren't ready yet. Your job was to keep a secure hold over the Rip."

"I could secure it if you would send reinforcements."

"All of our resources are currently being employed. Sending Agents here would only set us further back in our preparations. There's nothing I can do for you . . . yet."

Holly voiced the very word Shannon was thinking: "Yet?"

Madison much more hotly snapped, "How long does it take? You owe us."

Kovak nodded. "You're right. I'll admit that. See . . . understand that I'm extremely limited in the amount of information I can dissemi-nate." He glanced at his suited partner, then continued, "I don't have to tell you how ineffective our modern weapons are against ghosts. Fact is, we're outmatched in almost every way." He gestured to the man in the white lab coat. "In Project Alpha, we're developing a weapon that won't just level the playing field to give us a fighting chance; it'll tip the scale in our favor."

Curiosity lifted Madison's eyebrows. "What sort of weapon?"

The straw-haired partner cleared his throat. "We aren't at liberty to disclose specifics."

Madison's face hardened again instantly. Her shoulders braced, and she seemed to grow a few inches in height and hostility. Shannon was almost to the front of the crowd, but she faltered beside Vivian Tarrow, who had just backed up a step.

Shannon knew what to expect from her mom. Holly was cold,

strategic, cutting with precisely selected words. Madison, on the other hand, was hot and passionate, and she'd already proven she wasn't afraid to throw a strong punch. "You know why the ghosts went on the offensive? Because of you! They're retaliating because of what *you* are doing in your lab! You started this war!"

Kovak retorted, "In their Realm, we're slaves. Why shouldn't they receive the same treatment here?"

Holly looked away when he made eye contact with her. That was strange. Not once had Shannon ever seen her mom back down from a staring contest. Her eyes could drill just as deep as her words, doubling the damage to those who dared issue a challenge to the esteemed councilwoman. She never lost . . . until now. Now, she wasn't even competing.

Madison stared at Agent Kovak for a long moment, her arms folded tightly across her chest. "So, what? You're here to tell us this secret weapon you've been working on is finally ready?"

Kovak shifted, glancing at his partner again, who answered, "No. There was a . . . er . . . complication."

"Complication?"

Kovak backtracked, "Which is why we're here."

Madison barked out a bitter laugh. "You came here to ask us for help?"

"Yes, but—"

"No."

"Maddie—"

"Madison!"

"Whatever! I'm sure you haven't heard the news, but there's been a terrible accident."

"Believe it or not, we have our own problems to deal with."

"If you help us, we can finish the weapon and use it to help *you*. It's a trade-off."

Madison opened her mouth to argue, but Trey cleared his throat. "Um, Madison . . . maybe we should at least hear them out?" She fixed her glare onto her apprentice, who shrugged and meekly added, "We're in a tight spot."

"Except they never come through with their promises," Madison retorted, fixing another scowl on the three men before her. Kovak smiled mockingly.

"I know. But . . . it can't hurt to hear them out."

"I agree," Shannon's mom quietly added before Madison silenced her with a glare. Again, Holly yielded, and Shannon wanted to shake her and yell, *Who are you? Because you sure aren't acting like Mom!*

Kovak said, "Well, I'm glad to see someone here is reasonable." Madison scowled at him in frigid silence until he continued, "Here's the problem: we had eight test subjects in Project Alpha. The program has been so successful that Alpha was being transferred to a new facility dedicated entirely to the research and development of our new weapon."

"Oh, I see. So the problem is you have too much money and a brand new lab?"

The straw-haired man rolled his eyes at Madison's biting sarcasm as Kovak countered with forced patience, "No. We had to transport our test subjects to the new facility." He gestured at his suited partner and added, "Agent Byrn and I ensured every precaution was taken. Their powers were neutralized; the most dangerous one was sedated; the others were securely locked in cages. But there was a little accident."

"How little?"

Byrn reluctantly grumbled, "All our test subjects escaped."

As if electrocuted, Holly suddenly stood straighter, the intensity returning to her piercing green eyes. Madison demanded, "How did that happen? If they were so dangerous, why didn't you have them guarded?"

Kovak strained to keep his voice steady. "I elected against a convoy. Our goal was to move them quickly and inconspicuously. We don't want news to leak about our new facility. Top secret, Tarrow, got it?"

"And what exactly are *we* supposed to do about your blunder?"

"The crash was about ninety miles away from here. We believe it's possible the Alpha ghosts will come here, to Phantom Heights."

Madison blinked. "That's halfway across the state."

Holly calmly inquired, "And why do you suspect they might come here?"

Kovak met her eyes, and they locked gazes for several long seconds. He coughed and then cleared his throat, facing Madison instead when he answered, "We . . . think they're heading for the Rip."

Most people wouldn't notice the micro-reaction of their councilwoman, but Shannon recognized the slight narrowing of her mom's eyes and the almost imperceptible tightening of her lips at Kovak's hesitation.

Madison rubbed her eyes with her thumb and forefinger. "Let me guess, you want us to catch your fugitives before they escape into the Ghost Realm."

"We want you to be prepared and intercept them if possible."

"Well, in case you haven't noticed, there are hundreds of ghosts in Phantom Heights. How do you expect us to find and capture specific ones?"

"It may not come to that. We're hoping to contain them before they make it this far. And most of their powers, to the best of our knowledge, are still neutralized. They're traveling on foot, not to mention they're wounded from the accident, and—"

"How long ago was the crash?"

Agent Kovak shifted. "Almost two weeks now."

"And you still don't have them?"

Grudgingly, he admitted, ". . . No."

Madison laughed. "You got yourself in quite a mess. Bet you lost that bonus, huh?"

Kovak scowled. "Listen, those ghosts are crucial to developing the weapon."

"Kálos or moorlin?"

Trey, who had been glancing between the Agents and his ghost-hunting master, frowned. "What does that mean?" he asked.

The Agents looked down at him as one might regard an annoying child. Trey seemed to shrink beneath their scorn, and Shannon felt sorry for him when Kovak *tsk*ed, shaking his head with mock empathy. "Disappointing, Maddie. You haven't taught your apprentice what a kálos is? That's the most basic information a ghost hunter should know."

Madison's lips pressed into a dangerously thin line. Without looking at Trey, she answered, "You remember. Moorlins are the spirits of the dead—real ghosts. Kálos are the mortal ghosts that came through the Rip. We've been over this."

"Right," Trey croaked less-than-convincingly. "I remember now. Sorry."

In response to Madison's original inquiry, Agent Kovak replied, "Kálos, of course."

"Then there are plenty of others for you to replace the ones you lost. I know for a fact you have more than a thousand in your lab, and if you don't, there's an overabundance here to choose from." She gestured at the doors. "Take your pick."

Byrn shook his head. "Those ghosts were hand-picked for the Project, and they're a threat to humankind, so we need them back in custody as soon as possible. We can't afford to expend any more manpower than what we've already deployed."

"Then why don't you have the military track them down? Why come to us?"

"Because I want to keep this in network. No other branch of the government is trained to handle kálos. *You* are. Besides, we need them alive, and any other department would use lethal force."

"If they're as dangerous as you say they are, maybe they *should* be shot down."

"You're not getting it, Maddie. Half of the eight we lost are invaluable to our research. We need them back. *Alive*. They're no good to us dead."

Madison, much more somber now, asked, "You're sure they'll come here?"

Kovak nodded. "All sightings indicate they're heading this way even as we speak." The ghost hunter rubbed her mouth in deliberation.

"They'll seek out humans for food and water. We've had them isolated in the lab for so long they can't survive on their own. But they're afraid of humankind, and if anyone corners them, they'll lash out in a misguided act of self-defense. They're lethal, even without their powers. People will get hurt."

"If they don't have their powers, why are they so dangerous? What are you doing, training them?" She'd obviously meant it as a joke, but at Kovak's silence, she added, "Wait, you *aren't* training ghosts to fight, are you?"

"Of course not. That's ridiculous."

Madison scrutinized him. Shannon was unable to tell if he was being truthful, and based on the suspicious look etched into the ghost hunter's features, Madison couldn't tell, either. If it was sarcasm, it was well-masked. "If we find them, you'd better keep your end of the bargain this time."

Kovak nodded. "Dr. Anders will tell you what you need to know."

The man in the lab coat stepped forward, his hands deep in his pockets, shoulders slumped. "Shall we speak in private quarters?" he asked.

Shannon's mom was quick to reply, "I think that's a good idea. My office is upst—"

"No," Madison interrupted. She stood akimbo, feet firmly planted. "Anything you have to say can be said here."

Holly chuckled nervously. "Madison, this seems like a sensitive topic."

"I don't trust them. My whole raid team isn't going to fit in your office anyway, and I want everyone here to be a witness. No miscommunication." She glared at Kovak. "No question as to what was actually said if they go back on their word again. They can tell us all, or they can leave without our help."

Dr. Anders popped his gum and rolled his head toward his boss. "This is a breach of security."

Kovak waved his hand as if he couldn't care less. "Just get on with it."

Despite the call for urgency, Anders wasted several more seconds chewing while he watched Kovak. He sighed and faced Madison, Trey, and Holly. City Hall was so silent Shannon was sure she could hear Vivian's heartbeat next to her, so silent Anders's quiet voice reached every corner when he said, "Fine. Let me get straight to the point: I can't stress enough how dangerous these fugitives are. One in particular. He originated in Project Delta, where we crossed bloodlines to create a hybrid. This creature, which I cannot name for classified reasons and will refer to simply and truthfully as a monster, is enhanced in every way—senses, strength, speed. But he's violent, impossible to reason with. If the venom in his fangs gets into the bloodstream . . . well, death is a mercy. The venom turns the victim into a monster too. That's how they reproduce since they're infertile. Even a kálos will lose its powers and its state of mind when it transforms."

Shannon felt sick already. Now that he was discussing a comfortable topic, Anders's shoulders were no longer hunched, and his hands were clasped professionally behind his back. He continued passionately, "The goal of Project Delta was to create a kálos hybrid that would transform only partially into this creature, so it would gain the enhancements without losing its powers or intellect. We altered venom from our monster D1 and injected it into our first ghost D2, but our alterations were ineffective. The ghost transformed into a pureblood monster as well, just as bloodthirsty as D1 and with no retention of his powers. We adjusted the composition of the venom again, but our second kálos subject expired just minutes into the transition. Our third also perished."

Anders sighed. "D4 was a major loss. She was Level 4, two hundred years old, give or take. We were optimistic about her. The transition seemed to be going well, but while she became physically stronger, her power escalated proportionally. The body couldn't tolerate such a high power level; it destroyed her from the inside out before the transformation completed."

The silence in the gaps during his tale was suffocating. Anders murmured, "We learned from our mistakes. We needed a weak ghost so it wouldn't burn out, but after the death of D4, our investors were getting impatient. We brought in our fifth and final specimen of Project Delta. His divine power hadn't developed yet, and his young body was better able to adapt to the changes. The initially weak power level didn't overwhelm him when it surged as his body transformed. We created our first hybrid. But in the end, he was a failed experiment. Even though D5 maintained his basic powers, he still had the brutal animosity of the other monsters. I firmly believe our next attempt would have been successful, but Project Delta lost its funding, and we had to shut it down. Ah, if he'd only been able to talk, he might have been a success. We transferred this half-breed to Project Alpha about four years later, where he was renamed A6."

Dr. Anders's face was flushed with exhilaration. "A6 is truly incredible. When his body was reformatted to be stronger, his powers were super-charged too. A6 is the strongest, fastest, most powerful being to ever walk the Human or Ghost Realms. Are you aware of the categories kálos use to determine power level?"

Madison replied, "More or less. Level 1 is the lowest, 5 the highest."

Anders nodded. "That's right. After the transformation, A6 surpassed Level 5. You have to understand, it isn't possible for a natural-born kálos to be so powerful. Then again, he's not a true kálos anymore. We extended the scale to see where he would fall if it continued past Level 5. He's a 9. We couldn't even run tests on him at full power because he caused too much damage!"

Dr. Anders had to take a breath to calm himself again. He worked at his gum, as if mentally grounding himself. "Impressive as that is, A6 is still an animal. We never intended to release him into the real world. He kills; he can't help it. Killing is in his nature, and he has to kill to survive, which means as long as he's loose, many innocent people are going to be slaughtered. In the controlled environment of the laboratory, A6 is manageable, but out here, he'll be rampant. We hope to pinpoint his location as soon as he makes his first kill."

The crowd stirred, but nobody dared to speak for fear of missing a word. Madison said, "You actually created a monster like that and let it escape?"

"We didn't *let it* escape," Agent Byrn snapped.

"You still created it!"

"With good intentions. Can you imagine a new breed of super-soldiers with the power of A6? But now you know why we haven't told the public. It would cause mass panic if they knew a creature like that was on the loose."

Madison snorted above the rising murmurs of the crowd. "Are you kidding? Don't you think people will notice a crazed animal committing violent murders?"

"You see why we need A6 back as soon as possible," said Kovak. "In his case, dead or alive. Preferably alive, but I really can't see that happening." He shrugged and added, "Then again, I'm sure Dr. Anders would enjoy finally getting A6 on a dissection table in Omega, eh, Doc?"

The Agent in the lab coat didn't answer, but he failed to hide the grin that put creases in the corners of his mouth.

This is important, Shannon realized. The Agents wouldn't have come all this way otherwise. Vivian gave her a strange look when she spun on her heel and marched away from the conversation to the terraces leading up to the stage. She seized a marker from the tray beneath the whiteboard and used her sleeve to smudge away the arrows of the latest raid plan.

Dr. Anders continued, "Our initial fear was that A6 would track down the familiar scents of the other Alpha ghosts and kill them, but thus far we have no evidence they're dead. Let me clarify—you are *not* expected to confront A6. If he's sighted, contact us immediately. He has red eyes and fangs."

"Red eyes and fangs?" Trey echoed. "You just described forty percent of the ghost population." Madison nodded, her scowl deepening.

"A6 is more animal than kálos. He isn't capable of speech. Trust me, you hear his growl, you'll know. You've never heard a more terrifying sound in your life."

Red eyes, fangs, can't speak, growls, Shannon wrote.

Madison asked, "What's his Divinity?"

"He doesn't have one, thank God," Dr. Anders replied. "But Madison, don't think you can take him down. He *will* kill you. Do not confront him."

"You make him indestructible?"

"No, he *can* be injured and killed. But you won't be able to."

Visibly insulted, Madison set her hands on her hips. "And why's that?"

"Not for lack of skills," Anders assured. "A6 is just too fast. If you fire a gun at him, he'll sense the danger before you even pull the trigger, and he's quick enough to dodge the bullet. The simple fact is there's just no way to sneak up on him, not without incapacitating him first. The other primary targets are A1 and A2, but we want them for different reasons. A1 and A2 have passive Divinities and are no threat to humans."

"Then why do you want them back so badly?"

Kovak replied, "They're Mind-Readers, and I don't need to waste time explaining how much sensitive information they absorbed in a classified Project. We also want to retrieve them for their own safety. See, they're only ten years old, born and raised in the lab, products of our breeding program in Project Gamma."

Anders took over again: "We matched the twins' parents in the hopes of producing a powerful child to study throughout development. Their father was a Telepath, their mother a Technopath. We wanted a telepathic Technopath offspring, although we've since learned that despite our genetic manipulation, only one power can be passed down. Either Divinity would have been satisfactory, but instead we got twin Mind-Readers who have a knack for technology." Under his breath, he grumbled, "Not the first set of Gamma twins to malfunction. Anyway, they . . ." He glanced at Kovak, as though seeking guidance before adding uncertainly, "We raised them. They're very dear to us."

Madison scoffed. "*Please.* You mean they're your slaves, right?"

Agent Kovak's smirk widened into a smile; he didn't bother to rebut. "Mind-Readers make the best servants because all you have to do is think what you want and they obey."

Anders shrugged. "Gamma hasn't been very successful. None of the infants born there have been more powerful than a Level 2. For some reason, their powers just don't mature in the lab the way they should, and we've had some strange mutations. Now, back to the topic—our twins from Alpha have never even seen the outdoors. Our facility is underground—no windows. We can't believe they'd run away because they would have been in absolute shock. They may be psychologically damaged after such an experience. They always obey us and know there would be dire consequences for leaving, so the only explanation is the other Alpha ghosts must have kidnapped them."

"Or they just aren't as obedient as you think," Madison retorted.

Kovak snarled, "Listen to me, Maddie. If I told those runts to kill themselves, they would. They won't do a damn thing unless I say so. They did *not* run away."

Calmer than his superior, Dr. Anders said, "We taught them that ghosts exist solely to serve humans. They completely embrace that philosophy. If you find them and order them to come to you, they will obey. They'll be the easiest to catch, but we're afraid their lives are at stake. They don't have much time."

"Why?" Trey asked.

Anders smoothed a crease in his lab coat. "To prevent illnesses, we keep the lab completely sterilized. All visitors and staff have to disinfect before entering, and any staff member with even the slightest hint of a cold isn't allowed to come to work. Any test subject who becomes ill is immediately quarantined. Since the twins were born in the lab, they're extremely vulnerable, especially since they've never been vaccinated. We're afraid they'll die of an illness or infection, so you see, returning the twins to us would spare their lives. It's for their own good."

Agent Kovak added, "The other Alpha ghosts hate the twins. Wherever they are, the poor boys are no doubt being abused. Physically, mentally, emotionally. Probably sexually, too."

Madison raised one eyebrow at his casual tone but queried impatiently, "And they look like . . . ?"

"They're ten but small for their age. Light skin, brown hair, blue eyes. They are completely dependent on others. They have to be handed food and instructed to eat, or they'll starve. They can't survive on their own, so even if the other Alpha ghosts are abusing them, the twins will have no choice but to stay with them. Stockholm syndrome—the captive will bond with the captor. It's important to separate the twins from the others as quickly as possible and return them to the only place they've ever known."

Shannon neatly printed the description on the board.

Dr. Anders added, "Right, then there's also—"

Kovak coughed into his fist. "Mm-mm," he warned sternly, shaking his head.

Anders faltered, then continued, "So, those *three* are the primary targets."

Shannon turned, marker still in hand. Her mom coldly stated, "I thought you said *four* of the eight were irreplaceable."

Kovak finally met Holly's gaze, but he didn't answer. Anders glanced at him, then nervously evaded, "We want the others, of course, but these *three* are the most important ones. Now, based on behavioral observations, we believe A3 will assume the role of leader. But here's where it gets complicated because 3, 4, 5, and 7 are lethal. They won't seek out trouble like A6, but if cornered or confronted, they are more than capable of killing."

"I don't understand," said Madison. "I thought you were building a new weapon in Project Alpha."

"We are."

"Then why were you trying to make stronger, more powerful ghosts? And a breeding program? I thought the point was to eliminate ghosts, not make more. What the hell are you doing in there?"

"We have to study them in order to learn how to destroy them," Dr. Anders explained. "And if we raise ghosts from infancy, we can teach them our philosophies, make sure they understand their place in this world."

"Make them believe humans are superior," Madison rephrased.

"Exactly!" said Anders, completely missing her bitterness.

"You're insane if you expect us to catch these ghosts."

"*But*," Agent Byrn countered, "you'll have an advantage. There are some negative after effects of the tests we ran on them. We can't explain what causes these spasms, and as far as we can tell, there's no cure. These side effects incapacitate the ghost for about a minute until the spasm passes, giving you a brief window of opportunity."

Madison shook her head. "You make it sound so easy, but *you* haven't even caught them yet, and you know everything about them."

"They're eluding us," said Byrn. "Hopefully they'll make it here, think they're close to freedom, and let their guard down. They're expecting us to chase after them, not you. All we ask is that you keep your eyes open. Our ghosts are tattooed with identification numbers on their arms."

"What, that's it? A tattoo? What about pictures? Files? We need to know what their divine powers are. How old are they? How many males, females?"

Shannon's marker was poised over the whiteboard again, ready to record, but Byrn said, "We can't disclose that information."

Shannon frowned. She squinted to see across the room to Madison and her mom, who wiped her palms on her shirt and pressed, "You can't disclose a basic description for us?"

"No."

Madison much less courteously demanded, "Why not?"

"Because it might compromise the situation."

Through clenched teeth, Madison growled, "That. Doesn't. Make. Any. Sense."

"It doesn't have to," Byrn snapped. "If you catch a ghost, check its arm. You capture any of our ghosts, you get a reward. Simple as that. Understand?"

The ghost hunter said nothing. Although Kovak still wouldn't look at Shannon's mom, he did catch Madison's eye. "We might be willing to negotiate about that reward."

Agent Byrn looked at his watch. "We need to be going."

Kovak stepped forward, extending his hand in a friendly gesture. "So, you help us catch our ghosts, we finish the weapon, and then we take care of yours. Do we have a deal?"

Madison stared at his hand. Shannon capped the marker and set it in the tray, then slipped through the throng again. Part of her hoped Madison would say no and bat Kovak's hand away. He'd already proven that he couldn't be trusted. *Remember Cato!* Shannon wanted to scream in the silent room.

She emerged at the front of the crowd to watch the ghost hunter seize his hand, sealing her commitment. Shannon bowed her head. The Agent smiled—an expression that should have been reassuring. A sudden chill rippled across Shannon's skin, erecting goose bumps.

"I will warn you, if their powers are activated again, the levels are all over the scale. And they're deceptive; don't let their looks fool you. They don't look like killers, but they could strike you down in a matter of seconds, with or without their powers."

Kovak paused, then added quietly, "I've become very attached to those kids, Maddie. I'd do just about *anything* to get A1 and A2 back. Even if it costs me all the other Alpha ghosts, I want those two." When he let go of her hand, something shiny gleamed between her fingers. He leaned close and added, "That is your only hope against A6. Don't lose it."

The guards opened the doors for Byrn and Anders. Kovak, to Madison's clear displeasure, lingered near her. "I'll be honest with you," he said quietly. "Our test subjects have already caused mayhem on a massive scale. They took down all communications in a tri-state area for twenty-four hours. No cell phones, no landlines, no internet, no television. Radios were all static. There was mass panic. Satellites are still malfunctioning even as we speak. I have every branch of the government breathing down my neck. See, my lab rats also stole a very expensive computer from us, and we need it back. You know, you're very lucky."

"How so?" Madison snarled.

He looked up at the rafters. "Phantom Heights is so isolated you didn't even know all forms of communication went down outside of your little bubble. But I'd imagine it would have been a catastrophe if our fugitives had decided to shut down all power. They could have. The whole nation could have gone dark. Would your shield still operate? My bet is you would have been dead when the lights came back on."

He tossed a cell phone at her, and she caught it in one hand. "Use that to contact us." As an afterthought, he warned, "And understand that if my test subjects reveal information about the weapon to our enemies in the Ghost Realm, humankind will be in serious trouble."

He turned, overlooking Shannon and Trey and offering his hand to Holly, who seized it. "Good to see you again, Holly. Hopefully we'll be in touch."

He started to release, but she tightened her grip and leaned forward to whisper something to him. Shannon frowned. Her mom was facing the wrong way; she couldn't read her lips, but she saw Kovak's expression harden. He pulled his hand free and stepped back. "I'm afraid not," he said.

Holly turned her head just enough to the side for her mouth to be visible. "Agent Kovak," she hissed. "Please."

He paused to give her a tender smile that didn't reach his eyes. "You have nothing to worry about. Trust me." Kovak turned on his heel and followed the other Agents. The door slammed shut behind him.

"Pompous bastards," Madison muttered.

"But we're actually going to help them?" Trey asked uncertainly as a crescendo of murmurs rose in the wake of the strange visit. He slid the bar back into place across the door.

"We're not changing our routine, but if we happen to come across an Alpha ghost, then yeah, we'll take it down."

Holly wandered to the whiteboard on the stage. Shannon trailed just behind her shoulder. "Mom? What's wrong?"

"Nothing," she received in answer with a dreamy wave of the hand.

Shannon seized her mom's wrist. "Are you okay?"

"Yes. Why?" Her mom turned and smiled, but Shannon recognized it as the same front Holly used when posing for the news camera.

"Why wouldn't Agent Kovak look at you?"

The smile faltered. "Sometimes I think you're too perceptive for your own good."

Shannon donned a fake smile of her own. "Perceptive enough to notice when you're evading a question."

Her mom let the smile fall with her shoulders, but her brow furrowed, a sign of impatience and budding irritability. "All right, you win. I suspect it's because we had a disagreement the last time we spoke. Nothing you need to concern yourself with."

She swept a strand of hair out of Shannon's eyes and tucked it behind her ear. Shannon started to lean her cheek against her mom's warm hand, but it was already gone. Holly had turned away to study the list Shannon had written on the whiteboard.

Project Alpha

8 escaped

A6 half-breed: Red eyes, fangs, can't speak, growls

A1, A2: Twins, 10 years old, mind-readers, brown hair, blue eyes, obedient

Shannon, too, inspected her handiwork. She felt as though she'd been a poor scribe with so few details, but it was all the Agents had provided—just a story so full of holes there were no real characters. She jumped when Madison's voice came from behind: "What do you think?"

Holly made a show of turning her back on the whiteboard with a flourish, as if she couldn't care less. "I think this doesn't change our situation."

Shannon reread her notes, her back to the conversation but her ears attuned. Trey asked, "You think they'll keep their word this time?"

"I doubt it," Madison snapped. "But who knows? They might surprise us."

Wes joined them on the stage, his dark mood having evaporated in the excitement. "We shouldn't give them the chance to double-cross us again. I say we capture their ghosts and hold them for ransom until Kovak pays up." He laughed. "Level 9! Do you understand how much power that is? There hasn't even been a record of a Level 5 for hundreds of years."

Shannon turned as Madison uncurled her fingers to study the object Agent Kovak had given her. Nestled in her palm was a silver whistle.

Trey touched his weapon belt for security. "So, that *thing* can turn people into monsters just by biting them? Like a vampire?"

"Sounds like it," said Wes. "But I hate to tell you this, kid—there are plenty of other creatures besides vampires and werewolves that reproduce that way." Wes sobered in an instant. "He's screwing with the natural order. Hybridization between kálos and other species doesn't happen naturally. If Kovak is tampering with bloodlines . . . well, I can't blame kálos for getting worked up about it. But oh, what I wouldn't give to see a Level 9."

"Careful what you wish for," Trey cautioned. "A6 would probably be the last thing you ever saw before it killed you."

Madison ignored Wes's enthusiasm about A6 and turned to read over the frustratingly vague list. Shannon felt heat rise in her cheeks, again afraid that she'd taken inadequate notes. *That's all there is*, she reminded herself.

She surveyed Madison. The ghost hunter was grim, her anger replaced with weary resolution to a hopeless task. She muttered, "I don't care what Kovak is doing in his lab. But if his rats want to get to the Rip, they're going to have to go through me first."

— Chapter Eighteen —

Hero's Return

We stole through the night in silence, incomplete once again at seven. Axel had left us again yesterday when his health deteriorated. All week, Jay had tried to make him eat, but Axel insisted he wasn't hungry. What little he did eat, he chewed awkwardly, his teeth designed to puncture and rip rather than grind, and he forced only a few swallows before pushing it away and claiming he couldn't taste it.

Not long after, Axel had confided to me, "I just took a piss."

"Wow, thanks for that update," I'd muttered.

I'd started to walk away, but he'd rolled his eyes in exasperation and seized my cloak. "That hasn't happened in seven years."

I had stared at him for a few moments until what he was saying finally clicked. "Wait, you haven't gone to the bathroom since . . . ?"

"This is garbage," Axel had snarled, holding up some kind of packaged food I couldn't name. "You eat this shit your bodies can't process, so most of it's wasted."

"Well, sorry we can't all be as *evolved* as you . . ." I'd trailed off when Axel's face went blank and he clutched his gut with a soft groan. "Something wrong?"

Axel had moaned a little louder. "Damn it. I didn't think my bowels still worked . . ." he'd croaked. And then he was gone to expel the waste his body couldn't absorb from the "shit" Jay made him eat, which technically *was* actual garbage we had taken from a dumpster, so Axel wasn't completely wrong about that.

Jay had hoped Axel would be able to survive on human food, but by the end of the first week, it became clear that he couldn't; he complained that food was tasteless, water made him thirsty, and he was "pissing and shitting it all away anyways." Each day, we watched his pupils dilate and the dark circles become more prominent. He became restless and irritated before finally departing. He was going through his cycle twice as fast as he used to.

My thoughts kept gravitating back to his absence. He was more than capable of fending for himself, but still, when he wasn't with us, my nightmares shifted from cages and torture to conceived scenarios of Axel being captured. We would have no way of knowing. Every time he left, there was always a possibility he wouldn't come back. That, or he was out slaughtering dozens of humans, which I also didn't want to think about. When he returned, I couldn't help but scan him for blood.

An engine rumbled in the distance behind me. I turned. A pinprick of light was growing brighter in the darkness.

On our right, the land sloped up to a steep ridge. Whatever machine was heading our way, it was traveling on the path of metal rails at the top of the berm. A horn blared. The light was blinding, brighter than a car.

"What is that?" Ash asked.

She was answered by another blast of the horn. "Get down," Jay ordered. Obediently, we crouched low, taking shelter against the ridge. The ground trembled as the rumbling increased to a roar.

And then the mechanical beast was above us, speeding by in a whir of wind and noise. Kit and the twins squeezed their eyes shut and clapped their hands over their ears. I squinted through the wind to see metal containers flashing by on wheels of steel. My ears exploded when the horn split the air again, shredding my brain, like a Spasm turned into sound. I smashed my fingertips into my ears.

The machine, whatever it was, seemed to be passing by harmlessly. My ears were still ringing when the last container passed and the roar faded to a rumble slowly overtaken by the symphonic chirps of insects.

Only when the night was quiet again did I dare to rise. Kit wiped away tear streaks. RC, Ash, and Jay were pale, but the only casualty was the twins, who were suffering a severe coughing fit in the lingering dust storm. "What was that thing?" Ash asked.

Kit rubbed her sensitive ears and said, "I think it's called a metra."

I frowned. "Are you sure? That doesn't sound right."

"Metra," she said again. I couldn't think of a word to dispute hers, so I let it go. Whatever that thing was, I couldn't stop thinking about it. How could humans create something so powerful and unstoppable? Then again, after all I'd seen, why did I doubt anything humans could do? What they lacked in power, they compensated for with ingenuity.

I tilted my head back. I wanted to admire the stars, but they were hidden behind clouds. Tonight marked the fifteenth night on the run. The last town was far behind us, its lights invisible now. Where Jay was leading us, I had no idea, and I didn't think he did, either.

We had traveled through woods, open fields, and wetlands. We scoured towns like rats, avoiding humans, surviving on garbage and whatever we could steal. Once, we stumbled upon a thicket of wild berries that, with Axel's steadfast assurance they weren't poisonous, we'd gorged upon, although we had to learn the hard way that the green and pale ones weren't sweet.

Everything we did revolved around two concepts: survival and evasion. We were becoming efficient thieves, although I'd never be the master thief Kit was. I knew she used to be a street kid in a human city before she was captured, but I had no idea what a talent she had for "finding" valuable objects. In the first town we'd been in after our confrontation with *Them*, Kit had disappeared in the afternoon and returned at sundown, proudly dropping an armful of objects at our feet.

I'd curiously picked one up and opened it to find photographs, plastic cards, and human currency. Kit had beamed and announced, "We can buy food now."

None of us had known what to say, so we just looked at each other, then at the wallets scattered on the floor, then at Kit. Jay had knelt down and said, "Well, um . . . very good, Kit. You've got quite a talent. But things are different than they were for you Before. We can't let humans see us, so instead of stealing money to buy the food, doesn't it make more sense to just steal the food?"

Kit's ears had drooped. "I guess so."

"Besides," Jay had added, "no pick-pocketing. Stealing is bad. We can steal only what we need to survive. Okay?"

"Okay," she had echoed, although even as she agreed to his terms, I witnessed her hide something shiny behind her back.

We were falling into the routine of survival, learning as we went. How many miles we'd walked, I couldn't even begin to guess, but my blisters and sunburned cheeks told me we'd come far. Despite our close encounter with the metal beast, we continued to follow the railed path.

Finn sneezed, then croaked, "Can't we rest?"

"Not here," Jay answered. "There's no place to hide."

We were alone in the countryside as far as I could tell, but Jay had been paranoid after we had to hide from a pair of humans a few towns back. Nothing had seemed out of the ordinary at first. We'd heard footsteps and hidden, a drill we were becoming accustomed to.

But something felt wrong. My hands were clammy, and my heart rate was fast enough to make me light-headed. Maybe it was the way the humans were walking, the unusually careful way they placed their feet. What stole my breath was the sight of the ectoguns in their hands and the belts filled with ropes, knives, firearms, and other weapons with functions I couldn't guess. I even saw a muzzle swaying from the woman's hip, and that made every muscle in my body lock up. I'd had more than my fair share of experience wearing a muzzle, and I shuddered at the mere thought of being trapped inside one again. The humans wore combat boots; the woman wore tight pants and a green jacket, and the man was dressed in camo with a hat pulled low over his eyes.

"Ghost hunters," Finn had whispered.

I'd tensed, ready to grab him and Reese. I had expected them to run to the ghost hunters like they had tried to return to *Them* in the woods. But those two ghost hunters were not the twins' masters, and whatever thoughts my lab-brothers must have heard in the humans' minds caused Finn and Reese to recoil and cower. Jay had put his arm around each twin and held them close, and they didn't resist. "Are they looking for us?" he'd whispered.

"Yes."

We hadn't crossed paths with any ghost hunters since, but Jay still didn't like us to stop if we were out in the open. No resting allowed until we were safely hidden from view.

Reese hung his head. "Our feet hurt."

"I know," Jay sympathized.

"Our throats too," added Finn.

"We're *tired*," Reese whispered, rubbing his knuckles into his eye. He punctuated with a cough.

Kit chimed in, "And I'm hungry."

Jay took the backpack from RC and handed it to Kit so she could select something to eat. While she rifled through our stash, Jay knelt so Reese could climb onto his back. Ash allowed Finn to ride on her back, and we continued, Kit munching contentedly. When she started to stumble, I claimed the backpack and pulled her into my arms. Soon after, her breathing deepened, her head heavy on my shoulder and her arms dangling over my back. At dawn's first light, we left the metal tracks.

A cloaked figure stood stone-still at the verge of a thicket ahead, arms folded, waiting, as though it had known we'd come this way. A breeze swept its cloak from behind, carrying an ominous but familiar signature on the air. Normal people would have sensed the danger and avoided the being. Jay led us straight for it.

Axel didn't greet us when we halted in front of him. He glanced over his shoulder and said, "There's a town up ahead. You should reach it by this afternoon." Jay nodded with a sigh—the first sign of weariness he'd let us see. Axel shifted. "But it's not a normal town like the others. There are ghosts."

"Ghosts?" Ash repeated.

I added, "In the Human Realm?" My brain was so addled with fatigue and thirst that the meaning of Axel's words took longer to seep into cohesive comprehension.

Jay decided, "Let's check it out."

Axel turned, leading the way. Jay and Ash set the twins on their feet to walk on their own again. I would have continued to carry Kit, but she squirmed to be let down. We followed Axel into the wooded thicket.

The day waxed, and my strength ebbed with each step. We had a backpack still half-full of garbage food but no water to quench our thirst. My throat was so dry I could barely swallow.

Axel led us through another series of woods. The afternoon was dying when he finally halted at the top of a hill.

A desolate town crumbled below us. Far in the distance, in the center of the town, a green dome enclosed a white building. I squinted at it in confusion. It looked like a giant ectoplasm shield, but I didn't know of any ghost capable of producing one so monstrous, not even an Ectokinetic. Even if someone could, he would have burned out in a matter of seconds.

We hadn't seen any vehicles, and the pothole-riddled road didn't indicate frequent traffic, but a barricade had been erected to stop any potential travelers from going beyond this point. Jay leaned close to inspect the sign on the roadblock. "Danger," he read. "By order of the U.S. government, this area has been deemed unsafe for civilians. Enter at your own risk."

I was too busy scrutinizing a faded wooden sign near the road to pay much attention to the barricade. "Welcome to Phantom Heights," I read aloud, frowning as I tested the name out loud. "Why does that sound so familiar?"

"It was in your file," said Finn. He coughed again and rubbed his nose.

Reese finished hoarsely, "You came from here."

Jay's eyebrows shot up. "This is your hometown?" he asked, studying the ruined city with newborn enthusiasm.

I followed his gaze, searching for anything familiar. "Not the way I remember it."

"What kind of reception do you think we'll get?"

Lastday. All those people staring at me as if I'd suddenly transformed into an exotic, wild animal.

I hung my head and scuffed the toe of my boot against a rock. "Not a good one. I'm not welcome here, which means neither are you."

RC drew in a sharp gasp and fell to the ground in the claws of a Spasm. Over his yells, Ash noted, "It looks like ghosts drove the humans out."

"No," said Axel as RC quieted. "Humans are still there. But they're outnumbered."

Jay tilted his head in thought. "We can blend in with our own kind. We couldn't ask for a better hiding place." He started down the hill.

Reese inhaled rapidly twice, then sneezed hard. He sniffed and trudged after Jay. I warned, "No, wait, Jay—My, uh, the—I mean . . ." I cleared my throat—Finn and Reese jolted and turned their heads to face me—and finally spat out, "This isn't a safe place for us to hide. There's at least one ghost hunter here. Maybe more." I didn't want to think about Trey and wonder if he ever reached his dream of graduating from apprentice to ghost hunter, but I couldn't help it. My heartstrings twanged at the thought of my old friend. What hurt even more was that I couldn't remember his face.

Jay never broke stride, although he did glance at me over his shoulder. "Look at all the ghosts here. Apparently, they aren't very good ghost hunters."

The others followed him, but still I hesitated, feet rooted. Anxiety twisted my stomach into a knot. Not this place. I'd follow Jay anywhere but here.

The others were halfway down the hill when I reluctantly jogged after them. "Jay," I called weakly, grabbing his shoulder, "I really don't think this is a good idea."

He kept walking. "I understand the risks. We'll avoid the humans. If anything goes wrong, we can always run again."

"But my blood-family—"

Jay halted so suddenly I ran into him. He glared at me and demanded, "What about them?"

Just over Jay's shoulder, I noticed RC setting his left hand on his hip and narrowing his eyes at me. Ash and Kit both took a step back as if repulsed by the hostility, but a smirk dented Axel's cheek, like he fed on it. Jay, his voice low and lethal, seethed, "You want to find them?"

"What? No, of course not. After what they did to me? I'll never forgive them." Jay turned his head a little to scrutinize me. I swallowed and continued, "The first chance they get, they'll send us back to that place. I never wanted to come . . . here." I meant to say *home*, but I couldn't force the word out because this was not my home. Not anymore. I exhaled, trying to control my runaway heart. "If anyone recognizes me . . ."

Jay reached over my shoulder and tossed the hood of my cloak over my head. "There." He pondered for a moment, then announced, "I think it's best if we all wear our hoods. Kit, if anyone is around, stay in your fur, okay?"

"Why do we have to hide our faces?" asked Ash.

Jay threw his own hood over his head and marched forward again, and we magnetically followed. "Do you trust me?"

"Well . . . yes."

"All right then. If we want to be taken seriously, we don't want people to see us as just a bunch of kids."

I muttered, "Never mind the fact that we're powerless."

Jay disregarded my comment.

The buildings of Phantom Heights disappeared behind the trees as we reached the base of the hill. Each step closer to my hometown twisted my gut tighter and tighter. My shifty eyes couldn't settle in one place even though the eight of us were alone. We were walking in a deceivingly peaceful park. The grass was long, the mulch paths weed-choked. If I strained to listen, I could hear the sounds of the conquered town—subtle explosions and faint yells and once, a distant roar. But the park was abandoned.

Or so I thought. In the clearing ahead, a sentry stood watch on a pedestal. Kit saw it first and stopped. The rest of us hesitated, eyeing the figure with distrust. Human or ghost, it was most likely an enemy.

Axel rolled his eyes. "It ain't real."

True enough, the person in the clearing didn't move. Jay started forward again, and we trailed behind. We approached it from the side, and as we drew nearer and circled around to the front, I realized Axel was right; the person was made of metal.

The statue was mottled with graffiti. He stood defiantly with his legs spaced apart, his arms crossed, a plaque at his feet. His short hair was windswept. Something about the boy's face was eerily familiar. His lifeless eyes glared over the half-mask concealing his nose and mouth.

"Cato," RC murmured, ". . . that's *you*."

I couldn't take my eyes from the metal doppelganger. Was I really like that, so fierce and confident?

"Phantom: A Fallen Hero," Ash read aloud from the plaque. She looked up at my statue's stern face. "Hmm. That doesn't sound like they hate you. Looks like this statue is here to commemorate you."

I brushed my fingertips over the etched words. "Yeah, well, the hero didn't fall on his own. He was pushed off the edge."

"Well . . . maybe they regretted it?" she said.

Jay walked around my statue, studying it from every angle. "They called you Phantom?"

I closed my eyes.

The news story had been repeating all day. A bright-eyed, blonde reporter on the television screen gestured behind to the sidewalk, which was covered with glass and debris.

"This is the scene where a great battle just took place!" she pro-claimed. "Three children were assaulted by a ghost. Out of nowhere, a second ghost came forward and confronted their attacker. This isn't the first report of this mysterious ghost aiding humans. In fact, we have at least five confirmed instances, and more people are coming forward with similar stories. The public has begun to refer to this hero as Phantom as a tribute to his elusive nature and in honor of the town he seems determined to protect. But just who is this ghost who dresses in black and keeps his face hidden behind a mask? No one knows when or where he'll appear. What are Phantom's powers? Why is he defending humans? We don't have those answers. In fact, Phantom seems to be camera shy. We don't have any footage of him . . . yet. However, local

ghost hunter Madison Tarrow is skeptical of Phantom's true inten-tions."

The camera zoomed out to reveal a woman standing next to the reporter. Madison's expression was hard. She leaned toward the prof-fered microphone and said, "I don't know what game Phantom is play-ing, but I guarantee it's not in our best interest. He's either taking down his own personal enemies who just happen to be pestering hu-mans, or he's claiming our town as his territory. Because of his heroic actions, I'm willing to grant him some leeway. But as soon as he crosses the line—and I know he will—I'll take him down just like any other ghost."

The reporter reclaimed the microphone. "Thank you, Madison."

"Wait," said the ghost hunter. She pulled the microphone back to her lips and faced the camera. "I have a message. Phantom, if you're listening, go back. Your kind is not welcome in this Realm. This is your only warning. Go. Back."

She released the microphone. The reporter chuckled nervously and said, "But for now, at least, Phantom is considered a hero of the peo-ple. Stay tuned for interviews with the victims tonight at eleven. For now, this is Caslynn Swan, reporting live from downtown Phantom Heights."

I remembered a playful elbow in my ribs, Trey smiling, saying something about how I was famous now. His lips were moving: *This is awesome! You're a real-life superhero, Cato! Ms. Swan already inter-viewed Madison . . . Do you think she'll want to interview me too? I mean, I'm her apprentice. I'm kind of an expert too.*

Why couldn't I remember what his voice sounded like?

"You were abandoned by the very people you protected."

Jay's voice disintegrated the memory. I opened my eyes and rubbed the right side of my rib cage, still feeling Trey's elbow. "I gave them everything, and they turned their backs on me when I needed them." I couldn't stop gazing at myself in my former glory, the graffiti all too symbolic of just how far I'd fallen.

Axel mocked, "The Phantom of Phantom Heights. That's original."

"I didn't come up with the name," I snapped. At least, I didn't think I did.

Jay completed his circle and ended next to me. "Maybe this was their way of remembering what you'd done."

I wanted to leave this place. Leave all the fragmented memories behind me and never look back. "Who cares what it's for?" I said, turning my back on the statue and walking away. "It doesn't matter. That was a past life—one I might as well forget."

Footsteps in the grass told me the others were following. Axel muttered, "Maybe we should start calling you Phantom instead of Cato."

"Shut up, Ax."

Jay caught my arm. "Do you have any allies here? Anyone who might help us?"

I didn't answer immediately because I had to think long and hard about his question. I must have had at least one ally. But the faces in my memories blurred together. Again, I thought briefly of Trey, but even he never contacted me while I was in that place. "We're on our own," I whispered.

Jay didn't seem surprised by the grim proclamation. As we crossed the edge of town, I automatically dropped a step to let him take the lead. My footsteps crunched over a layer of glass. This place was haunting, but not in the familiar way. That was what frightened me.

Fences were patinaed and broken. Neglected landscape beds spilled thorns and weeds into overgrown lawns. Trees edging the crumbling street encroached on power lines. The houses were dark, even the streetlights curving over the road. The cars parked in driveways and on the streets probably hadn't been turned on in years.

This couldn't be my home. I always thought if I ever returned, everything would rush back to me and a light would be cast on the dark parts of my memory. Instead, the void was deepening. Nothing looked familiar. If the twins hadn't memorized my file, I wouldn't have believed this was once my hometown.

The street was deserted. I'd been so busy looking around that I hadn't paid any attention to where we were going. The road we were on led downtown toward the stroke of green arcing over City Hall's white bell tower. It was breathtaking. Whatever that dome was, human-made or ghost-made, it was the most alien thing I'd seen Outside. It was a beacon, a symbol of light and power. It drew our curiosity and pulled us toward it.

A clatter was the only warning before a large creature galloped from between the houses on the right. My first instinct was to brace myself. Automatically, the oldest crowded together to protect the youngest in the center, but the creature just whooped and galloped past us. Then another, and a third. They were startling—men but not, animals but not. Bows and quivers over their bare backs, tails swishing, hooves ringing on the asphalt.

We finally encountered ghosts as we traveled from the outskirts to downtown. At first, I was afraid. I expected them to attack us, but after the first dozen passed us with hardly a glance, I relaxed enough to observe them with wary curiosity. They were otherworldly. All wore cloaks, all colors, many styles, some so long they trailed on the ground, others at the ankle or knee or waist. Glowing eyes, skin white and black and every shade of brown in between. I even saw a woman with blue skin, orange hair, and a forked tail glide over our heads on papery wings of indigo, black, and orange.

A chariot rolled down the street, drawn by a chestnut horse with a pearly spiral twisting up from its forelock. It passed a man with a crossbow fused to his forearm, a cyborg who must be a Technopath, and ten identical brothers who were actually just one Replicator. Many ghosts had decorated their bodies with jewelry and piercings; I couldn't differentiate between dye, tattoo ink, and natural skin patterns. For the first time in the Outside world, our cloaks and uniforms fit right in. Nobody paid us any attention.

I scanned my surroundings for signs of human life. Did they flee this place, or were they all slaughtered? And my family—*I mean, my blood-family*—were they still alive? They didn't care if I was, so I shouldn't care about them either, and yet I couldn't help it. Where were they? What happened to them?

They disowned me, I reminded myself. *Who cares?*

And yet, my head drooped. If they did die, would I mourn them? *Should* I mourn them?

Our journey brought us to a cobblestone plaza. The fountain I remembered tossing pennies into as a kid had been filled with decaying human bodies, and what was worse, there was enough blood in the basin that the upper jets were shooting it into the air. The stench was overpowering. I was going to be sick, a worry that intensified when my thoughts jumped to the possibility that the bodies of my blood-family might be stacked in there. Could that be the reason my blood-sister never visited me?

Axel stared at the fountain, a frighteningly blank, placid look on his face. "Axel?" Jay asked. No response. He had to snap his fingers in front of the hybrid's face and call, "Ax, are you with us?"

"Huh?" Axel tore his gaze away and blinked to focus on Jay. "Yeah," he mumbled, embarrassed.

Ash whispered, "Look."

On the other side of the plaza was the Dome. A transparent shroud over City Hall, it emanated a green light that originated from the tip of the clock tower, casting strange shadows across town square and beckoning us like moths to the flame.

— Chapter Nineteen —

Home

Hypnotized by the unearthly light, we gravitated forward in a trance.

"What is it?" Ash asked, stretching her fingers toward the barrier.

"Don't touch it!" RC warned, but she'd already pressed her palm to the surface. I awaited her cry or a quick recoil, but instead, wonder lit her eyes in the green light.

"It's warm," she said. "It feels like a warm, smooth wall." Curiosity bested me, and I reached out to touch it, but to my surprise, I felt nothing. My fingers passed through.

Startled, I yanked my hand back. "How did you do that?" Ash demanded, pressing against the barrier. She was held back as firmly as she would have been if she were pushing against a solid wall.

Jay frowned and ran his hand down the transparent surface. RC made his hand intangible and pushed experimentally against the Dome, but even then, his hand hit a solid surface. Axel rapped his knuckles against it—no sound—and then he raised his hands over his head and slammed his fists down. He was strong enough to demolish a building with one hit. The shield didn't even waver. Only the swirls on the surface reacted to the contact.

None of their hands passed through the barrier like mine had. I tried again. My hand encountered no obstruction. I gazed at my fingers on the other side of the Dome.

The kitten pressed her ears back and stepped forward, body taut with caution. Her pink nose touched the shield. After a brief hesitation, she slunk forward through the barrier and sat down on her haunches across from me. I knelt and scratched her chin, the Dome's intangible wall between us.

"I don't understand," said Ash, stepping back. "How can you two pass through it while the rest of us can't?"

I retracted my hand, watching my gauntlet and then my glove emerge from the wall of the Dome until my fingertips passed and I was free. Not only did I not feel the physical shield, but I didn't detect any heat coming from it either. "I think it blocks ghosts," I hypothesized.

Jay countered, "But Kit's a pureblood, same as the rest of us."

My gaze traveled up to the curved edge above. "I guess Amínytes in their animal forms are an exception. And I'm a half-breed, so maybe it doesn't work on me."

RC pointed out, "But so is Axel."

I swallowed, a cloud of tension immediately condensing between us. Axel glared at me sidelong, his expression stoic. "I'm a different kind of half-breed," he said in a low voice that rumbled with a growl deep in his chest.

"Right," I said quickly. "With this thing on my arm, I might as well be human right now. This is a shield."

Jay studied the kitten sitting on the other side. "Hey, Kit," he requested, "could you change into your skin and walk back through?"

The kitten's body transformed in smoke, and then the girl was crouching on the ground. She rose and took a step toward Jay . . . and collided head-first with the barrier.

Kit staggered back, shocked, and her ears fell when she realized she was isolated on the wrong side. Her face crumpled. She pushed against the transparent shield and began to cry.

"Relax," Jay comforted. "Change back, okay, Kit-Kat? You should be able to come through again."

She whined but obeyed, her body shimmering to smoke again as she crouched down. The kitten darted through the barrier and leapt into Jay's arms, shivering after her ordeal.

The Dome was ghostlike but human-made. How odd, to find something made by humans in a town that seemed to have none besides the dead in the fountain. I wondered . . . if it was indeed a shield, what was it meant to protect?

I took a step, too quick to think, too quick to doubt, and I was inside. The green tint shifted so now City Hall was white and the world around me in all directions was green. "Cato, what are you doing?" Jay demanded.

I tipped my head back. I was near the bottom step looking up at the four columns. "*Cato!*" Jay hissed.

I ignored him and snuck along the steps, rounded the corner, then pushed my way through the shrubs along the side of the building to a window. Only a few clear shards were left in the edges of the frame, the glass replaced with wooden boards. Our little experiment had proven the shield stopped ghosts, likely ectoplasm too, but not other objects. City Hall had taken damage. I crept close, cupped my hands on either side of my face, and peered through a gap between the boards.

Calmer now, Jay asked, "What's in there, Cay?"

Was I really seeing what I thought I was? "A city," I whispered.

Hundreds of humans in camps of blankets, cots, and mattresses were clustered throughout the great hall. Was my blood-family in there? No, I shouldn't look, but I couldn't stop my roving eyes. My heart jumped into my throat; I thought, maybe, I saw . . .

Madison Tarrow turned her head my way at the same time my gaze settled on her, as if she somehow sensed I was there. I gasped and ducked, then turned back to my lab-family. Jay surveyed the abandoned town. "Not a whole city, I don't think," he said. "Just the survivors."

Too petrified of the ghost hunter to risk another peek, I cast a look back at the boarded window as I returned to my lab-family. "This is a ghost town in the Human Realm. What happened to this place? It looks like a war zone."

"I think it is." At our puzzled looks, Jay clarified, "Think about it. If ghosts are invading this Realm, that explains why *They're* trying to build the Weapon."

"But why here? What makes this town so special?"

Jay shrugged. "I don't know. It's *your* hometown; shouldn't you know?"

I had no answer. An uncomfortable wickedness had caused a smirk to manifest, and it widened into a twisted smile the longer I stared at City Hall. All this time, I'd felt cheated. I'd imagined my peers growing up, learning to drive, going to prom, worrying about college—normal teenage stuff—while my adolescence passed me by as I rotted away in a cage. Now I knew they didn't get to experience any of that, either. The pleasure I had at their miserable situation was wrong, but I didn't care. I didn't get to grow up with a normal life. Why should they?

"Can we go now?" Ash asked. "I don't like being so near all those humans, especially if there are ghost hunters inside."

We turned our backs to City Hall. Jay asked, "Where's Axel?"

RC replied, "He was here just a few minutes ago."

In unison, the twins pointed at a cloaked figure standing on the far side of the plaza. Axel didn't acknowledge us when we approached and stood beside him. He was staring at a tall chain-link fence topped with barbed wire, as if the intention had been to keep people out of a restricted area. But there was nothing inside—only a section of cobblestones that looked exactly the same as the rest of the plaza.

I caught my breath. I saw something and nothing at the same time, movement within the fence that my eyes couldn't focus on. It called me. A faint pull, as if all this time it, not the Dome, had been leading us here.

Jay said, "So, this is it. The place where the Realms meet."

I blinked a few times. Now that I knew what to look for, I saw it—waves in the air like heat rising from asphalt on a hot day. I squinted, hoping to see the shadowy silhouettes of the other Realm, but all I could discern was an unbroken view of the buildings disrupted by the shimmer.

Something about the portal was mesmerizing. After a minute, the novelty had lessened, and I stirred, increasingly aware of how exposed we were out in the open. I gently scratched at an itch near the port above my right temple while glancing at my lab-family. They were still captivated by the disturbance in the air. It must have been calling them stronger than it called me. My human blood diluted the pull.

A white butterfly with black tips and spots on its delicate wings fluttered in front of me. It slipped through one of the openings in the chain-link fence and vanished in the distortion.

Finally, thankfully, Jay broke the silence. "Our world is through there."

"No."

The others looked at me, surprised, but I'd surprised myself too. My gaze had been on where the butterfly disappeared when I said it, and I blinked before I faced my lab-family. Meeker, I said, "That's *your* world. Finn and Reese and Ash and I have never set foot in the Ghost Realm. We're already in our world."

Kit stepped back with a whimper. "My master's in there." Ash cocooned her hand around Kit's and soothed her with a gentle squeeze.

Jay faced the Tear again, then turned left to look at Axel and RC. The half-breed was standing with his arms folded, his eyes trained straight ahead. I wondered if he could see what I could not, if he was looking into the Ghost Realm. Without glancing at Jay, he said, "I don't belong in either world anymore."

The leader's gray eyes flicked to RC, who was holding his injured arm and also watching the Rip. RC shot a glance at Jay, then quickly averted his eyes again as he gave a one-shouldered shrug. "I'll follow you," was his only response.

Jay curled his fingers through the links of the fence. He'd claimed his world was on the other side, but I wasn't sure that was true anymore. He couldn't possibly remember it. He'd been at that place longer than I had. And besides, as dangerous as this Realm was, the Ghost Realm must be even wilder. Every Scout we'd faced in the Arena came from the other side, and that was just a small sampling of the monsters that roamed there.

"I think," said Jay, immediately capturing our attention, "we're safer here. This is where we should make our home. If we're forced to run, this will be our escape route."

Axel and the twins didn't seem to care, but RC, Ash, and Kit were nodding. "Whoa, wait a minute," I protested. "We're choosing between the Ghost Realm and Phantom Heights? If we're choosing to stay in this Realm, why can't we move on?"

"Because here, no one will notice us."

"And the ghost hunter?"

"Is in there." Jay nodded at the impressive Dome over City Hall. "As long as she stays in there, we don't have to worry about her. I get why you don't want to stay here, Cay, but look around. This is our best chance."

He was right, but I refused to admit that aloud. I crossed my arms tightly over my chest and glowered across town square just in time to realize we were being surrounded. Cloaked figures with glowing eyes were moving in. We pressed in closer to each other, nudging the three youngest into the center as the ghosts encircled our group. A low growl vibrated in Axel's throat.

The apparent leader of the gang stepped forward and sneered at us. "Yer trespassin'."

Axel leaned toward Jay and whispered under his breath, "He's only Level 2. We can take him."

Jay ignored Axel. "Sorry. We didn't know."

"Oh yeah?" taunted the leader. "Ya dint know this was Talon territory?"

"No, we didn't. Our mistake."

"Yeah, it is. And lemme guess, no one told ya there's a toll fer crossin' the Rip, either."

Jay protested, "But we didn't come through the Rip."

"Still gotta pay." The leader's smile faded as he observed our group. He tilted his head in uncertainty. "Yer dressed like kálos, but half o' yer eyes ain't bright. You human?"

Axel snarled, "Hell no, we ain't human."

The red-eyed woman nearest to the leader drew in a deep breath. Slits along the sides of her nose flared with her nostrils. She said, "They don't smell like humans, though they reek of this Realm." She pointed at Axel. "But something's odd about that one's scent." Her hand shifted to point at me. "Him too."

Jay backed up, throwing out his arms to protect the rest of the family. "Sorry for trespassing. We'll just be going."

"No we won't," Axel proclaimed.

I caught my breath. Ash hissed, "Axel!"

The gang leader narrowed his red eyes. "What was that?"

"I said, we ain't leaving," Axel challenged. "*You* leave."

Jay's hand shot out to seize Axel's arm. "What are you doing?"

The Talon leader laughed obnoxiously and turned to his gang, putting on a grand show for them. "Oh, sure! When the Eye stops turnin'!" As if given permission, the others chuckled. Kit pressed up against me, trembling, and I wished I had my powers to defend myself and her. I didn't even have a weapon. Ash reached over her shoulder, her fingers curling over her staff. RC's left hand disappeared into the pouch on his thigh.

Jay said, "I'm really sorry about what my brother said. He didn't mean it. We're leaving now."

"No, ya ain't," said the leader. He took a hostile step toward us. "I don't like you. Ya still gotta pay the toll, an' I'm not talkin' money anymore."

The Talon Gang pressed in on us, eyes of all colors glowing. Axel growled, teeth bared, revved for a fight.

The leader, if Axel was right, was actually fairly weak in terms of power. But even the passive Divinities could be deadly, and I was sure he'd earned the title of leader. I watched, wide-eyed, as he knelt on one knee to press his fist against the cobblestones. As he rose, his hand turned to stone that traveled up his arm. By the time he'd straightened to his full height, he was a sentient being made of granite.

Horrified, I retreated a step, bumping into Kit. *Bloody Scout, can Axel pick an opponent.* The leader of the Talon Gang was a Morphis.

With a battle cry, he rushed forward. The Morphis had more than a foot height advantage on my lab-brother. He veered back as he planted his feet, and then his stone fist was flying at Axel's face. I didn't care how tough Axel was; this was going to hurt even him.

Axel didn't blink at the stone giant bearing down on him. He casually extended his arm, palm out.

A ghastly series of *crack*s announced the moment Axel's hand closed around the Morphis's fist. The Talon Gang didn't move, and neither did we.

The leader let out a howl that echoed between the buildings.

Axel released him to watch his opponent's hand crumble. The Morphis sobbed and stumbled away from my lab-brother, clutching his hand as his stone body reverted back to skin and the granite pebbles raining on the cobblestones became drops of blood. "Oh, for the love of King!" he cried in agony.

The Talon Gang stared in shock at their wounded leader, and then their eyes settled on Axel, who cracked his knuckles and taunted, "Who's next?"

The others shifted uneasily, glancing between us and their leader. Axel took a threatening step toward the woman who had smelled us; she leapt back to reestablish a safe distance from the half-breed. Their bewildered terror was justified. Axel did not have the physique of a Strongarm ghost, and his eyes weren't glowing. He hadn't used a Divinity. The Morphis should have smashed my lab-brother into oblivion, not the other way around. That, and there was an eerie feeling in the air I couldn't quite put my finger on, and I suspected it was due to the strange energy Axel naturally expelled. It made the hair rise on the back of my neck and sent a plague of goose bumps down every inch of my skin. I could read the question in each gang member's eyes: *What is he?*

The Talon leader was on the ground now, blubbering like a baby. Axel let out a ferocious snarl that stole even my breath and made Kit hide under my cloak. The gang scattered, leaving their leader to stagger after them, his crushed hand cradled against his chest.

None of us moved. Ash didn't sheathe her staff, just gripped it tighter, skimming the shadows for more enemies. Kit emerged from hiding.

Jay rounded on Axel. "Have you completely lost your mind? You could have gotten us all killed!"

Axel scoffed. "They weren't even that powerful."

"That doesn't matter! Without our powers, we can't defend our-selves like we normally would."

The half-breed scowled and turned his head away from Jay's re-proachful gaze. "I wouldn't've let them hurt you," he grumbled.

"Our lives are not yours to gamble."

Axel scowled and glared at the Rip. I shifted my weight, uncom-fortable in the tense silence. Finn and Reese stared at their feet. Kit fidgeted with her pendant. Ash bit her lip and gazed up at the Dome. RC spun the disk in his fingers. He mumbled, "I guess if we want to make any allies, we'll have to keep them away from Axel."

Axel snarled at him, but it was Jay who snapped, "No Outsiders. Like Cato said, we're on our own."

He recommended we choose our new home somewhere in the out-skirts of Phantom Heights where there wouldn't be so many wanderers who might stumble upon our hiding place. We circled the ghost town in search of a place to claim as our own.

Axel sulked at the back of the group while Jay, RC, and Ash were busy searching. Kit, Finn, Reese, and I were content to lag behind them and absorb Phantom Heights. Certain buildings stirred echoes of mem-ories, usually just a sense of what it felt like to be in that place in a dif-ferent time. I peeked through the window of Joe's Bar & Grill and knew what it used to smell like inside. The hospital, a four-story build-ing downtown, warned me to keep away. I didn't have any specific bad memories of being inside, but it reminded me of the terrible place we'd escaped from.

We passed a two-story building with a sign that read *LeahRae Harris High School*. A memory, fresh and clear, knocked me out of time. I froze. I remembered standing here, right *here* on the sidewalk, except instead of Kit beside me, I was with Trey. His mouth was mov-ing. But . . . I couldn't remember what his voice sounded like . . . and I couldn't remember what he said. Actually, I couldn't even see him clearly. I knew it was him, but the figure lacked detail, lacked identity. He had faded from me while I was in that place. Now he was just an essence of a memory.

Kit's hand slipping into mine broke the trance. I blinked and turned away from the school. Even if Phantom Heights were still thriving, there was nothing for me in LeahRae Harris High. I was a fugitive. I couldn't go to college. Whatever career I might have planned back then, it was long gone now. I had no future.

The sky was darkening to a dusty violet. After hours of searching, we all agreed on an abandoned warehouse on the edge of town. The doors were barred shut from the inside, so Ash broke a window with her staff. After I climbed through and dropped to my feet on the other side, I rose to survey what appeared to be a manager's office. If the dust didn't tell me it had been undisturbed for a long time, maybe even years Before, the dented filing cabinets with their empty drawers agape, the chair with a broken wheel, and the bare desk were further evidence.

Jay was already opening a door. The rusted hinges ground together as a rectangle of darkness widened. My lab-brother stood in the doorway as the final squeals faded. We followed his silhouette. Before I even reached the doorway, I could tell by the echoes of his footsteps that it was a cavernous space.

We wandered into our new home. RC ducked excessively low to give the spider dangling in the doorway a wide berth. I kicked debris out of my way as my eyes adjusted. The arched roof suffered from gaping holes, letting in a draft but showing jagged pieces of sky, and that, I thought, was the most appealing aspect; we could see the stars. Puddles from the recent rain glistened on the floor. This place was abandoned and off the beaten track, and now it belonged to us.

Reese's wet coughs reverberated in faint echoes, disturbing a large rat that scampered along the base of the wall. Kit's golden eyes were trained hungrily on the skinny pink tail disappearing inside a hole, and I suspected we wouldn't have to worry about the vermin for much longer. Jay set the backpack down on the filthy floor and turned a full circle, taking in every detail. "It's not much," he said, "but I think this could work. Welcome home."

My mind rewound back to my old house with my blood-family.
No.

I shoved the memory away. When I thought of Home, I had to associate this place with the word instead of that house in the suburbs from Before.

I gazed out an opening in the wall. The Dome glowed faintly in the dusk over the skyline. The humans inside had turned their backs on me and left me to die in a cage. Now I was on the Outside, and they were the ones trapped.

I turned my back on the Dome.

I was Home.

— Chapter Twenty —
Captain of the Guard

A new start. That was what Jay promised we'd find here.

I looked at this town and saw something great that had fallen into ruin and chaos. When I stood in the debris listening to screams and explosions in a place that used to be filled with pleasant conversations and laughter, I was looking at a reflection of my own fall from grace. But Jay studied this same miserable place and saw a metamorphosis occurring— "Like a phoenix," he said. He saw our second chance in the ashes. I couldn't see it, but I trusted Jay, so I'd try.

We spent our first day scouring Phantom Heights for food. We avoided other ghosts. Outsiders couldn't be trusted, and with most of our eyes lacking the telltale glow of internal power, we worried about being mistaken for humans. Our first dinner that night consisted of old cans of soup, some sort of dried meat, and a bizarre type of fruit I was sure I'd never seen before. Ash and I had watched a ghost knock the hard, round shell on the ground. It split right down the middle and broke in half so she could snack on the colorful fleshy pieces within, but when we stole some of the intact fruit for ourselves, we couldn't figure out how to crack the shells. We knocked the fruit on the ground as we'd seen the ghost do, then again, harder, even flinging it against a wall and striking it with Ash's staff. Axel finally crushed the shell in his bare hands for us, but we knew there had to be a secret.

It took several hours before RC finally discovered the shell would crack open only if the small bulge of the apex was struck at precisely the right angle. With that knowledge, even Kit was able to crack one open with a light tap on the ground. I was certain the fruit hadn't originated in the Human Realm. I wasn't sure the dried meat I was gnawing on came from any recognizable animal in this Realm, either. Phantom Heights had acquired a new flow of alien food with its invasion.

Axel leaned against the wall with his arms folded, watching us gorge. Whenever he was offered food, he declined, muttering something about not being hungry and how pointless it was to take any of the food we'd worked so hard to collect.

Reese dropped the meat and clutched his stomach. "Jay," he whimpered hoarsely, the blood draining from his face.

His blood-brother finished, "Our stomachs."

With that announcement, the twins doubled over. Ash awkwardly patted Finn on the back as he vomited, but none of us knew what to do.

Axel scowled at them. "They've been running consistent low fevers all week, but their temperatures have been rising since this morning."

"They're sick," said Jay. The twins had finally emptied their stomachs. They groaned, foreheads beaded with sweat. Jay carried Finn to the nest of blankets in the corner. "They just need to rest."

I brought Reese to his blood-brother. They were shivering, tears cutting streaks. "What's wrong with us?" they whispered in unison.

They've never been sick before, I realized. It wasn't allowed at that place; anyone who exhibited symptoms was immediately quarantined, even those with negative reactions from experiments that could be mistaken for illness.

Jay assured, "People get sick all the time Outside. You'll be okay."

Finn moaned and rolled over. Reese stared up at the holes in the ceiling, struggling to understand what was wrong with his body. "Can you make us better?" he whispered.

Jay gazed down at them, a pitying look in his eyes. "No. I'm sorry, but you have to get better on your own. Rest. Your bodies will take care of themselves."

Reese closed his eyes, and an agitated sleep followed soon after.

The next night, Jay stayed with them while Ash, RC, and I slipped silently through the night like fish in black water.

Phantom Heights was chaos, and yet there was an order to the madness for those with the patience to observe it. Certain territories had been claimed by gangs. Fights that happened in neutral areas were generally not gang-related skirmishes. From the shadows, we witnessed multiple battles, and I drew the conclusion that oftentimes fighting went beyond anger or differences of opinion. Fights were honorable, a show of strength. The more you won, the higher your status.

Part of me—the ghost half, I supposed—longed to participate, but rationality kept me in hiding because for a ghost like me without even basic powers, a fight would mean certain death.

Smoke thickened the air and provided us cover. Ash and RC lingered a few steps behind me, letting me lead. I thought perhaps they assumed I knew where I was going, which I didn't. This town was as foreign to me as it was to them. Since they were both armed with weapons and I wasn't, I felt rather important, as if I had two bodyguards following me. Truth was, though, I didn't need weapons to be lethal, and neither did they, although it would have been nice to have *something*. I usually had weapons when I was in the Arena, and my hands felt strange being empty. I'd have to improvise.

I guided my lab-siblings through the smoke, my goals simple— avoid Outsiders; know which direction Home was; keep Ash and RC safe; find food and clean water to bring the twins.

We discovered the source of the smoke—a store had caught fire. Ash stared at the burning building with a peculiar combination of expressions all mixed into one pale stare. Her jaw was slack, mouth open as if horrified by the destruction and devastation the ravenous flames exhibited as they devoured everything. Her eyes were wide, wonderstruck, seeing a strange beauty in the pulsing glow that had ensnared her in a trance. Her eyebrows were drawn together, betraying guilt for daring to admire such a terrible sight.

"Ash?" I called. No response. Her hand was rising toward the flames, as if she wanted to touch them. I wondered if she saw the fire in present time or if she was reliving a blaze from her past. I touched her arm. "Ash, are you okay?"

She winced back into reality with a quiet gasp. "Yeah. Yeah, sure, I'm fine." She clutched her staff tighter and turned her back on the fire. With the flames behind her, she was a silhouette, her cloak blowing in the hot wind.

RC coughed and shielded his face with his left arm. Downtown was too crowded for my taste; it was hard to scavenge while avoiding so many ghosts. We retreated to the outskirts again where there was less activity.

The air cleared, and the stars reappeared. In the middle of a neighborhood intersection, I paused to look back at the skyline and the elegant arc of the green Dome in the haze. We had yet to see a human here outside the Dome, and that was fine by me.

My gaze fell back to ground level. The neighborhood was calm. A warm wind groaned between the dark, abandoned houses. Cars parked on the street had been sitting still for so long they were like behemoths sleeping under blankets of dirt, debris, and dead leaves, waiting for their owners to come wake them. The street sign on the corner was crooked. I wasn't paying much attention, and yet as I passed, my eyes caught the briefest glimpse: Spitler Ave and K St.

I stopped in my tracks. *Spitler and K.* I knew this intersection. I knew this street. Littered with garbage, bordered by empty homes, it was different from the image in my broken memory, but I knew it. Even without the street sign, I would have known. My eyes skimmed the decrepit houses until I found the one I was looking for—mine.

"Cato, come on," Ash whispered.

I didn't move. "Cay?" she queried in concern.

I stared at the tired building three houses down on the right that looked as abandoned as I was. I swallowed, trying to find my voice. "Go on without me," I murmured. "I'll catch up later."

"Why?" Ash asked, scowling, but I simply shook my head.

"I want to be alone right now."

RC reminded me, "But Jay said he doesn't want anyone out alone."

"I'll be fine." RC scratched his head, visibly distressed that I would go against our leader's wish, which prompted me to add, "I'll meet up with you by the school."

They exchanged glances, but finally, RC shrugged and returned to the shadows. Ash sighed, but after another moment of hesitation, she turned and jogged after him.

Flanking the ruined buildings, I analyzed the house with peeling gray paint as I made my way down the street. The white door hung at an odd angle like a loose tooth in a child's gums. The windows were boarded. The porch step creaked under my weight, and I paused to gaze up at my old home.

I set my open hand against the scarred wood and pushed. Warped hinges groaned as the door grudgingly scraped open. I held my breath, hesitating in the doorway before cautiously taking the first step into the dark house.

Excitement made me feverish; I'd dreamed of returning here, although this wasn't at all how I had imagined it. I guess I thought I'd be free, not a fugitive. I used to dream about opening this door to the same bright living room I'd left, my blood-family smiling behind me saying, "Welcome home!" after the long car ride away from that awful place. Mom would have let me ride in the front seat with the window down to blow away all the bad memories. And they—

Stop.

Why was I was daydreaming about a future that could never be? I was not free. My blood-family never came to claim me. And this was not the home I remembered.

The quiet room had a grimy heaviness to it, as if the thick coat of dust blanketing the furniture and swirling in lazy patterns through the air had the power to absorb sound and mute the house. The windows had been broken and then boarded up, but that must have been a long time ago because several weather-beaten boards had been knocked loose. Someone had ransacked the place and left garbage all over the floor. A staircase led to the second story. When I stepped forward, a *crunch* came from beneath my boot.

I paused, retracting my foot from the picture frame lying on the floor. I knelt for a closer look. The dust was so thick on the glass that I couldn't see the picture. I picked up the frame and smeared my thumb over the cracked surface to reveal three people smiling politely. A long crack ran diagonally from one corner to the other, dividing the family. I was on one side of the crack; my mother and blood-sister were on the other. Even locked in a photograph, I was separated from them. I was surprised to find this here, actually. I'd have thought my mother would have removed every trace of me from this house. Maybe Phantom Heights was invaded before she had time to do that. Maybe . . . that was the reason she never . . .

I knew better than that. I shouldn't make excuses.

My lab-family was like me in many ways. We'd all been discarded; in fact, RC used to call us The Forgotten Ones. Nobody on the Outside missed any of us. But none of my lab-siblings suffered the treason I did. They were all orphans or runaways or slaves. They weren't betrayed by their blood-families. When I closed my eyes, I could still see my mother's neat signature at the bottom of the custody transfer, a signature I recognized from field trip permission slips and poor test score acknowledgments for my math teacher. A signature I knew was authentic.

I sighed and set the picture frame down where I'd found it, then straightened and skimmed the room. My gaze lingered on a sofa with torn cushions bleeding white fluff.

I sat between my mother and blood-sister on the couch, holding a bowl of popcorn as a roaring lion announced the start of a movie.

I looked across the couch to where the television used to be, but it was long gone. There wasn't even a mark in the dust. I ran my hand over the arm of the sofa, leaving a trail in the filth, then journeyed into the next room—the kitchen.

My mother was scribbling in a notebook at the table. I dropped my backpack on the floor and opened the cupboard, hungry for an after-school snack.

Stomach rumbling, I reached up and opened the door to the cupboard, but I found only cobwebs and more dust. I left the door open and gazed around at the dark, abandoned room that used to be so bright. Sunlight used to stream through that window there, but now boards were crudely nailed into place to keep out the night, which, even so far away from the Dome, still possessed a faint green glow to cast eerie shadows. I turned to face a closed door. I knew steps led down to the pitch-black basement, but there was nothing for me down there. I wandered past a closet and a bathroom until eventually I circled back to the staircase that led upstairs. I set my hand on the wooden banister.

"Cato, you're going to be late for school!"

"I know! I'm coming!" I shouted back, slinging my backpack over one shoulder and sliding down the banister. I landed effortlessly on both feet and dashed out the door, calling "Love you, Mom! See you after school!" as she closed the door behind me, chuckling.

I missed them, and I hated myself for that. Time had scarred the wound, but it couldn't fill the void; all it did was trap the cold nothingness inside me. As I ascended the staircase, I habitually stepped over the creaky fourth stair. In the hallway, I paused to gaze into my mother's room, and then I continued on to the next.

The door was partially closed. I pushed, but something was blocking the other side. I squeezed through the opening to find my bookcase had fallen in front of the door. Novels littered the hardwood floor. I picked one up and flipped through the pages, stumbling across the sentences and finding to my surprise that I'd forgotten how to pronounce some of the words. I sounded a few out, my stammering childlike.

I set that book down and rifled through others that had spilled from the overturned bookcase. None were familiar. I was sure they were my books, but I couldn't remember ever reading them. I abandoned them in frustration.

My gaze settled on the bed. The mattress had been slashed by a knife or sword, and the blankets were wadded on the floor. The soft mattress gave beneath my hand. I sat, pleased by the familiar sounds of the springs adjusting to my weight, even though the cloud of dust made me cough. How many times had I fallen asleep on this bed? It must have been so blissful to be able to stretch out and sleep in any position I wanted, something I'd taken for granted before living in a cage so small

I could barely move.

I gathered the blankets and torn pillows so Finn and Reese might be a little more comfortable. As I straightened, I heard a muffled *thump* downstairs.

Nothing, I tried to convince myself. *Just the wind through the boards over the windows. Something must have blown over.*

The next *creak* sounded like someone closing the cupboard door I'd left open.

My eyes skipped over the room in search of a weapon. There was nothing practical here. I was better off trying to sneak out than standing my ground. I abandoned my spoils; they'd only hinder me. I could return for them later.

I slipped soundlessly through the door and eased my way, silent as a shadow, down the hall. *Please let it be Ash and RC.*

I crouched at the top of the stairs, listening. Another cupboard door slammed, and the intruder muttered, "There's nothing good to eat in this town."

It was a man's voice, definitely not any of my lab-brothers. My anxiety hiked another notch. He was in the kitchen. If I could make my way down the stairs quietly enough, I could sneak out the front door. Exhaling, I jerked the hood over my head and crept down, careful with the precise placement of each foot to avoid creaking.

I was only halfway down the stairs when the ghost emerged from the kitchen. I froze mid-step, staring at him. He stared back. His eyes glinted green in the darkness, his black hair tied in a short ponytail. I thought I caught a glimpse of a uniform, but his outfit was concealed beneath a full-length cloak with a tall collar as high as his earlobes.

He didn't move. Neither did I.

I dashed for the door. He was quicker than I expected, and I skidded to a stop at the end of the staircase. The intruder stood between me and my escape route.

"Well now, what do we have here?" he said, looking me up and down. Maybe it was my imagination, but his eyes seemed to linger on the white Alpha symbol on my chest for a second longer before they traveled on. I swallowed. If he came at me in a physical struggle, I might be able to overcome him, but if he used his powers on me, I didn't stand a chance.

The ghost didn't advance. Rather, he smiled. "You wouldn't happen to be one of the fugitives from Project Alpha, would you?" he asked, although his tone implied that he didn't expect an answer.

A slap across the face would have been less astonishing. "You . . . know about us?"

He nodded, gazing at me with an eagerness that made my nerves stretch tighter. "It's an honor to meet you. Please allow me to introduce myself—my name is Captain Hassing. Eh-lai." He extended his hand in a friendly gesture.

I suspected he wanted me to come forward and shake it, but I just gazed at his glove and made no move to step within striking range. "Captain of what?"

Hassing waited a few moments longer, but when I still didn't accept his hand, he lowered it and cleared his throat to bridge the awkward gap between question and answer. "The, ah, well, the Guard, of course." He seemed bewildered that his reputation didn't precede him. At my blank look, he added, "I'm in charge of both the Shadow Guard and the Prison Guard. I enforce the Law of Avilésor. Tell me, are you the leader?"

Avilésor? Reluctant to further betray my ignorance, I shook my head at his inquiry, and he seemed oddly disappointed that I wasn't Jay. "Well . . . that's all right. My employer is eager to meet you."

"Employer?"

"Azar." Hassing gave me a funny look. "Surely you've heard of *him.*"

"Sorry, no." Call it intuition or a sixth sense or whatever—this situation felt wrong. Besides blocking my path, Hassing hadn't made an offensive move, and yet the hairs on the back of my neck prickled. The back door was through the kitchen. If I could just get enough of a head start . . .

"Azar is a powerful man," Hassing boasted. "You should be honored he requested a meeting with you."

I was beyond confused now; I didn't know who this Azar guy was. Why would he want to meet with me?

All I could croak out was, "Why?"

Hassing smiled again. It didn't reach his eyes. "Azar wants to help you."

"That's . . . um, generous of him," I answered, unsure what else to say. I didn't trust authority, and I perceived Hassing's boss as someone with a lot of it. I'd had more than enough trouble with the human government; I didn't want to become ensnared in whatever government dictated the Ghost Realm.

The captain pretended to miss the uncertainty in my voice. "It is. Come with me to meet him."

I immediately and unconsciously slid my foot back, which shifted my weight into a more defensive stance. Hassing noticed, and his eyes flashed brighter for a fraction of a second, betraying his frustration. "There's no need to be afraid. Azar just wants to talk. It seems to me that having a powerful ally would be beneficial to you, considering your current position."

"I suppose so," I muttered noncommittally. "But like I said, I'm not the leader."

"It doesn't matter," Hassing growled, his impatience becoming more pronounced at my insistent hesitation. "Like I said, Azar is powerful, both as an ally and an enemy. Believe me, you don't want to make him your enemy. He'll speak with you first, and then you can put him in touch with your leader. You don't want to turn down this opportunity."

I shook my head.

Hassing took a step forward. "Come with me."

Although nothing in his tone had changed, the sudden advance was threatening. I backed away. "Ah . . . maybe we can talk later? I, uh, I can let the leader know Azar wants to speak with him. W-we can arrange a meeting for later."

Hassing's eyes glowed bright with frustrated intensity now. He took another step. "Azar doesn't like to be kept waiting."

Hassing reached for me.

The element of surprise was all I had; I lunged forward, batting his wrist away and delivering an elbow to the gut as I ducked under his arm and sprinted through the living room toward the kitchen.

"Ungrateful lab rat!" Hassing shouted. I yelped and leapt to the side as a section of the doorframe exploded in a flash of green light inches from my head. Smoldering splinters struck the left side of my face. Yikes, that was some seriously concentrated ectoplasm. Grade B at least, maybe even Grade A, higher than anything I'd ever been able to conjure. "I'm not going back empty-handed!"

I dashed through the kitchen and wrenched open the back door—thank a bloody Scout it yielded easier than the front door had—and vaulted off the deck and into the backyard. I whipped around the corner of the house, chancing a look back over my shoulder just in time to see Hassing emerge through the door and pause, his angry eyes searching for me. I wasn't quick enough; I knew he saw the edge of my cloak disappear around the corner.

A crackling orb of ectoplasm veered around the edge of the house. I gasped and ducked forward, losing my balance enough to fall hard on one knee. Ectoplasm zipped over my head and struck the siding in a green burst that left scorch marks. *What the hell? Since when can ectoplasm curve around a corner like that?*

I kept my momentum and scrambled forward on all fours for a stride before pushing off and lengthening into a full run down the street. The captain was close behind. He grumbled, "Cursed King, if I had Titon, this would be so much easier."

Whatever a Titon was, I was glad Hassing didn't have it at his disposal. I was regretting my decision to split up with RC and Ash, but I was reluctant to lead Hassing to our designated meeting place and put them in danger too. I altered my course, turning down a side street while Hassing huffed behind me. I was clearly faster, but I didn't know where I was going. I couldn't become intangible, so if I was unable to outmaneuver him, he could run me into a dead end. I whipped into an alley, my eyes on the Dome about a mile in front of me.

This was a stupid plan, but if I was right about the Dome, Hassing couldn't pass through it, just like my lab-siblings. It was risky for me to be inside it while all those humans were in City Hall, but it was the only safe place I could think of where Hassing couldn't touch me. He'd no doubt try to wait me out, increasing my chances of crossing paths with humans, but I'd figure that part out later.

No sooner had I decided on my course of action than a sharp prickle rippling across my skull sent me sprawling. The fall didn't even hurt; I was already lost in the pain. The Spasm flattened me from a full-speed sprint. I rolled on the ground, screaming, clutching my head as the world disappeared in the soul-shattering abyss of agony that turned minutes into lifetimes.

A breeze carrying the stench of garbage washed over my wet skin and churned my stomach. I shivered and opened my eyes to see a pair of boots in front of my nose. Swallowing, I peered up at Hassing looming above me, eyes blazing in fury. He was panting, glaring down at me, and I was done. He knew he had me, and so did I.

Hassing threw out his hand, shooting out a stream of green ecto-plasm. This wasn't an orb of condensed energy; it was a long, glowing whip he held in his hand, the end trailing to the ground and coiling at his feet, sizzling and crackling. I understood in that moment what his Divinity was. Hassing was an Ectokinetic.

"You had to make this difficult," he said in a low snarl. He snapped his wrist, and the ectoplasm lashed at me. It wound around my body, more like a snake than a whip, sparking pain in my nerves like a mild electrical shock as it constricted to pull my limbs inward and bind me. Hassing released extra power into it, ramping up the charge to punish me. I cried out.

Movement behind him caught my eye through a burning flood of tears and a glowing green haze. A cloaked figure sprinted down the alley. In one smooth move, it lashed out at Hassing with a sickening wet *thud*. Hassing grunted, his ectoplasm dissipating into thin air as he stumbled and raised his hand to his head. Blood glistened on his fingers. He stared at his hand in a daze, swaying.

The shadow never broke stride; it dashed past him and seized my wrist. "Let's go," said Ash, pulling me to my feet. In her other hand, her metal staff dripped with Hassing's blood.

Two uniformed ghosts appeared at the mouth of the alley. "Captain?"

Ash and I took off. As we dashed around the corner, Hassing shouted, "Don't just stand there! Go after them!"

"I don't understand what's happening," said Ash.

I leapt through a broken window. "That makes two of us," I answered as she dove in headfirst after me, then landed in a somersault and hopped to her feet. "Where's RC?"

"Fighting another one of those Shadow Guards. I told you we shouldn't have split up!"

Before I could argue with her, Ash let out a startled scream as one of the uniformed ghosts appeared through the wall, tackling her to the ground. The staff fell from her hand as they wrestled for control on the floor. Unsure what to do, I picked up the weapon. I couldn't use it as well as she could, but I could improvise.

Her attacker gravely underestimated her strength; Ash swung her elbow into his jaw and then kicked him away. She rolled backward over her shoulders and was on her feet again, and then her legs gave out and she collapsed with a squeal as she, too, succumbed to a Spasm.

When the ghost scrambled to his feet, I swung. The staff was solid metal but surprisingly lightweight. It smashed into the man's face. Not the prettiest counterattack on my part, but damn was it effective. With the solid *crack* of a broken nose, he fell back, a crimson mist hanging in the air for a moment. The words *home run* inexplicably bubbled to the top of my mind.

Ash was still writhing on the ground. Alarmed at the racket she was making, I crouched, holding her weapon and waiting for Hassing or the second Guard to appear. I experimentally twirled the staff, just as I'd watched her do a hundred times. It was awkward in my hands, light but too large for me to handle, but it was better than nothing.

Ash's screams had quieted to pathetic whimpers by the time the second ghost emerged. I tightened my grip on the staff. He faced me, and then his gaze fell to Ash on the ground next to his unconscious partner, a stream of blood pouring from his crooked nose. The newcomer hesitated, studying the weapon in my hands, and then his eyes lifted to my face. They were glowing.

I braced myself. He was using power, no question of that, but what was his Divinity? I took stock of the room, of my body, of my clear thoughts, searching for a change in something, *anything*, but nothing seemed to be happening. All this man appeared to be doing was scrutinizing me with glowing violet eyes.

He drew a short rod with a handle from his belt. "I'd rather not use this," he said, his voice calming, soothing, a glaring contradiction to his gentle threat. I clenched my teeth. I didn't know for sure what the rod did, but it reminded of the cattle prods *They* carried.

He continued, "You sh—"

A cringingly loud squeal of tires spinning on asphalt cut him off. We stared at each other, my own puzzlement mirrored on his face. He turned toward the broken window behind him where the sound was originating from.

No headlights, no engine revving. No warning. The shriek of the burnout stopped. In the next split second, I hooked my arm through Ash's and half pulled, half dragged her out of the way when a vehicle smashed through the wall as if it were possessed to drive without gas. Boards and debris exploded into the room ahead of the grill.

I hit the wall and shielded Ash with my body to protect her from the flying debris. She coughed and clutched me tightly. Wooden splinters were still raining when I hauled her up, and she'd recovered enough to stand on her own two feet. The Guard stirred beneath the crumpled front of the vehicle.

Without a single word or cue, Ash and I darted for the opening the car had created. We squeezed through the remaining half of the window frame to find RC waiting for us on the other side of the street. "We owe you one," I said as we crossed the road to meet him.

"I'll add it to your tally," he replied, stepping back so I could lead the way.

Kit fiddled with her Name in Ash's lap while I recounted our adventure. Axel was leaning against the wall with his arms folded, looking bored, while Finn and Reese watched with bleary eyes. RC was gazing out one of the holes in the wall, as if expecting to see Hassing outside.

I finished my story with, "Hassing said Azar wanted to help us."

Jay was silent, processing this development, but Axel leaned forward with sudden interest. "Wait, you're sure he said Azar?"

"You know him?" I asked.

"Know him? I'll rip the bastard's throat out!"

"Watch your tongue," Jay warned.

Kit's ears fell back. I asked, "How do you know Azar?"

"I don't know him personally," Axel growled. "Just his name. That son of a bitch—"

"*Axel!*" Jay scolded.

"—was after my parents. If we hadn't been running from him, my parents'd still be alive and I wouldn't be like—" he looked at his own hands in disgust "—*this*."

"Why was he after your parents?" Ash asked quietly.

"Hell if I know."

"Axel, *please*," Jay bemoaned. He exhaled and swept the hair from his eyes, then stared straight ahead in thought. "I doubt Azar really wants to help us; he's probably just interested in the Weapon. I think we should avoid him."

"Or stand up to him," Axel said as he cracked his knuckles. "I can track Hassing straight to Azar. He won't even see me coming. I'm-a—"

"Stop," Jay interrupted. "That's reckless, Axel. Reckless and stupid. You don't even have your powers."

"I don't need my powers. I'm strong enough now. I was a little kid last time, but now I can make Azar pay."

"He'd be a powerful adversary. Promise me you won't pursue this. It won't end well, Ax, and we need you here. Revenge isn't going to change what happened to you." Axel scowled and crossed his arms, which was as close to a promise as Jay could hope for. "I know you want to fight, but not this battle, okay? Let Azar fight *Them*. In fact, I wish him luck. But we're free now. We aren't a part of this war anymore."

I turned away. I'd like to believe that, and for a while, I almost did. But now, with both *Them* and Azar hunting for us, I didn't see how we could avoid this war forever.

War. It was hard to put our personal struggles into a perspective that big. My attention wandered to the youngest, the most innocent. Kit had pinched the cord above her pendant and twisted it so she could let go and watch the ivory spin. Finn and Reese had fallen asleep during our discussion.

I knelt by them. "Hey," I murmured, shaking Finn's shoulder. He stirred and opened his eyes. "Hey," I called again, and his gaze found me. "You hungry?" I offered him a crust of bread, but he shook his head. "No? But you haven't eaten all day." He didn't answer me. His eyelids slid lethargically over his dull eyes and then rose in one slow blink.

I turned to rouse his blood-brother. I had to call Reese's name several times before he awakened. His blue eyes flickered open, and when I asked him if he was hungry, I received a soft murmur of what at first I assumed was gibberish. Then I understood, and I requested, "English, Reese." He blinked, then whispered, "The threads kept wandering, so I tied them to him, and we can't untie them. But it's okay, because we can still hear . . ."

"What are you talking about?" I asked gently.

Reese was looking straight at me, but he was seeing something far beyond. "Follow the lights. She has brown hair, and there are flowers in the trash can. The lights. Five, zero, seven, one, four. But now *They* know. *They* know; something's wrong, but don't speak. Never speak. It's against the Rules. Zad? Zad, you're here. We have names. And, and you . . ." He trailed off.

Puzzled, I glanced over my shoulder. Nobody was there. I faced him again, and he was still staring at me, as if he thought I were somebody else. "No, Reese, I'm Cato. Who is Zad?"

Reese blinked at me. "Who is Zad?" he asked, genuinely perplexed by the question.

"I don't know. You tell me. Is Zad the lady with brown hair you were talking about? The woman who put the flowers in the trash?"

Reese whispered, "The code is five-zero-seven-one-four. It unlocks . . . You have to unlock it first. Five . . . zero . . . seven . . ." He was asleep again.

I leaned back on my heels. Finn and Reese were so small and malnourished they were frail even when they were healthy. Now that they were so colorless and weak, I was afraid they'd fade into spirits.

I rose and wandered back to the others. "Hey, Jay. Question," I said quietly so as not to wake the twins. "Was there ever anyone else incarcerated in Project Alpha?"

"No," he answered in surprise. He tilted his head with an inquiring frown and added, "Why do you ask?"

I shrugged. "No reason. Never mind."

I turned back to watch Finn and Reese sleep. Today, we'd added another enemy to our list. It was getting harder and harder to protect my lab-brothers, and right now they were fighting a battle we couldn't fight for them.

— Chapter Twenty-One —

Delirium

Their condition didn't improve during the night and following day.

Rain poured down in sheets, drenching Phantom Heights while the sky rumbled like the belly of a hungry beast. It was a cold, dreary night, darker than usual with no moon. Only the green glow emitted from the Dome far away over City Hall offered any source of light, but it was a cold, empty light that cast strange shadows and gave the underbelly of the clouds a sickly hue.

Water had soaked through my cloak, my pants, my boots—even, it seemed, through my skin. I closed my eyes and inhaled the smell of the rain. The others were still taking shelter at Home. I'd stayed with them for a while, watching the water droplets pelt the asphalt outside, but the moisture in the air and the twins' ragged breathing made Home smell of sickness until the stench grew nails that scraped at my throat with each breath and I couldn't take it anymore.

I emerged from a covered alleyway into the street again. Movement to my left—I pressed myself against the wall, crushing the book into my ribs to keep it dry and safe. I'd returned to LeahRae Harris High to find this for Finn and Reese. I'd like to say that I walked into my old school and everything came rushing back to me.

Instead, I tried to convince myself the reason I didn't remember it was because it had changed. The hallways were dark and deserted, lockers open, papers and books and pencils littering the floors. Maybe if the lights were on, and if students were loitering in the halls, and if the bell was ringing . . .

I was kidding myself. I had nothing more than a vague recollection of attending school. Wandering through a packed hallway with a stack of books in my arms, sitting at a desk scribbling notes on subjects that had long seeped out of my mind, eating lunch outside, and the bell. I did remember the sound of the bell signaling the changing of classes. I used to hear that bell in a dream and wake up thinking I was going to be late, but my eyes always opened to cage bars instead.

Introduction to Earth and Environmental Science by Professor D. Ryne was the book I'd scavenged from one of the classrooms. I would have liked to find more books, but when I rounded the corner, a tabby cat was sitting in the middle of the hallway—a sign that danger lay ahead. Raucous laughter echoed from the end of the hall, and I retreated.

Finn and Reese might not even be coherent enough to read, but I figured this book might cheer them up a little. One of us might have to try to read it to them, although our reading skills were rusty from disuse. But I was willing to risk embarrassing myself stumbling over the words if there was a chance it might help Finn and Reese feel better.

I peered around the corner. Three uniformed ghosts marched by, hoods up, their glowing eyes searching the shadows. Based on their uniforms, I was sure they were Shadow Guards searching for us. My throat itched; I pressed my fist to my mouth and held my breath to contain the cough. My lungs slowly emptied as the ghosts passed, and I eased around the corner, never taking my eyes from their backs. I darted across the street and paused again to ensure they hadn't turned and seen me.

They continued their patrol, oblivious to my presence. One perk of being human—ghosts couldn't sense me in this state like they could my lab-siblings. The downside was I couldn't sense them either. Holding the book beneath my waterlogged cloak in an attempt to keep it dry, I dashed through the rainy night, splashing through puddles. The drone of the storm covered my quiet footsteps. A simultaneous flash-*boom* lightning bolt struck a giant rod on the tallest building nearby, making me jump in thunder's bellow. No wonder so few ghosts were out on a night like this.

The emerald Dome shimmered behind me, brilliant as ever against the dark sky. I ran away from it into deeper darkness where there was little light to guide my way.

This town was becoming familiar to me again, not from memory, but because my daily scavenging had given me the chance to discover the best hiding places, the streets less traveled, the areas where the human raid team was most likely to target, the buildings that were uninhabited, and the buildings that housed ghosts now. I knew the secrets of this town better than I ever did in my life Before. Phantom Heights was more of a home now than it had ever been. It sheltered me, provided me with food, offered refuge from my enemies.

I ducked into the shelter of an alcove and paused, peering through the storm in search of prying eyes glowing in the darkness. This was the most crucial part of my journey; I couldn't lead enemies to Home. My patience knew no bounds with the importance of this task. I crouched, still as a statue, waiting, searching. My feet started to tingle from losing blood circulation.

I pursed my lips and whistled one long note.

A full minute crawled by, and then movement drew my attention. A black cat crossed the road. If it had stopped and sat down, that would have been a signal of danger, but it kept going, which meant all-clear. I rose and slipped back into the rain.

A pair of stray cats scattered as I paused beside a broken window. The rain had slowed to a drizzle, a fine mist that clouded the hazy air. I scrambled through the opening, careful to avoid cutting myself on the glass shards still embedded in the frame.

I landed in the office, tossed back my hood, and shook my sopping hair, sending drops of water spraying across the room. The door swung inward under my push, opening into the cavernous warehouse.

Rain leaked with a steady *drip, drip, drip* into the plastic industrial drums we'd found, five in total we had placed beneath the biggest holes in the roof. The twins were lying in their usual place in the corner. Kit crouched on the balls of her feet nearby, watching them with her ears pinned. Jay was busy sorting our supplies, and Ash, whose wet body was steaming from a trip outside, ruefully twisted her auburn hair to squeeze water out. RC was sitting with his back to the wall, sharpening the blades on one of his silver disks. Axel sat cross-legged as if in meditation.

I paused, my gaze settling on Kit and the twins. Finn and Reese seemed to be asleep, but they were talking. Their voices murmured in unison, eerie in the somber warehouse. "Zero . . . three . . . two . . . three . . . two . . . zero . . . one . . . seven . . ."

"Hey. What's wrong with Finn and Reese?" I asked.

"Bot's broken," said Axel without opening his eyes.

Jay, who was in the process of breaking a pastry into even pieces, paused to glare at him. He'd never approved of the nickname Axel gave the twins—Bot, because he claimed they were robots.

I had to admit, the nickname wasn't totally undeserved. To the untrained eye, Finn and Reese experienced zero emotions and no empathy, and they absorbed knowledge as if downloading it directly into their brains. It didn't help that their fingers sometimes twitched when they were anxious, which Axel claimed was proof they were robots because their hardware was malfunctioning—to which Finn humorously corrected the cause would more likely be a malfunction in circuitry, not hardware. That didn't help his case.

All in all, Bot wasn't a bad nickname when considering other terms of endearment Axel had been known to use on various occasions.

Jay replied, "They're delirious. They've been spouting off codes for a while now. Even when we wake them up, they just open their eyes and keep reciting numbers." He handed a chunk of pastry to each of us.

I set the book down and accepted my share. Axel simply held up one hand to refuse when Jay offered, so Jay gave it to Kit instead. She ripped her intense gaze away from Finn and Reese, but she was on the verge of tears as she sank her fangs into her meal.

I picked off a moldy bit and flicked it aside before eating. Ash, RC, and Kit polished off their pieces. Jay ate almost all of his share, but he left a mouthful and handed it to Kit, who gazed up at him, smiling in gratitude before she shoved it into her mouth.

Jay dipped a bowl into a barrel of rainwater and raised it to his lips.

He filled it again and handed it to me. I swallowed the cool water. "I'm worried about them," I said, nodding at the mumbling twins as I passed the bowl back.

"Seven . . . two . . . three . . . nine . . . one . . ." they continued to murmur, stirring restlessly. Their faces glistened with sweat in the dark room, lit by a flash of lightning outside. "Nine . . . one . . . three . . ."

"There has to be something we can do for them," said Ash as Jay dipped the empty bowl into the drum again and handed it to her.

"Six . . . two . . ."

"I don't know what," Jay replied wearily.

I watched Finn and Reese mutter in their sleep, mindlessly reciting complex codes from memory. When I touched Reese's forehead, heat radiated from his skin. He no longer had the ports embedded in his skull, but he still bore the scars; I could see the round marks on his shiny skin.

I took a threadbare blanket and worked at the fabric until I could tear two long strips away. These I dipped in the rainwater and folded, then draped across the twins' foreheads. The only reactions I received were more whispers of random codes that meant absolutely nothing to me. I solemnly placed the book in the corner to await their awakening.

Sometime in the early morning, their fevered thrashing stilled and they fell silent. We were all relieved, and we made sure not to disturb them so they could sleep and recuperate.

By mid-morning, I was crouching by the broken window again, staring Outside. The sun reflected in the puddles left from last night's storm. All of my lab-family, even Axel, was Home. Bright days like today weren't ideal for traveling around town.

At the quiet *kerplunk* of a bowl being dunked in water, I turned away from the window. Jay carried the bowl to the twins, whose chests rose and fell with shallow, labored breaths. "Hey," Jay called softly, kneeling between them. "Finn? Reese? Are you thirsty?"

Neither boy responded. Jay frowned. He set the bowl on the floor and gently shook Finn, but our lab-brother didn't move. "They won't wake up," Jay whispered, panic heightening his voice. We approached, staring in horror at the twins. Only Axel remained by the wall. RC paused to linger hesitantly a few yards away while Ash, Kit, and I gathered around Jay and the twins.

"What's wrong with them?" Ash asked. "Why didn't they get better?"

None of us had an answer. Jay pulled Finn into his lap, still trying to wake the boy. The skeletal twins were sickly pale, sweat glistening on their ashen skin, dark circles shadowing the hollows of their eyes, their bodies somehow even more frail than usual. "Come on," Jay pleaded, gently shaking Finn again. "Please wake up."

Axel said the words the rest of us were too afraid to admit aloud: "They're dying."

Kit's lower lip began to quiver; she knew what death was. RC backed farther away, as if suddenly afraid the twins were contagious. Jay shook his head fiercely. "No. I can't just sit here and watch them die. We have to do something."

"There's no one to help us," I realized in a numb monotone. "The only ones who might be able to are the humans, but you know they'll turn us over to *Them*."

RC said, "It'd be more merciful to let them die than send them back to that place."

"Azar?" Ash suggested. "He . . . did offer to help."

Axel snarled, "No."

"Can't we just find them some medicine?" she asked.

"We don't know what kind of medicine they need," Jay said miserably.

I added, "Plus they throw up anything we give them."

"So . . . there's nothing we can do." She closed her eyes as grief twitched her brow.

Kit crawled forward and buried herself in Ash's arms for comfort. RC stared at Finn and Reese as if memorizing their faces to say goodbye already.

"It's not fair," Kit whispered. "We escaped. They can't die. It's not fair."

"I know," Ash choked out, stroking Kit's hair. "It's not."

An idea was forming in my mind. It was insane, full of countless risks, but the pieces began to come together.

"Humans *can* help," I thought aloud.

Jay shot me a look. "You just said they'd turn the twins over to *Them*."

"Not if we have something of theirs," I stated slowly, the final piece fitting into place.

The others stared at me. "What do you mean?" Axel demanded.

Jay's eyes widened in sudden realization as his arms tightened around Finn's fevered body. "You want to blackmail them."

I nodded, pleased that Jay had caught on to my idea so quickly.

"Mmm, that'll make them mad," worried Ash. RC watched me with a dejected look on his face, as if afraid to even dare to hope because he'd already given up.

"But it could work," Jay muttered. "The only problem is it would have to be something valuable. Those humans don't have many more possessions than we do."

I nodded slowly. "What if we took a person?"

"A person?" Ash echoed.

I swept my gaze around the circle, meeting the eyes of every one of my lab-siblings. What I was about to suggest was crazy, dangerous, and to be honest, downright idiotic considering our pitiful status as fugitives without powers. My confidence started to waver. Jay must have noticed, because he leaned forward and said, "Cato, I'm willing to do *anything* to save them. Do you understand?"

I met his intense eyes. Yes, I did. That was what I'd been counting on from every single person now staring at me, waiting. I had a specific target in mind, one that wouldn't be easy to obtain.

"I bet the daughter of a ghost hunter will be good enough leverage."

— Chapter Twenty-Two —
Abduction

Kidnapping Vivian Tarrow would be no simple task. In fact, short of our lucky escape, it would be the hardest feat we'd ever attempted.

Thus far, we'd been meticulous about avoiding the humans. As Axel put it, "We're about to go piss off a ghost hunter while we don't have our powers. Of the top ten stupidest things I've ever done . . . You know, actually, this'll probably rank around number four."

Ash asked what the stupidest thing he'd ever done was, but Jay's grumble of "I don't think I want to know" kept Axel quiet with nothing more than a mischievous smirk to leave us guessing.

Taking inventory of what we had was discouraging. No twins meant no advantage of mind-reading, we were short two sets of basic powers, and we had no access to ECANI, not that it would have been much help anyway. Ash had her staff, which was good only in a direct fight, and we definitely wanted to avoid that. Jay and I were powerless and weaponless. Axel was strong and fast and unstoppable, but if we sent him in, he was likely to accidentally hurt or kill Vivian. So that left Kit with her full powers and RC with half of his and the bladed disks— a Level 1 Amínyte who was too small to fight, and an injured, half-blind Telekinetic who could move only small objects within a limited radius and had restricted movement of one arm.

Jay had taken me aside right after my announcement and asked, "Are you sure about this?" I'd told him it was the only way. He'd nodded, but skeptically, and said, "Okay. I just have to know your head is where it needs to be."

"It is," I'd dismissed.

"Cato." The seriousness weighing down my name finally made me turn to face him. "We're crossing a line, and once we do, there's no go-ing back. Are you sure this is what you want?"

I'd been so swept up in the excitement I hadn't had time to slow down and think. My lab-family would be facing brand-new adversaries. I'd be facing familiar faces from Before. And most importantly, by doing this, I'd be revealing to my mother that I was in Phantom Heights. She let *Them* lock me up and throw away the key. I was sure she knew by now that I'd escaped, but if she didn't already know I was here, she would soon.

"This isn't about what I want."

"Isn't it?" He'd fixed me in the scope of his steely gaze. "If we're going to take this risk, I need to make sure we're doing it for the right reason and not some crazy revenge scheme."

"It's crazy all right, but this isn't about revenge," I'd answered, although even as the words left my mouth, my heart started beating a little faster. "While we're in Phantom Heights, our biggest enemy will be Madison, and the only way to cripple her is to take the one thing she treasures most. Anything less, and Finn and Reese will either die or be sent back to *Them*. Trust me, Jay."

The revenge was just an added bonus I kept to myself.

Ideally, we would have spent several days studying our target, iden-tifying the weapons the humans used, planning how to counter their attacks, and memorizing their formations as they scavenged in the ruined town. But ideally, we wouldn't be forced into this situation to begin with. Time was infuriatingly short to pull off a stunt that could very well put us back in the hands of *Them* and evoke the wrath of Madison Tarrow.

We didn't waste the precious time we had. Every second was spent strategizing. We knew the last raid yielded less than usual from the aerial supply drop, and soon—probably today before dark—the humans would be forced to leave the safety of the Dome to scavenge for more supplies.

We'd watched the raiders enough times to know that Madison would be leading the primary team, and at her side would be her apprentice. The half-moon meant the werewolf would be with them for protection. Vivian almost always accompanied the main raid team numbering anywhere between fifteen and thirty humans, most of whom weren't ghost hunters but did carry weapons and knew how to use them.

"What if Vivian isn't with them?" Ash asked.

"She will be," I insisted.

Ash stared me down. "But what if she isn't?"

"Then we target the apprentice."

My mind needed to be focused, but I couldn't stop it from wandering while Jay was talking. Vivian Tarrow or Trey Selman. Either way, I was about to come face-to-face with my past, and either way, we were going to be in Madison's crosshairs.

After an hour of suggestions and arguments, the plan was sketchy at best, full of potential miscalculations and errors and what-ifs. Before we had time to hammer out the details, Axel reported the raid team just stepped through the Dome, and Vivian was part of the fifty-eight.

"Fifty-eight?" I repeated in horrorstruck disbelief. "Why? They never go out in teams that big."

Axel shrugged. "They didn't split up this time."

As if the odds weren't already stacked against us. My heart sank.

We turned to Jay. His shoulders sagged, and he exhaled. "Finn and Reese don't have enough time for us to wait for the next raid. We stick to the plan."

Jay and Ash each scooped one of the boys into their arms. Neither Finn nor Reese so much as groaned or fluttered an eyelid—not a good sign. I wished they'd ramble codes again.

RC, Kit, and I faced Jay, Ash, and Axel. For a moment, the two groups held eye contact. Ash stroked Finn's cheek. "We can't leave them alone."

"We have to," I said. "That's the only way it'll work."

RC reached into his pouch and drew the silver disk, which he pushed into Finn's limp hand. He had to fold the boy's fingers around it. "So they know we didn't . . ." he began, but his voice caught in his throat. He bowed his head.

Jay nodded his approval. Kit shifted forms in a swirl of black smoke and scampered away from our feet. As if we could outrun the pain of losing our lab-brothers, RC and I dashed after her, feeding off the adrenaline to give us strength and propel us forward. Axel stayed behind with Jay and Ash; he'd meet us after the other four had arrived safely at the Dome.

Up ahead, Kit scurried out of sight. RC and I kept low, darting through the shadows. The plan was imprecise but simple—Jay and Ash were taking Finn and Reese to the edge of the Dome, where they'd leave the twins for the raid team to find. Axel would protect them en route.

RC, Kit, and I were to locate the humans and tail them. Jay and Axel would rendezvous with us for the attempt on Vivian while Ash stayed near the twins to protect them until the last possible second.

RC slowed and raised a finger to his lips. A white cat was sitting in the middle of the road ahead of us. I nodded and followed RC through an open doorway as we adjusted our course to skirt the ghosts in our path. Once we were clear, we took off again, dashing silently through the twilight.

We sprinted on, stopping only once when RC succumbed to a Spasm. His terrible screams haunted the night. I dragged him into the debris and then knelt to smother his screams with my palm. He thrashed in my grip, unaware I was even there.

Upon hearing his cries, Kit reappeared, slinking around the corner with her ears pinned and her tail drooping. She sat down on her haunches and watched somberly until RC was able to stagger to his feet, and then we were running again, chasing the black-and-white kitten. In front of us, figures moved in the fading light.

I skidded to a halt, reaching out to seize RC's cloak as he ran past me. He stopped, and I pointed to the street ahead, where a group of people trekked perpendicular to us, guns in hand. We detoured down a side street, now parallel to the raid team. Kit continued on ahead to trail them at a closer distance.

We'd never dared to venture this close to the raid team before, and watching them turned me cold with fear knowing these humans were armed with weapons specifically designed to injure or kill creatures like me. And we were about to leave our lab-brothers with these same heartless people who let *Them* take me, a half-human, away to be tortured. Why wouldn't they do the same to two pureblood ghosts?

Vivian, I reminded myself. *They'll save one of their own.*

I sullenly predicted, "The others should be at the Dome by now."

RC nodded. We followed the raid team, maintaining a safe distance downwind in the shadows of the early night. A gray cat stayed near us, a calico slinking around the corner farther ahead, no doubt part of Kit's scouting array.

Leading the humans was a furry creature slinking along on four massive paws, nose to the ground. I recognized Madison at the front of the group behind the werewolf, her apprentice predictably by her side. Seeing them in the flesh made my heart fly. I had a flash of a memory, a quick image of Madison facing me with hatred in her eyes as I stared into the depths of her ectogun. She'd hunted Phantom then, and she'll hunt me now, especially after I've stolen her daughter.

Some things never change, I thought bitterly.

Our target trailed on the right flank of the team near the front. Somehow we'd have to isolate Vivian, which wouldn't be easy. My eyes were fixed on her slim figure in the deepening dusk, and my heart fluttered at the prospect of seeing her again when I'd been sure I never would. I remembered those green eyes of hers staring at me on Lastday when the doors closed. What I couldn't remember was her voice, and knowing I might have another chance to hear it was more than I could have ever asked for.

My eyes flicked up to the silhouette standing on the roof above the raid team. I pointed up at Axel, and RC inclined his head. It was time.

The raid team moved slowly, relying on the poor light to mask themselves. Each raider had a weapon drawn, safety released, finger on the trigger. Nighttime raids were always the most stressful; although the raiders could hide in the darkness, they couldn't see their enemies who lurked in the same shadows. A flash of glowing eyes would give them only seconds to react.

Vivian licked her lips. Everyone was on edge, and the nervous energy was contagious. She couldn't shake the crawling sensation that she was being watched. But every time she turned, no one was there.

City Hall was far behind them. The danger increased with each step farther away from the entoplasm shield, and morale was already low. The raid earlier that morning hadn't gone well. The blue and green teams had rendezvoused at the drop site according to plan, but halfway through loading the truck, they came under heavy fire, forcing a retreat. They'd not only lost the supplies and several raiders, but also the truck.

This mission was to retrieve the truck and restock, but something felt wrong, although Vivian couldn't put her finger on *what* exactly. She was sure the supplies were long gone, and more than likely, there was a trap waiting for them at the truck. This was a suicide mission.

Ahead of her, Trey pivoted and discharged his weapon at a pile of crates, sending a green explosion of wood flying in every direction.

"Trey!" her mom hissed, throwing up her arm to deflect the shrapnel away from her face. Immediately, every ectogun was trained at the crates. A black-and-white kitten scampered into the shadows near the blast.

The nose of Trey's weapon tilted downward. He swallowed, staring at where the tail had disappeared. "I saw something move."

"Believe it or not, I don't think that cat is much of a threat."

The wolf, who had stopped at the sound of the blast, huffed and turned away, his nose to the ground again. Madison sighed and led the group after Wes. "You have to have a clear head," she lectured as her apprentice trotted to her side.

"I know."

"If you don't take one of us down with friendly fire, the very least you'll do is attract enemies to our position."

"I'm sorry."

Vivian exhaled and pressed her hand over her hammering heart. "Hey," she murmured, seizing Trey's shoulder. He lagged so they were abreast. "Do you feel like we're being watched, or is that just me?"

Trey nodded. "Yeah," he agreed, skimming the deepening shadows. "I've been feeling jumpy ever since we left."

Vivian froze at a sound nearby. She whirled and pointed her weapon into the darkness. The man behind almost ran into her, and Trey halted. "What?" he asked, stopping beside her. He swept his ectogun in front of him with a level of expertness that made her feel a little safer having him at her side. She remained motionless. She could have sworn she saw a flash—maybe a glowing eye?

But nothing was there now . . . or was something invisible? Vivian pried her left hand off the ectogun so she could fumble for a pair of glasses in a pouch on her belt while trying to hold the weapon steady in her right hand. She slipped the temples over her ears. Through the lenses, her vision shifted to infrared.

She aimed at the blur of movement, but the ghost who had been crouched against the wall had already disappeared through the brick.

Vivian lowered her ectogun and pulled the glasses away from her eyes. Trey asked, "Was anything there?"

She hesitated, then glanced away when she answered, "No."

"That was way too close," Jay muttered under his breath.

We were on a rooftop overlooking the events unfolding below. From here we could see the smoking pile of wood where Kit had nearly been shot. We could see the shadowy alcove where RC had been forced to use his precious reserves to become invisible, then intangible to escape Vivian's sharp eyes. And we could see the procession of armed humans making their way through the alley, led by the giant werewolf.

Axel crouched at the edge of the roof like a predator waiting to pounce on unsuspecting prey. Actually, that was a chillingly accurate comparison.

This plan was starting to seem like a bad idea. Who was I to think we could go up against the armed raid team without our full powers? Was it cockiness or desperation that made me believe this was even feasible when the idea first took root? Now I grappled with the inevitability that all we'd accomplish was losing someone else right before the twins faded from us forever.

I muttered, "Maybe we should fall back and try again during the next raid after we've had more time to plan this through."

Jay ran his fingers through his hair. "We don't have that kind of time. What do you think, Ax?"

Axel tilted his head, studying the humans far below. "I think it'd be fun to go hunting," he murmured, more to himself than Jay. A tiny, longing smile made an appearance. "And I think I'd be really good at it."

"No hunting," Jay said firmly.

"Mmm, I know," Axel lamented, though he ran his tongue over his fangs while eying the raid team like a delicacy.

I seethed, "Would you focus, please?" I left it at that, although I would have liked to admonish him for taking this so lightly. Didn't he realize how important this was, how easily it could go wrong, how we were going to lose at least two lab-siblings if we didn't pull off a nearly flawless abduction?

Axel shrugged and muttered, "What? Jay asked what I was thinking."

Jay apparently had opted to ignore Axel at this point. "One opening. That's all RC needs."

"He could eclipse her," I said. "I know I vetoed that idea before, but—"

"It's too late. We're not changing the plan now."

I bowed my head. Eclipsing was a basic power all ghosts had because it was tied to intangibility, and while it wasn't a terribly draining power, it was tricky, one I'd used only once and avoided ever since. In theory, all you had to do was become intangible and step into someone else's body to take control. Eclipsing a ghost was risky because if the host was stronger than the eclipser, he could overpower and expel the intruder. Eclipsing a human, in comparison, was easy. They couldn't fight back.

The problem was, our power manifested in our glowing eyes. If RC eclipsed Vivian, her eyes would glow violet as long as he was in her body. Surrounded by a group of armed raiders headed by a ghost hunter and a werewolf, there was no way an eclipser would go unnoticed, and RC would find himself in serious trouble if he couldn't make a quick getaway. He wouldn't be able to use any of his abilities while in a human's body.

Still, as risky as it was, the way things were going now, it might be simpler for him to turn invisible, sneak up behind Vivian, become intangible, eclipse her, and run like hell. He didn't have those power reserves, though, not with that neutralizer still attached to his arm. Invisibility and intangibility used at the same time would drain someone at full power.

Jay thought aloud, "We just need a diversion so RC can make his move."

My courage was buckling. I wanted to retreat before it was too late, even though I knew any delay would cost Finn and Reese. "How are we going to do that?"

Axel turned his head to glance slyly at us. "Don't gotta," he said, nodding down. "A diversion just showed up for us."

Shouts came from behind, and the raiders whirled to defend themselves when a group of ghosts appeared out of nowhere, blocking the way they'd just come. There were no peace negotiations, no exchanging of words. Both sides opened fire. Glowing orbs of ectoplasm flew through the air from the hands of the ghosts and the barrels of the humans' weapons.

Madison knelt between her daughter and apprentice, closing one eye to focus on her target when she pulled the trigger. The shot would have been dead-on if the ghost hadn't raised a shield at the last possible moment to deflect it. More ghosts, drawn to the sounds of the battle, were appearing through the walls.

Madison's hair blew into her face as a breeze swept over her from behind. The light from the moon was extinguished in shadow; she gazed up to see the underbelly of the massive wolf as he vaulted over the knot of humans and, snarling, dashed boldly into the group of attacking ghosts. A blast of red ectoplasm struck Trey in the shoulder, spinning him around from the force. Vivian crawled forward until she was leaning over him, ectogun level, though she didn't shoot.

Madison found Emerton on the flank. "Chief, we need a route!" she called as she removed a silver canister from her pack and pulled out the pin with her teeth, then tossed it over the heads of the raid team. Smoke erupted from the cylinder, engulfing the ghosts.

"Here!" Emerton called as he threw open a door and started ushering raiders inside.

"Five o'clock!" Madison shouted over the coughing as enemies fell in a cloud of fog. She backed in after the raiders, still firing at the shadows staggering in the smoke.

"Get up," Viv urged Trey. She holstered her ectogun and threw his arm over her shoulder. Madison paused in front of them as a shield.

Trey groaned but leaned into Vivian, using her strength to rise. She guided him to the door.

Madison followed them in and slammed the door shut behind her. Compared to the chaos from which they'd just escaped, the old Kuhns Theater was muted and quiet. Madison breathlessly issued orders to her team: "Chase, Val, bar the door. Christene, I need a lookout at the window. Emerton, watch my six. Ectoguns at the ready. If you see *anything* coming through the wall, open fire; don't wait for my order. Understand?"

Her raiders nodded as a woman and a teenage boy shoved an arcade game in front of the door. Emerton stood at Madison's back with his ectogun aimed into the shadowy depths of the building while she surveyed the other raiders.

Casualties seemed to be minimal. Johanna had minor ectoplasm burns on her face. Dani was inspecting her torn jacket, but she herself didn't seem to be harmed. Trey was shaken and pale, but at least he was on his feet with Vivian's help. Madison yanked down the fabric of his shirt and ran her fingers gingerly over the discoloring skin. He gasped at her touch.

She released her apprentice. "Doc'll have to examine it when we get back; there's nothing we can do here." She did a quick head count before she surveyed the building. Broken-down arcade games and empty glass cases stripped of overpriced candy bars lay buried in veils of cobwebs. Velvet-coated stanchions and black posts had failed to corral the onslaught of sudden visitors, and most had been toppled and trampled on the floor.

"We need to move before they regroup," announced Madison. Wes let out a low whine. He was hunkered low, tail curled between his legs. "What's wrong?"

He growled as he morphed into partial limbo, still so much more wolf than man that his words were garbled when he rasped, "I don't know." His eyes darted. "I smell something. I don't know what it is, but I have a bad feeling in my gut. I feel like we're in danger."

The raiders gripped their weapons tighter and turned in circles as if afraid of unseen monsters pouncing while their backs were turned. Vivian stepped closer to Madison, who skimmed the room and saw nothing out of the ordinary, but the contagious lack of morale in her team sparked her irritation at the culprit. She snapped, "Of course we're in danger, Wes. We're always in danger when we leave City Hall."

"This is different," he whimpered just before the transformation back into a wolf completed. He bowed his head like a dog expecting a beating.

Chase asked, "Should we go back?"

"No," Madison asserted. "Wes, as much as I respect your instincts, we've come too far to turn back now on nothing more than a gut feeling. We're moving forward. Take point." She called over her shoulder, "Green team, up front. Blue, on six. We're taking a detour."

Wes padded forward in the lead, his tail still curled between his legs. Trey was unsteady, but he caught up to Madison as she passed the deserted ticket podium. She glanced at him as he fell into step beside her. "Can you still shoot?" He nodded grimly. She sighed. "Wes's instincts haven't steered us wrong before. What do you think? Should we head back to City Hall and give it another try tomorrow?"

They passed through the doorway into the aisle. The dust was thick here, coating the cloth seats and filthy carpet. Madison coughed as they trod down the aisle toward the stage, passing rows upon rows of empty theater chairs. There was still a faint scent of buttered popcorn beneath the heaviness of the dust, and her boots peeled off the sticky floor with each step.

Trey shook his head. "No. We have a mission. We shouldn't turn back just because he smells something he doesn't recognize."

"I agree, but . . . I've had a bad feeling too. I know I'm not the only one. Everybody's jumpier than usual. There's a strange feeling in the air."

Trey made the mistake of shrugging and then scrunching his face in a painful grimace. He opened his mouth to answer, but he was cut off by an ear-shattering scream of panic.

"*MOM!*"

Madison whirled to find Vivian struggling in the air. Raiders backed away from her, watching in shock as enchanted ropes slithered up Vivian's torso like serpents. Wes snarled, but he was as unsure as everyone else; his glowing yellow eyes skipped over the abandoned theater in search of an unseen enemy. Trey raised his weapon.

"No!" Madison pushed his ectogun down. "You'll shoot Viv!"

"Help me!" her daughter cried again.

The ropes went taut, yanking Vivian's limbs close to her body and stopping her struggles.

Madison set her infrared glasses over her eyes. They should have allowed her to find the invisible ghost attacking her daughter, but . . . nothing.

"Mom—!" The cry was cut short as a blindfold and gag encircled Vivian's head. Where was the ghost? It had to be there, invisible, but the infrared wasn't detecting it!

There! A hand grabbed Vivian's ankle from the floor. Madison aimed, but just as her finger touched the trigger, the ectogun flew from her hand and clattered between the seats. Her daughter was sinking through the floor.

"*Viv!*" Madison made a wild leap. Her hands missed Vivian's hair by inches as she landed hard on her stomach. Her daughter was gone; she'd disappeared straight through the floor. Madison slammed her fist against the stained carpet. "Stairs," she cried in a panic, rising, her frantic gaze searching. "We have to get down there!"

Wes had already bounded up onto the stage and vanished around the curtain. "Wes!" Madison called. She sprinted after him, setting her hands on the stage and vaulting up in pursuit. The loud *crash* of a door slamming open sent her heart into her throat. She shoved the heavy curtain aside and found a doorway leading down into the dark. Blind, one hand gripping the railing and the other fumbling for the flashlight in her belt, she made her way down the stairs, raiders on her heels.

"Wes?" she called. A beam clicked on behind her, and then she gripped her own flashlight and turned the beam down to the bottom. "Vivian?"

Madison reached the end of the stairs. Her beam skipped over long-forgotten props of wooden trees, city skylines, and country fences, the paint faded and peeling beneath shrouds of cobwebs. Rows of clothing racks housed costumes ranging from Victorian gowns to gaudy circus outfits. Lighting equipment, obsolete soundboards, brooms and buckets—her light danced over the graveyard of lost theater lore, more lights joining hers in a mesh of disorienting beams in the dark . . .

Until Madison's light froze on a still, naked figure lying on the floor. The other beams gravitated toward hers, illuminating the body. Voices whispered behind her, but she couldn't hear the words over the hammering of her heart. Madison rushed to the naked figure.

"Wes?" she called as she dropped to her knees and shook his shoulder. He groaned, his eyes flickering open and fixating on her face. "Cooper, what happened? Where's my daughter?"

"I don't know," he groaned. "I was hit from behind, and Vivian . . .

Vivian . . . I don't know where she is. I don't know what hit me."

The werewolf grimaced and tried to change back. Fur sprouted from his skin and his face lengthened into a snout, but he couldn't change any further than limbo, and he reverted back to his naked human form again.

"Madison?" Trey asked uncertainly.

She leapt to her feet. "Somebody help Wes up and let's go!" she shouted, shoving her way through the crowd and dashing up the stairs.

Trey was on her heels instantly. "Where?" he asked. The others were right behind as they burst through the door and made a direct course for City Hall. Madison's footsteps pounded on the pavement of the empty street, and although she knew she was in plain sight for an enemy to spot, she was too distraught to care. She was putting her whole team at risk, but they had chosen to follow her into the open.

"Back to get more volunteers and weapons to hunt down whatever beast kidnapped my daughter!" She wove between the dead cars on Main Street, sliding across the hood of the last one to save the extra second it would have taken to go around. Her chest was tight with worry and grief, too tight; she was suffocating. Her vision was swimming. She'd lost her husband and one child, now her daughter? *Never*.

She had to beat them to the Rip. The only use a ghost had for a live human was to sell in the slave trade. If Vivian was taken into the Ghost Realm, she'd be gone for good.

Madison's gaze was on City Hall's doors when she noticed two small figures lying on the ground outside the shield. She stopped short. Trey slammed into her; other raiders managed to stop or alter their course just in time to avoid the collision.

Trey was saying something, probably apologizing, but Madison couldn't hear him. Blood pounded through her ears. Everything else was muted, as if she were underwater. She bent forward. The figures were children—two of them, unconscious at her feet. They were sickly thin and at first glance appeared to be corpses. She didn't recognize them, and after being trapped inside City Hall for a year and a half, she would have known if they were from Phantom Heights.

She was too flustered to process this discovery. Children? Where did they come from? If they were human, how did they get here?

If they were human . . .

What if they weren't?

A crumpled piece of paper was tucked under one kid's hand. She pried the note free. An icy chill swept over her body as her heart stopped, freezing time with it.

If thay di, so dos Vivian

Madison's jaw clenched. Her whole body started to quake.

"What is it?" Trey was asking, but his voice sounded distant, as if he were speaking to her from the end of a long tunnel. She couldn't breathe. Was this really happening? She stared at the kids lying at her feet, trying desperately to comprehend.

"Madison—"

"Shut up, Trey, just for two seconds, would you?" Trey blinked and stepped back in shock. Madison knelt down; she could apologize later.

One close look at the kids, and the blood left her head so quickly she nearly fainted. The boys were identical twins with brown hair. Both wore dirty gray sweatpants and light gray T-shirts with a symbol on the fronts—*α*.

Madison was too afraid to check their arms because she knew what she would find.

A1 and A2.

<hr>

RC leaned against the wall, panting. Moving his right arm so much had caused the jagged pieces of his neutralizer to shift, and now his arm was bleeding. His face was pale beneath jewels of sweat, his left eye as dim as the rest of ours now. "Almost burned out," he whispered as he swiped the back of his hand across the stream of blood trickling from one nostril.

His voice was far away. I stared at the girl sitting at his feet, her arms and legs bound together, her eyes covered by a blindfold, her mouth gagged. She was sobbing quietly. I wanted to touch her shoulder and comfort her, but I was paralyzed, transfixed, unable to process what we'd just done. She was so scared that my touch probably would have done more harm than good, anyway.

Jay, RC, Axel, Kit, Vivian, and I were in a closet, waiting. Kit didn't look much better than RC after using most of her power reserves to phase both him and Vivian through the wall into the basement of the building next door.

Only Vivian's muffled sobs perforated the tense silence until Axel unleashed a heavy sigh and shoved the door so hard it broke free of its hinges and slid across the floor. Our prisoner flinched at the loud sound amplified by echoes. Axel strode out without a look back.

Although he hadn't said a word, his reaction was the cue we'd been waiting for—confirmation the raid team found Finn and Reese. Jay said, "Let's move." He nodded at me and added, "Carry her."

I blinked. "Me?"

"Yes, *you*," he snapped, uncharacteristically short on patience.

He picked up Kit and turned away with RC, leaving me alone with Vivian. I swallowed hard. Vivian's dark hair fell in a tangled curtain over her face. I closed my eyes, remembering the way she'd looked at me on Lastday. That single moment right before the doors closed and sealed me in solitary darkness, her wide eyes gazing at me, drinking in my face one last time, as if she'd somehow known I wouldn't be allowed to return.

I crouched in front of her. My hand drifted toward her, but she seemed forbidden, like a dream that would disintegrate if I touched her, and I hesitated.

Gingerly, as if she were made of glass, I scooped her into my arms. Vivian went rigid and sobbed harder. I frightened her, and that broke my heart. Scaring her wasn't my intention; it was a consequence I'd foolishly overlooked. But I'd come up with this crazy plan, and now I had to commit to the repercussions. I didn't know if my heart was beating too fast or not at all because I couldn't feel it anymore.

I lifted Vivian off the ground.

My prisoner.

— Chapter Twenty-Three —

Cold

If thay di, so dos Vivian

Madison crumpled the note in her fist and pressed the back of her hand to one of the twins' sweltering foreheads. "We need to get them to Doc. Trey, go inside and shut off the shield."

"What?"

Madison raised her head to meet Trey's shocked gaze, her eyes burning with angry tears. "They're ghosts. Kálos. We can't just walk in with them while the shield is up."

"Then *why* are we taking them inside?" he seethed.

Madison held up the note. "Because Viv will die if we don't." Trey clenched and unclenched his fists, his teeth grinding at the prospect of bringing ghosts—*enemies*—into the sanctuary, but he stomped through the shield and up the stairs, then pounded on the door until the bar slid on the other side. Trey stormed into City Hall.

The raiders had gathered in a crescent to surround her, necks craned. Madison lifted one of the twins and cradled him in her arms. He was limp and lightweight—way too light. "Someone pick up the other," she ordered. Emerton obeyed without question. Madison waited, impatience mounting while she stared at the transparent green shield. Finally, it flickered and disappeared.

She hurried up the steps and through the open doors. "Turn it back on, Trey!"

The crowd inside parted, staring at Madison as she strode down the aisle toward the low stage with the boy in her arms. Trey, who was standing in the corner, pulled a lever to reactivate the entoplasm shield. Beneath their feet, the generator returned to life with a sputtering hum

251

in the basement. The green tint from outside cast a sickly light on its prisoners once more.

A thin woman with dark cocoa skin and graying hair pulled back into a bun was arranging two mattresses on the stage. Her name was Dr. Alexandria Crawford, but to everyone in Phantom Heights, she was known simply as Doc.

"Trey says you have some new patients for me?"

Madison lowered the boy onto the mattress; Emerton did the same on her right. Doc knelt down to study the twins.

"What is going on?" Trey demanded. Wordlessly, Madison held out the scrap of paper for him to take. "If they die, so does Vivian," he read aloud.

"We just found A1 and A2," Madison whispered. "And Kovak's runaway lab rats abducted my daughter." She turned to the doctor. "Please tell me these kids will be all right."

Doc leaned back to study a thermometer she'd just removed from A2's mouth. "106.2. If I don't break these fevers, they won't last through the night. Lily?" Doc turned to the man and woman lingering nearby waiting for orders. Lily Lisle and Shay Barr were the only two nurses left from Doc's original staff. "Bring up the hospital equipment from the basement. They need IVs. Shay, I need you to get cold compresses from the freezer."

Her nurses hurried to complete their tasks. Doc began to remove the twins' filthy shirts, which persistently clung to their damp, mud-scabbed skin. "Looks like they've been through hell and back," she said.

Trey muttered, "I thought Agent Kovak said they're ten."

"They're unhealthily small for their ages." Doc pushed open an eye and shined her light into it. "No response," she muttered. She pried open the boy's mouth and shined her light inside to view his throat.

Lily was trying to insert a catheter for an IV into the back of his hand. "They're too dehydrated," she said, her normally cheery voice edged with frustration after another failed attempt. "I can't find the vein."

"I'll do it," said Doc. "Put the compresses under their armpits, behind their necks, and on their foreheads." She expertly inserted the catheter and taped it down, then moved aside so Shay could connect it to the end of a clear tube feeding into the fluid bag while she tried to find the vein on the boy's brother.

In a trance, Madison watched the doctor and nurses work over their new patients.

If they die, so does Vivian.

No. She couldn't lose her daughter too. Not after losing her son just a couple of short years ago, and her husband before that. She would be alone in the world, and she wouldn't be able to bear it.

"Madison?"

Her eyes narrowed. She would kill the Alpha ghosts. She would hunt them down and rescue her daughter, then kill them in the slowest, most painful way possible. And then she'd deliver their bodies to Agent Kovak to dissect. They had no idea what a terrible enemy they'd just made. They would regret crossing her; she'd make sure of it.

"Madison?"

A gentle hand on her shoulder brought her back to reality. Trey was standing in front of her. "You okay?"

Madison ran her hands through her hair. "They have my daughter," she whispered. "I don't know what to do." She was no stranger to this cold, helpless feeling. The last time she'd been trapped in it, Phantom Heights had fallen, and she had watched, lost, letting it happen. It had taken her too long to pull herself together then. The déjà vu made her shudder. "I don't know what to do." Had she already said that?

Her apprentice patted her arm in sympathy. "We'll get her back."

Madison noticed the way he held one arm stiffly at his side. "You're hurt."

"I'm okay." He gazed at the two young fugitives. "Viv thought we were being followed." He swore softly. "Why didn't I stay right beside her?"

Madison squeezed her eyes shut. "I should have been able to save her," she whispered, her voice catching.

Trey shifted, as if considering embracing her, but he refrained. A much less gentle hand latched onto Madison's shoulder and spun her around to face the wrath of a slim, raven-haired woman. "Have you lost your mind?"

Madison shoved her away. "Back off, Holly."

"You brought *ghosts* inside the shield!"

"I didn't have a choice. They have Vivian."

"And that justifies putting the rest of us in danger?"

"I have to rescue her."

"It's too late. She's probably already dead." Madison winced, and Holly continued, "There's no point in even trying. We don't do hostage negotiations, remember? I'm sorry for your loss, but I'm not going stand by and let you drive us all to ruin trying to save a dead girl."

In one fluid move, Madison had the end of an ectogun resting between the councilwoman's eyes. "I haven't lost her yet, and don't think I won't shoot you."

Holly froze, her hand still outstretched for the phone in Madison's belt. She straightened. "You aren't fit to lead right now."

"I know what I'm doing. Would you let these kids die?"

"These 'kids' aren't kids, Madison. You're talking about them as if they were human. Why can't you see them for what they really are?"

Madison stepped closer to Holly until their faces were inches apart. "I know exactly what they are. If we call Kovak, it will be on *my* terms."

Trey backed up a step. Holly, unfazed by Madison's fury, met her gaze. "I see," she said icily. "So your daughter is the only life worth saving, is that it? Anyone else is just a casualty?"

"I care about every single life that was lost."

Holly scoffed in her face. "That I find hard to believe. Maybe you've forgotten you were a ghost hunter before you were a mother."

"I haven't forgotten *anything*, including my morals."

"Your *morals*?" Holly seethed in a low-volume hiss. She pointed at the twins. "If you don't hand them over to the Agents, you might be the reason Kovak can't finish his weapon in time. You're potentially condemning millions of people to death or slavery, all to save *one* person. You're telling me that's in line with your morals?"

Madison snatched the note back. "If our roles were switched—if it were *your* daughter's life at stake instead—what you would do, Holly? Would you sacrifice her?" She holstered the ectogun at her hip.

Holly didn't answer the question. Under her breath, she muttered, "A demon will still grow up to be a demon."

"You want to kill two helpless kids, Holly?" Madison called, purposely drawing attention.

She made a grand show of drawing her Glock and offering it to Holly, whose eyes darted over the onlookers. "That's not what I said."

"But you want to let them die, right?"

"Do you think saving them now will mean they'll show mercy on us when they're older and we're at war with their kind?" Madison waved the gun in a wordless taunt. Holly's whole body started to quiver with rage. "But you're the *expert*, right, Madison? You know everything. Have you even seen their homeland? What kind of world they come from?"

"Have *you*?"

Holly simmered at her.

"Mom?"

Madison's heart leapt. She and Holly both turned toward the voice. When Madison realized the speaker was Holly's daughter, not hers, a rush of hot tears blurred her vision. Shannon's eyes flicked from Madison's face to her gun, then to her mom.

Holly looked away from her daughter's gaze and directed her wintry glare onto the twins instead. "Do what you want. They'll be dead by morning anyway." She stormed away. Shannon cast an apologetic look at Madison and followed her mom. Hand shaking, Madison returned the gun to its holster.

Trey solemnly touched the back of her wrist in silent support.

Shay muttered, "They still aren't responding, Doc."

"Is it contagious?" asked Madison. Her concern was not for A1 and A2, but for the townspeople who would be devastated by a viral outbreak.

"Believe it or not, I think we're dealing with a common cold," said Doc.

Madison stared at the half-dead figures. "That is *not* a common cold."

"Do you remember what the Agents said? These kids were born in a sterilized lab. Infants have antibodies passed down from their mother, but if she also lived in such a clean environment for most of her life and then they spent ten years without exposure to germs, I can't imagine their immune systems have many, if *any* antibodies to defend them. I think their bodies don't know how to fight this infection, so their fevers keep rising. Pneumonia is probably settling in. They're dangerously dehydrated and literally burning up."

"You have to save them."

Her voice level and calm, Doc said, "I am doing everything I possibly can, given the resources and circumstances. Right now, I'm just trying to get them stabilized. That's our first step."

"Hey," Trey interrupted, "what's that?" He knelt and pried a silver object from the boy's hand, then took a step back to study his discovery, flipping it over and frowning. "It's some kind of disk."

Madison held out her hand. As he passed it to her, he asked, "Do you plan to contact the Agents?"

Madison glared at the boys barely clinging to life. She glanced at the odd silver disk in one hand, the threatening note in the other. Holly's words echoed through her mind, but she answered, "Not yet."

Hassing stood before Azar, his gaze on the Warden's feet. "So," Azar said, unspeakable threats lingering beneath the surface, "two kálos without their powers bested you, your lieutenant, and two of your top officers."

The captain swallowed and shifted. "I underestimated them."

"Clearly."

Hassing remained silent, accepting the criticism. The Warden, still far too calm, inquired, "Any updates on Officer Rendlen's condition?"

"The Healer had to reconstruct his nose. He's still in recovery."

"I want to speak with him as soon as Leah releases him."

"Yes, sir."

Azar exhaled slowly. "I don't like being disappointed." Hassing cringed, still unable to lift his gaze to meet Azar's condemnation. "However . . . your failure might not have been a total loss. Let's count it as an intelligence expedition. What can you tell me about them?"

Hassing looked up in shock. Azar was giving him another chance?

Unfortunately, he didn't have an answer. "Well . . . ah, not much, sir. I couldn't sense the boy's presence at all, not even when he was a few feet away from me. The woman I did sense about three seconds before she knocked me into tomorrow."

"And Lieutenant Cisco was unable to identify their Divinities?"

"That's correct, sir. The boy's eyes didn't glow at all, which makes me—uh, *us*, I mean—suspect technological interference from the Agents. Cisco couldn't sense their power levels, Divinities . . . nothing. If they hadn't been dressed the way they were, we would have mistaken them for humans."

"What about the prisoners themselves? Are they old?"

"They were dressed in full cloaks. Hooded. I didn't get a good look."

"Surely you noticed *something*. You keep saying *boy*. How young was he?"

"Young enough to have no facial hair."

Azar started a slow pace in front of the window, his body a silhouette before the gold-and-orange sky. "Probably hasn't reached his second coming of age. Anything else useful?"

"They're fast," Hassing muttered, still amazed by how effortlessly his quarry had dashed through the shadows. "I was expecting weak prisoners."

"Can you confirm all of them are in Phantom Heights?"

"No. Only three were confirmed, but it's reasonable to assume the others are there as well."

"In that case, Rayven can return. I want you to go after the Alpha fugitives again. *Carefully*. If we can forge an alliance, I want to do so. No use sending Cisco again if his Divinity won't work on them; he'll manage the forces here in Avilésor while you head the team in Cröendor. How much time do you need to select your Shadow Guards?"

Hassing didn't even need to think about his answer. "The recovery team under the command of Officer Jana."

"Where is she now?"

"To my knowledge, she's stationed up north near Lake Mulzon. Salek, if I'm not mistaken."

Azar nodded. "Send for her team. All resources are at your disposal."

"And Titon?" Hassing asked hopefully. His prey was fast; having a mount to ride them down would give him a better chance.

"Except that one. Valdenars don't exist in Cröendor. I still want you to keep this as quiet as possible, and Titon will draw attention from both humans and kálos. Now, debrief Cisco, contact Officer Jana, and get to work."

"Thank you, sir." Hassing bowed as he backed away.

As he turned to walk out, Azar called, "Hassing?"

The captain licked his lips and pivoted.

"Don't fail me again."

— Chapter Twenty-Four —
Not Human

Madison woke with a start. Dawn had softened the light of the ento-plasm shield so it wasn't as cold and eerie on the skeletal faces of its prisoners. She blinked a few times, disoriented. She'd fallen asleep?

She scrambled to her feet. Doc, who was kneeling next to two piles of blankets, rose when she saw Madison watching.

Madison swallowed, staring at the bundles. "Is—are they . . . ?"

Doc backed away. An invisible tether attached Madison's unblink-ing eyes to the bundles. Were they moving? Her legs felt like lead, but she somehow forced them to move forward in a trance. *Please, let them be alive, let them be breathing, please let them be alive . . .*

She ascended the terraces and looked down upon the two boys. Doc had removed the cold compresses sometime in the night. The twins' eyes were closed, skin ashen. She couldn't see a telltale rise and fall of their chests.

No . . .

The world tilted. Madison fell hard on her knees. Her chest con-stricted with grief because their deaths meant her daughter was prob-ably lying dead in the middle of a street with her throat slashed open. Tears spilled and dripped off her chin. Hands shaking, she brushed the damp hair from the forehead of A1.

His brow furrowed at her touch.

Madison's eyes grew wide. "Hey there," she cooed, running her thumb along the boy's cheekbone. His eyelids fluttered, opening just enough to reveal slivers of his cobalt irises beneath the dark lashes. Hope flooding through her, she tilted his chin up.

"I don't think he sees you," said Doc. She stifled a yawn. "Fevers finally broke at about three in the morning. They're reacting to touch, but their eyes aren't focusing yet, and they haven't spoken."

Madison stroked his cheek with a mother's soft touch. His eyes closed again as the weight of his head settled into her hand. "He's so weak."

"Yes. Even if they weren't so sick, they're severely malnourished and underdeveloped. I have to say, I'm shocked by their poor condition. I know the Agents said their fugitives from Project Alpha are vicious killers, but if the others are in as bad of shape as these two, I can't imagine they're half as threatening as Kovak would like us to believe."

"They managed to sneak past a werewolf, two ghost hunters, and the entire armed raid team to kidnap my daughter. Obviously, the others are more lethal than the twins."

Madison bit her lip, worry blossoming at the thought of what those killers might be doing to Vivian. If they hadn't already slit her throat, they could be torturing her, defiling her . . . Madison couldn't bear the dark images being born in her mind. "So, they're going to live?"

Doc rubbed her eyes. "Their chances have increased. I have to keep the fevers down and get them rehydrated. There's definitely fluid in their lungs. Without bloodwork or a chest X-ray, I can't give you an official diagnosis, but my bet is pneumonia. I have them on antibiotics." She set a comforting hand on Madison's shoulder. "They've already shown improvement. It's a good sign."

Madison slid her hand out from beneath A1's cheek so she could sit back on her heels. When she raised her head, fierce determination had charged her right down to her cells. "Then that means I'm free to rescue my daughter."

Doc's grip on her shoulder tightened. "I don't think that's a good idea. The Alpha ghosts set the rules, and we have to play by them. For now, anyway." Madison was silent, letting the doctor's words sink in. Doc knelt beside her newest patients again. "You know, if I didn't know any better, I'd think these kids were human."

"They're not human," Madison said dryly.

"Will you please look at their eyes and tell me what you think?"

"I *hunt* ghosts. I don't give them medical attention."

Doc fixed her with a steady stare and reminded, "Vivian's well-being depends on theirs."

Madison sighed in resignation. She tilted A1's face and gently lifted an eyelid. "You're right. His eyes are dull." She refused to say *humanlike*, but they were. Without prior knowledge, Madison had to agree these ghost kids were indistinguishable from human kids.

She wasn't surprised to hear Wes's voice—of course the nosy werewolf was eavesdropping—explain, "That's not uncommon when a kálos is ill."

Madison said nothing. She didn't even want to look at him right now. He could have saved Vivian, but he'd charged forward without taking stock of his surroundings and let himself get whacked in the head. He'd been the only one to directly confront Vivian's kidnappers, and he'd lost. He'd lost *her*.

She slipped a small scanner out of her weapon belt and waved it over A1's body from head to toe, then scanned A2. Their power reserves registered at less than Level 1. Madison stared at the sleeping twins for a moment more, then rose and returned to her mattress.

Trey, hands thrust deep in his pockets, meandered over and seized the round object by her feet. "I saw you examining this last night. Know what it is yet?"

"It's a metal disk with a hole in the middle. That's it."

Trey scrutinized it. "Why would the Alpha ghosts leave it if that's all it is? Maybe there's a camera in it, and they're watching us."

"There's no camera lens. No switch. No button. No panel, no screws, no nothing." She took the disk and ran her finger along the edge. "The only marking I've found is this slit around the perimeter. I can stick the tip of my knife into it, but the inside feels solid."

Trey took it back, unconvinced. "It doesn't make sense."

"I don't know, Trey. I just don't know. I can't . . . I can't think straight." She gazed through her tears at the sleeping twins, silently despising them for bringing this misfortune.

Vivian sat in the shadows with her knees drawn to her chest and her arms wrapped around her legs. High above her, early morning light was cutting its first rays through a small, grimy window, the height of which led her to believe she was being held underground somewhere in the industrial district. The room had a certain dampness to it—a cold, dirty, abandoned feeling that seeped into her bones and added to her misery. There was another small room with a toilet and sink in it, but the plumbing didn't work. Still, it was better than nothing, although the smell was starting to make her nauseous.

She was alone. Her captors had untied her but left her blindfolded and gagged. Vivian had lain perfectly still long after the door closed and the lock clicked into place. She'd listened to the footsteps above her until the paralyzing terror seeped out of her muscles and she was brave enough to sit up and remove the gag and blindfold.

Her stomach rumbled, but fright churned it with nausea so she wouldn't be able to eat even if there was food. Sometimes she heard screams coming from the floor above, both male and female. One had even sounded like a child. The screams would last for a minute or two before fading to an eerie silence, leaving Vivian to the horrors of her imagination. Were people being tortured up there? Was she next?

Every time she heard a sound, she froze, her heart hammering.

But no one came.

Her mom would find her. Right now, the raid team was probably following Wes, who was tracking Vivian's scent. Imagining the rescue party was a slight comfort. In the meantime, though, the loneliness was unbearable.

Mom will come, she told herself. She closed her eyes, imagining her mom running down the stairs and throwing open the door to rescue her.

Her eyes opened. There *were* approaching footsteps on the stairs. But they were not running eagerly; they were slow and deliberate.

They stopped on the other side of the door. A bolt slid. The knob turned. The rusty hinges creaked as the door opened, and then a shadow slipped inside.

Vivian gulped, watching in a terrified stupor that froze her body again. The figure paused, studying her. The Alpha symbol on the chest of his dark outfit was white and easy to identify in the shadows. A black cloak was clasped around his neck; the hood covered the top half of his face. A silver whistle dangled on his chest.

Vivian had enough experience with ghosts to know his eyes not glowing indicated he had no power right now, just as Agent Kovak had predicted. She tensed as the fugitive approached. That automatic stiffening finally reawakened her muscles to move. As he drew nearer, she crawled backward until her spine hit the wall. He was only a few feet away, within striking distance. She turned her head and held her arm up to shield her face. "P-Please don't hurt me," she begged, trembling. "Please . . ."

Clink.

Vivian remained frozen for a few more seconds before she dared to lower her arm. The ghost was straightening, still staring at her from the shadowy depths of his hood. At his feet were a can of soup and a bowl of water. Vivian gazed at his offering, then peered up at him. He turned without a word and walked away.

Her heart still kicking her ribcage, Vivian stared at the food again. The door creaked. "Thank you," she called.

The ghost froze in the doorway. Slowly, he turned his head to stare at her. He seemed beyond confused that she, a human, had expressed gratitude to him, a ghost. She shifted uncomfortably under his scrutiny, and even though she couldn't see his eyes, her crawling skin could feel their penetrating stare.

He turned away and closed the door behind him, then bolted it. Left alone again to eat her meal, Vivian seized the can and lifted it to her lips. *At least,* she thought as the cold barley soup hit her empty stomach, *they don't plan to starve me to death.*

Although what they wanted with her, she had no idea.

— Chapter Twenty-Five —

Shadow Rider

"Talk some sense into her," Holly demanded.

Mayor Correll shrugged. "It's her call. There's nothing I can do."

"That's funny, I don't remember electing Madison Tarrow as mayor."

Correll stroked his bushy mustache, which was now an obnoxious size on his face after his rapid weight loss coupled with a lack of maintenance. Holly thought it looked like an ugly caterpillar devouring his lip and getting fat before metamorphosis. The patchy beard he'd sprouted below it didn't enhance his appearance. Correll lowered his voice and said, "I'm sorry. All ghost-related issues default to Madison's judgment. You'll have to appeal to her, not me."

"But you have the power to relieve her of duty. Put Chief Emerton in charge."

He shook his head. "I'm sorry."

Holly let her breath out in a huff and turned her back on him.

A group of giggling kids darted in front of her, forcing her to back up a step. Two girls and a boy were running from a boy with a blue bandana tied over his nose and mouth. "You can't escape!" called the bandana boy.

The other three halted and spun to face him, giggling. He dramatically raised his hands and pointed his open palms at the two girls, who both gasped and pretended to freeze. The ringleader then thrust his hand toward the boy, who grunted and fell on his back as if struck down by invisible ectoplasm.

"I am the great and powerful Phantom! Who else dares to challenge me?" cried the masked boy, punching his fist triumphantly into the air.

Holly recognized him. His name was Andy Kaminski. His mother, Nikki, was the secretary for city council. Holly marched forward and seized Andy's arm harder than she intended, pulling him back. "You stop that," she said as she yanked the bandana away. Andy opened his mouth to protest, and she shook him. "I mean it. Go find your mother right now."

The other kids meekly hung their heads, but Andy scowled and jerked his arm free. "What did we do wrong?"

"You . . ." Holly was acutely aware that she was attracting unwanted attention. "You're going to disturb them." She gestured at the twins. Andy, now subdued and remorseful, followed the motion of her hand with his eyes, and then he, too, bowed his head. "You have to be quiet," she scolded. "No more roughhousing."

"Sorry, Mrs. Jennings," he mumbled.

Holly crushed the bandana in her fist and glowered at Andy as he tromped to his mother. Only after the last onlooker averted his eyes did she release a deep breath to calm herself.

She stared at the twins, who, despite her warning to Andy and his rambunctious gang, hadn't stirred. They were so thin, so sickly, so harmless . . . but they weren't. They could be very dangerous. What a pity they hadn't passed away in their sleep; their deaths would have uncomplicated this little situation Holly now found herself in. She started to chew on her fingernail, then abruptly yanked her hand away. It had been years since she'd conquered that nervous habit. Why did these kids hike her anxiety so high?

They might know.

She shook the thought from her head. No, they couldn't . . . Could they?

Of course they might. They were Kovak's pets. Even if he hadn't told them, they were Mind-Readers.

They know . . .

Holly backed away from them. No, there was still a chance—a slim chance, but a chance nonetheless—that these slave kids didn't know about Cato, and she would be damned if they awoke to glean the truth from her mind. If they exposed her, the town would exile her.

She slipped her fingers inside the front of her blouse to feel the warm golden cross on a thin chain above her heart. God hadn't answered her prayers last night. She had begged Him to end the twins' suffering on Earth, both for their sake as well as her own. But it was not His will, so now she prayed, *Father, I humbly seek Your protection and guidance. I—*

"It must be absolutely maddening," a voice hissed in her ear.

Holly jumped. Wesly Cooper was standing behind her shoulder. She clenched her fist around the cross. *Amen.* Voice steeled, she answered, "What, watching Doc waste our resources on a pair of demons who will likely repay the favor by killing us someday?"

The werewolf smirked. "No control. Losing all your authority to Maddie. How does it feel to be powerless, Councilwoman?"

Now that Holly's heart rate was calming, her mind was sharpening. She stared straight ahead, refusing to grace him with even a glance. "You think I've lost all my power? Careful now, Cooper. You're going to get yourself in trouble." She narrowed her eyes and lowered her voice even further. "You're a guard dog, nothing more. If you slip off your leash, you're gone. I'm sure Agent Kovak would be happy to give you a new home."

"Is that really your call now?"

She bristled. Cooper had always kept his head down and his tail between his legs, metaphorically speaking. He'd never outright challenged her before. She seethed, "Would you like to test me?" and walked away before he could call her threat empty. *It wasn't*, she reassured herself. True, the council had been unofficially dissolved, but she was *not* powerless.

City Hall was abuzz with chatter, all revolving around the same topic—Vivian and the Alpha ghosts. People were constantly trying to catch a glimpse of A1 and A2, and Doc had to shoo away curious onlookers who wandered too close. Dissent was rampant in the crowd. Hundreds of humans had been slain; why should the survivors deplete their precious resources to save just one? No one except Holly dared to speak such thoughts near Madison, though.

The ghost hunter was, as Holly had predicted, still pacing back and forth in front of the stage, stealing glances at the blankets where the twins slept. Cooper leaned against the wall, arms folded, eyes following Madison's path. He taunted, "You're going to fall through the floor if you keep that up."

Madison grumbled, "I should be out there looking for her."

Holly rolled her eyes. Cooper yawned and said, "We can't win, Maddie, so we might as well just play along."

"*Madison*, Wes. I hate the name Maddie, and you know it." She sighed, then turned to look Holly in the eye. "Okay. I'm calling the AGC."

Holly lifted her eyebrows. Had she heard correctly?

Doc, who had been sitting on the steps next to Trey, warned, "Think very carefully before you do anything rash."

Cooper peeled himself away from the wall. "You don't think the Alpha ghosts are keeping an eye on us? You turn the twins over and Vivian is dead, you realize that?"

"I disagree," said Holly. "Agent Kovak has resources we don't. He can rescue Vivian. Let him help us."

Thank the Lord the Mind-Readers weren't conscious because in truth, she had no interest in a rescue operation. She reckoned two scenarios were likely. The first and simplest was that Vivian was already dead. If she was truly in the custody of violent killers like Kovak had said, that possibility was probable.

And yet, the more Holly read over the list her daughter had written during Kovak's visit, the more suspicious she became. Holly was more interested in what *wasn't* written, and a lot was missing. Why? How could the Agents possibly expect Madison to catch the Alpha ghosts if she didn't know what she was hunting?

Holly was too afraid to seriously consider the only answer that made any sense. Regardless of whether her worries had merit or were just the tortures of a guilty mind, Holly's only option was to gently tug on Madison's strings and convince her to let Kovak clean up his mess.

And Vivian, if she was still alive and had happened to learn a secret Holly had buried two years ago, would somehow have to be silenced, but Kovak could fix that. He had before.

Her pressure seemed to be working; Madison pulled the phone out of her pocket. Cooper blurted, "Maddie, Kovak already destroyed part of your family. Are you really going to let him destroy the rest of it?"

Madison froze. Holly scowled and said, "Or he might redeem himself."

"Not likely. He's responsible for the death of your son. If you make that call, I guarantee your daughter's blood will be on his hands, too."

Holly clenched her fists, silently cursing the meddling werewolf.

Madison hung her head. She croaked, "I'm out of options." Although Cooper was vehemently shaking his head, she rationalized, "Even if he can't send in an extraction team, he knows his fugitives. We can get advice. He can tell us how to get her back." She pressed her thumb to the first number.

Trey leapt to his feet. "Don't!"

The phone flew from her hand and smashed into the wall. Madison stood in shock, jaw slack as plastic pieces and microchips clattered to the floor in a sudden and eerie quiet so heavy it seemed to have acquired a substance.

She glared at Cooper. "You do that?"

He looked just as surprised as she did. "Huh? No, how could I?"

Madison wheeled to Trey, who shook his head with a puzzled shrug. Behind her apprentice, one of the markers by the whiteboard began to levitate.

Holly gasped and took a step back. Madison drew her ectogun. Trey, who thought she was aiming at him, closed his eyes and flinched. *Shoom!* A blast of green ectoplasm whizzed over his shoulder and struck the marker down.

Trey cracked an eye open, peered at her ectogun, and then turned to stare at the destroyed marker. "What the hell?" he whispered. He stumbled back with a gasp when another marker rose. The cap popped off, and the marker began to write.

Shannon trotted up the steps and seized Holly's hand. "Mom, please get away from the board." She pulled, but Holly held her ground.

"I'm not afraid of them."

"Please. Mom, *please.*"

Holly backed up but stopped before reaching the steps. She pulled her daughter inward and wrapped her arms around her. "What's happening?" Holly demanded.

Madison set the infrared glasses on the bridge of her nose, searching for the wielder. Her eyes continued to dart, unfocused, as if she couldn't locate a target . . . as if the marker were floating of its own accord. The ghost hunter lifted the glasses to stare in horror at the words printed on the board:

Vivian wil sufer sereus conseqenses.

Holly read the sentence three times before she redirected her attention to Madison for a reaction. Trey was aiming all over the place. "Where's the ghost?" he demanded, finding nothing to shoot.

"Not here," Madison murmured. She stepped forward. "We're inside the entoplasm shield. There's . . . no way it could have gotten in." She reached for the floating marker and waved her hand beneath it, then over. Frowning, she seized it in her hand and held it for a few seconds. As soon as she let go, gravity reclaimed it, and it fell with a clatter.

She read the misspelled sentence on the board. Cooper hissed, "I told you they were watching." He eyed the ruined cell phone on the floor and rubbed his head, which no doubt still ached from his last confrontation with the fugitives from Project Alpha.

"The disk," said Trey. "There must be a camera in it."

"No," Madison replied, pulling it out of a slot in her weapon belt. "I've had it in here whenever I'm not tinkering with it." Her eyes were trained on the words on the board, her alarm visibly evolving into hatred as the wrinkles in her forehead deepened. She glanced at the security camera in the far corner of the room. In one move, she leveled her ectogun and fired. The camera exploded in a burst of green light and sparks.

People ducked, covering their heads. Holly instinctively tightened her hold on her daughter, using her own body to shield Shannon as they both sank to the floor in a crouch. "What is wrong with you?" Holly demanded. "Those cameras haven't been turned on in years."

Madison pivoted, firing four more shots clear across the room to destroy the final cameras. City Hall was deathly silent as the pieces of the last camera fell to the floor. Madison holstered her ectogun. "Better safe than sorry."

Holly rose and extricated herself from Shannon's grasp on her arm. She wandered across the stage to the nearest window. It, like all the others, had been covered with boards to protect against non-ectoplasmic projectiles, but the planks were decrepit, and a few were missing. She set her hand on the boards and squinted through the gap. Outside, the green surface of the shield swirled in lazy currents. Beyond the shield's edge, the shops were dark and abandoned.

"I don't see anything," Holly reported.

Madison glared at the sleeping twins. "I hate them. If it weren't for them, Vivian would be safe with us right now."

Quietly, Cooper said, "Maddie? They're just babies, you know. If you look at the average life span of kálos, these kids are very, *very* young." The ghost hunter clenched her jaw and shook her head.

Doc reasoned, "You can't blame them for what the other Alpha ghosts did."

"Yes I can," Madison snapped. "I can blame them for whatever the hell I want." She kicked the marker, and it skittered across the floor and into the corner.

Doc watched Madison cry in frustration. "I want you to see something."

"I'm not in the mood right now."

Doc approached the twins and patiently requested, "Come here, please."

Madison glared at her, then stormed over to the two boys. Holly's curiosity bested her, and she drifted closer too. Shannon took a step to follow, but Holly waved her away. Her daughter lingered, retreating only when Holly gave her a stern look.

Doc pulled back one of the blankets and pointed to A1's hollowed ribs and jutting hip bones. "They haven't eaten in a few days, but this didn't happen over that amount of time. This is long-term starvation."

She indicated the back of A1's hand where the IV was inserted in the middle of a dark bruise. "Their blood isn't clotting properly, plus they have a Vitamin D deficiency, as well as other essential nutrients and minerals."

She lifted A1's limp hand to display the scars circling his wrists. "From being bound and struggling against the restraints," she explained. Holly and Madison had both seen enough, but the doctor continued, "See all these bruises here on the torso? Some of these were made by the accident, I'm sure, but look at these fainter ones. I'd imagine most of them were made by being repeatedly hit and kicked. Here, on his arm, you can see someone grabbed this kid hard enough to leave individual finger marks."

Madison said, "So the Agents were right. The other Alpha ghosts abused the twins."

"Actually, these injuries are too old. I believe it was the Agents who abused these kids. And I'm not done. The twins are so malnourished I have no doubt many of their injuries resulted in fractured bones that never properly healed. It wouldn't surprise me if they're suffering from early arthritis. And look at this."

Doc parted A1's chestnut hair to reveal a hidden scar that curved around his head like a trail through a forest. "He had surgery. Looks to me like a few years ago, the Agents shaved his head, peeled back his scalp, and popped off the top of his skull to take a look at his brain. Now, in my opinion, it's highly doubtful the operation was medically necessary. Both twins had this procedure done, probably more than once."

"What made those marks?" Madison inquired, pointing at a line of five round scars evenly spaced across his forehead an inch below his hairline.

"Put your fingers here. Do you feel the indent?"

Madison nodded. "They drilled into his skull? Why?"

"Sometimes doctors need to make burr holes for medical emergencies to relieve pressure, but these scars form a perfect ring around his head, twelve in all, and both boys have them. This was no medical procedure."

Doc sat back on her heels and gazed sadly at her newest patients. "This isn't how you're supposed to treat children. If a test has to be run on a child, you speak gently and try not to scare him, then reward him afterward. Holding him down and restraining him is the worst way to administer tests. They must have been terrified, and to be honest, I'm concerned about how receptive they'll be to treatment when they wake up."

Holly tried to swallow the lump in her throat but couldn't; it gagged her. She had to turn away. Doc was too busy watching Madison's reaction to notice. "I know you're frustrated about Vivian, but we can't send these kids back to the AGC. They were abused, neglected, starved, beaten, and subjected to painful and unnecessary medical experiments, and their only crime is they aren't human. There has to be a way to rescue your daughter without sacrificing them."

Madison gazed at the unconscious boys. "Still," she choked out, "it's their fault Vivian is in danger now."

"No, it's the fault of the other Alpha ghosts who took her."

"But if they hadn't gotten so sick in the first place . . ." Surely she realized she was being ridiculous, but she needed someone to blame.

Doc countered, "And if the Agents had given the twins proper care, they wouldn't have gotten so sick. If you have to blame someone, blame them."

Madison hung her head. "Kovak is our best shot at getting my daughter back."

"They have a history of betraying us. If we surrender the twins, we have no leverage and Vivian is dead."

Holly said quietly, "It's a calculated risk. He could be your only chance to get her back alive. Don't be rash in your decision."

"He doesn't care about us," Madison whispered. The resignation in her voice was final; any window of opportunity to convince her had passed.

"Besides," Cooper drawled over their shoulders, "I'd rather keep the twins and interrogate them to learn what Kovak is up to. I bet he's got some dark secrets he doesn't want anybody knowing about."

Holly stiffened. When Madison grumbled, "I'm not interested in that," Holly gave her a sidelong glance in relief.

Cooper scowled. "We have a chance to—"

"I *don't care!*" Madison shouted. "Let the ghosts go to war with the Agents; I just want Vivian back!"

"You can't see the bigger picture," he grumbled.

"No, Madison is right. Vivian is our priority right now," said Doc. "I know it seems like our hands are tied, but remember this blackmail scheme works both ways. The Alpha ghosts, for some inexplicable reason, want these kids alive. Since our new friends seem to be keeping an eye on us, my hope is that if we show our patients kindness, they might reciprocate it to Vivian."

Vivian stirred from an uneasy sleep. She froze, listening in horror to the echoing screams of a girl on the floor above her. Who were the Alpha ghosts torturing now?

She wrapped her arms around herself and shivered. Her fingers touched her wrist, but when she remembered her bracelet was gone forever, emptiness solidified into tears.

Finally, the bloodcurdling screams from above subsided.

Vivian's stomach rumbled. She rolled onto her back, staring up at the ceiling and feeling sorry for herself. She couldn't remember the last time she'd been isolated like this, not since privacy became a luxury that ceased to exist when City Hall boarded its windows and permanently activated the entoplasm shield. The voices, the subtle sounds of bodies shifting, the heat, just the *presence* of other beings was a comfort.

Solitary confinement was causing madness to fester. Already, she desperately missed the soothing sound of her mom's voice, and Trey, how he used to sit next to her and twist his Rubik's cube while rambling off new facts he'd learned about the Ghost Realm, stupid stuff like how vampires never aged and couldn't turn into bats, or that imagii were spirits only children could see. To her surprise, Vivian realized she even missed Wes and the puppy whimpers he would make when he fell asleep in his wolf form near the full moon.

With a sigh, Vivian rolled onto her other side, her gaze focusing on a small pile a few inches from her nose. She sat up. Where had these come from? She traced her fingers over the spine of a book, then lifted the novel in wonder, running her thumb over the gold letters of the title, *Shadow Rider*. She hadn't seen this book in years.

Grinning faintly, Vivian set the book in her lap and reached out to touch the corner of her pillow, then the softness of her fleece blanket. A pair of glass eyes watched her, and she picked up the worn teddy bear. "Hello, Tessie," she whispered. She laughed aloud at the familiarity of her forgotten childhood bear. In this miserable, damp place, holding this memory of a happier time brought her peace.

But Tessie had been left in her room at her abandoned house. All of these items had been. How did the Alpha ghosts know where she lived?

Vivian shuddered, unnerved as she touched the book again. Yes, it had been her favorite, but they couldn't have known that . . . Could they?

Something moved near the wall . . . or so she thought. She scanned the gloom for a shadow out of place, skin crawling now that her mind had been infected with the thought of being watched, but her only apparent company was a small, furry creature that scampered along the far wall and vanished into a hole. Rats. *Great.*

Beside the remnants of her past were a bowl of water and a chunk of bread. She set Tessie in her lap and seized the bread, then broke a piece in her fingers as she contemplated. The fact that the Alpha ghosts were showing her kindness must be a good sign, but since she didn't even know why she was here, she couldn't begin to speculate what was happening outside her little prison. Vivian popped a piece of bread into her mouth.

Her chewing slowed. The texture wasn't what she'd expected. The bread was tougher, chewier, and kernels cracked between her molars. She swallowed. This wasn't *real* bread—at least, not the kind from her own Realm.

She settled back against the wall and reached for the book. Printed on the inside front cover in a messy scrawl were the words:

Viv—

Happy 15th birthday. Have an adventure!

— Cato

Vivian gazed at the scrawl for a long time. Her birthday was the fifteenth of May, and it had been an unseasonably warm spring day, most of which she'd spent under a redbud tree by the lake reading this book while nibbling at the half-melted chocolate bar that had accompanied it.

"An adventure," she whispered, then shook her head. "I don't think this is what you had in mind, Cato." Her fingertips traced the faint etches where the ink had stained the paper. Yes, back then, she had wanted an adventure. Now, she wished she could go back to that time, back to when everything was simple and her adventures were sealed away in novels, and all she had to do to escape was close the book.

She touched Cato's words one more time, then flipped through the pages, inhaling the familiar and soothing fragrance of the book. A faded receipt from C-Sully's Café that had served as a bookmark fell from between the pages and fluttered to the filthy floor next to her knee. Tears instantly burned her eyes. The car accident that claimed her dad's life felt so distant, but she still remembered the night before when they had dined in the corner booth of the café as snowflakes danced on the other side of the frosted windows. It was the last time the four of them sat together as a family.

Her isolation enveloped her. She took a deep, calming breath to keep her misery dammed, then shoved the last piece of bread into her mouth and started reading the marked page—the chapter where the heroine was alone and defeated, locked away in the dungeon of a black castle . . .

— Chapter Twenty-Six —

Name

I passed through the thin barrier of the Dome. It was like an illusion—imposing, impressive, but not real. Not to me.

My hood was thrown low over my eyes as I snuck to the edge of City Hall. The black-and-white kitten leapt onto the windowsill, and I pressed a finger to my lips. Kit bobbed her head in understanding.

I peered through a gap between the weathered boards. The room didn't trigger any memories. It consisted of two levels, the overhang of a balcony jutting around three of the walls. The survivors had set up camp, and most of them were congregated in small groups around blankets and mattresses. The cold green light from the Dome made them appear . . . ghostly. As if they were fading.

I should have recognized most of these people, but their faces lacked familiarity, and the longer I lingered inside the Dome, the more danger I was in. If Madison caught me, she'd skin me alive for stealing her beloved daughter.

I pressed my fist to my mouth and clenched my throat to contain a cough scratching to escape. My gaze skipped to the far end of the room where three terraces rose up to a short stage and a dark-skinned lady knelt beside two piles of blankets. I had to quietly clear my throat before I was able to whisper, "I can't see them." Kit flicked her ears and tilted her head up at me. "Let's see if we can get a better view."

She hopped down and trotted after me on silent paws. We crept along the edge of the building, keeping low to prevent our shadows from passing over the boarded windows.

Kit was the first to reach the last window, and she jumped onto the sill. A few planks had fallen away throughout the course of City Hall's beatings. I didn't want to risk anyone glancing at the window and seeing my face between the boards, so I stayed low and peered through the quarter-inch gap between the lower planks that were still clinging to the frame on rusted nails. Now we were positioned right next to the low stage.

Finn and Reese slumbered beneath the blankets. Their faces were deathly white, dark circles hollowing out their eyes to give them a skeletal appearance. But they were alive, and that was a blessing. They slept side by side on their backs a few feet apart . . . No, that wasn't how they liked to lie. Why were they being kept apart on separate mattresses? They preferred to sleep on their sides, physically touching each other, even if it was only their fingers. None of us liked to sleep on our backs—that was a vulnerable position, one we were often restrained in.

These humans didn't know how to care for my lab-brothers. Finn and Reese still lingered on death's doorstep, and yet it was this slight injustice that hiked my blood pressure.

The IV implanted in each boy's hand extinguished my irrational anger. Seeing the catheters, tubes, and bags of fluid conjured horrific flashbacks to Quarantine. In the corner, scowling down on Finn and Reese, stood none other than Madison Tarrow, the infamous ghost hunter of Phantom Heights.

I counted at least four guns holstered in her weapon belt. As soon as my eyes settled on her, I stiffened with a deeply embedded fear, and yet, a disconcerting sense of satisfaction filled me when I imagined the look on her face in the moment she'd realized what had happened. I hadn't lied to Jay; revenge was not the driving force behind my plan. But it was so satisfying to know how deep my strike had been to my old enemy who had tried to kill me more times than I could count. I had the power this time. *I* had hurt *her*.

A newfound fear paused my dark thoughts as I observed the way she glared at Finn and Reese. There was another potential consequence of my plan I'd failed to take into consideration. We'd crossed an invisible but clear line by kidnapping Vivian. No doubt Madison had never been so pissed in her life. What if she directed her rage toward my defenseless lab-brothers?

She was holding something in her hand. It reflected green light off the Dome in quick flashes as she turned it between her fingers. Once I realized what it was, the anger rekindled so strongly inside me that I felt my power stir against the neutralizer. She had RC's disk. We'd left that so Finn and Reese would know we hadn't abandoned them.

Give it back! I wanted to scream at her. For a moment—just a moment—I felt the green power boil to life, and I knew when Kit looked up at me and cowered with her ears back that she must have seen both of my eyes flash green before the metal band on my arm smothered the hot power once more.

I clenched my hands into fists. There was nothing I could do. I couldn't stand up to Madison. I couldn't protect my lab-brothers. I couldn't even let them know I was nearby.

Kit pawed at my fingers until I unclenched them and lifted my hand enough for her to crawl underneath. I stroked her, my eyes still fixed on the crack between the boards. My gentle fingers caused her to start purring despite her worry. I leaned my forehead against the board, watching the twins sleep. *This was the only way to save them*, I miserably reminded myself. *We'll get them back.*

Kit crawled out from under my hand and nudged me with her nose, reminding me that we needed to leave. We'd come only to check on Finn and Reese, and now that we'd affirmed they were as well as we could hope, we had to return to Home.

My feet were cemented in place. I hated leaving my lab-brothers alone to face the doctor's needles and probing fingers under Madison's spiteful watch. Turning away took every ounce of willpower.

Several blocks away from City Hall, Kit changed from fur to skin and walked beside me. She had added some color to her dingy gray outfit with a pair of indigo arm sleeves and matching wraps to cover her heels and calves.

"Cato," floated her timid call. I glanced down at her. She held up her arms until I lifted her, and then she draped her arms around my neck and rested her cheek on my shoulder. "You're scared. So's Jay and RC and Ash."

"Not Axel?" I inquired, not even bothering to deny her claim that I was afraid.

"I don't know. I can't read Axel." When she sighed, her breath tickled my neck. "Why are you scared?"

"I'm just worried, that's all."

"About Finn and Reese?"

I turned my head away from her to cough before I answered, "Yes. And you, and everybody else."

"Why?"

I didn't reply immediately. Behind us, the Dome painted a green arc above the skyline. "I want to protect you."

"From what?"

I stroked her tangled hair. "Everything. *Them*, Azar, humans. And I don't want the mistakes I made Before to hurt you."

Kit twisted her body so she could lean in front of me. I stopped again, staring into her golden eyes. She set her open hand on my cheek. "I can protect you too."

I smiled and bowed my head. Her eyes closed as our foreheads met. "I love you, Cato."

I planted a kiss on her forehead. "I love you too, Kit-Kat."

Nestling deeper into my arms, she stuck her thumb in her mouth and suckled softly. "Hey, Cato? I like Vivian."

"Yeah? You haven't even talked to her."

"But I watch her. She's pretty, and I think she's nice. Can we keep her?"

The smile I forced was really more of a grimace. "No. She's just visiting for a little while until Finn and Reese come back."

"Oh." The thumb plugged her mouth again. I carried her through town, my thoughts on the small body I was holding. All I wanted to do was keep her safe. My heart ached with the knowledge that I'd had these very same thoughts when I carried Finn away from his cage, and now he was in more danger than ever. I'd failed him.

A cat was sitting in the middle of the road, so we took a winding, indirect route to avoid Outsiders before safely reaching Home to find RC and Jay sorting the supply of food we'd scavenged earlier today. Jay rose to his feet and dipped a tin into the drum of rainwater. RC struggled to use one of his blades left-handed to open a can of soup. His injured right arm had been causing him more and more pain lately, the wound red and festering. The blade slipped, and RC threw his disk on the floor in frustration, then closed his eyes and leaned his head back with a sigh.

I set Kit down, knelt beside him, and pressed the backs of my fingers against my lab-brother's cheek. He shied away from my touch, but then he relaxed once he realized who I was. "RC, you have a fever."

Jay turned at my proclamation. Without opening his eyes, RC insisted, "I'm fine."

My gaze shifted down to the ruined neutralizer cutting into his right arm. "We have to get that thing off you."

I reached for it, but RC's left hand shot out and seized my wrist. "Don't touch it."

"He's right," said Jay. "It'll cut deeper and make the injury worse."

"But it's infected," I argued. "Doing nothing will make it worse too."

No answer from either of them. I took the can from RC, seized the disk, and worked the blade beneath the lid to pry it loose. He watched me work, and it was then I noticed how dull his left eye was. It should have been glowing by now, but it never sparked back to life after his near burnout kidnapping Vivian.

"Hey," he said, "you still got my other one?"

"Yeah."

"Let me have it." He held out his hand, eyes on the pouch buckled to the outside of my thigh.

"Why? You still have two, and I thought you didn't want this one."

"What do you care?" he snapped. "It's useless to you anyway."

He was right, and I wasn't in the mood to argue, so I handed it over. RC suddenly gasped and recoiled—a spider was crawling down the wall on stilt legs. Kit pounced, smashing the arachnid with her open palm. RC exhaled and set his hand over his heart, muttering, "I hate those creepy little bastards."

Jay glared at him for the language choice.

"I'll protect you," Kit sang, leaning in to give RC a quick kiss on the cheek and then skipping away on a mission to destroy every spider in our Home. Not even RC could smother a fond grin as he watched her. That was the first time I'd ever seen him look at her like that.

I smiled. Spider-slaying was a low-risk job perfect for Kit, although I did wonder if there were any venomous spiders in this region. I passed the open can to Jay, who looked me in the eye and asked, "Would you like to take this to her?"

I hesitated, seriously considering his offer. I longed to see Vivian up close and hear the sound of her voice again. That was, in a tiny, insignificant way, part of the reason I'd chosen her of all people to take, and now she was right beneath my feet.

But no, I couldn't face Vivian. The lives we shared Before didn't matter; I couldn't afford to get too close to her. I shook my head. "No."

Jay studied me. There was no way he'd missed my hesitation, but he turned away without question. I watched him go, my heart heavy. I was having a hard time deciding if I was relieved or depressed by my choice.

Vivian raised her head when the door creaked open and a dark form eased through the opening. Her visitor closed the door and hesitated, studying her before deciding it was safe enough to approach. She couldn't tell if this was the same ghost who had given her food before, but regardless, she kept her resolve. Wiping her moist palms on her crusted jeans, Vivian set Tessie aside and stood.

Immediately, the ghost halted. He wasn't afraid of her; of that she was certain. Rather, he was wary. After all, she was only human—powerless and weaponless—and, if what the Agents said was true, she was no match for him in a physical fight. Both of them knew it.

He remained frozen. She waited, as patient as one would wait for a stray dog to approach. Standing had thrown him off, since every other time he'd come she had either been sitting or sleeping. But, apparently reaching the conclusion that she had no intention of confronting him, he crept forward again.

Vivian remained perfectly still, afraid of spooking her visitor. A silver glint on his chest caught her eye, and she recognized the whistle resting on top of the white α. He stopped well out of her range, then knelt down and set a can of soup and a tin of water on the floor.

"What's your name?" she asked quietly.

The ghost rose, then stood like a statue and studied her with calculating intensity. Vivian didn't move. She was afraid to hold out her hand for a handshake or even breathe. He hadn't spoken a word to her since she'd been brought here, but she hoped if she could get him to talk, she might learn why she was here and what he planned to do with her.

A full minute of tense silence passed, and then the ghost turned and strode away. "Wait!" she cried, dashing ahead of him and sliding to a stop in front of the door.

His hand had been outstretched for the knob, but he leapt back with impressive reflexes, quick as a cat and just as light on his feet. He clenched his jaw and folded his arms. "Please, move," he said quietly, icily, spacing the words apart so a threat lingered just beneath his polite command.

His voice. *"Carry her."* She remembered him. He must be the leader.

Vivian stared into the depths of his hood where his eyes were hidden in shadow, glaring at her. She was surprised by how young his voice sounded. Of course, youthfulness was difficult to gauge since the life span of a human hardly compared to the life span of a ghost. He could be older than her great-grandparents for all she knew, but he certainly wasn't old by their standards. She bravely lifted her chin and replied, "Please tell me your name."

Again, he sized her up. "I don't want to hurt you," he answered softly, "but I will if you don't move."

Vivian hesitated. She knew he could really hurt her, even kill her. But she'd also seen the way he kept his distance. She read him to be more passive than aggressive—a glaring contradiction to the Agents' description of him, although she had no doubt he was more than capable of killing. And she was being foolish enough to confront him right now.

Still, she wanted to get through to him, to make some kind of connection, and knowing his name would be the first step. She clenched her fists, deciding a few bruises would be worth knowing the name of her captor.

"Just your name. You do have one, don't you?"

Silence answered her. Would he slap her across the face? Punch her in the gut? Pin her to the door by the throat? Her body tensed involuntarily. *I shouldn't have pushed so hard*, she realized as the silence dragged on.

He took a step forward, and she braced herself.

To her surprise, the ghost seized her shirt and firmly but surprisingly gently moved her to the side. She marveled at how effortless the maneuver was, how strong he must be despite his appearance. After all, now that they were standing face-to-face for the first time, she saw now that he had only a few inches of height on her. His build was impossible to tell in the poor light under his black cloak, but he didn't seem to be excessively muscular.

She scowled but made no retaliation, fearing a much stronger blow should she interfere a second time.

Her captor opened the door and took a step, then paused. He turned to look back at her. "Jay," he said, then closed the door behind him. The bolt slid into place on the other side.

Vivian leaned thoughtfully against the wall. Jay. The Alpha leader who fed her, gave her water, brought her books to read and Tessie to keep her company, and didn't harm her even though she had provoked him. There was, she decided, much more to Jay and the other Alpha ghosts than the Agents wanted her to know.

I flipped through the pages of *Introduction to Earth and Environmental Science* without reading. A student had printed **Mrs. Snyder 3rd Period** in the top corner of the first page. The sheets of paper cascaded under my thumb.

I paused and turned a few pages back to return to the illustration of the water cycle that had caught my eye. My throat clenched. I could hear the twins asking, *"Is this called water, or rain?"* That seemed so long ago. *"So . . . are there pipes inside clouds?"*

I let the pages fall again. I'd really wanted to see the looks on the twins' faces when I presented this to them. They might have even smiled. Knowing I may never have the chance to give them this book sank my spirits so low I felt as if gravity had doubled and was trying to pull me through the floor.

The final page fell from my fingertips. I reversed and flipped from back to front. When the last page settled into place again, I paused to study the list of student names on the inside front cover: Kevin Murray – Therese Luce – Deb Stipp – Jennifer Dawn – Rich Kiebdaj – Gigi Miele – April Center – Shannon Jennings – Laurie Wink.

The penultimate name popped off the page and caught my breath.

Shannon Jennings

The cursive name illuminated a dark part of my memory like a quick flash of lightning that left an afterimage even when I closed my eyes. I brought the book closer to my face and squinted at the signature.

A door slammed, making me jump. Jay leaned against the basement door and tipped his head back with a slow exhale. "What's wrong?" I asked, subtly closing the book and slipping it behind my back.

He massaged his temples. "Vivian stood between me and the door and refused to move. She's getting bolder, and I don't like it."

RC had been sitting with his back slumped against the wall, but he opened his eyes to exchange a concerned look with Ash and me. Axel was sitting nearby with his arms folded and his eyes closed. He was listening to us, but his focus was tuned to sounds far out of our range on the other side of town where Finn and Reese were lying inside City Hall. Without opening his eyes, he said, "Actually, she was terrified of you."

"She held her ground."

Axel opened his eyes. "She was so scared I thought she was going to piss all over the floor."

Jay shot me a stern look. "Scared or not, if she attacks me, I *will* defend myself," he warned.

Feeling the need to apologize for our prisoner's actions, I mumbled, "Sorry."

Jay didn't acknowledge my apology, but I knew he heard me. He muttered, "They're going to be so terrified when they realize they're all alone surrounded by strange people in a strange place."

None of us were surprised by the shift in topic. "They aren't alone," RC said. "Axel is almost always listening, and I can intervene again if anything happens."

His words offered little encouragement, as he himself wasn't looking so well. Jay shook his head. "They'll still be scared. They'll think we abandoned them."

"We didn't have a choice," I said quietly. "They would've died."

None of us were capable of pacifying Jay. He started to pace.

"Jay," Ash soothed, "we're going to get them back. Arena's Honor." We all knew what was really on Jay's mind. Ash was just the first to say it aloud: "I promise this family isn't going to fall apart."

Jay buried his face in his hands. "This family can't break," he said, his muffled voice cracking behind his palms. "I can't let it."

"You know what, Jay?" snapped RC. He staggered to his feet. "Sometimes I get real sick of you saying the word *family* like it's the holiest word in the world. You wanna know something? Families aren't perfect, and they *do* fall apart, whether you like it or not."

Jay halted in his tracks. He and RC stared each other down.

"Please don't fight," Kit begged. "Brothers shouldn't fight."

"And how would you know that, Kit?" RC fired back.

Tears sparkled in her round eyes, and her lower lip quivered. RC turned with a disgusted grunt and stormed into the office, slamming the door shut behind him. The echo rang through the warehouse. In its dying reverberations, Jay said, "Axel?"

"Yeah, yeah, I'll go babysit the moron," said the half-breed with a roll of his eyes. He rose and made a grandiose show of stretching his arms above his head before casually strolling after RC.

The silence after his departure was suffocating. Ash, Kit, and I stared at Jay, who was still gazing at the door, his brow drawn in sorrow rather than reciprocated anger. Ears back, Kit approached him and slipped her hand into his, but he turned his back on us and crossed his arms, staring out one of the holes in the wall.

"Jay?" Ash called meekly. "He didn't mean it. He doesn't feel well, and he's scared about Finn and Reese, and he's just trying to prepare himself in case they . . . in case . . ."

She lapsed into silence. I swallowed and filled the void with the empty promise, "We'll get them back."

Jay just shook his head.

— Chapter Twenty-Seven —

Patients

Madison's tongue poked between her lips as she worked the tip of her pocketknife into the disk. The hole in the center had no opening on the sides; only the outside slit offered any chance of popping it open. She was hoping to dismantle it and learn what was inside, but she'd been working at it for an hour with no results to show for her efforts.

"Oh," drifted Doc's soft voice. "Hello there."

Madison caught her breath and rose to get a clear view of Doc kneeling next to one of the twins. The boy didn't answer her. His dull eyes roved in confusion as he tried to gain his bearings, and he shifted weakly in alarm.

"It's okay," Doc soothed. "Shh, you're safe. Can you tell me your name?"

His vacant gaze rose to find her. Again, he didn't answer. "C'mon," the doctor encouraged with a warm smile. "What's your name?" He blinked once, then slid his hand out from under the blanket. He turned his palm up to reveal $\alpha2$ tattooed into the pale flesh on the inside of his forearm.

Doc ran her finger over the ink. "Yes, I see your tattoo. I want to know your real name."

A2 made a fist, studied the tattoo in confusion for a moment, then offered his arm again and gazed up at the doctor. "Okay. We'll try again later. My name is Dr. Crawford, but you can call me Doc. You are very, very sick. I know you don't feel well, and I know you're probably scared, but I'm here to help you. The Alpha ghosts left you in my care so I can make you feel better."

A2 demonstrated no emotion, no hint of surprise or interest at what he'd just been told. Madison loomed over Doc's shoulder and growled, "Just to be clear, you are prisoners, not guests. Got it?"

"Don't frighten him," Doc chastised. She smiled at her newest patient. "Will you let me help you get better?"

He blinked but didn't respond. "All right," she relented. "I'm going to give you a quick checkup now. I know you've had some bad experiences, so I don't want to frighten you." She dug into her pocket and pulled out a penlight. When she shined the beam into his eyes, he squinted and tried to turn his head away, but she gently seized his chin and tilted his face toward her.

"Easy, now. You're okay. Eyes are a tad brighter, but still too dull," she murmured, swapping the light for a thermometer and requesting, "Could you please—?"

A2 obediently opened his mouth before she'd even finished the sentence.

"Oh. Well, thank you," she said in surprise. "This won't hurt a bit. I promise. I just need to put this under your tongue, and it'll tell me your body temperature. Okay?" She folded back the blankets and set the end of her stethoscope on his bare chest. He flinched when the metal met his skin. "Sorry about that. I know it's cold. I can listen to your heart and lungs with this. Pretty neat, huh? Do you think you could—?"

A2 inhaled, but the sound was raspy, and the breath triggered a deep, croupy cough that racked his whole body. Doc shook her head. "I was afraid of that. Instead of deep breaths, could you please breathe norm—Oh. My, you do what I ask before I even finish asking. You're an excellent patient," she praised as the boy started breathing normally. She listened to his wheezing. "Still fluid in the lungs."

Doc held out her hand. Lily, who had picked the thermometer off the floor and disinfected it already, passed it to Doc so she could slip it under his tongue again.

Doc set her hands on her patient's abdomen and applied pressure. "Does it hurt when I press on your tummy?" A2 squeezed his eyes shut in a grimace and moaned softly. "Okay." Doc pulled out the thermometer and glanced at it. "101.8. Still higher than I want. Now, will you please open your mouth for me and say *ah*?" she requested as she withdrew a tongue depressor.

He opened his mouth but remained silent. Doc set the depressor on his tongue and shined her light into his mouth. "That sore throat must really hurt," she sympathized. "Can you say *ah* for me?" she asked again. The boy's brows drew together. The request seemed to confuse him.

Madison's impatience was unbearable. "Ask him where Vivian is."

Doc scowled and removed the tongue depressor so he could close his mouth. "He doesn't know."

"You don't know that until you ask."

Doc looked down again just in time to witness A2 pull the catheter out of his hand. "No, no," she scolded gently. "I know IVs are no fun, but it has to stay there so you can get better." He squirmed feebly when she reinserted the catheter. "Don't fuss now. A little bit of trypano-phobia, huh?"

"What's that?" Madison demanded. "Is it fatal?"

Doc glanced over her shoulder. "Considering it's a fear of needles, no. Lily, will you please bring some gauze and wrap his hand? I think it'll be best if he can't see the catheter. Do the same for his brother."

She relinquished her patient to the nurse, who knelt down with a roll of gauze. A2 watched Lily wrap a long strip around his hand. The nurse taped it in place and set his hand down on his chest, and Doc leaned over to pat it in reassurance. "Just relax," the doctor soothed. "Let us take care of you."

Too exhausted to even move his head, he closed his eyes again.

Madison knelt beside the twins and settled in, waiting. Watching. For more than an hour, she barely moved, stiffening whenever either boy so much as breathed out of rhythm. Finally, her patience had fully eroded, and she gently stroked A1's cheek, then squeezed his limp hand. He stirred, his fingers twitching inside hers. When she realized what he was holding, A1's eyes flew open and his hand jerked in sur-prise before he retracted it.

Madison let go. "Hi there."

His blue irises flickered weakly like a dying candle at the end of the wick. Madison stiffened and reached for her holster.

"What are you doing?" Doc demanded, stepping forward.

"His eyes are glowing," said Madison, drawing her ectogun in defense.

"He's reading your mind," Wes said through a yawn. He stretched on his cot and folded his hands behind his head. "Remember? They're Mind-Readers."

Madison froze. Sure enough, A1 hadn't moved. Now that she thought about it, he didn't have the strength to so much as lift his head, let alone draw enough power to attack. She lowered her weapon. Wes added, "Mind-Readers are harmless. Trust me, I have a friend in the Ghost Realm who's a Telepath."

"What does that have to do with mind-reading?" Madison snapped, the ectogun lowering a little more.

"The powers are similar. Every Telepath is a Mind-Reader, but not every Mind-Reader is a Telepath. Believe me when I say these two have harmless, passive abilities. Why don't you put the gun away? You're probably terrifying the poor kid."

Madison obliged, although A1's half-opened eyes were still trained on the ectogun in her holster even after her hand retreated. She offered him an unconvincing smile. "Listen, I have a very important question for you. The other Alpha ghosts took my daughter. Do you know where she is?"

He blinked. The effort needed to keep his eyes open was draining his last bit of strength. But Madison was not going to let him go back to sleep until she had her answer. Finally, he moved his head once to the right, once to the left.

"Okay, then can you tell me where the Alpha ghosts were hiding before they brought you here?" This time when the boy shook his head, the movement was barely perceptible. Discouraged, she snapped, "Can you tell me *anything* useful?"

A1's eyes closed. "Wait, wait," Madison pleaded. She gently but firmly shook him until his eyes fluttered open once more. Madison slid her hands beneath his limp body and shifted her position so she was sitting behind him, supporting his deadweight. Wet coughs made his diaphragm convulse. Madison held him tight until the bout passed and his head rested on her chest with a miserable groan. She reached into her back pocket and pulled out a folded piece of paper, which she opened and held in front of A1's face.

"This is a map of Phantom Heights," she said, directing his attention to the paper. "I want you to look at it very closely and point to anyplace that looks familiar. If you do that, I promise I'll let you go back to sleep for as long as you want, and I won't bother you."

A1 coughed hard, his whole body heaving. He whimpered as the second wave of painful coughs finally subsided. Madison accepted a damp cloth from Doc and pressed it to his forehead.

"Madison, this is too much. He needs to rest."

"The map," she pressured, ignoring Doc. "Please. I know you can do it. Agent Kovak told us what good boys you are. Please, show me on the map where my daughter might be."

A1 squinted at it. He studied it for so long Madison had to keep checking to make sure he was still awake. Finally, he raised his hand and touched his fingertip to the paper. Madison peered over the top of his head to see where he had indicated, then sighed in disappointment. "Yes, City Hall. That's where we are now. Do you recognize anyplace else?"

He seemed to understand she was displeased with his answer. He studied the map again before pointing to another place—Alvarez Park on the southeastern side of town. "Anywhere else?" she pleaded.

A1 could barely keep his eyes open. He lifted his hand as though to point to a new location, but he hesitated, moved his hand, then hesitated again. His hand fell. "Okay," Madison relented, setting the map on the floor. "Thank you for trying. You can go back to sleep now."

A1 exhaled, and his head lolled as he closed his eyes. Madison meant to set him down immediately, but the weight of his head against her bosom, and the shallow rise and fall of his chest, and the innocent peace in slumber made her want to not disturb him. She let him doze in her arms.

She watched him sleep, his labored breathing rattling his chest. This wasn't the first time she'd held a sick child, and right now, with his eyes closed, he did look human. Innocent. Could a kálos, she wondered, be raised as a human? Or would the lust for violence persist despite the upbringing?

She hesitated, then brought her trembling fingers up to his face and stroked his cheek. Had anyone else ever done that to him before?

Madison closed her eyes and hung her head. She started to hum the lullaby she used to sing to her own children, but she managed only the first three notes before the rest lodged in her throat, the fourth note ending in a long sigh. She planted a tender kiss on the boy's hot forehead before she gingerly lowered him back onto the mattress, and then she leaned back on her heels, swallowing a frustrated scream as she snatched the map and crumpled it in her fist.

"Patience," Doc reminded her.

"Patience," Madison echoed bitterly, rising to her feet.

Patience, Vivian prepped herself.

She remained seated this time when Jay came to bring food. Tessie was good company, but she wanted a real person to talk to, someone who would answer. With nothing else to do in the empty room, she'd spent her time reading, thinking, pacing, occasionally dozing. But mostly thinking. Her plan was both stupidly simple and simply stupid— win her captor over.

This time when Jay entered the room, she didn't move a muscle. He closed the door and hesitated, as expected, to gauge her reaction and take note of the surroundings.

She smiled, remembering her mom had once told her a smile could be a powerful ice-breaker. Instead, it triggered Jay's suspicions. He'd started to approach, but he paused again. Vivian smothered the smile, frustrated already. He was so darn skittish!

She waited patiently while he came forward, set the soup and water on the floor, and rose. Finally, she spoke, keeping her voice soft and respectful. "Jay, would you please eat with me?"

The question definitely caught the ghost off guard. He stared at her in surprise, then cocked his head slightly, as if wondering if he'd heard correctly. Encouraged that he hadn't simply ignored her and left, she continued, "It's just that, I mean, it's really lonely down here by myself. I thought . . . maybe . . . you could dine with me?"

Jay didn't move. Vivian was unsure how to interpret his behavior. How strange that such a powerful, dangerous ghost was scared of her. Sure, she was the daughter of a ghost hunter, but he was a walking weapon, and yet he was afraid of an unarmed human. What could the Agents have possibly done to him to make him like this?

To her grave disappointment, he turned without a word and strode away. She waited for a few minutes after he'd left, staring intently at the closed door on the other side of the room, and then, admitting defeat, she sighed and reached for the soup.

Vivian paused, tin can raised to her lips, at the astonishing sound of the door creaking open again. She set her meal down and sat up straighter as the cloaked figure re-entered, a fruit in hand. He approached her but stopped well out of arm's reach.

Vivian breathlessly encouraged, "You can sit."

Jay grudgingly complied. Rather than sit cross-legged like she was, he seated himself on his knees and the balls of his feet, ready to leap up in a moment's notice.

Vivian took a gulp of cold chicken noodle soup. She hadn't planned to get this far, and now that Jay had actually joined her for dinner, she wasn't sure how to begin. The next few minutes of quiet were broken only by the sounds of Jay biting into the crunchy skin of the fruit and Vivian quietly sipping her broth. Though she couldn't see his eyes in the shadow of the hood, she could feel him watching her, his gaze unwavering, and so when she cleared her throat, it was more for her own benefit to break the silence than to command his attention.

"Ah-hem . . . I, uh, I've met Agent Kovak before," she began. Jay took a deliberate bite, otherwise unresponsive. "He used to work with my mom."

The only response was quiet chewing. She added, "I don't like him. He's a real piece of work, isn't he?"

Jay finished chewing. Swallowed. Took another bite.

This wasn't working; they weren't connecting through a common enemy. She bit her lip and stared at the broth in her can. "I knew somebody who was taken to the AGC. He, um, he was . . ."

She bowed her head, unable to continue. Jay blew a sigh of annoyance at the dismal conversation and stood.

"Jay?"

He paused.

This was it; Vivian had to make him see her as human. Okay, poor word choice. Not human per se, but a living creature with a name and a life worth sparing. She looked him in the eye and said, "You never even asked my name."

"I already know your name, Vivian."

She caught her breath, first flustered, then frustrated, her idea withering. New tactic: she stood, pushed her shoulders back, and puffed her chest to look as intimidating as possible. "Okay, so you know my name, but you obviously don't know who I am. My mom is a *ghost hunter*. You understand, Jay? Now, if you let me go right now, I *might* try to talk her out of killing you."

"I know who Madison Tarrow is." Stupefied yet again, Vivian stood in silence, her jaw slack. The Alpha leader turned away.

"Wait," Vivian called, her voice small and scared enough to make Jay look back. "Is there something you want from me?"

"No."

Thoroughly confused, she asked, "My mom, then? If you demanded a ransom, she'll find a way to pay it, whatever it is. I know she will."

He continued to study her. She was unnerved by the way he observed and calculated, thinking every answer through carefully before speaking, if he chose to respond at all. He didn't miss a single detail. Finally, Jay exhaled. "This is a little more complicated."

She crossed her arms. "How much more complicated?"

He answered her question with one of his own: "How much do you know about us?"

Vivian blinked in surprise. She considered being bold and telling him she knew everything, but she decided Jay was not a person to lie to, so she reluctantly admitted, "I know Project Alpha is where a secret weapon is being developed. Eight of you were being transported when there was an accident and you escaped. You, I'm guessing, are A3, and you're the leader. All of you are, well, you're . . . you're killers, except ten-year-old twins who were with you. And there's a hybrid called A6 on the loose probably killing a lot of people. Um . . . that's about it, I suppose."

Jay gauged her sincerity. "That's all you know," he said. It was both a statement and a question. She nodded. Jay licked his lips before explaining, "The twins got very sick. They were dying. Humans were the only ones who could save them, but we knew they would report us, so—"

"So you kidnapped me to blackmail them," Vivian finished. "I understand now. I'm your leverage to keep my mom from contacting the Agents."

Jay nodded. Hesitant now, he said, "Your doctor . . . she's good?"

A faint grin twitched Vivian's lips. "She's the best. Doc will do everything she can. Trust me, the twins couldn't be in better hands. But, um . . . if they, you know, don't make it . . . ah . . . what happens to me?"

His cold silence terrified her. She shuddered, tears filling her eyes. He didn't have to say it: she was expendable. Even if the twins survived, it would be much easier for the Alpha ghosts to dispose of her than it would be for them to try and take her back to City Hall.

But Jay wouldn't kill her, would he? Sure the Agents had warned that the Alpha ghosts were heartless and cold-blooded, but Jay didn't seem . . .

She couldn't even finish the thought. Jay didn't have to kill her. All he had to do was order another Alpha ghost to do the job.

She was sobbing now, but Jay displayed no empathy. As she hiccupped into a momentary silence, he said, "Let's hope they don't die."

He turned away, leaving Vivian alone in the dark basement with only Tessie to comfort her. She buried her face in the bear. "I have to get out of here," she whispered into the wet fur. "I have to escape before they kill me."

— Chapter Twenty-Eight —
Static

A1 and A2 thrashed in fevered sleep. Finally, after Nurse Lily's insistent pleading, Doc roused them to end their suffering.

"Hey," she said softly, "you're okay. It's just a nightmare. You're safe." She touched A1's arm, and he jerked awake. As soon as he saw her, he shied away, squeezing his eyes shut and cowering. "I'm not going to hurt you," said Doc, visibly shocked by his reaction. The boy opened one blue eye and peered at her. Doc reached for him again, slower this time. Again, he cringed away.

A2's limbs were tangled up in the blankets, and he squirmed in silent distress. "Hey, easy now," Doc soothed. "It's okay. Shh, you're okay." Slowly, he comprehended the blankets were not restraints, and his panic ebbed to bewilderment. He touched the blanket, then realized his head was resting on something soft, and he brought his hand up to touch the corner of the pillow as though it were a puzzling object he'd never encountered before.

Doc smoothed out the ruffled blanket. "I'm sorry I can't bring you to a clean hospital that's nice and quiet with a real bed. I wish I could." Calmer now, the brothers gazed up at the doctor, listening to her pacifying voice. "Why don't you go back to sleep?" she said, pulling the blankets over first A1, then A2. Lily situated herself next to them for nightmare duty.

Trey watched from the bottom step, then turned his attention to his ghost-hunting master sitting in the corner with her knees drawn up to her chest and the silver disk in her hand. He approached to sit next to her. For a moment he was silent, respectful of Madison's frustration. He cleared his throat. The words blurted out: "Agent Kovak said knowing the difference between kálos and moorlins is the most basic information an apprentice should know."

A1 and A2 had roused abruptly, and Lily was tucking them in again. Madison frowned, as though Trey's words had to travel across a great chasm to reach her, and then she had to surface from her deep thoughts. She turned her head to look at him, and he gazed back with intense focus so she'd know he was serious.

"I'm sorry. I should have explained the difference a long time ago. I guess I thought it would be easier to refer to kálos as ghosts when we first started your training. It's my fault; I'm sorry."

"I'm not mad. I just want to learn. If kálos aren't dead, then they aren't really ghosts, so why do we call them that?"

Madison rubbed her hand down her face as she gathered her thoughts. "People have always told ghost stories. True ghosts are, by definition, the spirits of the dead. Usually souls travel to whatever world is after ours—whether it's heaven or another afterlife of some sort, no one really knows, I guess. But sometimes love or hatred or restlessness holds someone back, and those souls remain as moorlins in the worlds of the living. The kálos we fight possess every power of a moorlin and then some; the difference is they were born mortal. Their hearts beat, and we can kill them."

"And the Ghost Realm isn't really the spirit world, is it?"

"No. It's a misnomer from when the first kálos in this Realm were mistaken to be spirits of the dead. The terms *kálos* and *moorlin* are used only by the professionals who study them. Most people simply refer to both as ghosts."

"Then, shouldn't we be called kálos hunters instead of ghost hunters?"

His master managed a half-hearted smile. "If you want to be technical about it, yes." She twirled the disk between her fingers. "You know Tears are small portals that form between the Ghost Realm and ours. Most exist for only a few seconds, some a few days, and then they vanish. Have you ever noticed a weird shimmering in the air, usually over a road?" Trey nodded. "Those aren't heat waves."

His eyes grew wide. "Those are Tears?"

"They're actually quite frequent but so short-lived creatures rarely pass through either side. And what you probably assume is a mirage of water on the road? What you're actually seeing is a glimpse of a body of water in the Ghost Realm. Tears still form all over the world. Phantom Heights earned its name long before the Rip showed up here because this place has always had frequent Tears. The Rip seems to be a permanent one. As far as we know, it's the only one to last this long. I just wish it had formed somewhere else."

Trey was silent for a moment. He mumbled, "I'm sorry I'm not as good a ghost hunter as he was." He knew better than to talk about her son; the words had just tumbled out. At least Trey hadn't broken the unspoken rule and said his name aloud in Madison's presence.

"No, don't say that." She put her arm around his shoulders. "You're a great ghost hunter. You'll learn; you have an awful lot of potential too."

Trey liked to think so, but a voice at the back of his mind told him he would never measure up. He dropped his head. He could see it in Madison's eyes every time she looked at him, how she loved and hated him. How she drew him close like a son and then pushed him away because she was afraid he might come to replace the one she lost.

Sometimes the guilt alone drove him mad. He couldn't help but wonder if the death was partially his fault; if he and Cato hadn't kept such elaborate secrets, maybe there wouldn't have been a funeral in Alvarez Park, and Madison wouldn't cry at night, and Vivian wouldn't be too downtrodden to notice how perfectly her hand fit inside Trey's when he worked up the courage to take it.

The looks Madison gave him sometimes made him suspect she secretly blamed him too.

"Did you know the morning I lost him, I'd yelled at him?" He looked up to see her eyes glistening. Haunted, Madison whispered, "That's not the last conversation I wanted to have." She sighed. "If I'd been a little more involved in his life, he might still be alive."

"It's not your fault." Silently, he added, *I think it's mine.*

Madison swallowed hard. "I try to tell myself that every day. But I can't make myself believe it. I should have been able to protect him. And now Vivian . . . I failed again." Madison closed her eyes.

She wouldn't survive if Vivian died. Trey could see now how frail she was beneath the hard exterior. The worry was cracking her. And if she couldn't lead, then who? He? Wes? They wouldn't survive without Madison guiding them forward, but now Trey realized it was Vivian who gave the ghost hunter the willpower to keep going. Take Vivian, destroy Madison, and the domino effect would be disastrous.

Eager to shift topics before his role model completely shut down, Trey cleared his throat again. "Um . . ."

A1 and A2 bolted up. Their glowing blue eyes settled on Trey, who stared back at them for one second, two, three, and then their gazes fell and they yielded as Lily gently pushed them back down to return to the land of slumber.

Trey finished quietly, "I still feel ignorant about ghosts—I mean, kálos. If I'm going to be a ghost hunter, I gotta know this stuff, right? You said people incorrectly call them ghosts, so . . . what are they really?"

Madison's sigh had the undercurrent of a groan, as if she were in pain. "No one really knows what kálos are. Ironically, we call them ghosts, and yet really they're the polar opposite. See," she explained at Trey's blank stare, "moorlins are invisible in our Realm. They have to expend a massive amount of power and energy to be seen or to become solid enough to touch an object, even for a fraction of a second. And a kálos . . . ?"

Trey nodded. "I get it. A kálos has to deplete power reserves to become invisible or intangible."

"Exactly. According to their legend, moorlins are their ancestors. One story is that a long time ago, there was a couple so in love nothing could keep them apart. Then the man died tragically, but his love was so strong he remained in this Realm as a moorlin. He was so passionate that he was actually able to materialize his ethereal form. The dead man and his living lover bore a child—the first kálos."

"Do you believe that story?"

"It's romantic, but no. I don't think it's probable."

"How long do they live? Kálos, I mean."

"About nine hundred years, give or take. Kálos children grow at the same rate as human children, which is why the twins, who are ten, do actually look like ten-year-olds. Their childhood is fleeting. In their early twenties, the aging process slows way down to a ratio of ten to one in comparison to ours. By that, I mean the aging on my body in a year's time is equivalent to the aging process on the body of a kálos in a . . . decade," she finished quietly.

Trey frowned, listening. Conversations throughout City Hall died as others became aware of the sound. In a few moments, the only noise in the crowded room was a quiet ringing.

"Is that a . . . cell phone?" Wes asked.

Madison's head snapped to the far corner where the phone Agent Kovak had given her was vibrating and ringing. Eyes wide, she rose and strode to it, shoving the disk into a slot in her weapon belt.

"I didn't think it would work after the Alpha ghosts smashed it," said Trey as he stood.

His ghost-hunting master picked up the phone, but she just stared at it. "Madison," Doc warned, standing protectively over her two patients, "if you answer that, just . . . think carefully about what you say. For Vivian's sake."

Madison glanced at the doctor, then lifted the phone to her ear. "Madison Tarrow speaking."

Trey crept forward. City Hall was deathly silent now, just the residual hum of the generator in the basement. Every eye was on Madison, who said after a brief pause, "Yes, I can hear you, but barely. There's a lot of static. Can you hear me?"

Her eyes danced as she listened, and then they fell on A1 and A2. Trey recognized the indecisive furrow in her brow.

Doc folded her arms and shook her head with a warning scowl. When Madison hesitated and sought Trey, he also shook his head. *Don't do it*, he thought at her, as if she could read minds like the boys still fast asleep at Doc's feet.

Madison's shoulders slumped. "No," she croaked into the phone. A few seconds later, she repeated louder, "*No.*"

She closed her eyes and bowed her head as she listened. "Agent . . . Agent Kovak, you're cutting out. Please repeat that." She adjusted her grip, which was all that was holding the cell phone together. "We, uh, we must have bad reception. Could you repeat what you just said? What about a cat?"

She yanked the phone away from her ear, wincing at the static storm that was loud enough for Trey to hear from several feet away. When the noise died down, she hesitantly put the phone to her ear again. "Agent Kovak? Are you there? I must have misheard—you said one of the Alpha ghosts is blind?" She frowned. "Blind in . . . what? I can't hear you. Hello?"

"Blind?" Wes blurted. Madison snapped her fingers at him to shut up. Wes turned to Trey instead and whispered, "Did she say one of the Alpha ghosts is blind?"

Trey shrugged to say *I don't know* without the risk of also receiving an irritated snap from his ghost-hunting master.

Wes grumbled, "That's kind of an important detail to leave out."

Madison turned dangerously pale as the color drained from her cheeks. The cell phone slipped from her fingers. When it struck the floor, it broke into pieces.

"What? What did he say?" Wes demanded. Madison shook her head, too traumatized to answer. He gripped her by the shoulders, giving her a firm shake. "Maddie, what happened?"

"They . . . three of them . . . We aren't safe in here."

"What?"

"Three of the Alpha ghosts can pass through my entoplasm shield."

Wes gawked at her, silent in the rising buzz of anxious conversations behind them. He released his grip and took a step back. "Did he say *how*?"

She shook her head, and he stalked to the boarded window to glare outside where the swirling green currents meandered across the barrier.

"He kept cutting in and out," said Madison in a monotone. "And there was a lot of static. All I made out was one of the Alpha ghosts is blind and three can breach my shield, but I don't know if that's with or without their powers."

Doc gazed down upon her sleeping patients. "Should we set up a guard system, do you think?" she asked. "At night?"

Wes growled softly. "If they even think about coming in here, I'll rip them to shreds."

"I don't think they will," said Trey. "They've been careful to avoid direct contact with us. They'd be outnumbered, and they're smart enough to know that."

"They better if they know what's good for them," said Madison.

Councilwoman Jennings gracefully ascended the terraced steps and seized Madison's arm. She hissed something in Madison's ear.

"What?" Madison asked as Trey subtly maneuvered into earshot.

His eavesdropping didn't go unnoticed—Mrs. Jennings fixed him with a cold glare—but she must have decided his apprenticeship allowed him to be privy because she whispered to Madison, "*A6.* Cato could pass through your shield. If one mutt can, chances are another could too."

"Shh!" Madison surveyed the crowd over the councilwoman's shoulder. "You want to start a panic? There's nothing I can do, okay? I have no idea what sort of monster the Agents concocted."

Mrs. Jennings lowered her voice even more. "We'd be trapped in here. If that *thing* gets in, it'll—"

"Kovak doesn't know where it went." Madison turned away to face the boarded window. "If we're lucky, it's far, far away from Phantom Heights."

Axel, with his usual amount of kindness, understanding, and insight, gave me the helpful advice to "chill the fuck out before you piss your pants, Cato" as I walked down the stairs.

Jay glared over his shoulder. "Hey! Watch your mouth." Gentler to me, he asked, "You all right?"

I nodded, my heart flying out of control. Every cell in my body rejected the idea of going underground, but Vivian was down there. Jay reminded me, "She doesn't know. As long as you keep the hood over your face, she shouldn't recognize you. But it might be best if you don't talk, just in case."

I nodded again. My throat hurt anyway, as if I'd swallowed a nail that had lodged in my esophagus, so I'd keep quiet.

We stopped at the base of the stairs, and Jay slid the bolt on the door. I trailed after him into the room, my gaze immediately alighting on the teddy bear sitting next to a book open on the floor, its reader temporarily interrupted in the middle of the story. Vivian was nowhere to be found.

Jay and I both wandered in a little farther. His attention was on the closed bathroom door on the far side of the room. He handed me the water and bread we'd brought for the prisoner and made his way to it. "Ms. Tarrow?" he called uncertainly.

Something was wrong. My excitement dropped to a sickening sense of foreboding. I sensed a shadow moving behind me, and I turned to glimpse a figure dashing through the doorway. She'd been hiding behind the door when Jay swung it open.

All caution about speaking in front of her was wiped from my mind. "Jay!" I yelled, dropping the meal and sprinting after her.

Vivian glanced once over her shoulder at me but never broke stride as she took the steps two at a time. She hesitated at the top to gain her bearings and locate the exit.

What she found instead was hooded Axel standing in front of her with his arms folded and his legs braced. "Where d'you think you're going, doll?"

Vivian whimpered and held her hands up in surrender as she took half a step back. I pounced, tackling her from behind. We crashed to the ground, and the air rushed out of Vivian's lungs in one *oomph* as my weight settled on top of her. I straddled her, pinning her wrists down.

"Please, I'm not resisting. I'm sorry. I'm *so* sorry. Please don't hurt me."

RC and Ash pulled the hoods over their heads and rose. Ash drew her staff, but I had Vivian under control now.

"That was very stupid, Ms. Tarrow," Jay said dangerously as he emerged from the staircase.

"I know," she whispered, trembling beneath me. "I know, and I'm sorry. It won't happen again. Just, please don't hurt me. I'm sorry."

"I don't need you to be sorry. I need you to behave, and this will be easier for all of us."

"I'll behave. I'm so sorry. I'll be good. I will; I promise." Despite her insistent apologies, I maintained a firm grip on her wrists. Her words quivered with fear, but even so, the sound of her voice brought a rush of memories back to me—of sitting at a table outside LeahRae Harris High, of walking down the sidewalk with backpacks slung over our shoulders, of sitting on a pier skipping stones on a glassy lake in summer's heat.

Jay instructed, "Let her go." I did as I was told. She remained limp on the floor, her body shaking with sobs. "Get up," Jay commanded. His authoritative tone sent a chill down my spine. I'd never heard him deliver orders like that before.

"Okay," she whispered. She was slow in her movements, making extra effort to show us she was being compliant. Once she was on her feet, Jay wordlessly pointed to the doorway she'd just escaped from. Vivian nodded in understanding and walked toward it, her hands still held up in surrender. Jay trailed after her.

I watched the pair of silhouettes vanish into the gloom. I wasn't sure what I'd expected, but that wasn't the first encounter with Vivian I'd hoped for. I pressed my hand against my chest to contain my heart.

At the end of the stairs, the door closed. The lock slammed back into place. Our prisoner was once again secure.

— Chapter Twenty-Nine —
A Thief's Business

"Where are my patients?" Doc demanded.

Wes, who had been dozing in the early dawn, opened his eyes to find the blankets on the stage abandoned. He stood, more perplexed than alarmed. The twins were too weak to walk out the door, and anyway, they couldn't as long as the entoplasm shield was still active.

His first response was to seek out Maddie and gauge her reaction. That was always his first response; after all, a ghost's best chance of survival was to stay one step ahead or behind a ghost hunter. Wes may be a weir, not a kálos, but the same survival guide applied.

Maddie stared at the deserted mattresses with barely contained horror. Doc set a cup of water and an empty bowl on the floor, her eyes trained on the IV bags. She followed the clear tubes and peered behind the podium, whereupon she let out a sigh and her shoulders fell with relief. Maddie rushed to her side.

Wes sauntered over to find that sometime in the night, the twins had crawled from their mattresses and were now sleeping on the floor in the podium's shadow, their bodies curled into tight little balls, backs pressed against one another. Odd that they'd prefer the hard floor to the mattresses, but then again, Wes would bet his entire fortune Kovak hadn't let them sleep on a real bed, so the floor must be a more familiar setting.

Joints creaking, Doc knelt down to slide her hands beneath A1's frail body and lift him up. The boy shifted in her arms, and his eyes fluttered open. "Good morning," she cooed as she carried him back to the mattress.

Wes looked down at the kid's brother. He was willing to carry the boy, but no rush; he waited a few seconds, and sure enough, Maddie came forward to do it before he had to exert himself. A2 stirred in his sleep but didn't awaken as he was carried back to his makeshift bed and laid down.

Wes took a step after them, but he hesitated, his eyes drawn down to a small, round object tucked in the shadow of the woodwork. He tilted his head. Out of habit, he cast a look around to make sure no one was watching when he knelt to study the tarnished penny. Tails-up. Bad luck for those who believed in it. He flipped the penny to Lincoln's head so he could read the date: 1992. *Worthless.*

Wes left the penny on the floor heads-up for some superstitious fool to find. He rose, his full attention on the twins again. Doc propped her patient upright in her lap and brought the cup to his lips. When the water touched A1's throat, he coughed, water spraying and then dribbling from his mouth. "Okay," she soothed, pulling the cup away.

When the coughs subsided, she tried again. This time, he was able to swallow. "There we go. I bet that tastes pretty good, doesn't it?"

He reached weakly for the cup when she pulled it away. "Not yet. We need to make sure you can keep that down before you can have any more."

"And if he can?" Maddie asked.

"Then we've taken a big step toward recovery."

"Spoke too soon," said Wes with a nod at A1. The boy's face was as white as a sheet, his brows drawn. Doc snatched the plastic bowl and held it in front of him as he vomited.

"Okay," she murmured, "just let it all out. Okay. You're okay." Her head wagged with disappointment. At the sound of his brother's misery, A2 opened his eyes.

For the next hour, Wes had to listen to A1 suffer from dry heaves. The convulsions of his empty stomach weakened his already feeble body until he didn't have the strength to even lift his head, which lolled like a newborn's. Lily held him in her lap so she could support him when another bout racked his body. "I know it hurts, baby. I know," she crooned. He was shivering, chilled in cold sweat, tears streaking his face.

Finally, his stomach settled, and he lapsed into an uneasy sleep. Lily rocked him in her arms, waiting to ensure the dry heaves had passed before she lowered him back onto the mattress and tucked the blankets around him.

His brother was lying on his side with his head turned away, his half-opened eyes trained on the gauze around his hand. He stroked it with the lightest touch, obsessed with the catheter even though he couldn't see it.

Maddie stared at the boys, her emotions written all over her face. Motherhood had softened the ghost hunter's hard edges toward these particular kálos. Wes, on the other hand, observed them passively. He was never a father, never had any interest in such a job. He was too restless to settle down and raise children. Who could tame a wolf, after all? The moon was his mistress. And while he did pity the twins for the suffering Kovak had wrought, he didn't look at them like others did. They saw children; he saw answers to valuable secrets.

Doc said, "I'm concerned they still aren't talking."

Yes, that was also a concern of his. How could anyone coax answers from them if the kids wouldn't speak?

Maddie said, "The Agents didn't say anything about them being mute."

Doc grumbled, "The Agents didn't say a lot of things. My fear is there might have been some brain damage in the accident." She seized her penlight and knelt beside A2. "Don't pull that out," she warned sternly. He blinked and moved his fingers a few inches away from the gauze. Doc gently shifted him onto his back, but he resisted weakly and tried to roll onto his side again.

"Hold him, please," Doc requested. Lily grabbed A2's wrists while Shay pressed down on his ankles. A2 didn't struggle, but he started shivering.

"You're all right," said Lily. "We aren't going to hurt you."

A2 continued to tremble, his whole body shaking. His eyes were squeezed shut, teeth clenched in expectance of pain.

"Hey," Doc soothed. "Hey now, just relax. Easy. I don't know why you're upset, but there's no reason to be. You can read my mind. You know I'm telling the truth."

A2's breathing was still rapid, but his shivers subsided. At a nod from Doc, Lily and Shay released him but remained poised to grab him again. Except for his chest moving, the kid had stiffened into a statue.

Doc clicked her penlight on and shined the beam of light into the right eye, then away, then into it again to observe the pupil response. "Normal," she said, performing the same exercise to his other eye. "I want you to keep your head still and follow my finger with your eyes." The boy's blue eyes followed her index finger as she traced a path through the air. "Also normal."

Doc pulled the blanket away. "I want you to wiggle your left toes." He did. "Now raise your right arm." He did. "Can you blink three times?" He did. "Please touch your nose." He did. "Now say *ah*." A2 just stared at her, visibly puzzled by the request.

Doc shook her head. "There doesn't seem to be anything preventing them from speaking." A2 rolled onto his side again. This time, Doc didn't force him onto his back. She studied him for a moment, then reached out to touch the procession of scars on his forehead. The kid shrank away from her as though he wanted to disappear into the mattress. "Can you tell me what happened to you?"

A haunted look shadowed his face. When Doc's hand touched his skin, he squeezed his eyes shut, curled his fingers into fists, and went completely rigid, every muscle locked.

Doc traced the small scars with her forefinger. "I'm not going to hurt you."

A2 remained frozen until her hand retreated. Lily set a cup containing a few swallows of water next to Doc, who moved it closer to A2. "When your tummy feels well enough to try some water, you can drink this. Okay? I'm leaving it right here for you." She rose and pulled the blankets over his body again, then left him in peace.

A2 ignored the water and scooted closer to his twin until they were touching, and then he curled into a fetal position, his fingers brushing the gauze and his gaze fixated on his hand again. He was still staring at the covered catheter when his eyes closed.

Wes remained where he was, arms crossed, watching them sleep. They frightened him. Not because they were powerful, which they weren't, or because they were dangerous, which, again, they were not. It was where they'd come from that unnerved him. They were living proof the Agents were committing unspeakable atrocities against kálos at the AGC. Not that such news was a surprise, but still, it was unsettling to see the evidence right in front of him. Humans criticized the violence spreading from the Rip, but who was really the villain? Was it the kálos causing destruction and kidnapping humans for the slave trade, or was it the Agents imprisoning kálos, breeding them like animals, and torturing them for the sake of building a weapon to destroy them all?

Wes yawned and looked away from the twins to survey the humans prattling throughout City Hall. A1 and A2 were the first kálos to be protected in the safety of the entoplasm shield, the first to be accepted in this town after Phantom. The stupid half-breed had gotten himself wrapped up in the glory of heroism. Not that he'd ever let it go to his head—actually, he'd been quite humble—but he'd made the mistake of playing superhero instead of treating the job as a business.

Wes was smarter than that. He'd lurked in the shadows for years, using his powers and connections to stock up on wealth while using his human façade to forge valuable networks with powerful people so when the time came to cash in on favors, he had a whole list to choose from. And then, only when the humans were driven to such desperation that they would do anything to survive, *then* he had revealed himself.

He would never be loved as Phantom had been, but this was a business arrangement, nothing more. He wasn't a hero, and he didn't care that people glared at him behind his back and called him a thief, for he *was* a thief, and he'd readily admit that. The thief had prevailed when the hero fell.

There was a good reason for that. He'd been careful, and he was still careful. He'd let Maddie hold his leash, as long as she didn't keep it too tight. Better to be a guard dog than a lab rat. As long as the people of Phantom Heights needed him, he was safe from the Agents. That was something Cato hadn't understood until it was too late.

Wes's gaze wandered. Certain faces in the crowd attracted his attention. There was Mayor Correll, a stout, blustery man who still liked to walk around offering handshakes and encouragement even though he'd really surrendered his leadership to Maddie in this time of crisis. Wes used to share an occasional drink with him and talk his way through the web of politics. There were other notables too, like Police Chief Emerton and Councilwoman Jennings. Each had been in a position of power before the shield went up, and each had been carefully selected, researched, and cajoled over the years. Wes had dedicated a lot of effort to ensure he stayed in their favor.

That didn't do him much good now. Such a waste of time, cultivating those connections. Maddie was the only one on whose good side he needed to be at the moment. Correll hadn't made a critical decision in at least a year; Emerton was a key member of the raid team but no longer had the authority to make an arrest; and Jennings couldn't pass any legislature that might inhibit Wes's freedom.

Now there were new players. These Alpha fugitives thoroughly intrigued him. How bold they were, attacking the combined raid team and striking him down in his wolf form while whisking away a ghost hunter's daughter from under her own nose. *I'd like to meet them*, he decided. How, he wasn't sure yet, but they were going to have to show themselves if this trade actually went down. They had answers. Maddie was a fool for not wondering what the Agents were up to. Information was currency, especially with the building hostility.

Trey strolled past him, breaking Wes's vacant stare. Wes focused on the guns holstered around the teenager's waist. Point proven. War was on their doorstep.

Even in human form, Wes had sharp hearing, good enough to hear Trey ask, "Do you still hate them?"

Wes turned his head away, pretending not to hear, but his eyes narrowed as he listened for Maddie's answer. "Have you seen the way they look at people? There's no life in those eyes." Her voice caught. "Ghost or human, how can people hurt children like that?"

Her answer satisfied Wes more than he would have thought. He liked discovering soft points in the ghost hunter's armor—one missing chink in the chain mail was all he needed to start pulling it apart link by link if the need arose.

Trey said, "I agree. It's one thing to fight ghosts that attack humans, but torturing innocent kids who haven't committed a crime yet?"

"The Agents would argue that they'll grow up to be bloodthirsty ghosts someday, and a lot of humans would agree."

Wes waited, listening. A figure appeared in front of him, hands on her hips. "Eavesdropping, Wes?" Maddie demanded.

He blinked innocently at her. "Huh?"

"Right," she spat, pushing something hard against his chest. "I've been over every inch of this thing. Do you know what it is?"

He leaned back, hesitant to touch the silver disk in case it was actually made of silver. Gingerly, he took it out of her hand, braced for burns on his fingers. No pain, not even a tingle; if there was any silver in the alloy, it was diluted enough with other metals. "I haven't the slightest idea," he said, turning it over. "I've never come across anything like it in the Ghost Realm." He had to tailor his words. Speaking to humans, he called it the Ghost Realm; speaking to kálos, he called it Avilésor. Such was the nature of his half-life—half in this Realm, half in the other.

Maddie snatched it from his fingers. She studied the smooth metal face broken by the hole through the center. "I was thinking of giving it back to the twins."

Trey said, "I don't think that's a good idea."

"They might know what it does."

"It could be a weapon."

"No, I don't think so. Agent Kovak said the twins are harmless, and I believe him. Even if it is a weapon, I don't think they'll use it."

Wes seized the opportunity to apply his most sincere expression and add, "We'll never know what it does otherwise."

313

"It's risky," Trey insisted, glowering at Wes. While the apprentice did a better job of masking his disgust than Maddie, he still made it clear he didn't trust the lunos, although Wes really didn't care. Trey wasn't worth the effort of winning over. Not yet, anyway. When he was older and actually a threat, then Wes would try harder, but not now.

"It is," Maddie agreed. "But that kid had this for some reason, and I want to know why." She held the silver disk up and stared at her reflection. Wes watched the sleeping twins.

Why indeed.

Jay and I were more cautious this time when I opened the door. It swung slowly, and the two of us hesitated at the threshold, seeking our prisoner before we entered. Vivian, who had been pacing anxiously along the far wall, quickly threw herself into a seated position. She'd been on extra good behavior after the stunt she pulled yesterday. She didn't realize how lucky she was that Axel hadn't dragged her back to the basement by her hair.

I stood guard in the doorway while Jay ventured into the room. Behind my back, I gripped the contours of Vivian's ectogun. I didn't actually know how to use it; I surmised all I had to do was pull the trigger, but I wasn't sure. It was meant to be a scare tactic if our prisoner became aggressive. Vivian Tarrow wasn't exactly your typical damsel in distress.

She opened her mouth as Jay drew near, probably either to apologize again or just to talk because her teddy bear wasn't enough company for a girl who had been living in crowded conditions for so long. Before she could say a single word, Jay gasped and dropped the bowl.

Realizing what was about to happen, I took a hesitant step forward, but I stopped. I couldn't go to Jay and leave the door unguarded for our prisoner to make another break for it. All I could do was watch, frustratingly helpless.

Wide-eyed, Vivian stared in horror as he fell to his knees, clutching his head and screaming. "Oh my gosh!" she cried, leaping to her feet.

A shadow breezed past me, and then a figure was crouched between Vivian and Jay. Vivian stepped back and hit the wall.

Axel's snarls and Jay's screams echoed in the basement. At least I understood what was happening; poor Vivian was plastered to the wall, petrified and bewildered.

Finally, Jay's yells faded to pitiful moans. From under the hood, Axel kept his gaze fixed on Vivian without so much as a glance at his fallen lab-brother. His growls never ceased, not even to pause for a breath.

"I'm okay," Jay said hoarsely, pulling himself up to his knees. Axel glared at Vivian for another moment, then stalked past me and disappeared up the dark staircase.

Vivian gawked at my lab-brother, who surveyed the contents of the bowl scattered across the floor. "I'm sorry," he mumbled as he staggered to his feet. "I'll get you more food."

"Jay?" said Vivian uncertainly. "Are . . . are you hurt?"

He returned to me, his footsteps dragging with newfound exhaustion. I stepped aside to let him pass. Before I closed the door, I glanced back at Vivian. She slid down the wall until she hit the floor, gazing at the spilled food and water with wide eyes until she squeezed them shut.

I closed the door. Jay was a few steps up, leaning against the wall, his head down. I locked the door and waited. Finally, he dragged his hand down his face and looked back at me. "Bad timing for a Spasm, huh?" he half-heartedly joked.

"Is there ever a good time?" We walked up the narrow staircase together. I pushed the door open and let him pass, then followed behind and closed the door.

Ash was busy dividing our rations under Kit's impatient watch. Jay went to wash the bad taste out of his mouth with rainwater, and Ash nodded at the far wall. "Hey, Cay, RC's asleep. Can you wake him so he can eat with us?"

I nodded and set the ectogun down, then went to kneel beside our dozing lab-brother. My eyes were pulled magnetically to the inflamed injury on his bare arm. I nudged his shoulder and called, "RC. Hey, wake up. It's time to eat. RC?"

His eyes remained closed, his breathing deep and even. Panic surged through me. "RC!" I shouted, shaking him roughly.

He frowned and opened his eyes, taking a moment to focus on my face. "*What?*"

I exhaled in relief. "Bloody Scout, don't scare me like that." His left eye was as dull as mine. His face sheened with sweat, and when I touched his cheek, I exhaled in concern. "You're burning up. If you don't get better soon, we'll have to take you to the humans."

"You can't do that. If I leave, you lose your communication with them. And you know Madison would torture me to find out where we're keeping Vivian."

"Not if hurting you would put Viv in danger," I countered.

RC scoffed. "How much leverage do you think she's worth?"

"But you need help."

He closed his eyes. "There's nothing these humans can do."

My mouth went dry once I realized what he was saying. The only people who could remove the neutralizer were the ones who'd put it on him in the first place.

— Chapter Thirty —

Nighttime Secrets

"Begin."

I stared up at the speaker high above, where His *voice had issued from. "What's going on?"*

His voice deadened to a monotone, Jay replied, "They didn't tell you?"

I shook my head.

Ash said, "Winner gets to eat."

"Winner of what?" I demanded. "I don't know how to play this game."

She raised her head to glare at me from across the Arena with her smoldering eyes. Her grip tightened on the staff. "I'm sorry," she whispered, raising it and advancing on me . . .

I gasped, straining to see in the blackness. The waxing moon drifted in and out of sight behind green-tinted clouds. Ash, Jay, RC, and Kit were sleeping. There was no sign of Axel; he must be out in the town. But I knew he wasn't far. Actually, I'd bet anything he was near City Hall right now.

I stared up at the ceiling, its height not unlike the Arena's, but at least from here, I could see the sky. When we were at that place, we were separated in cages. I always fell asleep with my back pressed against Ash's and my fingers curled through the bars to feel Kit's fur. Touching them kept me sane because I knew I wasn't alone in the dark.

We still thrived on that mindset even though bars no longer separated us. My foot was pressed into RC's back; Ash's arm was draped over my stomach; Jay was upside down with his shoulder against mine; Kit was curled into a tiny ball of fur between us.

Slowly, carefully, I disentangled myself from the group. An irritating itch at the back of my sore throat made me cough. I sniffed, rubbed my nose, fastened my cloak, and tossed the hood over my head as I crept to the door leading to the basement. Each step had to be carefully placed because my lab-siblings were light sleepers. They could slumber through my nightmare-induced thrashing because they were used to it, but they would hear me sneaking in the dark if I wasn't careful.

I pretended I was Axel as I moved—silent and undetectable. There were times I envied his natural abilities. Then I remembered everything he'd lost to gain those abilities, and I immediately regretted thinking such thoughts for even a second. He'd knock me across town with one punch if he ever knew. Good thing he wasn't a Mind-Reader.

I almost tripped over the pyramid of soup cans Kit had stacked in the middle of the warehouse, narrowly recognizing the form in the dark and skirting at the last possible second. Kit had proven to be a natural when it came to foraging. She was bringing in most of our food now. When I found a package of stale crackers, Kit showed me up with a whole box of pastries. The ghosts probably didn't even notice the little kitten raiding their stashes after clowders of cats had scouted the town for her so she knew the best marks to hit. I hadn't told anyone, but I'd seen Kit hide something shiny in the wall on more than one occasion. Food wasn't all she was pilfering, but I didn't want Jay to be mad at her. She was probably stealing from thieves anyway, so what was the harm?

My heart was already out of control from the close call with the cans. Opening the basement door silently was harder than I thought it would be; it took me a full minute to coax it open without the hinges squeaking. I pried it partway and tiptoed down the steps to the locked door at the bottom.

I stopped. I didn't know what I was doing down here. The more I was around our prisoner, the more complicated this became. It'd be easier to leave her locked up alone. Hopefully she'd be gone soon, and we'd have Finn and Reese back. There was no point in visiting and getting attached to her now.

And yet, her presence called me stronger than the Rip.

I slid the bolt, and the door swung open to blackness. I stood in the doorway for a long time to let my eyes adjust until I was able to discern the form of a person lying against the wall on the far side of the room. This was as far as I had planned to come, and yet I was like an addict unable to reach my high. I couldn't see her from here. This was a bad idea, very bad, very stupid, and Jay would have every right to pummel me for this if Axel didn't beat him to it, but I stepped inside and closed the door behind me.

She didn't move. I took a long breath and released it twice as slowly, then crept across the room. By the time I reached her, blood pounded in my ears. She slept on, the steady sound of her breathing soothing, her chest rising and falling peacefully. She looked both child-like and ancient at the same time. Survival had taken a toll on her.

A rush of sinful satisfaction coursed through me with the realization that her normal life had ended when mine did. She knew now what a blessing it was to have a bed, to eat a full meal every night, to have a future . . . and to lose it all. Her suffering brought her closer to my level. Maybe I wasn't such an outcast from these humans after all.

I knelt beside her. The book was lying next to her wrist, opened with the spine up and the pages down to mark her place. She must have been reading before the light faded.

Vivian was the first Outsider from Phantom Heights we'd had direct contact with, and I had so many questions for her. I wanted to ask her about Lastday. What happened after the doors closed? What did people say about me?

I couldn't ask her any of those questions, not without betraying who I was. Jay said she didn't know I was here, but I found that hard to believe. I thought the moment we revealed our presence in Phantom Heights, everyone would know I'd escaped and returned. Now I was starting to wonder if only one knew. I couldn't even begin to imagine how deep my mother's conspiracy was threaded. She wanted me to stay a secret buried forever. *He* had told me she'd asked him to throw away my key, and I didn't know what measures she was willing to take to ensure that happened.

The question was, how much did Vivian know?

She was watching me. I started at the sight of her open eyes, and yet she was perfectly calm. She didn't move. "Why are you here?"

A rush of heat flushed my cheeks. I shrugged. "I don't know," I croaked, rather startled by the huskiness in my voice. I tried to clear my throat, but I was congested and couldn't unclog my vocal cords, so I continued, "I couldn't sleep, so I thought—"

"No. I meant, why are you here in Phantom Heights?" As if sensing my uncertainty, she sat up and clarified, "You were stranded almost ninety miles from here. That's a long way to travel."

I heaved my shoulders. "I think the Rip called Jay. He led us here." *I'm actually having a conversation with her. Bloody Scout, is this real?*

Vivian's head tilted. "Just Jay? Not you?"

I started to shrug again, then refrained from the repetitive action. "I can't sense it as well as the others. When I'm close I can feel it, but from a distance I just don't feel that pull."

"Hmm. Well, that's not good. How can you find your way home if you can't sense Tears?"

A bitter chuckle almost escaped before I swallowed it. Home? A Tear couldn't lead me Home. "It doesn't matter. I don't have a home to return to."

"I'm sorry, but I still don't understand why you can't sense Tears. Is there something wrong with you?"

She hadn't meant it to be abrasive, and yet I bristled. "No, there's nothing wrong with me. I can sense Tears, just not as well." I'd never been sensitive about being a half-breed, but something about the phrase "wrong with you" nettled me. There was *nothing* wrong with me.

Her eyes watched me in the dark, and somehow they softened the ice built up around my heart. The anger, the hatred, it was an automatic response. It was how I'd survived, but the truth was I could never hate Vivian. Not even if she followed in her mom's footsteps to become a ghost hunter and looked at me through the scope of a gun. She could despise me all she wanted—she might for all I knew—but I could never hate her.

"Have you ever killed anyone?"

Her sudden question startled me out of my thoughts. "Huh?"

"Agent Kovak told us you—"

"*He* was here?"

She shot me a curious look and answered slowly, "Yes."

"What, ah . . . what did *He* tell you?"

"He thinks you're dangerous. Are you?"

"Huh. Yeah, I guess I am."

She leaned back, not out of fear, but so she could better size me up in the dark. "What's your Divinity?"

"Doesn't really matter." I shifted the cloak off my right arm so she could see the metal band around my biceps glint in the faint moonlight. "Right now, I'm not so different from you."

She squinted at the neutralizer. "What's it feel like, to have your power locked away like that?"

I dropped the cloak, and it fell like a curtain over my shackle. "Like somebody scooped out all the substance in your chest and turned you into a cold, empty shell that can never be warm again."

She didn't look too sympathetic. "Agent Kovak seems to think you're dangerous even without your powers. That's why I want to know—have you ever killed anyone?"

"Yes," I answered truthfully. I remembered the first time I'd taken a life. I was standing in the Arena, the body of a Scout lying at my feet, blood darkening its singed red mane. In mesmerized horror, I had watched the creature's death throes, its claws flexing and scrabbling at the concrete, its scorpion tail thrashing, then curling stiffly as the tattered, leathery wings folded. Its amber eyes were wide open. The life slowly faded from their vacant gaze as the pool of blood spread across the Arena floor toward the drain.

There was such power in taking a life. Such guilt. Even after the blood was washed away in Detox, it stained the mind forever.

"How many?" I simply stared at her. "C'mon, it's not that easy to take a life. How many have you killed?"

"Nineteen," I said without needing an extra second of deliberation.

"Humans?"

"No." But I was obligated to add, "Not yet," because if I ever had to choose between the life of a human and the lives my lab-siblings, I knew what my choice would be.

I expected my answer to scare her, but she said, "Not yet, huh? Do you plan to?"

Feeling unusually coy, I told her, "I haven't decided."

She nodded. Her bravery impressed me, but what else should I expect from the daughter of a ghost hunter? True to her nature, she boldly informed me, "I've killed too. Except my number quadruples yours."

I laughed. She still did it! After all this time, Vivian really hadn't changed that much. Indignant at my chortling, she snapped, "What?"

The laughter triggered a mild coughing fit. Once it passed, I explained, "When you lie, you tilt your chin down and look to the right."

"I do not!"

"Do too."

Now self-conscious, Vivian made a point to look me in the eye. "Even if I do, that's not a reason to laugh at me."

"I'm sorry. I'm not laughing at you. But you aren't a killer." At least, she didn't used to be. She'd fired her ectogun hundreds of times, but I'd bet her real gun, the one loaded with bullets, had never left its holster. "How, um . . . how are you?"

She gave me an incredulous look. "Seriously? You kidnapped me, you're holding me hostage, you've threatened to kill me, and you want to know how I am?" I stared hopefully at her, unsure how to answer. She sighed and admitted, "You know . . . all things considered, I've actually been worse."

"That's good," I blurted. I received a sharp look in response. "Well, I mean, um, not *good*, but . . . you know what I mean?"

She studied me for a few breathless seconds. Then the faintest grin dented her cheeks, and she nodded while turning her gaze downward. "Yeah. I do."

"Question." She stiffened and gave me another strange look, braced for me to pose it. "Are you . . . um, a-are you an apprentice now?"

I held my breath. She looked up at the ceiling and said, "No." She bit her lower lip. "Jay said you kidnapped me to save the twins."

"Yes," I said, my voice breathy with relief at her answer.

"Why?"

I frowned at her, annoyed by the way she kept lobbing simple questions that somehow left me speechless and confused. "What do you mean *why*?"

"Don't you hate the twins? They helped the Agents experiment on you."

I inhaled and sighed. Yes, Finn and Reese had partaken in torturing me. Yes, based on that logic, I should hate them. But they were victims just as much as I was. I wasn't innocent; I'd hurt Jay and RC and Ash in the Arena, and they had hurt me too. "It's hard to explain, but they're like brothers to me. Wouldn't you want to save your brother?"

Even in the dark, I noticed how deathly pale Vivian suddenly became. "How did you know I had a brother?"

I stared at her, and she stared at me, both of us locked in shock for different reasons. "Had?" I whispered. "You *had* . . . ?"

She silenced me by holding up her hand. "I don't want to talk about him."

"Oh. I . . ." My thoughts had ground to an abrupt halt. "I'm sorry." It seemed to be the only semi-appropriate thing to say. *Stupid.* What was I even sorry for?

"Do I know you?"

She fired the inquiry like a bullet. One question, and she'd yanked the ground out from underneath me, sent my mind reeling. *Shit.* "Kn-know me? Why, w-why would you ask that?"

"I don't know, you just seem . . . really familiar for some reason. What's your name?"

I couldn't breathe.

Jay once told me, "*They*'ll try to unname you and make you believe you are A7, not Cato. Don't let *Them*. You have to remember who you are."

I hated my lab name. I was not A7-5292, no matter how hard *He* tried to reprogram me to believe I was. But I couldn't tell Vivian my true identity. I grimaced when I claimed that my name was A7.

"A7?" Vivian repeated. She sounded as disgusted by the name as I felt. "No, I mean your real name. You do have one, right?"

Cato. Cato, Cato, my name is Cato! I wanted to scream at her.

I hung my head and muttered, "You can call me A7."

Saying that aloud killed a piece of my soul. I couldn't look at her.

"No offense, but that is a *terrible* name." My eyes lifted to her face. She tilted her head, scrutinizing me in the darkness. "Seven . . . How 'bout I call you Seph for short. That's marginally better."

It took me a few long seconds to realize my mouth was hanging open, two seconds longer to find the sense to close it. I swallowed. She named me. She looked at me, and she determined I was more than just a numbered lab rat. I was a *person* worthy of a name.

A deep ache made my chest clench. I thought I'd moved on. I thought I could face Vivian without any of the old attachments. I wasn't supposed to love her anymore.

My fingers twitched. I wanted to push my hood back and speak my real name. Maybe she'd accept me. I had doubts before, but now . . .

I remembered holding Kit in the hay when she asked if she was a good sister. And RC stopping the dart mere inches from my face, Ash falling to her knees from the breathtaking beauty of a sunrise, Axel standing between us and the Talon Gang, Finn and Reese with a stone and a leaf in their hands, asking if the objects were alive. I thought of Jay saying, "Do you trust me?" Maybe I should ask him if *he* trusted *me*. Was it worth the risk to the family that took me in when I was nothing, all for this one human?

No. It wasn't.

I so desperately wanted to believe that one person, *this* person, never forgot me, but I had to remember who she was. This was not the Vivian I knew, just as I was not the Cato she once knew. She was a raider, and she'd already mastered skills that put her on the path to an apprenticeship in ghost hunting, whether she ever planned to follow in her mom's footsteps or not. She never even wrote me. I'd like to make myself believe Madison had prevented her from contacting me, but at the same time, I knew Vivian was resourceful. She could have found a way. I wanted to trust her . . . but I couldn't.

"You know, Seph," she said, interrupting my thoughts, "you didn't have to do this." At my puzzled silence, she clarified, "Kidnap me. I understand why you don't trust humans, but all you had to do was ask for help."

I wasn't sure if I should laugh or take her seriously. She leaned forward. "Please take me back. I promise we'll still help the twins. You have my word."

"Your word I'll believe. It's Madison's I don't."

"Mom would never hurt kids, ghost or human."

A great sadness filled me as I stared at the naïve girl in the darkness. She'd never been the one on the wrong side of her mom's gun. "I know what Madison is capable of."

Vivian scoffed. "You're biased because you're a ghost. You don't know her like I do."

"Oh? And you think you're unbiased? If you had even an ounce of ghost blood in you, I guarantee you'd see an ugly side of her you'd never imagined."

She stubbornly shook her head. "You're wrong."

"You know what, forget it. We're never going to agree."

"Fine. Just tell me the truth—are you really going to kill me?"

I was silent for a long minute. I may not have the clairaudience of Axel, but I'd detected the tremor in her voice. My answer wouldn't appease her. "If everything works out the way it's supposed to, neither of us has to worry about that. Okay? Just be good and do what we say, and you'll be fine."

A neutral answer Jay would have approved of. Vivian seemed to accept it. But she abruptly changed the subject once again by snatching her stuffed bear and accusing, "You took this from my room."

A paralyzing cold stole my body. Me? How did she know it was me? She couldn't possibly . . . Maybe I was reading too far into this.

Maybe she meant *you* in the collective plural. That must be it. There was no way she could have known it was me specifically. I challenged, "So?"

"*So*, how did you know where I lived?"

She was starting to ask too many questions. I wasn't the best liar, and I was afraid of too many inconsistencies if I tried to weave tales for her. I rose and told her, "Enough. Go to sleep."

She crossed her arms, resentful that I'd given her an order. "I *was* asleep. You woke me up."

"Then go *back* to sleep," I said, although I was fighting a smile.

She lay back down with an indignant *huff* that made the grin break free. I turned my back to hide it. I crossed the room and opened the door but paused, staring into the pitch black of the empty staircase. I couldn't resist one look back. Vivian's eyes were closed, her toy cuddled in her arms as if she were a child again.

She'd looked at me with fear in her eyes. But it was the same fear she'd have for a human. She was afraid of me because I was holding her hostage, not because I was a ghost or a half-breed or a monster. She saw people for who, not what, they were, and I loved that about her. It was dangerous, I knew, to love a human again, especially this one from the past I was better off leaving far behind.

"Good night, Vivian," I whispered.

I pulled the door closed behind me.

Holly pulled back the blankets. Her shadow fell over the twins, shielding them from the eerie green light leaking through every crevice into City Hall.

Behind her back, she gripped the ectogun she'd pilfered from a sleeping raider. She'd never actually fired one herself, but kneeling beneath a boarded window and tilting the gun up to the light had revealed the safety switch and the trigger, and that was all she needed to know. Aiming wasn't going to be an issue, not at the range she would be at.

The moment she touched the ectogun to A1's forehead, his eyes opened. She'd expected him to recoil as he always did when Doc tried to handle him, but he lay perfectly still, staring up calmly at her as if he'd expected this, his blue eyes faintly aglow.

Holly had been observing him long enough to know how to wordlessly command him to use his Divinity. She cleared her throat. His reaction was immediate and expected; his eyes flared brighter. He was in her mind. She thought (or imagined) that she felt his consciousness brush against hers like a feather.

Lips pressed tightly together, she formed her thoughts into words as if about to speak them: *I know you can talk.*

A1 blinked, and while the gesture may have been innocent, Holly took it as an affirmation.

There is a half-breed in the lab. Not A6, a half-human. His name is Cato.

She focused on Cato. She'd intended to paint a picture of how he used to be, but she couldn't. All her mind would conjure in the heat of the moment was the last time she saw him. Dressed in all black—gloves, combat boots, running pants, sleeveless athletic shirt—he stood dazedly on City Hall's portico, his eyes—one blue, one green—unfocused, vacantly wandering across the faces watching him. He winced every time a camera illuminated his features.

Do you know who I'm talking about?

This time, there was no mistaking a genuine reaction; A1's eyes danced to the side for a moment before they returned to meet Holly's gaze. She caught her breath, her terror temporarily disrupting the clarity she'd been cultivating in her mind. She had been sharpening her thoughts into a javelin intended to pierce the Mind-Reader with one stream of consciousness.

He's not a Telepath, she had to remind herself. He could hear only her current thoughts. He couldn't search her subconscious, and that was where she'd tried to bury the one question she was afraid he might discover—*do they know what I did?*

She had to focus. The moment she let her mind wander, this little

Mind-Reader might learn a lot more than she wanted him to.

Focus.

She narrowed her raging thoughts down to, *Where is he? Which Project did Agent Kovak put Cato in?*

"Are you going to pull the trigger?"

Holly's fingers tightened around the ectogun. That wasn't what she had expected A1's voice to sound like. It was deep, too masculine for his age, too close to her ear. A1's eyes flicked just slightly to stare at someone over her shoulder. Holly didn't turn. She knew who it was.

Wesly Cooper, his voice low and suave, murmured, "If not, I hope you realize you're wasting your time. You can't bluff a Mind-Reader. He knows, even if you're not sure yourself. And believe me, it doesn't take a Mind-Reader to see that you don't have the courage to pull the trigger."

Her lips barely moved when Holly hissed back, "Courage? Is that what it takes to shoot a kid?"

"Whatever it is, you don't have it, do you?"

The hand holding the ectogun had developed a tremor. Holly swallowed hard and stared at A1, at his eyes, at the blue irises glowing in the dark. If she could just focus on those, on the knowledge that he wasn't human, then she could steel her heart enough.

But she couldn't look past his small body, and the frail way his chest rose and fell, and the wide eyes set in a child's hollowed face.

The werewolf extended his hand toward the ectogun, but Holly held it out of reach. "Back off, Cooper."

"What were you asking him?" Even in the dark, she could see his white teeth shaped into a smile. "Were you interrogating him about Kovak's secret weapon? Because I would love to be a part of that conversation."

"It's none of your business," Holly seethed. A1 still hadn't moved, hadn't even reacted to the werewolf's arrival. He just lay still, watching the exchange.

Cooper's teasing smirk hadn't faded since Holly had approached him earlier that morning. "I need a favor," she'd announced.

The grin that had dented the werewolf's cheeks made Holly's stomach turn. He'd answered in an oily voice, "I don't do favors. Small services, now those I'll do, but I charge a fee."

It had been all Holly could do to not roll her eyes. She'd stroked the jagged edge of her thumbnail. The compulsion to chew it off was intolerable. "I need you to bring something back from the next raid."

"Oh?"

"A nail file."

Cooper had gaped at her. "A *nail* file?" She'd returned his gaze with frigid composure despite the rising heat of embarrassment making her perspire. "Seriously? You do know we target food on the raids, right? And medical supplies? Not cosmetics."

"One tiny little nail file shouldn't weigh you down."

"Councilwoman, how delightfully shallow of you. I do enjoy seeing your true colors every once in a while. But I did mention a fee."

"I think this will cover it." Holly had held up a single dull penny.

He'd scoffed. "You're joking."

"Not at all. This is a wheat penny. 1934." She'd noticed the way he had straightened. Then it was her turn to smile. "They don't make pennies like they used to, do they? Not since 1982, unless I'm remembering my history wrong?"

He had shoved his hands into his pockets with a careless shrug. "A penny's a penny," he'd muttered, although the way he'd eyed it assured her she was correct. "Whether it's made of copper or zinc, it's still one cent."

"One cent here, maybe. But copper carries a lot more value in the other Realm, doesn't it?"

"And how would you—?"

"I have a theory. See, there have been unexplained bank robberies all over the country. Agent Kovak suspected ghost activity, but ghosts have no need for human currency, do they, Cooper? But *you* would. And I bet all it cost you was a few copper pennies to pay your hired thief."

Finally, his cocky smirk had vanished. Holly had leaned close to whisper, "So far, I'm the only one who's put two and two together. Would you like to keep it that way?"

He had snorted softly. "You have no idea how expensive that nail file you just bought is."

Holly had pocketed the coin and replied, "It's yours once you bring me what I ordered."

Conducting such petty business with the conniving werewolf was one matter; now he'd caught her trying to interrogate A1 in the middle of the night. The last thing she needed was blackmail over her head from the likes of Wesly Cooper.

She glared at A1, cleared her throat, and thought, *You will not tell a soul about this.* She redirected her glower onto Cooper. "You listen to me, mongrel. This didn't happen. Got it? And if you say otherwise, you're going to wake up neutered. Am I clear?"

He continued to smile at her, his self-assurance rekindled now that the scales had tipped. Holly stood quickly, and he rose slower to face her. She stared him down, but her confidence was wavering, and before she lost her dignity, she wheeled and marched away, gripping the ectogun tightly with regret.

Damn Cooper.

That may have been her only chance, gone.

— Chapter Thirty-One —

Jack

A1 and A2 stared at the disk lying on the floor. Their knees were drawn to their chests, chins on their arms. Every few minutes, one of the boys would reach out and touch the silver surface.

Madison stood several paces away, observing the way their fingers possessed a nervous twitch that caused them to drum against their legs as if typing on an invisible keyboard. She'd thought they would be able to activate whatever secrets the disk held, but no. It was still just a plain, ordinary piece of metal with a hole in the center and a slit around the outside.

Returning the disk to them had triggered the most interactive response from them yet, but it still didn't answer any questions. Madison had waited to present the disk, giving the twins time to recover a little more and herself time to think through the potential consequences. She'd had Wes's blessing but not Trey's, and that wasn't reassuring. She had vowed to keep the disk until the boys were healthy enough for the IVs to come out, although that had been a traumatic experience for them.

"Easy," Doc had said. "Hey, don't hold him so tightly, Shay. All right, all right. That's enough. Let him go."

Shay had released A2 and held his hands up in surrender. "Okay," Doc had soothed. "Hey now, you're okay. I'm sorry. I know you don't like being held down on your back."

As soon as the nurse let go, A2 had rolled onto his side again and curled in on himself like a wilted leaf. Shay had asked, "What do you want me to do, Doc?"

"I can work with him on his side. Give us some space," she had said, waving him away. A2 had flinched at the motion of her hand. "My goodness," she'd mused. "You act like I'm going to torture you. I'm just trying to take that catheter out of your hand. Isn't that what you want? No more needles. I promise. And I'll give you a reward for being so good."

Her hands were gentle as she unwound the gauze. He'd squeezed his eyes shut, his body rigid while she slid the catheter from his vein. "There we go," Doc had said brightly.

A2 had opened one eye and glanced at his hand, then opened his other eye and held his hand up to inspect the sinister wound—a tiny puncture mark and a dark bruise. "Easy, right?" Doc had chimed. "The worst part is over."

As promised, the boys were rewarded with a treat, which turned out to be chicken broth. Shay had propped the patients up with pillows while Lily and Doc sat cross-legged to spoon-feed the twins, who didn't seem to have appetites and didn't want to open their mouths. Doc had bargained, "Let's make a deal. I want you to eat half of this. That seems fair, don't you think? You need to get your strength back." And yet, neither boy opened his mouth until she gave the clear yet gentle order, "Open."

Their reactions had broken Madison's heart. At the first taste, their eyes had grown round with wonder. They'd stared at the nurse and doctor, dumbstruck. They'd clearly never tasted anything like it before, but it was just broth, nothing special, which made Madison wonder what Kovak had permitted them to eat during their lifelong captivity.

A2 had looked at his brother, who had gazed back at him, eyes flashing. "Do you get the feeling they're talking when they do that?" Trey had asked.

"Sure," Madison had answered. "They can read our minds; why wouldn't they read each other's?"

The boys did indeed seem to be having a silent conversation. A1 had cocked an eyebrow as A2 narrowed his eyes ever so slightly, their eyes aglow. Madison had hidden the strange disk behind her back when she approached.

"Hey there," she'd greeted, revealing her hand. The brothers had glanced at her and away again submissively. But they'd glimpsed the disk in her hand, and the twins audibly gasped. Though they had hastened to look away from it, she'd noticed how their eyes kept gravitating back to the disk. She held it out to A1. "This was found with you. Does it mean anything?"

Both twins had stared at the disk with unwavering intensity, not the least bit concerned about the broth anymore. A1 had reached uncertainly for the disk, but then he'd hesitated with his hand still outstretched, glancing at Madison before his eyes settled back onto the disk again. He'd waited, frozen in that position, as if in need of permission before he was allowed to move.

"You can take it," she'd encouraged. He had seized the disk with the greatest care, gazing at the metal as though it were the most priceless material in the world.

When Madison had leaned closer, A1 had clutched the disk protectively to his chest as if afraid she would take it away from him. "What does it do?"

He didn't give her an answer.

She'd been observing them closely ever since, hoping they might unlock a secret compartment or activate a hidden switch. But they treated it more like a security blanket, keeping it close and occasionally touching it for reassurance.

Aware of someone approaching to stand beside her, she said, "They're kind of sweet, aren't they? In a tragic sort of way."

"You aren't getting attached, are you?"

"Holly," she said with a start. "I . . . I'm sorry, I thought you were Doc." Holly didn't answer, and, desperate to alleviate the tension, Madison added, "Listen, I was thinking . . . What if we named them?"

"That's not a good idea."

"Kids shouldn't have numbers for names."

"Except they aren't yours to name. You're going to trade them for your daughter, remember?"

Madison took a shuddering breath. "You're right." She nodded at the whiteboard, which was blank except for the list scrawled in the corner. "They haven't contacted us in a while." In her company's maintained silence, Madison added in a whisper, "I wish I knew she was okay."

"I know you want to gun down everyone in your path and bring her back. What you need to remember is we're not soldiers. We're survivors, and our job is to keep surviving until the real soldiers come."

"I'm not sure they ever will come. And I don't want to put my faith in Agent Kovak."

Holly warned, "Let's remember who the real enemy is."

"Who, *them*?" Madison snapped, jerking her head at A1 and A2.

Holly took her time to select her words. "While I agree what happened to them at the AGC is deplorable, I like to believe Kovak had a good reason. His methods may be questionable, but his motives are true—humankind's survival. Ghost kids are sacrificed to save the lives of human kids. Don't forget, ghosts torture our children for the fun of it."

"You say that like it's a fair trade. They torture our kids, so we torture theirs? Is it easier when you differentiate between *ghost* and *human*? That doesn't change the fact we're discussing the suffering of *children*."

Holly raised her hand as if to touch Madison's shoulder, then thought better of it. "I know what a burden it is to lose a child. I truly do hope Vivian is returned safely. But if she isn't . . . her sacrifice won't be forgotten."

Madison clenched her jaw. She watched A1 touch the disk again, then draw his hand back to rest on his knee. She noted, "I haven't seen you try to interact with them."

Holly's expression hardened immediately. "I have no intention to."

"Why? You aren't afraid of them, are you?"

"Those two? Hardly." She did admit, "I don't like the idea of somebody listening to my thoughts."

"Do you have something to hide?"

"It's principal. They have no right to invade my privacy."

Doc approached her patients, and Madison seized the opportunity to escape from Holly.

A2 snatched the disk as they approached. "Hello," Doc greeted pleasantly despite the cold reception. "You look better. Are you feeling better?" Unsurprisingly, she received no response. She unscrewed a bottle and bent down, explaining, "I've got some medicine for you to take." She measured pink liquid into a spoon and offered it to A2, who eyed it suspiciously. He opened his mouth and allowed her to spoon the medicine in.

Immediately, he made a face of revulsion. "I know it doesn't taste good, but it will help you get better." She turned to his brother with another spoonful.

A1 gazed up at her in dread, his lips pressed firmly together. "Open your mouth," Doc gently ordered. Reluctant but obedient, he did as he was told, eyes closed in preparation for the awful taste. He grimaced and shuddered as the spoon retreated. Doc watched him for a moment. "Come on," she coaxed. "You have to swallow it."

He did, then shook his head and stuck his tongue out.

"Thank you. Now, I need you to swallow this decongestant and then chew this. It's Vitamin C. It's going to help you." After her patients followed her instructions, Doc handed each boy a cough drop. "These will make your sore throats feel better. You suck on them. Don't crunch them, understand?" The twins popped the lozenges into their mouths and used their tongues to experimentally push the cough drops around their mouths.

Satisfied, Doc rose to her feet with a soft groan, leaving her patients to continue staring at the floor while they sucked on their cough drops. Madison caught Doc's arm as she passed. "Listen, Doc, I have a favor to ask. I want to take one of the twins out with—"

"Absolutely not," Doc interrupted sternly.

Madison let go, feeling as dejected as a child being reprimanded. "You didn't let me finish."

"You are not taking one of the twins out with the raid team to try and find the other Alpha ghosts."

Madison's eyebrows crept up in astonishment. Doc shook her head. "Honestly, you're willing to put them in danger out there? What do you think the Alpha ghosts will do to Vivian if they discover you let one of the twins be injured or killed?"

"He'll be guarded."

"So was Vivian."

Madison glared at her. "*Or*, maybe the Alpha ghosts will try to steal him back, and I'll have a chance to capture and interrogate one."

"My patients are not strong enough for a field trip outside. They aren't going anywhere." She marched away without a look back.

Madison exhaled, her gaze wandering back to the twins. They looked so wretched sitting there. People had tried to induce them to talk—Lily, Shay, Doc, Trey, Wes, even some of the local kids. But A1 and A2 never responded. All they did was sit and stare at nothing with those downhearted expressions. The poor boys had probably reached out for years in desperation, seeking attention, but they were denied every time and treated like lab animals instead of people until they'd withdrawn into themselves so deeply they were now socially under-developed beyond repair.

Their powers complicated matters. Yesterday morning, Doc had knelt to wake them and discovered that their lips were moving in their sleep. When she touched A2, the boy's eyes had snapped open, but they didn't see; they flicked frantically back and forth, vacant, his mouth forming silent words. "Madison?" Doc had called in a panic. "Wes? Something's wrong."

Wes's solution had been as simple as calling, "Hey!" and snapping his fingers in front of the boy's face. A2 had blinked rapidly, focused on Wes, and closed his mouth, although he looked completely lost. The werewolf had smiled at him and said, "Welcome back."

"What did you do?" Doc had demanded. "What was wrong with him?"

"Nothing," Wes had answered as he stood. "There are a lot of peo-ple—a lot of thoughts to hear. He just needed a little help to separate his mind from theirs. Most Mind-Readers in the Ghost Realm have some instruction from a parent or teacher. I'm betting these poor bastards never got a lesson in Mind-Reading 101."

It was a miracle the kids hadn't descended into absolute madness by now. Madison wandered closer and sat down where Doc had been kneeling. The boys didn't move. "Please look at me." Their shocking blue eyes glanced up at her and back to their feet in less than a second.

Madison reached out to touch one's hand, but he subtly withdrew it out of her reach before she could set hers on top of his. She cleared her throat—he stiffened expectantly and raised his head to finally meet her gaze, his eyes glowing—and revealed a baseball cap from behind her back. She couldn't remember if it was A1 or A2 who had been wearing it when she first found them. Actually, she couldn't even tell them apart right now unless she inspected their tattoos. She offered it to the closest twin. "Here."

He hesitated, but his eyes were still glowing, and once he understood what she wanted, he accepted the hat and put it on backward. When he brought his hands back down to his lap, she glimpsed his number—A2.

Against Holly's advice, she took a breath and said, "Listen, I was thinking . . . You need names. How about . . . mmm . . . Andrew? Or Nate? Those are good names. Do you like them?"

"Maybe Jack?" Holly taunted from a few yards away.

Madison grimaced. "Not Jack," she choked out. "Could we call you Andrew and Nate?" The twins' reactions were subtle, almost unnoticeable, but Madison thought she saw the slightest wrinkles of disapproval etch into their foreheads. "No? Okay, you can think about it. Maybe I could make a list for you to pick from."

Their response was less than enthusiastic; it was nonexistent.

Hassing stood on a rooftop gazing out over the ruins of the human town. Rayven's talons pricked his left shoulder through his cloak, which swayed in the acrid breeze. "Anything yet?" he asked, glancing down at the cloaked figure sitting cross-legged beside him with her head bowed.

Officer Jana opened her eyes. "Something is knocking them right out of the sky," she said, holding up the black heap of feathers she'd been cradling in her lap. "A shadow that smells like death."

Rayven made a noise in his throat. Hassing glared down at the broken body of a crow, its ruffled feathers stirred by another gentle gust. He clenched his fists. His Divinity pulsed; sparks of green ectoplasm jumped across his knuckles. "That's a vague and useless analysis that doesn't help us."

Jana's glowing blue eyes peered up at him from beneath her hood. "I've never been given an unknown target before. It's impossible to focus on somebody if I don't know who I'm looking for." She stroked the bird's head with her thumb. "Let me concentrate. I'm trying to trace the connection back to the shadow that took his life, and it's the most obscure link I've ever attempted considering this poor bird didn't even know what hit it."

Hassing turned his back on her. "Find those fugitives, or it'll be your head and mine."

"No pressure," she muttered, bowing her head again in concentration.

Above, a murder of crows flew low over the town and alighted in a maple. "One for sorrow, two for mirth," Hassing recited under his breath, remembering the rhyme from childhood. *Three's a marriage, four a birth. Five is good luck; six is not. Seven a secret whose answer is sought . . .*

Jana gasped and clutched the dead crow tighter.

"You found them?"

Her eyes were wide open but glowing, which meant she was using her remote-viewing Divinity. She could still see, but she was also watching another scene. "He's looking right at me," she whispered.

"Who?" Hassing demanded. At her blank look of horror, he added, "It's a coincidence your target happens to be looking this way. He can't see you."

"He can, though. He just told me so."

"What?"

Jana blinked hard to sever the vision. Rather pale, she twisted to look up at him. "He was wearing a hood, so I couldn't really see his face. But I felt it—he was staring *right at me*. That . . . that's never happened before."

"And it didn't happen this time. Remote-viewing is passive," Hassing reminded her. "There's no way—"

"It *did*. The target's back was to me at first. Then he turned, like he felt me watching and was trying to find me, and then we made eye contact. He said, 'I see you.'" She shuddered.

"What did he look like?"

She gazed at the lifeless bird in her hands. "I couldn't say for sure. He was dressed in black, wearing a hood. I couldn't see his eyes. Which . . . is weird. They weren't glowing. But he was definitely staring at me; I could feel it. No facial hair. Young. Pale skin. That's all I can say."

"You're sure he's a kálos if his eyes weren't glowing?"

"I'm not sure of anything."

Hassing wandered to the edge of the roof and gazed across the town, causing Rayven to tighten his sharp grip to maintain his balance. "Do not use your Divinity again."

"What?" He heard Jana rise. "But Captain, I can't devise a strategy for my team if I can't—"

"If the fugitive really is capable of detecting when you're remote-viewing him, that's a prime opportunity to feed us false information. And that's a bigger risk than having no information at all."

"But Captain—"

He swiveled his head to give her a solid glare. "That's an order, Officer." She slumped in defeat.

Hassing winced when Rayven's talons dug into his shoulder as the bird crouched, then took off, wings flapping. He cursed and grabbed at Rayven, but the feathers slipped through his fingers. Hassing summoned his Divinity, letting it warm him from the heart of his core. The heat flowed freely to his fingertips when he snapped his wrist, and a whip of crackling green ectoplasm cut through the air. The concentrated energy caught the Amínyte, and with a yank, Hassing pulled the bird out of the sky.

Rayven squawked when he hit the rooftop. "Not so fast, you waste of feathers," Hassing growled, dragging him closer. Jana averted her gaze.

Rayven transformed in a swirl of black smoke, but Hassing maintained the ectoplasm bonds. The slave's nostrils flared, golden eyes blazing. "Master expects a report."

"And you'll give him one. But you're going to exclude some details. You'll tell Azar the fugitives are killing off your spies and Officer Jana has been unable to establish a full remote link. You won't say a word about the lab rat who spoke directly to her when she was observing him. And you will *not* tell Azar I ordered a cease to Jana's reconnaissance. Am I understood?"

Rayven glowered at him. Hassing let the nearly solid Grade B ectoplasm degrade to a sizzling current of Grade F, causing Rayven to go stiff and bite back a groan. He contained his pain admirably. No doubt plenty of practice.

Rayven went limp the second Hassing let the ectoplasm dissipate. "Am I understood?" he repeated.

"Yes," Rayven grumbled. He transmuted in smoke again and lifted off.

Hassing watched the black bird with the white-tipped wing ascend over the buildings. As Rayven passed over the maple tree down below, the murder of crows lifted into the sky again with a ruckus, following in his wake.

Eight brings change, and nine's a curse. Ten, beware, and brace for the worst.

Hassing shook his head, imagining Azar pacing in his office, waiting.

Waiting for him to bring the Alpha fugitives.

The Alpha fugitives he couldn't find.

— Chapter Thirty-Two —

Errand

When Vivian awoke, she made a horrifying, humiliating discovery that caused her to lock herself in the bathroom and cry. She stayed there until she heard the door in the outer room open, and she knew Jay had brought her lunch. Still sniffling, she unlocked the bathroom door and cracked it open. "Jay?"

She could make out his form in the gloom. He paused and stared at her, and she nearly broke down in tears again. "I . . . um, I need . . . Jay, I need a tampon," she finally admitted. "Or a pad, or *something*. Toilet paper isn't really working."

Jay continued to stare at her. She could feel the temperature rising in her cheeks until her whole face was on fire. All she wanted to do was slam the door shut again and lock herself away, but she had to swallow her pride and stare back at Jay, waiting. He still didn't speak. The mortification was dissolving into resentment that he seemed to be purposely shaming her.

Finally, he asked, "You need what?"

"A tampon or pad," she repeated. "Please. I'm bleeding."

"You're injured?"

"What?" She scowled and opened the door a little wider. "No. I'm on my period." He continued to gaze blankly at her until she sighed in exasperation and said, "There's a girl in your gang, right? I saw her upstairs. Could I speak with her, please? She'll know what I'm talking about."

Still perplexed, Jay turned slowly, then watched her over his shoulder while he returned to the door. Vivian glared at him until he closed and locked it. His footsteps ascended the staircase on the other side.

Vivian ran her fingers through her hair, tears burning her eyes again. She wiped them away on the sleeve of her jacket. This was so embarrassing.

She did her best to ignore the discomfort of toilet paper wadded in her underwear while she waited. And waited. What was taking so long?

No sooner had she crouched down in the corner to ease the cramps than she heard faint footfalls on the steps. The person hesitated on the other side of the door. Slowly, Vivian rose. She held her breath for another few seconds.

Then, finally, the lock clicked, and the door inched open.

This Alpha ghost was nothing like Jay. While the leader had been overly cautious every time he entered Vivian's prison, this one was more skittish than a deer. She peeked inside first, then crept in. She used her foot to close the door behind her because both hands were occupied with a long metal staff clenched in front of her body.

The two girls critically surveyed one another from across the room. Vivian couldn't see the Alpha ghost's face, but she noticed long, dark hair spilling out of the hood. The girl wore a black sports bra under her cloak, showing off her smooth, strong abdomen and tapered waist. She had the figure Vivian had always lusted after.

Vivian had been uncomfortable before, and now she felt what little self-confidence she had left dissolving. She'd always thought of herself as barely sub-par. Pretty, more or less, but not quite beautiful. She'd never had the confidence to dress in clothing that exposed her midriff like that.

The Alpha ghost didn't move, didn't speak, didn't acknowledge Vivian in any way, leaving the introduction up to Vivian, who cleared her throat and said, "Hi. Um, what's your name?"

"Ash." She tightened her grip on the weapon.

"Ash," Vivian acknowledged. She'd halfway expected her to answer with a number like Seph had last night—that experience had been so dreamlike Vivian still wasn't entirely sure it had even happened—and she said, "Uh . . . well, this is an awkward introduction, but I, um, I need . . . girl-to-girl, it's that time of the month, so . . . can you spare a tampon?"

Ash stared at Vivian with confusion equivalent to Jay's. "What?"

Vivian sighed with exasperation. "A *tampon*. I started my period, okay? I need a tampon!"

Her voice rang in the closed room, and Ash took an uneasy step back. Vivian glared at her, fuming. Ash had a gorgeous body and likely a pretty face to match—although Vivian enviously hoped not. Her breasts were filled out, and her hips had an attractive curve. She'd definitely already crossed the adolescent threshold. Was this clueless act for the sole sake of humiliating the prisoner?

The answer hit Vivian rather suddenly. She remembered something she might have heard while halfway listening to her mom, something about ghosts coming of age. Ash could be old enough to be Vivian's grandma, but it was possible she wasn't old enough to reproduce yet. Pregnancy wasn't possible until, what, like a hundred years old or something, if Vivian was remembering correctly. Did she remember her mom saying a ghost came of age twice? Ash might have a post-pubescent body with a prepubescent reproductive system due to the skewed aging ratio compared to humans.

Vivian hung her head with a defeated sigh. What was she supposed to do now? Strip from the waist down and crouch in the bathroom for the next week?

Her gaze landed on Tessie's glass eyes staring up at her from the grimy tiles. Vivian snatched the teddy bear and held it up. "You know where I live," she stated, holding Tessie out as proof. Ash neither confirmed nor denied the proclamation. "I know I'm not in any position to ask for favors, but if you could go back to my house and look in the upstairs bathroom, there should be a pink box with a picture of a running girl on it. You'll find it in the cupboard above the sink. I really, *really* need that box. And maybe you could grab a change of clothes from my room while you're there?"

Ash shifted the staff to one hand and reached up to sheathe it across her back, revealing her smooth underarms. Vivian was certain a fugitive didn't have time to worry about luxuries such as shaving one's armpits while living on the streets. Just another example of how ghost bodies were different from human bodies, even if some ghosts did look almost human. *Lucky bitch*, Vivian caught herself thinking jealously. Ash probably didn't have to shave her legs, either.

Vivian folded her arms tightly across her chest, suddenly paranoid this demi-goddess ghost girl might somehow be able to see the nests of armpit hair under her jacket, or at least suspect and judge. Embarrassed on every level, Vivian turned her head away.

Ash set her hand on the doorknob. "I'll tell Jay what you want."

"Thank you." Ash was already out the door. Vivian called after her, "Tell him it's really important!"

The door closed, and the lock slid into place on the other side.

Vivian wandered back into the bathroom. She stared at the cracked mirror above the sink. Her reflection was blurred behind a layer of grime. She stepped closer and used her sleeve to clean a patch, then scrutinized her face with a critical eye. Her eyebrows needed plucked, a pimple had formed on her left cheek, and more than a year's worth of dirt had darkened her skin tone a few shades. What she wouldn't give for a bar of soap, a hairbrush, a razor, and a pair of tweezers.

She sighed, eclipsed in the light of Ash's perfection even though she'd never even seen Ash's face. She wrapped her arms around her midriff and turned away from the mirror.

I opened the cabinet door and skimmed the shelves inside. "Pink box," I muttered. "Let's see, a pink box . . . Oh. This must be it." I seized it and held it up.

"That ain't pink," Axel disputed.

I frowned at the box. "What are you talking about? Yes it is."

He interlocked his fingers behind his head and dismissed, "Whatever you say."

I pointed at it and added, "Besides, here's the picture of a running girl. What, are you color blind or something?"

Axel scoffed. "Compared to me, *you're* color blind. If that's the color you think is pink, fine."

I tilted the box, studying it. "What do you s'pose Vivian needs this for?"

"I dunno."

We both leaned closer. I opened the box to peer inside at a bunch of wrappers. I pulled one out. It was long, and whatever was inside felt cylindrical. I tore open the wrapper to find a plastic tube, rounded on one end with a straw and a string on the other. I tugged on the string, which didn't seem to have an effect, so then I experimentally pushed against the straw. From the rounded end of the cylinder, white fluff emerged. "Think it's a weapon?" I asked.

Axel hummed a sing-song version of *I dunno* and heaved his shoulders in a shrug. I tossed the object down the hall to see if it would explode or transform into something dangerous. It rolled to a stop in the middle of the hallway and just sat there. Axel and I waited, staring at it. Finally, he said, "Humans are weird. Let's go."

"Hold on," I said as I closed the box. "Viv asked for a change of clothes."

I wandered into her room. It didn't look as though anything had been moved since the last time I was here when I found the bear and book on her bedside table. Axel followed and leaned against the doorframe. "*Viv?*" he mocked.

My cheeks warmed, and I kept my back to him while I knelt to pick a drawstring bag off the floor. "What?"

"Just sounds a little casual. You think she calls you *Cay*?"

Probably not. Actually, she probably didn't think about me at all.

I elected not to answer.

Vivian had an abundance of clothes, which whoever raided the house before had tossed throughout the room when emptying her closet. I shoved a pair of stretchy black pants into the bag with short boots.

Axel continued, "No, wait, she doesn't call you Cay, does she? She doesn't even call you Cato."

Oh no. I could hear the smirk in his voice when he finished, "It's *Seph* now, right?" I was so mortified I couldn't face him. He sniggered. "That's adorable."

The heat burned my whole face, spreading down my neck and scorching the tips of my ears. "Don't tell anybody." I shoved a tank top, two bras, a handful of underwear and socks, and a jacket into the bag.

"Why?" Axel challenged. "Keeping secrets? Don't want Jay to know?"

"Please, Axel?" I implored. I still couldn't look at him when I grabbed the hairbrush off the dresser. I felt his presence right behind me. I didn't want to, but I lifted my face to look into Vivian's mirror and meet his red eyes, as if facing his reflection might be less intimidating than the real person.

It wasn't.

"A piece of advice, Cato," he said in a low, deadly voice. "Don't do anything that might jeopardize this family."

I turned away from the mirror and snarled under my breath, "I'd never hurt our family."

He didn't answer. When I looked up, he was already heading out the door. "Come on. I'm bored."

Relieved, I followed him into the hallway. He reached the staircase and jumped the whole flight of stairs, landing as light as a feather at the bottom.

Determined to prove my own stealth and speed, I took the steps two at a time and joined Axel on the landing. I thought I was quiet, but to him, I might as well have tromped down the stairs. I could never impress him.

He was already waiting by the front door. I took the last two steps and hesitated, my attention drawn toward the kitchen. "What's wrong?" Axel asked.

I crossed the living room and paused in the doorway to the kitchen, my eyes wandering. "Wanna share what you're looking for?" Axel grumbled over my shoulder.

"Weapons," I muttered, venturing into the kitchen and opening drawers.

"You got weapons, dumbass," Axel reminded me. He folded his arms and leaned against the doorframe.

He wasn't wrong; I was wearing Vivian's weapon belt. I still hadn't fired her ectogun yet, but it was nice to know I had access to it while I was roaming this ghost town. There was another gun I hadn't examined yet, plus three small canisters in the belt—I was pretty sure they'd belch out smoke if I pulled the pins—as well as a pocketknife, a lighter, a stun gun, a Tazer, and a pouch of little square gadgets whose function I still wasn't sure of. Not quite my taste for a weapon arsenal.

I yanked open the drawer next to the sink. That was what I'd been looking for. I seized two handles and lifted up a pair of cutting knives for Axel to see. The smooth blades gleamed when a ray of sunlight through the boarded window struck them.

He raised one eyebrow. "Those ain't gonna replace the weapons you're used to fighting with, you know."

I held one knife in each palm, weighing them. The shape was wrong, and the balance, and they were a little too heavy, but this was the closest substitute to the dual blades I favored in the Arena. "I just need a little practice."

"Uh-huh," he said doubtfully. I stepped toward him, then hesitated, my eyes drawn back to the locked basement door. Madison's home laboratory. My palms immediately moistened, and my feet turned cold.

"There could be better weapons down there." Axel's voice in my ear made me jump out of my skin.

I had no doubt I'd find weapons down there . . . and who knew what else. Fear flared in me at the thought of even opening that door. "These'll work," I said, striding past Axel for the front door. I felt rather than heard him following close behind.

I sheathed my new knives in the belt and shouldered the drawstring bag, proclaiming with forced cheeriness, "Bet this'll make Vivian happy."

I opened the front door, and Axel slipped past me. "What do you care?" he said. "Ash is gonna be the one to give her all this stuff."

My spirits fell. "Huh?"

"*Viv* asked for Ash, remember? And if Ash doesn't give this to her, Jay will. Either way, it ain't gonna be you."

347

I ignored the way he said *Viv* just to irk me and shrugged with what I hoped came across as carelessness, although I could never pull off that attitude as successfully as Axel. "Whatever."

Axel smirked and eyed me sidelong. I stared determinedly forward. Our mission had been a success, and even if I wouldn't be the one to deliver the spoils to our prisoner, knowing Vivian would appreciate the gift eased my guilt a little after we'd traumatized her. It was a slight sense of satisfaction in light of the situation that had been darkening all of our thoughts these past few days: RC was getting worse.

We'd all been feeling more and more helpless watching RC's fever burn him alive. Kit wouldn't leave his side, and Jay had been pacing so much I'd swear he was wearing a track in the floor. Nobody would say it aloud—we'd risked everything to save Finn and Reese only to be losing RC. Not even the humans of Phantom Heights could help us this time, and even if they could, we had nothing left to gamble. *They* were the only ones who could save RC.

I shifted the bag on my shoulder. I knew I had to focus on getting Finn and Reese back, but even after the welcome distraction Vivian had provided, my mind was fixated on the infection in RC's arm. At this rate, RC was going to die, and there was nothing I could do.

— Chapter Thirty-Three —

Rubik's Cube

Shannon folded her legs and seated herself next to Trey, who was so focused on the Rubik's cube in his hands he didn't notice her until she said, "Hey."

His concentration broken, he jerked his head up and blinked at her like some nocturnal beast in the sunlight. He had traded his optical goggles for his glasses, the lenses magnifying his eyes and adding to the effect. "Oh. Hey."

They sat in silence for several long minutes. He turned the rows on his cube, and Shannon appreciated his quiet presence while she collected her thoughts.

"I couldn't pull the trigger," she finally said. Trey paused long enough to glance at her from the corner of his eye. She bowed her head. "That day I went with the raid team, everyone else acted, but I couldn't do it. Does that make me weak?"

"No." He turned one rotation and then inspected the squares to see how the patterns had changed. "Violence doesn't equal strength."

Shannon scooted a little closer. "How do you do it?"

Trey heaved a deep sigh. "You see them as people, don't you? You have to learn to look at them differently. It's easier to shoot the ones that look like monsters. The ones that look like humans are harder. But they're not human, and they want to kill you. That's what you have to remember when you need to pull the trigger."

"How do *you* do it?" Shannon repeated. "I looked at them, and I saw Cato, and I couldn't shoot."

"I see Cato every time I have to shoot a ghost. But then I remind myself they're not like him. And if Cato were standing next to me, he wouldn't hesitate to shoot them, so neither should I."

Shannon nodded slowly. She understood, but she knew in her heart if she ever found herself in that situation again, she still probably wouldn't be able to pull the trigger. She drew her knees to her chest and watched A1 and A2 sleep.

"You see them as people, don't you?"

How else was she supposed to see them? No, they weren't human, but that didn't mean they weren't people. And right now, with their surreal blue eyes closed and their chests rising and falling in slumber, they did look human.

"It's easier to shoot the ones that look like monsters."

Her best friend Amber's eight-year-old brother, Andy, had tried to play with A1 and A2. It was a simple game of catch, but the results were pathetic. Andy had tossed a ball to A2, who saw it coming and reacted by throwing his arms over his head and cowering. The ball had bounced off his back and rolled down the steps.

Andy had retrieved the ball and said, "No, you're supposed to catch it, then throw it back to me. It's a game." He'd tried again with the same outcome. A2 didn't even try to catch the ball. Andy had then tried rolling the ball to A1 to see if he would roll it back. The kid didn't move. Only his eyes had shifted to follow the ball as it rolled toward him and bumped against his knee.

"I've never seen a person so broken before," Shannon murmured. Trey peered at her, then followed her gaze to the twins. She swallowed hard. "Do you think . . . Cato . . . ?"

He pushed the glasses farther up the bridge of his nose and glared down at his puzzle. "I try not to."

Shannon nodded. "Something's been bothering me. I was hoping you might be able to shed some light for me."

"I'll try. What's up?"

"I just . . . I don't know, thinking about Cato, and ghosts, and all that's happened to us . . . Mom believes ghosts are demons from the outermost layer of hell. Is . . . is that what you think? That they're demons?"

Trey set the Rubik's cube on the floor. "Honestly, I'm still trying to figure out what I think." Shannon bowed her head. He continued, "But I can tell you what Madison thinks."

"She's a Christian, right?"

"I'm not sure. We've never discussed religion." Trey twisted so he could face Shannon. "When I first started training, Madison drew two overlapping circles on a piece of paper. Remember those Venn diagrams we used to do in elementary school?"

She nodded.

"Madison said it was just a theory, but one circle represented our Realm and the other circle represented the Spirit Realm—heaven, hell, the afterlife, whatever you believe. The middle area where the two circles overlap is the Ghost Realm. Madison says it's a Realm where the spiritual and the physical can coexist."

"So, she doesn't think ghosts—well, *kálos* I guess—are demons."

"Right. They're more like mortal half-spirits."

Shannon nodded slowly, digesting the idea. "I think I like that."

Trey gave her a crooked grin as he picked up the cube. "What's neat about Madison's theory is, who's to say there are only two circles? I think there could be dozens, even hundreds of other Realms out there, and they probably overlap in different places. Some might be a little in the Spirit Realm, and some a lot more. It's hard to imagine."

"Yeah."

"Madison thinks it's a plausible theory. She's encouraging me to write a thesis on it someday. You know, assuming I can catch up on my studies."

"That's exciting." Shannon glanced around to make sure no one was listening, then leaned in and whispered, "Listen, I had an idea."

"Yeah?" He was focused on the Rubik's cube again and didn't look at her.

"Yeah. The twins are Mind-Readers, right? I bet they know what really happened to him at the AGC."

"Who?"

"You know who."

Trey froze. Still refusing to meet her gaze, he muttered at his cube, "We know what happened to Cato."

"Do we?" She leaned closer. "Really?"

He stared at the Rubik's cube a few seconds longer, then finally lifted his head to look at her. "Did you try asking them?"

She shook her head, then tucked a strand of hair behind her ear. "Mom forbade me. She won't let me go near them."

"Seriously? Then wait until she's not paying attention. I know you're not a fan of breaking rules, but—"

"Haven't you noticed? She watches them more than Mrs. Tarrow does."

"Doubt that. Madison hardly ever takes her eyes off them."

"Look," Shannon whispered, barely moving her lips. Trey, seeming to understand her unspoken call for subtlety, bowed his head and shifted his eyes to find her mom. Sure enough, she was strategically placed a few rows from the stage in a position where she could keep an unobstructed watch over A1 and A2 without being noticed by Madison and Doc.

"She's obsessed," Shannon whispered. "She watches them like a hawk. I mean, I know she doesn't trust ghosts, but I can't imagine she's afraid of them hurting anybody."

Shannon studied her mom. The dark circles hollowed out her eyes, the worry lines in her forehead carving a little deeper each day. Silver-gray hairs streaked through the black. Shannon wanted to hit rewind, to remove the obsessive and paranoid glint from her mom's eyes, to replace the frown lines with a smile, to be small enough to fit completely in her safe arms again and naïve enough to believe her mom would do anything to protect her.

"Your mom is . . ." Trey trailed off.

"I know." Shannon shrugged. "Like it matters. They can't talk anyway."

"I think they can. They just haven't been given a reason to."

She offered him a kind smile. "You're worried about Vivian."

He closed his eyes in a grimace and leaned his head back against the wall. "How can I not be? If she's still alive, she's a prisoner of cold-hearted killers, and who knows what they're doing to her right now?"

"You love her, don't you?"

His eyes flew open. "What? No. Why would you say that?"

"Come on, I've seen the way you look at her."

Shannon watched his ears turn vermillion, the color spreading to his cheeks. "Was I that obvious?"

"To everyone but her." Shannon reached out and took the Rubik's cube from him. She was pretty sure Cato had given it to him years ago, and it had never been solved since the day Trey first turned the rows out of place. He could cheat by peeling off the stickers, but he didn't. She turned the cube over. "Why don't you just tell her?"

Trey shrugged. "Cato." Shannon set the cube back in Trey's palm and gave him an inquisitive look. "Every time I think I'm ready to con-fess to her, I see Cato, and, I don't know, I feel like I need his permis-sion before I can have a clear conscience. That's stupid, right? It's not like he . . . I mean, Vivian . . . I just . . . I feel guilty somehow, you know?" He shook his head and resumed his task of turning the rows. "It's stupid," he muttered under his breath.

Shannon said, "When Cato was in his right state of mind . . ." She trailed off and started over. "The Cato we remember would want you to be happy. And Vivian. And if that means the two of you end up to-gether, I'm sure he'd be happy. In fact, I bet he'd be proud of you. You're turning out to be a great ghost hunter."

Trey scoffed. "I wouldn't say that."

"That day I snuck out with the raid team, you were so brave. Braver than I could hope to ever be."

Trey twisted the cube, head down, eyes fixed but unseeing. "I must hide it well, then. You know something? Every time the teams go out, I'm terrified. Not of dying, but rather that Madison will be hurt or killed, or Chief Emerton. I'm expected to fill the position as team lead-er if one of them dies. And I . . . I can't. I'm not ready." His knuckles turned white around the cube's edges. "I'm sorry."

"Why?"

"Because I shouldn't have said that. Madison wants me to be a leader, and leaders can't admit things like that."

Shannon leaned her head back to stare up at the rafters. "Trust me, I know. We're just kids pretending to be adults. You don't have to apologize."

Trey nodded. "Thanks. Hey, you know, talking about that day . . . Why *did* you decide to sneak out with the raid team?"

"Oh. Like I said, just, get some fresh air, stretch my legs. You know." Shannon let a sigh escape. "When you were a kid, did you ever run away from home?"

"No."

"But didn't you ever think about it? Not seriously enough to actually do it, but just wonder how long it would take anyone to notice you were gone . . . who would worry, who would miss you?"

Shannon's eyes were still on the rafters, but she could feel Trey looking at her sidelong behind the lenses. "Did *you* ever run away?"

She turned her head to meet his concerned gaze. "The raid was the closest I've ever come." She set her hands on her knees and rose.

Trey watched her waist-length hair sway with each step as she walked away. She wasn't returning to Mrs. Jennings; her destination led her to Amber instead, a pretty blonde girl who had been in his English class the last semester before the school shut down.

He studied the cube still cupped in both hands. Red, white, yellow. That wasn't right; the red had to be the middle square so it lined up with the middle red square of the second row. Trey turned the top row of the Rubik's cube once to the right. Now it was orange, red, blue.

He puffed air into his cheeks and let it out slowly; what was supposed to be a distraction to keep his hands and mind busy was quickly becoming a headache. He wanted to chuck it, but settled for slamming it onto the floor. When he looked up, he encountered two pairs of glowing blue eyes.

Trey gasped, so startled by the intensity of their gazes that he couldn't help himself. He'd been sure they were asleep—it was only dawn, after all—but as soon as the connection was made, the twins severed it and looked down at their feet again.

Trey stared at them, waiting for their eyes to flick back up. When it became clear they knew he was watching and didn't intend to raise their heads again, he twisted to look around. No one except Council-woman Jennings was paying any attention to him or the twins. Convinced it had definitely been him they were watching, Trey faced forward again.

He fiddled with the puzzle, eyes constantly shifting between the cube and the twins. They were Mind-Readers, and they knew exactly what he was doing, and yet they couldn't help themselves; more than once, he caught the blue eyes transfixed, not on him but on the cube in his hands, though they looked down again as soon as he looked up.

It was a game, trying to catch them in the act of watching. After a few minutes, he stood. Immediately, they gazed down at their toes. Their faces were composed to betray no expression, no emotion, no way to know what was going through their heads. Their silent, melancholy moods were unnerving—kids weren't supposed to behave like this. Even the human kids living in City Hall would make up games and tell stories and chase each other and laugh.

Trey ascended the steps and knelt in front of A1 and A2. Their eyes were glowing even though they didn't look up at him. He felt nothing when they were in his mind—no probing, no second consciousness in his head—but it was unsettling to know they were listening to his innermost thoughts.

Trey swallowed, realizing they knew he thought their powers were creepy. Self-conscious, he held out his hand, the Rubik's cube balanced on his palm.

He'd expected one or both of the boys to grab it, but neither moved. The three remained frozen until Trey began to feel uncomfortable. Mrs. Jennings's eyes were boring into his back. "Here," he mumbled, holding it closer. "You can take it."

One of them cautiously raised his arm. He hesitated before reaching for the colorful cube, looking questioningly at Trey. "Go ahead. Take it."

Gingerly, as though the cube were made of glass, the boy gripped the Rubik's cube and took it into his hands. He gazed at it, intrigued, as his brother peered at it from the side.

Trey shifted, acutely aware that more people were watching now. *As if the situation weren't awkward enough without an audience.* He cleared his throat and pointed to the cube. "The, ah, goal is to make all the sides one color. Um, see, you twist the rows."

The boy holding the cube made no attempt to experiment by turning it. Trey licked his lips. He indicated the center square. "I've never solved it, but I know the middle square tells you what color that side is supposed to be. Like, this one is red. That means when it's solved, this side will be red."

Not surprisingly, he didn't receive so much as a nod of acknowledgment. "Okay, well . . . you can play around with it for a while if you want. So . . . yeah." He rose to his feet and walked away.

Vivian would have been the first person he'd go to and confide, "Well, that was a disaster." But she was locked away somewhere, possibly dead.

No. No, he shouldn't think like that. He jumped when hot breath tickled his ear and a masculine voice praised, "Nice work."

Trey peered at Wes over his shoulder. "Huh?" The werewolf jerked his chin at the stage. Trey turned to see the twins leaning together, turning the cube to study it from all angles, twisting a row to see how the patterns were affected. "Oh. Well, that's—"

"Good. We get them to open up, and maybe they'll tell us what's going on in that mysterious lab."

Trey scoffed. "Right. Because I'm sure they're dying to tell us all the secrets their masters are hiding." Despite the sarcasm, his heart skipped a beat when he remembered Shannon's theory. His eyes darted to Mrs. Jennings. Her icy emerald eyes were staring right back at him. Shannon hadn't been exaggerating when she'd claimed her mom was obsessed about any interactions with the twins.

Trey gulped and turned back to Wes, who said, "We'll see. Those kids can answer a lot of questions."

"Except they obey humans, and I bet they don't consider a were-wolf to fall under the human category." Wes scowled, eyes flashing yellow ever so briefly before they returned to their normal mud color. He turned to leave.

"Wes, wait," said Trey, seizing the werewolf's arm so he didn't have to be alone under Mrs. Jennings's scrutiny. "I have a question I've been wanting to ask you. What's a passive power?"

Wes arched an eyebrow. "You're asking for an example or a definition?"

"Well, I don't know. You'd mentioned that the twins have passive powers . . . and I don't really know what that means. Madison was explaining to me about kálos and moorlins, but she never mentioned passive powers."

"Ah." Wes turned back to face Trey. "You're asking what the difference is between active and passive. Basically, it's how kálos classify their Divinities. Passive powers affect only the ghost and no one around him. So, for example, the twins are Mind-Readers. Do you know when they're reading your mind?"

"No."

"And are you affected in any way when they read your mind?"

"Uh, no."

"So, mind-reading is a passive Divinity. A good example for perspective would be shape-shifting. It doesn't matter what form the Shifter takes because changing shape does not affect you or the environment in any way."

"Okay, so that means an active Divinity *does* affect other people or the environment?"

"Right. Elementals, for example, physically change the environment when they use their abilities. Those are active Divinities."

"A kálos can *not* have a Divinity, right?"

"Sure. Not many, but there are some."

"What if one has a Divinity but not the basic powers?"

"Then it isn't a kálos," Wes answered without hesitation. "There are no special circumstances; you either have all the basic powers and are a kálos, or you don't and you aren't. The entire social hierarchy is based on their power levels. Passive Divinities are weaker than active ones."

"Whoa, hold up. What do you mean by power levels?"

Wes paused. "Power is limited," he explained more slowly. "Using it in any capacity drains the user's reserves, but how quickly depends on how much the kálos has to begin with. A powerful kálos can remain invisible longer, and his shields can withstand more force, and his ectoplasm can be concentrated or degraded at higher extremes. All of this is determined by his Divinity. Active powers are strongest. Kovak mentioned different levels, remember? Levels 1 and 2 are usually the passive powers, like our two young friends over there. Active tend to vary between Levels 3 and 4."

When Wes didn't continue, Trey said, "I thought the spectrum went all the way up to Level 9."

"No, you're thinking of what they said about A6, who is an anomaly. The highest is Level 5, which is extremely rare. As of right now, there aren't any known Level 5s in the Ghost Realm, but historically that range has been occupied primarily by Telepaths and Elementals."

"Cato's Divinities were active, right?"

"That's right." Wes's gaze drifted out of focus. "Two divine powers is an unheard-of phenomenon. He was something special."

"What level was he?"

Wes shrugged. "Probably Level 2 when Kovak took him, but he was still growing. With two powerful active Divinities, I'm guessing he might have matured at a Level 4, maybe even a Level 5 unless his human half diluted his power. One can only speculate. Anyway, active and passive—does all that make sense?"

Trey nodded, processing the new information. "Yeah."

"Good. If you want to be a ghost hunter, you need to understand the creatures you hunt . . . just as long as you never point your guns at me." He clapped Trey on the shoulder and, before he walked away, growled, "I mean it."

Trey stared at the werewolf's back. He didn't harbor the disdain for

Wes a lot of people had. He was able to look past the swagger to see the valuable teachings Wes could offer, even if he was an ass sometimes.

Trey reclaimed his seat by the wall where he watched the twins turn his Rubik's cube over and over. They passed it back and forth, studying it intently as though it were the most intriguing object they'd ever seen. Their eyes glowed as they communicated silently with one another.

Bored, Trey slumped against the wall. How strange, the normalcy that had settled over this life. He watched raiders dismantle and clean their weapons. A group of kids played tag around adults' legs. A mother braided her daughter's hair. Up on the balcony, Mrs. Solwitz, the former principal of LeahRae Harris High, was telling a story to a captivated audience comprised of both children and adults.

Trey draped his arms over his knees. Sometimes, in this place with these refugees, it was hard to remember the fire that used to drive him. Before the town was lost, before Cato was taken away, before Phantom even existed, Trey had been training. Ghosts had always fascinated him. They could control the weather, move objects with their minds, temporarily switch souls between bodies, and so much more.

He'd studied hard when he was young, desperate to prove to Madison he was serious about becoming an apprentice. A week after his thirteenth birthday, she made it official. And then a year later, he noticed his best friend's eyes had changed. One green, one blue, and they glowed with new internal power. Suddenly, Trey found himself in the midst of the greatest secret ever. The race was on. Cato was learning to control his powers, growing quickly, and Trey had to catch up. He couldn't do what Cato could, but that was okay; he'd have to learn to supplement his lack of natural abilities with weapons.

Trey's thoughts drifted. He remembered a day in Alvarez Park. Back then, there wasn't a statue, and nobody called the clearing Hero's Hollow. The sun was high enough to cast its warmth into the center of the clearing.

Cato was in a foul mood. "Question," he said.

"Answer," Trey replied automatically.

"How long do you think I'll be grounded?"

"Probably forever," Trey teased. His grin faded at Cato's sour look. *"Here's a thought—maybe if you told Ms. Tighe you were Phantom, she wouldn't have given you an F on your algebra test."*

"For your information, asshole, I didn't fail. I got a D."

"Minus." Trey ducked Cato's playful punch, which evolved into a spontaneous wrestling match. They were rolling in the grass, Trey on top, then Cato, then Trey again, and this time he stabilized his balance to stay on top. Cato squirmed, but Trey had a tight enough grip to keep him pinned. *"You know, if you're going to be a hero, you'd better get stronger."*

His friend smirked, and then his surreal eyes were glowing. The colored contact that made his right eye appear green couldn't conceal the blue glow when he tapped into his power. Trey's hands passed through Cato's wrists, and the half-breed rolled away. He was on his feet while Trey was still on his hands and knees. *"And if you're going to be a ghost hunter, you'd better figure out a better way to catch a ghost."*

Trey laughed good-naturedly and stood, brushing the grass from his jeans. Overcome with the serenity of the summer day and their promising future, he stretched his arms over his head and proclaimed, *"You and me, Cay. One day, the two of us are going to run this town."*

Trey closed his eyes. Nothing was the way it should have been. Cato was gone, and now Vivian was gone too, and Trey hadn't even told her. It might be too late; she might never know how he felt. More importantly, he might never learn her feelings for him.

As always, as soon as the thought took root, he saw Cato glaring at him, both eyes blazing green, face wrinkled in disapproval.

Trey clenched his fists. It wasn't fair! How much time had to pass before he could think of Vivian without thinking of Cato? How Trey used to wait at the street corner every morning for Viv and Cay to walk to school, and how they'd walk the whole way back together. And he'd go down the basement stairs to Madison's lab, casting a longing look over his shoulder while Cato and Vivian spread their books on the kitchen table, thinking maybe it wouldn't be so bad to fail math if it meant he would need to be tutored too. What would Cato say if he knew his true feelings?

"Now who's the hopeless romantic?" he probably would have teased.

A faint smile made Trey's lips twitch. He'd lost count of how many times he'd taunted Cato whenever he caught his best friend lost in thought while watching his crush from afar across the schoolyard.

"You've got some talent, you know. Picking the one girl you can never be with."

"Why do you say that?" Cato fired back, immediately defensive. *"I'm not that far out of her league, am I?"*

"Oh. I'm sorry; I thought you knew. Wow, okay, um, I have something really important to tell you."

"What?" Cato asked, a hint of desperation in his voice.

Trey had to fight to smother a grin. *"I don't want to alarm you, but . . . you're a ghost."*

The grin broke free the moment Cato's wide-eyed confusion hardened into a scowl. *"Funny. Jerk. But so what? Phantom is a hero. Girls like heroes . . . don't they?"*

"Yeah, girls like heroes. The girl's family? Not so much. Her mom isn't going to accept a ghost, even a half-blood like you. Sorry, Cay. That's one blessing you'll never get."

"We'd keep my other half a secret."

"You really trust her that much?"

Cato bowed his head, reluctantly yielding for the moment, but Trey noticed how he still watched longingly from the corner of his eye.

That felt like a lifetime ago. God, they were so innocent back then, daydreaming about asking girls to prom and stressing about algebra tests. Trey would have given anything to rewind back to those days. He started tapping his fingers anxiously against his thigh. Twisting the Rubik's cube, even if he couldn't solve it, was a good stress-reliever. It kept his mind from wandering so much. He raised his head to see if the twins had tired of it yet.

He gasped. His frustration forgotten, Trey stood and dazedly approached them. Sitting at their feet was the Rubik's cube, each side a solid color. "How?" he croaked. The twins blinked at him, offering no explanation.

Trey snatched the cube and scrambled it again, then handed it to A2. "Show me," he said, sitting down. It had taken the boys more than an hour to solve it the first time, but Trey was willing to wait as long as necessary.

A2 yawned and turned the cube over in his hand, barely glancing at each face. Trey watched in amazement as A2 began shifting the rows so fast Trey couldn't keep up. The boy didn't even look at the Rubik's cube. He seemed to have learned all the secrets of the puzzle, so now all he had to do was skim over the cube once, and he knew where each piece was supposed to go; it was just a matter of putting it there. In less than twenty seconds, the cube was solved again.

"Please," Trey begged, "you have to teach me."

But the twins remained as silent as ever. A1's head nodded down, then jerked up again. He blinked to stay awake.

"They need to rest," Doc called from the far side of the stage where she was sorting her supply of bottles.

Trey took possession of the Rubik's cube again. "I don't understand. I've been playing with this thing for years, and I haven't come close to solving it."

A2's breathing was already slow and even, congested snores issuing from his open mouth. His brother was watching Trey with half-opened eyes. Within a few seconds he, too, was lost in slumber. The mental exertion had taken a toll on them.

Trey rose. Those kids had just solved his unsolvable puzzle, and he'd never know their secret. He watched them sleep.

If only their powers were reversed and he had the ability to read *their* minds . . .

— Chapter Thirty-Four —
Final Vote

Morning's light warmed the golden grasses of the prairie, a small miracle no prisoner in the subterranean fortress would ever know. In his office, Agent Kovak roared, "It just doesn't make any *sense!*" as he threw a pencil cup at the wall. Pens, pencils, and highlighters scattered across the floor.

Agent Byrn, lock-jawed and stone-faced, lingered in the doorway. He watched a pencil roll to a stop against the toe of his shoe. "I agree," he said flatly. "A6 should have killed someone by now. A lot of people, actually."

"He can't survive without killing." Kovak started to pace. "There have to be bodies; we just haven't found them yet."

"The murders would have made headlines."

"I know. And the others . . . Their trail went cold too."

"I doubt the runts are alive at this point," Byrn predicted solemnly.

Kovak shot him a look of daggers that he would dare to make such a suggestion. "Until we find their corpses, we assume they're alive."

Byrn ran his hand down his face. "If kálos catch wind of what we're doing here . . ."

"They won't."

"The twins know every secret, every goddamn file! If that information gets into the wrong hands—"

"It *won't*. The runts won't breathe a word, and you know it."

"No? We never thought they'd crash the Grid either, but they did."

Kovak whirled, flinging his arm out to backhand a glass of water off the corner of his desk. Byrn kept quiet until his business partner's rage had cooled enough for him to safely inquire, "What about Tarrow?

You think we can trust her this time?"

Kovak was silent for a moment. "Hard to say. She's unpredictable. Then again, our subjects haven't acted according to our predictions at all, either. They may not even be headed in that direction anymore."

"A7 concerns me, though. He still has ties to Phantom Heights."

"I know. But even if Maddie betrays us, Holly won't."

"Phantom Heights has changed. You think Holly hasn't?"

Kovak smiled at him. "I bought her loyalty a long time ago."

"Loyalties change, too."

Kovak let out a dark chuckle. "I'm not worried about A7. I severed all his ties to that place, and even if he did go back . . . Trust me, Holly won't want him discovered any more than we do. That would be a mess I know she doesn't want to clean up."

"You don't think we owe it to her to give her some forewarning?"

"We don't owe her anything." Kovak lowered himself back into his chair. "You know something? I almost miss the runts."

Byrn let the tension fall from his shoulders now that the danger of being in the throwing radius seemed to have passed. He nudged the pencil with his foot and eyed the rivulets of water trickling down the wall to collect in a puddle by the empty glass still rocking on its side. Apparently Kovak had forgotten *someone* would have to clean up the mess with the runts gone. "Hmph. I miss them organizing my paper-work, but that's about it."

"Can you divert as many resources to Project Alpha as possible so Dr. Anders can continue their research?"

Byrn nodded. "I'll have to pull some strings with investors, but I should be able to. It'll take Anders a decade to accomplish what A1 and A2 did in a few years, though. Especially without ECANI."

"Maybe not. They set the groundwork already; all Anders has to do is continue what they started. I won't stop looking for them, but we need to keep working, with or without the original Alpha subjects. The clock is ticking."

Agent Byrn turned away. "I'll make some calls."

Wes yawned. He stretched his arms high over his head and twisted his body to crack his stiff back. Boredom didn't suit him well. He felt like taking a nice, leisurely stroll around the lake in Alvarez Park. What was Maddie going to do, tell him no? He wasn't a dog to sit by her side at all times. If he wanted to leave, she wasn't going to stop him. She could complain—and probably would—but she needed him to come back.

What kept him here was not the thought of Maddie's disapproval, but reluctance to miss out on any new developments. Wes had no intention of missing even the slightest hint of excitement if the twins decided to talk or the other Alpha fugitives made contact again.

He slumped against the wall and watched Doc hold out a spoon. A2 leaned away from it. "Come on, you've been such good patients so far. You need to swallow this." A2's blue eyes flickered between her face and the spoon lingering in front of him. She moved it closer until it was almost touching his mouth. He parted his lips in reluctant submission. "Wider."

He complied, allowing her to administer the medicine. He shuddered and squeezed his eyes shut. When he swallowed, he gagged.

"Thank you." She turned to A1. "Your turn." His brows drew together, and he shook his head in a way that was more pleading than defiant. "I'm sorry. I really am. I wouldn't give this to you if I didn't think it would help."

A1 rolled his lips together. Doc commanded, "Open." And there it was—he couldn't disobey a direct order, no matter how gently Doc gave it. Wes took a mental note of that. He wondered what the kid's reaction would be if instead of requesting, "Will you please speak?" someone ordered, "Speak now." Maybe Doc and Maddie had been too gentle. Maybe Holly had been on the right track when she threatened the kid with a gun to his head. Kovak had clearly beaten the crap out of the boys over the course of their lifetime. Perhaps they were capable of speaking, but thus far nobody had triggered the right pressure points with the right amount of force.

So noted. Filed away for future reference.

Doc capped the bottle and started to rise, but she hesitated when A2 went cross-eyed and inhaled sharply twice, about to sneeze. She yanked a tissue from her pocket and pressed it into his hands. But it was his twin brother instead who, without warning, sneezed hard, throwing his face into his hands.

Doc remained motionless for a moment, glancing between the two boys. A2 exhaled, showing no further sign of sneezing. A1 lowered his hands and sniffed. Slowly, Doc reached out, took the tissue from A2, and handed it to A1, who accepted it and blew his nose. Doc rose and backed away, still observing her patients.

"There's something odd about those two," Doc murmured.

She'd pulled the thought right out of Wes's mind. He made another mental note to ask his telepathic friend about the mind-reading relationship between identical twins, if such a topic had ever been studied before. No doubt Ero would be interested in that conversation.

Maddie asked, "How long until we can get Viv back?" just before she bit into a stale cracker.

Wes's gaze jumped to the ghost hunter sitting on the middle step. She chewed, waiting for an answer, and when none came, she looked up at Doc, who was frowning at the twins. They had settled down back-to-back and closed their eyes, the disk cradled in A2's hand. All they ever did was sleep, waking up only to take medicine and stare blearily around City Hall before nodding off again. They were still so thin, their skin sallow, dark circles under their eyes. But their breathing was slow and steady now, and their eyes glowed as they were supposed to, and Maddie's scanner had confirmed their power reserves were up to Level 2, which was normal for a Mind-Reader.

Wes had to admit Maddie's question was valid. He couldn't see these kids improving much more beyond their current state, not with the limited resources available to Doc.

At Doc's hesitation, Maddie swallowed her mouthful. "What's wrong?"

Doc met her gaze and then turned away. "You have to understand that they're extremely underdeveloped and malnourished. They need long-term care in order to—"

"Doc, that's not what I asked."

Doc pursed her lips, shook her head, and reluctantly answered, "They're still incredibly weak but, ah . . . well . . . I suppose their condition is stable enough to trade back now."

Wes straightened with renewed interest. He studied Maddie, who was scrutinizing Doc with cautious optimism that was quickly fading. The news should have made her laugh or weep with joy, but something in Doc's haunted voice forbade relief. "Isn't that a good thing?" she asked.

Doc remained motionless. "How badly do you want Vivian back?"

"Why?"

The doctor raised her eyes to meet Maddie's. "Because the twins will probably die."

"But you just said they're stable."

"Yes. But they're going to need antibiotics, supplements, basic medical care the Alpha ghosts can't provide for them. Their bodies are just too weak, too vulnerable to illnesses. They haven't even been vaccinated. For now, in my care, they're stable, but after we send them back, their fevers will probably spike again. Most likely, they'll die."

Maddie stared blankly at the tiled floor. "So . . . you're saying it wouldn't matter if we kept them for a few more weeks. Or months. We have to sacrifice their lives to save Vivian."

Doc's nurses were listening nearby. "Doc?" Lily inquired. "There has to be something we can do."

Doc rubbed her hand down her face. "I don't know what."

Shay shook his head in despondent acceptance. "We did everything we could. What happens after the fact is out of our hands."

Trey scratched his head and said, "What if we talked to the Alpha ghosts and explained? I mean, they brought the twins to us in the first place because they didn't want them to die, right? So they must care about them."

Maddie shook her head. "They won't let us keep them. I know they won't. And I don't want Viv to suffer because we try."

"So, what, then? We send them off to their deaths?"

Wes shifted. "I have an idea." *A rather brilliant one*, he wanted to add. It had just struck him like lightning in the instant all the planets aligned.

Holly rolled her eyes. "Oh, no!" Maddie exclaimed as she clambered to her feet. "No way. You're going to end up making the situation ten times worse with whatever you're scheming."

He shrugged one shoulder. "I'm a businessman, Maddie. I have a special talent for making deals people can't refuse. Hear me out."

"No commitments."

Wes grinned. "Okay, what do the Alpha ghosts want more than anything?"

"Uh, the twins alive?" said Trey.

"No. *Freedom*. Am I right?"

"Yeah, sure," Maddie answered impatiently.

Holly crossed her arms and glared suspiciously at him, but even her icy distrust couldn't diminish his exhilaration. He continued, "And what do *we* want more than anything?"

"To be out of this place and have our normal lives back."

"Right. So, why don't we help each other?"

Maddie stared at him. "I'm not following you."

Holly narrowed her eyes, which made Wes suspect she *was* following, and she didn't like where this was going. He explained, "It's a simple trade. We have contacts with the Agents, right? We can find a way to give the Alpha ghosts back their powers. Then we check in with the AGC from time to time and tell them their fugitives aren't in Phantom Heights."

Maddie snapped, "And why in the world would we do something idiotic like that?"

Wes smiled again. "Because in return, we demand they help us get rid of this infestation in Phantom Heights."

"Mercenaries," she summarized.

"Exactly!"

Holly interrupted, "Absolutely not."

"Why?"

She braced her weight onto one hip. "Do I need to waste my breath with an answer? We want to drive ghosts *out* of Phantom Heights, not invite them in."

Wes retorted, "Well, your methods haven't been very successful, have they?"

Holly leaned close to Maddie and hissed, "This is a bad idea."

"He does have a point, though," Maddie replied, barely moving her lips.

"Ghosts are our enemies; I don't need to tell you that. You know what it's like to have a ghost kill someone you love." Maddie closed her eyes in silent acknowledgment. "We can't trust ghosts, especially not Kovak's."

Wes said, "Of course we don't *trust* them. This is a business deal."

Maddie faced him again. "What even makes you think they'd be willing to bargain? They hate humans."

"They're also just as desperate as we are. The Agents are still on the hunt, and those lab rats don't stand a chance against other ghosts. Without their powers, it's only a matter of time before someone catches or kills them. They know it too. So, we offer them the one thing they need, and—"

"—and they take their powers and run," Maddie finished, "leaving us right where we started. They aren't going to keep their word. What did you plan to do, shake on it?"

Wes countered patiently, "Not if they have an incentive to stay."

"Such as?"

"First of all, like I said, we'll mislead Kovak. If the Agents stay clear of Phantom Heights, the Alpha ghosts will feel safer here. That by itself could be incentive enough. And let's face it, they're cunning. I mean, look how long they've evaded capture with such minimal resources. Plus, their kidnapping scheme was rather genius."

"Genius?" she repeated. "No, it was *stupid*! If they thought they could cross a ghost hunter and get away with it, they're not all that bright."

"No, think about it. They needed leverage to make us cooperate. If they'd taken anyone else, you would have ignored the risks and chased after them, right? They specifically chose Vivian because they knew you'd be too afraid to put her in harm's way. Face it, Maddie, they played you."

She leaned back, her cheeks burning. "So they're smart," she admitted. "What does that have to do with incentive?"

"They can be reasoned with, I hope. We need to provide them with the indisputable fact that the twins will die unless they get the medicine they need—medicine we can provide if they accept our terms."

Doc was nodding thoughtfully in contradiction to Holly furiously shaking her head. Maddie lingered in indecision. Trey watched his ghost-hunting master, his vote tied to hers. But in the end, Maddie's vote was the only one that mattered. Wes said, "See, it's perfect! We can trade the twins for Vivian, just as planned, and then we'll give the Alpha ghosts daily amounts of supplies. They'll have no choice but to stay and get more the next day."

"It does actually sound like a good idea," Trey quietly persuaded.

Maddie adjusted her weapon belt while she thought. "In theory. But do you really want a group of killers living in our town?"

"Right," said Wes, "as opposed to the polite, law-abiding ghosts currently living in our town. Besides, if we hold the medicine, we hold the leverage this time. They attack any humans or fail to do their job, and we don't give them what they need. Plus, I bet the threat of a phone call to Kovak will get them to do just about anything."

"There are a lot of risks with that plan, Wes," she muttered. "They kidnapped my daughter . . . without their powers. Who knows what they're capable of *with* their powers? I have a bad feeling about this."

"Desperate times call for desperate measures."

"If the deal falls through for some reason," Trey added, "we could always call the Agents as a backup plan."

"Oh sure, because the Agents have been so helpful over the years," said Wes. He turned to the crowd. "I think we need a vote. Who wants to bargain with the Alpha ghosts?"

Wes was smiling even though adrenaline had his heart racing. Risky play, trying to circumvent Maddie's authority, but if he could convince a majority of the townspeople to agree with his plan, that might be enough to sway her.

But people were uneasy and confused about his call to action, their eyes darting to see if anyone else was willing to vote in favor of his proposition. Nobody was brave enough to raise the first hand. Not a good start.

Holly stepped onto the stage. "Let's realize what exactly we're deciding here. Mr. Cooper wants to make an already lethal gang of ghosts even more dangerous and then trust their word that they'll protect us. These are ghosts our own government placed a bounty on because they are a public threat. They've been caged in a laboratory for who-knows-how-long, and I'm going to wager a guess they don't harbor kind feelings toward humans. They kidnapped one of our own and threatened to slaughter her. Do you trust them with your lives? The lives of your children?"

Wes wasn't irritated by his challenger. On the contrary, he relished the competition. He opened his arms to the crowd. "I'm asking you to take a risk with me. Don't we take risks every day? How is this any different? We actually have a chance to rebuild our lives if we play our cards right."

The crowd stirred with nervous excitement. A few bold hands went into the air while people deliberated quietly. Holly murmured under her breath, "A public debate? Big mistake, Cooper. You're not a politician."

"A position that could have suited me well," he retorted with a smile. "But I found much better success outside the spotlight."

"*I* represent the people and their best interests."

"Will that be your new campaign slogan?"

"You're just a dog barking at the end of your chain. You're playing *my* game."

"If you're so confident, what's the harm in a little competition? Afraid you won't get your way, Councilwoman?" He raised his voice and stated, "You once trusted a ghost to protect you. I know these are different circumstances, but it worked before. Can our current situation be reversed if we employ not one, but seven mercenaries to take the hero's place?"

Excitement rippled through the crowd. "If you are referring to Phantom," Holly frigidly replied, "you seem to have forgotten one tiny detail: he was half-human. These ghosts don't have a drop of our blood in them. You want to hire terrorists as bodyguards and pin a hero's cape on them, but they are pureblood enemies without regard for human life. You can't deny that."

"I agree," Wes answered to everyone's surprise. "But we aren't looking for heroes. Like Maddie said, they'll be mercenaries. This is not an alliance. We're paying for a service. It's nothing more than a business deal."

"We don't even know if they're as powerful as Kovak claims. Face it, we don't know anything about them, really."

Wes beamed at his competitor and marched across the stage.

"Hey!" Doc protested when he threw back the blanket, seized A1's arm, and hoisted the kid onto his feet. A1 blinked, bewildered from the rude awakening. Doc seethed, "Wesly Cooper, don't you dare harm my patient."

"Wouldn't dream of it," he replied sweetly, his eyes finding Maddie to see if she would intervene. She watched passively, not even resting a hand on a weapon. A1 hunched his shoulders and tucked his chin down, uncomfortable finding himself the center of attention.

Wes held up the kid up by his arm, which was so thin that his fingers completely encircled the biceps. "You sure don't look like much, but I bet your friends from Alpha are stronger than you, aren't they?" A1 stared at his feet. "*Aren't they?*" Wes repeated, tightening his grip.

A1 grimaced and inclined his head once. His brother, awakened by his twin's distress, sat up to watch.

Wes used his other hand to grip the nape of A1's neck and force his head up to face the crowd. "Agent Kovak told us your friends are powerful warriors. Is that true?" A1 hesitated, but when Wes applied a little pressure to his neck, he inclined his head again. "Have you seen them fight?" A single nod.

"How?" Holly challenged. "You think Kovak lets his test subjects roam the halls unsupervised?" She fixed A1 in her crosshairs and said, "He denied training them; what opportunity could you possibly have had to see them fight in a real battle?"

A1 glanced at her, then abruptly dropped his gaze. Wes reminded, "Yes or no questions, Councilwoman." He leaned closer to his captive and asked, "Did Kovak train them to fight?"

The kid's vibrant blue eyes danced over the crowd but locked onto no one in particular. He shook his head. Wes let go of his neck but maintained the tight hold on his arm. "I don't suppose the specifics are important right now. What I and everyone else wants to know—are they any good?" A1 bowed his head but nodded while staring at his bare toes. "Are they powerful?" Again, he nodded. "And do you think they'll be willing to make a deal with us?"

A1 thought for a moment, then barely jerked his shoulders. Wes let him go and faced his audience again. "There's your answer. The Alpha ghosts are powerful and know how to fight. Now, who's ready to take our lives back? Let's reclaim Phantom Heights! Show me your hands— your courage! Come on, raise 'em high!"

More hands rose. Mayor Correll voted in favor of the deal. As soon as Police Chief Emerton's hand went up, so did those of almost all the raiders. Doc raised one hand while gently placing the other on A1's shoulder and steering him back to the mattress to sit down. Even Trey's hand rose. To Holly's clear dissent, her daughter's hand was in the air.

Maddie clenched her fists at her sides. For once, she and Holly were united. "I don't like this," said Maddie. "Whose side do you think they'll take when war breaks out? What then, Wes?"

"Then we use them until they breach our contract, and when that happens, we sell them out to the highest bidder," he replied.

"Have you forgotten what they did to Vivian?"

"Of course not. But like it or not, we need them, and they need us." He grinned. "We can keep them on a tight leash, right?" He surveyed the sea of hands. "Hmm, that looks like more than half, wouldn't you say, Councilwoman?"

Holly shot him the foulest look she could muster while she steamed under the humiliation of losing at her own game.

"Guess it's settled, then," Wes declared, facing the onlookers and raising his arms with the grace of a performer. "The Agents left us here to die. We're collateral damage. I think it's high time we claim the penance they owe us." The whole crowd stirred, and a few *whoops* answered.

A2 raised his fingers to his mouth; Doc gently swatted his hand away before he could start biting his nails. A1's brow wrinkled in alarm that Wes was speaking ill of his masters. Wes raised his voice: "We're still waiting for the aid Agent Kovak promised us more than two years ago. He doesn't know it, but he's about to repay his debt to us."

Wes was treated to enthusiastic applause. He held his hands up, basking in the attention, and waited for the volume to die down before he became appropriately solemn. "This will be an all-or-nothing deal. If even one person contacts the AGC, you've betrayed us all." He turned his head to fix Holly with a critical glare.

Fuming under the implication and the townspeople's accusing stares, she folded her arms with a cross *huff* and grumbled, "I don't condone this deal. You want to betray our own government for a group of dangerous fugitives." Her glower shifted from Wes to the silent crowd watching her. "But . . . I've always represented the interests of the people—" she couldn't have missed Maddie rolling her eyes "—and the people have spoken. I won't be the one to betray them."

For now, Wes silently finished for her. He didn't need the Divinity of mind-reading to know she was playing another one of her strategy games. "Maddie?" he implored.

The ghost hunter shot him a bitter look from the corner of her eye. "You've all made your decision crystal clear," she grudgingly answered. "My only role from here on out is to enforce it."

Wes clapped his hands together, causing the twins to flinch. "All right! Let's make a deal."

Maddie shook her head. "I still say it's a bad idea, but I've been outvoted. Since you're the 'businessman,' and you 'make deals people can't refuse,' I'll leave the negotiating to you."

"How do we contact them?" asked Trey, looking down at the twins for an answer.

"They're watching us, remember?" said Wes, turning to the white-board behind the stage. Apprehensive silence settled over the crowd.

"Hey!" Wes shouted, his voice ringing in the great hall. "Alphas! We need to talk!"

The final echoes of his call faded to silence. The marker didn't move.

Neither did the onlookers.

The seconds stretched to a minute, and people started to shift. Wes's confident smile faltered. He'd been so certain that would work.

As Holly opened her mouth and took a breath, probably to complain that it would be more entertaining to watch grass grow, the marker rolled over the edge and landed on the floor. The cap popped off, and the marker levitated.

— Chapter Thirty-Five —

Negotiation

Vivian is redy to kum hom

Maddie glared up at the security cameras she'd destroyed, then turned a slow circle. "How the hell are they doing that?" she whispered.

A1 and A2 were mesmerized by the marker. They probably knew the trick; too bad the bastards were mute. Wes, completely absorbed in his role of negotiator, clasped his hands professionally behind his back. This was his territory now. He shouted, "I'm sorry to inconvenience you, but we need to discuss this deal!"

No need to yel. We can heer you. And the deel dos not chanj

Wes blinked in surprise, then cleared his throat to regain his composure. The twins stared keenly at him. His response was in a whisper so soft only those in nearest proximity could hear him say, "Oh no, I understand."

He waited to see if the fugitives would request him to speak up, but instead, the marker scribbled:

Your redy to trayd?

Wes's eyebrows rose. He pressed his hand over his mouth and asked under his breath, "Can you hear me now?"

Not a single person in City Hall had been able to hear that. Wes had barely been able to hear his own voice muffled behind his palm. Everyone's eyes were trained on the levitating marker, waiting. It remained motionless.

Then wrote:

Yes

Wes gasped and took a step back. The crowd shifted with equal unease at the results of his experiment. Raiders drew their ectoguns half a second behind Maddie and Trey.

"What the hell?" Trey muttered under his breath. "I thought they didn't have their powers."

Maddie shushed him. She directed her attention to the twins and accused, "You're communicating with them."

A1 rubbed his sore arm, but both boys stared at the floor and shook their heads no. The marker scribbled:

You caled us for a resin

Still shaken, Wes gestured at A1 and A2 and answered at normal volume, "You want the twins, and we want Vivian. But you see, we were hoping you might be interested in a new deal."

The marker hovered in the air for a moment.

Then it fell. It landed on the ground with a clatter, where it rolled a few inches and came to a standstill.

Wes stared at it, devastated. They'd balked at his proposal already? Did he just ruin the original trade too? Maddie would turn him into a fur coat for this.

The eraser rose from the tray and swept the board clean, then settled back into place before the marker levitated again and scrawled:

No. We wil tak them and leev

Wes let out a shaky breath to recompose himself. "All right, fine. That was the deal. But you should know they'll probably die."

He let his words hang in the air.

Explane

Wes gazed at the twins, who glanced at him for a moment before their vacant stares drifted back to the marker. "Dr. Crawford says they're susceptible to illnesses. She saved them this time, but they need vitamins and supplements and antibiotics, which you can't provide for them. They may be stable now, but if you take them back with you, they'll get very sick again."

Your rong. We can get watever thay need

"How?" Wes challenged.

We can steel

"Oh, I see, you'll just steal what you need. Sure. Except it isn't easy to get medicine, and you don't have your powers. And you're being hunted. And you don't know what kind of medications they need. In fact, you might even give them the wrong medication and kill them."

The marker dropped into the tray so the eraser could rise and sweep across the letters. The corners of Wes's lips tugged upward in a confident grin as he closed in for the kill.

"But we can get you the medicine . . ."

". . . and your powers."

A heavy silence replaced Axel's final words.

I stared straight ahead, struggling to comprehend. This wasn't how my plan was supposed to pan out. The resolution was supposed to be final—Finn and Reese would be healthy so we could release Vivian, reclaim our lab-brothers, and then decide where to go.

Jay's jaw was clenched. "How?" he asked suspiciously.

Ash was still at Home to guard Vivian, but the rest of us were at the edge of the Dome, close enough for RC to have a visual through a gap where a couple of planks were missing over the window. The Telekinetic raised his hand, tracing the word in the air with his finger. Inside City Hall, the marker followed the same path.

Axel parroted Wes's words: "You need something to remove the device that neutralizes your powers, right? You can't walk into the AGC, but we can."

"No," Jay muttered, "this isn't right. There must be a catch."

Axel shook his head. "I wasn't listening to the humans 'til I heard the werewolf shout. I don't know what they were talking about before that."

Jay gave him a withering glare. "You weren't paying attention? What if something happened to Finn and Reese?"

Axel, realizing his blunder, hung his head. In his defense, Jay couldn't possibly expect him to be attuned to the twins every single second, especially now near the end of his cycle when his health was deteriorating and his focus was lax. Axel had been preoccupied with a pair of Shadow Guards who had ventured a little too close to Home and almost obliviously strolled through our wall.

"Cato?" Jay implored.

I blinked. I hated when he did that—turned to me first because I was half-human. Their actions and customs were just as bewildering to me as they were to my lab-family. The humans weren't reacting at all the way I'd anticipated. "I have no idea what they could want. I would have thought they'd be eager to get rid of us."

Axel muttered, "Reese is looking this way."

"We're too close," Jay said. "They know where we are."

I ground my teeth. I was confident Finn and Reese wouldn't volunteer our location, but if given the order, all they had to do was point, and raiders would charge out of City Hall. *We're here*, I thought, just in case they were attuned to my thoughts. *And we missed you. But we can't bring you Home quite yet. Please wait.*

"Plus," Axel said suddenly, raising his hand, "did you know the Agents asked us to contact them if we sighted you in Phantom Heights?" We all tensed. "Well, we might tell them we haven't seen you. You're not here. You never came this way."

"Lie?" Jay asked.

"Nope," Axel said quickly to redeem himself. "Not yet, anyway."

Everything about this was wrong. "We should just trade Vivian for Finn and Reese and then leave," I advised. "That was our original plan, and I think we should stick to it."

Jay traced his finger around one of the ports in his forehead. "But they're offering us our powers. We'll never have another opportunity for that. And if we don't get RC's neutralizer off soon . . ."

I glanced at RC, who was leaning against the transparent Dome with his eyes closed. His ashen skin sheened with sweat. We couldn't pause the countdown to remove the band from his arm, and this scheme seemed like the only feasible way to save him. But the too-good-to-be-true offer had my gut churning with unease. "I don't like this."

"Me either," said Jay. "I don't trust them. Ask what the catch is," he instructed RC. Our lab-brother opened his eyes to blink lethargically at Jay before he pulled away from the Dome and squinted at the white-board through the window. He raised his hand again to control the path of the marker with his mind.

"Wes is reading," Axel reported, staring intently at the boarded window. The rest of us could catch only minimal glimpses where boards were missing, but Axel's eyes could see past the visible spectrum. I didn't fully comprehend how his vision worked, but I assumed the images were formed with multiple layers, from gamma rays to radio waves and every spectrum in between, maybe even beyond the known limits. Even if every board were in place, Axel would have a clear view inside City Hall.

"No catch," he said for Wes, "just a fair deal. We do all that for you in addition to providing you with the medicine for the twins, and you do something for us in return."

"What?" Jay asked, distrust heavy in his voice.

RC printed the word on the board. We waited anxiously until Axel continued, "We promise protection from the Agents in exchange for your protection from kálos. Let us rebuild our town. This can be your home, too, where the twins can get the medical attention they need and the Agents won't look for you here."

Jay snorted and told RC to write, "There are hundreds of ghosts out here. We'd be expected to fight them all?"

Wes's answer: "Don't forget there are two ghost hunters and a lunos here to help you."

Jay muttered, "Not much help."

Once RC passed the message on, Axel growled, and yet it wasn't his typical growl; I was sure he was still playing echo for the werewolf. "Look, it's a great deal, and you'll never get another one like it. We're offering you the only chance to get your powers back so you can defend yourselves from your enemies. You'd be fools not to accept our generous offer," Axel finished. Jay's gray eyes danced in thought.

"It does sound like a good deal," RC mumbled.

"Of course it does," I snapped. "That's the point."

"But we'll have our powers," said Jay, thinking aloud. "If we have to run again, we'll be able to defend ourselves. Right now, we're pretty helpless."

The offer was too tantalizing. "They know we're desperate," I said, trying to make him see reason. "They know we don't have many options."

"I know. But you're right; we *are* desperate. And we're out of options. This could be our only chance to get that thing off RC's arm." He looked at each of us in turn. "What do you say?"

Axel scoffed. "I ain't doing it."

"Why?" Jay demanded.

"'Cause I ain't gonna be a guard dog that comes running when a human snaps his fingers."

I rolled my eyes, and he whirled on me. "*Don't.*"

"What?" I shot back. "You think the rest of us want this? Believe me, Ax, the last thing I want to do is make a deal with them. But Finn and Reese need us to do this, and so does RC."

"I don't care," he snarled, stepping toward me in a manner threatening enough to make me retreat a step. "I am *never* letting humans have control over me ever again."

Jay watched us half-breeds square off against each other. Eyes still closed, RC monotonously implored, "Please don't."

Axel ignored him. "I still say we're better off stealing whatever Finn and Reese need."

"Wes is right—we don't *know* what they need!" I cried. "How can we steal medicine for them if we don't know which medicine will make them better?"

"I'd rather take that chance than be a slave. But why don't you just admit it—you want to play hero again."

"Bloody Scout, you're a real idiot sometimes, you know that? And how do you plan to get the neutralizer off RC? You think you can pull it off before it severs his arm? That infection is going to kill him!"

"Technopathy," he tossed out.

His suggestion surprised me enough to warrant a hesitation of brief hope before my brain started countering with faults. "And where do you plan to find a Technopath?"

"I don't know, the Ghost Realm?"

"That doesn't do Finn and Reese any good."

Axel shrugged. "If they get sick again, we'll find them a Healer."

"We don't have time to go traipsing around the Ghost Realm looking for a Technopath and a Healer! Does RC look strong enough to you?"

Calm and collected while my temper was flaring, awakening my hot Divinity for a moment before my neutralizer smothered the power flow, Jay intervened, "We have no money and nothing valuable to trade. The only thing we have is the exact price the humans just requested."

Axel snarled, "Fuck humankind."

Jay pleaded, "Axel, your family needs you."

"You all fight, then. I don't care. But I refuse to do what *They* created me for, Jay, and that's fight for the sake of humans. If you make this deal, you're making it without me."

I shook my head. As much as I didn't want to feed Axel's giant ego, there was no denying that losing the asset of the fastest, strongest, most powerful ghost to ever exist was a devastating blow.

Jay heaved a sigh. "Fine."

"*Fine?*" I repeated.

Jay met my gaze. "I can't force Axel to care about the well-being of his family."

Axel rounded on him. "You know what? Fuck you too!"

Jay resisted the bait for an argument and instead asked, "Cato? RC?"

We exchanged glances. Nobody said a word. Nobody nodded. Our silence was answer enough.

Jay bowed his head. "RC, tell them . . . tell them we won't start fighting until we have the twins and our powers. If they come through with that, then . . . we have a deal, I guess."

Axel crossed his arms and turned away, growling and cursing under his breath. My stomach turned, sickened by the knowledge that RC was sealing our fate with a few words scribbled on a whiteboard.

"Jay," I choked out, his name catching in my throat. I stared at the transparent swirls made by the condensed energy of the Dome. "You do realize you're making this deal with the people who betrayed me?"

Jay wouldn't look at me or the others. "I know."

I'd never heard his voice so heavy. It weighed down on me, suffocating me, crushing me. He was right—we were out of options.

Wes smirked when he read their answer. "You made a wise decision. Tell us what we need to do to restore your powers."

The marker began to move again. Wes waited patiently while a crude picture was drawn depicting a clamp with a handle and a square top.

This is wat you need to bring us

Wes nodded in understanding. He hadn't noticed the twins rise, but one of the boys had wandered forward and now stood in front of the whiteboard, his eyes trained intently on the words. Wes asked, "Where will it be?"

Dont kno. Thats your problem

"Right, of course it is," Wes grumbled. "So, how about we trade now, and we'll give you the first dose of medicine. Once you have your powers, the other deal goes into effect."

No. We wil trayd everything at onc so you cant go bak on your werd

"We won't!" cried Maddie.

Thats the deel. No negoteating.

"I need proof she's alive."

383

Wood you like us to send you a finger?

"Don't you dare!"

Then youll have to tayk our werd. Also we need sumthing els

Her arms crisscrossed over her chest. "Now you're pushing it." After receiving no response, she said, "What?"

Suplys to treet an injery

The hard lines in the ghost hunter's face softened. She turned to Doc, who inquired, "What's the nature of the injury?"

Infecshun

"I'll see what I can do."

Wes noticed Maddie wasn't looking at the marker anymore. She was focused on A2, who hadn't followed his brother to the whiteboard. He was standing on his tiptoes at the window, his fingertips curled through a gap in the boards and his eyes squinting through the crack, trying to see something, or some*one*.

Maddie was fast. She snatched an ectogun out of her holster and dashed for the doors, shoving people out of her way. Trey was already on her heels. She hauled the bar to the side and used her full weight to heave the door open.

Wes sprinted after them. Behind him, the marker fell to the floor as if a string holding it had been cut.

Maddie didn't make it far. She halted in the middle of the portico, gazing at a lone person standing in the center of town square staring back at her. He was dressed in a long-sleeved black shirt with a white *a* symbol emblazoned on the chest. Black pants, black boots, a black cloak with a hood covering his face. He was nothing like the twins. His posture alone was indicative of his self-confidence and his physical strength.

Wes lingered in the doorway, blocking anyone else from joining the ghost hunter and apprentice on the portico. Something was wrong. Very, very wrong. The air didn't taste right, didn't feel right. *Run*, his instincts told him. *Flee. Hide.*

"Maddie," he whispered.

She raised her gun and aimed at the fugitive. "Don't. Move," she seethed at the stranger.

Wes's skin itched. His blood pulsed warmer, faster. The wolf thought he was in danger, and it stirred beneath his flesh, urging a transformation so he would have teeth and claws to defend himself.

A gentle breeze stirred the fugitive's cloak. He didn't answer. He was not attacking, not defending. Just standing there. Waiting.

Wes frowned and glanced over his shoulder. At the far end of the hall, A2 turned away from the window, his shoulders slumping. His attention had been on the window; not once had he looked toward the doors. The range of his mind-reading ability wasn't far enough to detect someone in the plaza.

Wes shook his head. The figure in town square had been a distraction while the others escaped.

By the time his attention returned to Maddie's adversary, her ecto-gun was pointing at the empty square.

"Where'd he go?" Wes asked.

"That's the question," she muttered with her back still to him. "I blinked, and he was gone . . . without his powers. His eyes weren't glowing." She glanced at him over her shoulder. "I really hope you know what you're doing."

The encounter had tightened Wes's stomach with unease. He'd never sensed a creature like that before. What was it? A kálos, or something else?

Less confident than he'd been a few minutes ago, he promised, "You'll see. This will work."

— Chapter Thirty-Six —

Cat and Mouse

The knife hit the wall handle-first and clattered to the floor. I didn't bother to pick it up. I'd been throwing my new knives for an hour and still hadn't come close to mastering them as weapons. Axel was right; they were nothing like what I was used to. They weren't made for fighting.

I stretched my arms, which were sorer than I'd expected from the knife-throwing, and approached Jay. He didn't acknowledge me when I sat beside him. My eyes rolled up to the holes in the ceiling so I could analyze the aging daylight. "Think they made it by now?"

"It's a long drive," he replied wearily.

He rested his chin on his knees and said nothing more. He was still resolved to the decision, as was I, but it was eating at our every thought and turning our stomachs sour. To be honest, only part of me hoped the humans could actually steal the disabler from *Them* so we could save RC and the twins.

The other part of me hoped they'd fail so we wouldn't have to go through with this deal.

"Please come with me," Trey begged.

Wes shook his head. "No way. I'm not going in there. I'll be right here when you come out, but this is as far as I'm going."

Trey scowled and threw open the car door. He stepped out into the cool, damp air, and when he slammed the door, the sound echoed down the long tunnel. With a diameter of more than a hundred and fifty feet, the tunnel was wide enough to accommodate an eight-lane freeway.

Trey felt like an ant creeping through the pipes beneath a giant's lair. The tunnels were a complex maze that would have confounded them if Madison hadn't drawn a map.

Wes's red Camaro looked like a toy in front of the massive steel doors barring the way. The passenger window rolled down. "Hey," Wes called from the driver's seat. Trey turned. "Get the device. But see if you can find out some more information on our new friends while you're in there."

"Yeah, fine. Just don't take off unless I'm in the car with you."

"Hurry up. I don't want to be here any longer than we need to be."

Trey approached the sinister doors. The hollowness of each footstep was amplified in the tunnel, and the overhead lights distorted his shadow. A breeze made the hairs on the back of his neck stand up. He peered upward, searching for the ventilation system he was sure was responsible for the breeze and the eerie whistle haunting the tunnels. The lonely quiet was disconcerting to someone who hadn't experienced silence in a long time.

Trey knew from Madison's map that they were far below a prairie wildlife reserve in this godforsaken empty stretch of the Midwest. Trey wasn't even sure which state he was in anymore. No GPS this far underground.

He stopped at the doors, tilting his head back. He wiped his moist palms on his jeans. Had Cato stood here?

Once the idea sank its barbs into his mind, Trey could think of nothing else. He closed his eyes and pretended, whether it was true or not, that his sneakers were in the exact footprints as his best friend's.

I'm not here about Cato, he had to remind himself. *Not this time. Project Alpha. Vivian.*

He took a deep breath and opened his eyes to face the ominous doors. At eye level was a small black box with a speaker and a button, which Trey pushed. A buzzer sounded, and then a female voice said, "This is a restricted area. Please state your business."

Trey fought the urge to scoff and roll his eyes. They knew he was coming. He was certain they knew the second he and Wes drove down the overgrown dirt path in a patch of woods and entered the tunnel's ramp. Invisible camera eyes had been watching them every inch of the nerve-wracking hour-long trip through the winding passages that slowly took them deeper and deeper underground, farther and farther away from civilization. If the intimidating voice turned him away now, it would be a long trip with nothing to show, and it might cost Vivian her life.

Trey licked his lips and answered, "Hi. Hello. Um, my name is Trey Selman. I . . . I was hoping to speak with Agent Kovak."

"Do you have an appointment?"

"No."

"Please schedule an appointment and come back at the appropriate time."

"What? No, I can't do that. I've come a long way. He'll want to talk to me. Tell him Madison Tarrow's apprentice is here."

"One moment, please."

Trey scuffed his shoe on the smooth surface of the tunnel, his heart pounding. The AGC made his skin prickle with unease, and he was human. He couldn't imagine the fear it evoked in ghosts—*kálos*. He had to start using the correct term.

Trey jumped when the woman announced, "Agent Kovak will see you."

"Thank—" His voice was barely more than a squeak. He had to clear his throat. "Thank you." The doors unlocked with an automatic *clank*. They parted slowly, gears grinding like a goliath's growl reverberating through the tunnels.

Trey stepped through, tipping his head back to watch the giant doors move apart. By the time he looked forward again, he realized he'd entered a strange courtyard. Ten-foot steel spikes loomed from the ceiling like man-made stalactites to contain . . . what? A dragon?

Maybe, Trey thought in a daze. *Or something worse.* Now that he thought about it, the Agents had more than just gho—*kálos*—locked up in there. Project Delta was proof of that.

To the right was a single door, equally massive, that probably lifted up when it opened. To the left were rows of transport trucks, the same kind, Trey realized with a sinking stomach, that took Cato. In fact, one of those trucks was probably the one that carried his best friend away.

Trey shuddered and faced forward again. This pair of doors looked much more inviting than the door on the right. These were sleek, modern, and human-sized. They parted automatically at his approach with a quiet *whoosh*.

Trey cautiously stepped over the threshold, but he jumped and whirled at the sound of the first set of doors colliding with a hissing sigh of the gears and a *clank* of the lock. Trey entered the AGC to face a receptionist—Bridget, according to the nameplate on her desk. The wall behind her was a mosaic of screens reeling security footage. One of the screens near the bottom right corner showed Trey standing in the middle of the room. Another revealed a red Camaro parked in the tunnel. Most of the cameras, as Trey had suspected, surveyed tunnel sections, but a few showed the endless expanse of a prairie, just as Madison had said.

Other than the wall of screens, the lobby looked . . . normal. Trey almost forgot he was deep underground. Warm light from wall-mounted lamps gave the cream walls a cozy glow. A couple of chairs faced a table in the corner where ghost hunters or other rare visitors could wait and read magazines. The ceiling was only a few feet above Trey's head, much more to scale than the monstrous empty tunnel outside. In fact, Trey almost could have convinced himself he was in a waiting room at an office. Almost.

Bridget smiled a perfect smile with perfect white teeth. "Good afternoon. I'll have to ask you to disarm before you meet with Agent Kovak."

"Huh? Oh, right, sorry." Trey unbuckled his weapon belt and set it on the counter. Without the familiar weight around his waist, he felt much too light, as if he'd just removed the anchor keeping him earthbound.

Bridget took his belt out of sight, and Trey chastised himself for not counting his weapons and e-zaps to make sure all would be accounted for later. His gaze wandered across all of Bridget's knickknacks in her workspace. She had several bobblehead dogs constantly nodding at her next to framed photos of a stern man in a lab coat and three little kids—two girls and a boy. The wall by Bridget's desk had been decorated with finger paintings signed in crayon by the young artists: Megan, Justine, and Ismael. Bridget's pen cup was filled with a rainbow of color to match her coffee mug, which actually had a rainbow on it.

Bridget slid a clipboard across the counter, reclaiming Trey's attention. "You'll need to wear this visitor's badge at all times. Make sure you return it before you leave. Also, you need to sign in here. And this is a confidentiality form saying if you share any restricted information, you are subject to indefinite imprisonment. Have you been ill in the past week?"

"No," Trey answered, scribbling his signature on the sheet of paper.

"Not even the slightest sniffle or sneeze?" she pressed.

"Nope."

"Okay. If you'll please proceed to the sterilization chamber . . ."

Trey tensed. "The what?"

Bridget chuckled. "Not to worry, it sounds much more sinister than it actually is. We have many test subjects here, Mr. Selman, and we don't want any germs or viruses you've brought from outside to get them sick. Just walk through the chamber, and ultraviolet light will kill any foreign microbes on your body as you pass through. It won't hurt a bit. I promise."

Trey nodded, clipping the visitor's badge to his jacket as he approached the closed doors. Bridget pressed a button, and the doors separated to reveal a narrow hallway filled with long tubes of neon purple lights. Trey entered, then flinched when the doors closed behind him.

He took a deep breath and walked forward. The charged air made his skin tingle and the hair rise from his arms. The sensation was uncomfortable, but, as Bridget had promised, painless.

He walked to the closed doors at the end of the hallway. He was still searching for a button or handle when they slid open automatically, granting access to a brightly lit hallway. The floor was linoleum, the walls and ceiling painted white. The place had a sterilized odor, like lemon-scented cleaner and formaldehyde. Two men in white lab coats passed by, talking animatedly while studying a clipboard.

"Trey Selman."

Agent Kovak, who had been waiting near the doors, proudly gestured down the hallway. "Welcome to the AGC. Walk with me. Let's chat."

Trey swallowed hard, inclined his head, and walked alongside the Head Agent. He wasn't sure he'd ever been in such close proximity to Kovak before and was acutely aware that the Agent had a full head of height on him. Kovak, his usual suit covered by a white lab coat, strutted with a strengthened air of confidence. He was definitely in his element here. "This is a pleasant surprise," he said. "I never expected to see you here, especially not arriving in such style."

"Huh?"

"Camaro." Trey gawked at him. "Smooth ride. Beautiful finish. Not something I thought I'd see roll out of Phantom Heights these days."

Cameras, Trey remembered. Agent Kovak had probably watched them coming from miles away. *He's messing with me.* Trey kept his composure and replied, "Wes keeps it outside the Heights."

"Long walk," Kovak commented.

Trey didn't bother to answer that he'd ridden on the back of a werewolf to reach the garage well outside city limits, not that Kovak would have believed that tale anyway. His head rolled as he took in the bleak scenery. "I thought there'd be more ghosts."

"I beg your pardon?" Kovak asked with a forcedly cheery smile.

"I mean, from Project Gamma. Like the twins."

The Agent adjusted his tie. "Ah. Yes, well . . . A1 and A2 were very special."

"Because they're Mind-Readers? That's not exactly a rare power."

Kovak studied Trey from the corner of his eye. "Tell me, what brings Maddie Tarrow's apprentice all the way out here?" Trey could see the eagerness in his eyes—he hoped Trey brought tidings of the missing test subjects.

"I want that reward."

"Do you have our fugitives?"

"Not yet."

"Do you have any information about their whereabouts?"

"No."

Agent Kovak's grin wavered. "I don't think you understand the concept of a reward."

"That's why I'm here. Madison isn't taking your proposition seriously, but I am. I was hoping maybe if I knew a little more about the Alpha ghosts, I could figure out where they went."

Agent Kovak chuckled humorlessly. "We know everything there is to know about them, and it hasn't helped us track them down. Does Maddie know you're here?"

"Yeah. She's not happy about it, but I don't care. I'm sick of how we live, and I want to do something about it. Catching your ghosts and getting that reward is our best chance."

"You could have just called."

"Well . . . yeah, but . . . I also wanted to see the lab. I was actually wondering . . . Do you have any internships?"

The Agent's eyes widened fractionally. "Internships," he repeated. Trey nodded. "Maddie isn't treating you well?"

Madison, Trey almost corrected, but instead answered, "She taught me a lot. But I feel like she's holding me back. I could be a great ghost hunter with the right master. After the loss in her family, she just isn't as . . . dedicated."

Loss. That was the easiest way to say it. Because it was Agent Kovak's fault, and Trey couldn't give him the blame he deserved, so they would both pretend a person was lost. Not dead, just lost.

Though Kovak couldn't have missed the word choice, he said, "And you believe you can be more successful here?"

"Yes, I do."

Agent Kovak was quiet for a moment, considering. "You want a job here even after the ordeal with Phantom?"

Trey coldly stated the line he had been rehearsing the whole trip:

"Ghosts belong in a lab."

Cato wasn't a ghost, his conscience automatically rebutted. He shoved the thought to the very back of his mind and locked it in a vault. But then an image of A1 and A2 surfaced, their blue eyes blank and their skin shrinking over fractured bones, and Trey had no faith in his statement at all.

"And you don't hold us responsible for the death of Maddie's son?"

This time it was direct. No word play, no pretenses. Again, the answer was so well-practiced Trey had to be careful not to recite it too quickly. "It was an accident."

He didn't believe that for a second. The question was, did Kovak?

The Agent's stony expression offered no insight. Trey gulped. Lying wasn't his strongest skill, and, unable to read Agent Kovak, he felt like a mouse whose tail was trapped beneath a cat's paw while the feline played with its food. "Tell me, are you interested in the ghost hunting or the research?"

"Hunting." That answer wasn't even a prepared one, and yet it slipped out with quick confidence. Trey took a breath to slow down and finish, "I don't want to be cooped up in a lab all day. I enjoy fighting ghosts."

"Then take my advice—get out of the ghost-hunting business."

Trey frowned. "Why?"

"Because the work we're doing here will put an end to the need for ghost hunters. It's a dying business. If you want an internship to conduct research and program computers, then by all means, apply here. We'll consider you. But ghost hunters won't be in demand much longer."

"Because of the weapon being developed in Project Alpha?"

"That's right."

"Can I see it?"

"Absolutely not. It's classified."

"Then, can you show me how the neutralizer bands work?" Agent Kovak eyed Trey, who continued, "I mean, the Alpha ghosts do still have their powers neutralized, right?"

"As far as we know."

"I'd like to see where they lived. Then I'll leave so you can get back to work."

Kovak absently twisted a gold ring on his finger. "All right, Mr. Selman. You want a tour of Project Alpha? Right this way."

They stepped inside an elevator, where Kovak pressed a button with the symbol α.

The button began blinking, and the elevator descended.

"We're already underground," Trey observed. "How deep does the AGC go?"

"The classified Projects are lower. The less sensitive ones are closer to ground level."

"Not much security to get to the classified ones."

Agent Kovak smirked. "You see that lens right there? It scanned your visitor's badge and my retina the moment we stepped inside. If you'd been alone in here and pressed that button, even if you were wearing that badge, an alarm would have been triggered."

Trey squinted suspiciously at the lens. "Oh."

"Do you know why we prefer retinal scanners to fingerprints or keycards?"

The way Kovak was looking at him made Trey feel as if the answer was ridiculously obvious and he was expected to know it, but he sheepishly shook his head. Kovak tapped his temple and answered, "Eyes. A Shifter can assume the form of anybody who works here, and while it can replicate the person right down to the thumbprint, a Shifter can't change its eyes. That's how you identify them; even when assuming the body of a human, they'll retain their glowing eyes."

Trey nodded. He was pretty sure he'd read something like that in one of Madison's books. He should have known the answer, but his taut nerves were blanking his mind with the single-mindedness of his task.

His heart shot into his throat at the sound of a quiet *beep*. The elevator settled to a stop, and a woman's disembodied voice announced, "Level Alpha."

— Chapter Thirty-Seven —
Project Alpha

The doors opened to a deserted hallway. The lights were dimmer in this hall than they had been in the last one, probably because Alpha was currently unoccupied.

Agent Kovak strode down the corridor, Trey trailing behind and gazing at closed doors as they passed. "What's in these rooms?"

"Quarantine is down there at the end of the hall, which is where we send subjects who are sick or injured. Every Project has its own Quarantine wing, which has its own elevator so the doctor's assistants can access each level without leaving the wing. That room there is the Arena. To your left is where we conduct the majority of our experiments, and the door next to it is where we study the effects of exposing a ghost to its weakness. This door leads to a staircase that would take us up to the Arena's observation room."

They were heading for the double doors at the end of the hall, opposite to what Kovak had identified as Quarantine. The doors slid open when they drew near. "This," Agent Kovak explained, flicking the light switch, "was where the Alpha ghosts lived."

Trey stepped inside. The dark room came to life, lit by bright fluorescent lights. Seven small cages lined the far wall. Over each cage was a plaque that read A1, A2, and so on to A5, then A7 and A8. A large cage labeled for A6 was separated from the others. Trey approached it, critically analyzing the thin metal bars.

"I thought A6 was super-strong."

Agent Kovak flipped another switch, and the cage began to hum softly. "Don't touch it," he warned. "I activated the electric current." He picked up a small metal tool and tossed it onto the cage. Trey leapt back with a startled gasp when a blinding spark flashed. The tool clattered against the wall.

"That didn't kill him?"

Agent Kovak chuckled. "A6 is not easy to kill. Although he's still an animal, he's smarter than the other two Deltas. He didn't electrocute himself nearly as often as the purebloods."

"Pureblood . . . *whats*, exactly?"

"Mr. Selman, Project Delta is classified, as is Project Alpha. The only reason I've allowed this tour is the Project is temporarily vacated. Be careful what you ask."

"Sorry. Can you tell me what A6 looks like?"

"Red eyes and fangs," Kovak replied once more.

Trey scowled. "A little more specific than that. Scales? Claws? Fur? Does it walk on four legs, or two?"

Kovak shrugged. "A6 is not likely to be seen. If you do catch a glimpse of him, you'll probably be dead before you even know what hit you. You'll sense A6 before you see him. He has, shall we say, a rather ominous aura. You can't hide from him. Even if you kept every muscle perfectly still and held your breath, he could hear your heart beating, smell your sweat, see your body heat. He is the perfect predator."

The Head Agent gazed mournfully at the empty electrified cage. "As much as I hate to kill what I've created, we'll probably have to destroy A6, which is a pity, but we still have the serum that turned him. We could always make another one."

"Can't recreate Cato, though, can you?"

The words blurted out before Trey had time to realize the consequences. Kovak's eyes locked on him even though the Agent's head didn't turn. "You're right," he said softly. He gazed at the half-demon's cage again. "A6's transformation was carefully orchestrated and monitored. Your friend was a freak accident. The odds of recreating those exact results are astronomically low, and unfortunately, I'm not allowed to experiment on humans to try."

Kovak turned his head to freeze Trey in his dark, piercing gaze. "You don't have anything you want to tell me about Cato, do you, Mr.

Selman?"

Trey took the time to inhale, then exhale before committing to words. "You asked me two years ago. I told you then, I wasn't there when the accident happened."

"And two years ago, I couldn't tell if you were lying to me."

"I wasn't then, and I'm not now."

"Mm-hmm." Kovak adjusted the band on his watch. Trey eyed him warily, somehow inexplicably suspicious that he'd given the wrong answer to a misinterpreted question. "I think time will tell where your loyalties lie." Kovak flipped the switch again, and the hum stopped.

Trey wandered over to the other cages, stepping over two small squares of tape in the middle of the floor. "Are these cages electrically charged too?"

"No need. Their powers were always neutralized, except the twins, and they never left their cages without permission."

Trey crouched down. "I'm not sure a dog could fit comfortably in here." He glanced at the Agent. "May I?"

Kovak shrugged. "If you really want to."

Trey crawled into A7's cage. He struggled to pull his long limbs in, and then he crouched in the confined space. He squirmed a little, trying to find a semi-comfortable position in the cramped quarters before he decided there was no way to accomplish such a feat and crawled out again. "Tight space," he said.

Agent Kovak answered with nothing more than a smirk.

"What's this for?" Trey asked, tapping his finger against a sensor on top of the cage.

"It's activated by a keycard. Sends a low voltage through the bars. It's completely painless; all it does is make the muscles lock up for a few seconds to give us time to remove and restrain the subject."

"Oh. So, they spent most of their time here?"

"When we weren't running tests on them, they were here."

"What about the neutralizers?"

Agent Kovak walked over to a cabinet and opened it to withdraw a metal band and a device that resembled the crude picture drawn on the whiteboard in City Hall. Kovak held up the band. "Would you like to see how it works?"

Trey tensed and took a suspicious step away. Kovak chuckled. "It doesn't hurt." Grudgingly, Trey removed his jacket and held out his right arm. Agent Kovak slipped the band over Trey's fingers and slid it up to his biceps. "It will tighten," he forewarned, wrapping both hands around the band and twisting in opposite directions.

Immediately, it constricted like a living creature. Trey grimaced. It didn't hurt, but it was uncomfortable. "Try to pull it off," Agent Kovak challenged. Trey seized the band and tugged.

The band responded by tightening like a python. Already, Trey felt a cold tingle in his right fingers. He released the band, and after a moment, its grip loosened. "Okay, get this thing off me," he said.

Agent Kovak fitted the clamp over the neutralizer band. He flipped a latch on the clamp, and a red light blinked on. He slid the latch downward. The metal warmed, and the neutralizer released its hold.

Trey pulled it loose and rubbed his arm, his eyes roaming the room for cameras. One over A6's cage. He didn't see any others.

Kovak said, "You see why the Alpha ghosts can't remove their neutralizers?" He held up the clamp. "Without this, it's impossible. Can't phase them off, either. We incorporated vidon into the design. Have you ever heard of a vidon spyder?"

"No," Trey admitted, eyeing the lens in the wall. Was the camera on? Without test subjects to observe, it probably wasn't. Or it was on but not being closely monitored.

Kovak set the band and clamp down on the counter. "We found a dead one a few years ago and extracted its webbing to study. Fascinating creature. Can you guess what it likes to eat?"

Trey, who was now fixated on the clamp, shrugged. Kovak shook his head. "Kálos," he said, disappointed that Trey wasn't remotely interested in playing his guessing game. "These giant spiders have evolved the ability to spin webs kálos can't phase through. We're working on manufacturing synthetic vidon in Project Zeta. It would be groundbreaking for ghost hunters if we could find an economical way to mass-produce it."

"That's really cool," Trey muttered, although he couldn't force enough enthusiasm to satisfy Kovak, who sighed and turned away.

"Did you have any more questions?"

Trey eyed the clamp, his adrenaline pumping. He needed more time. "Yes. Um . . . so, what . . . what was the Alpha ghosts' diet?" He made a show of shoving his arm into the jacket sleeve, his back to the camera.

"Their *diet?*" Kovak repeated in a tone that betrayed his mounting impatience. He huffed at the ridiculous question and bent down to open one of the lower cabinets. Trey made his move. He sidestepped and leaned forward, pretending to struggle with fitting his other hand into the sleeve, using the jacket as a screen while his hand reached for the clamp . . .

Kovak straightened too quickly, forcing Trey to retract before the Head Agent faced him again with a small, sealed plastic container in hand. "Here," he grunted, tossing it at Trey, who caught it in one hand. "Cheap, easy to buy in bulk, convenient to store, and doesn't spoil. It's basically a ground-up paste of the bare essentials. Alphas 1, 2, and 8 got the standard meal, but 3, 4, 5, and 7 were given a specialized blend with extra protein."

"Why?" asked Trey as he peeled back the cover just enough to dip his finger into the gruel. It felt gritty, and he didn't want to put it in his mouth, but if the Alpha ghosts ate it on a daily basis, it couldn't be that bad, right? He sniffed his finger before licking the paste. Although he'd been braced for the worst, he actually couldn't taste much of anything. The mixture had an unpleasant texture on his tongue but lacked flavor, good or bad.

Kovak glanced at his watch, not even bothering to hide his boredom. "Because we needed those four to be in better physical condition. Now, is that all?"

"Yes," Trey mumbled, eyeing the clamp again.

"Then I'll show you out."

Trey followed, smoothly exchanging the cup of paste for the clamp on the counter as he passed. He tucked his trophy into the inside pocket of his jacket. "Can I see some of the other rooms?" he asked, zipping the jacket as the doors shut behind him.

Agent Kovak considered. "I don't see why not," he said, turning left. The doors opened, and Trey entered an indoor arena.

He tilted his head back. The ceiling stretched high above him, more than enough room for a ghost—kálos—to fly, or some other creature, for that matter. Halfway up the far wall was a long window.

Agent Kovak gestured to the center of the room. "This is where they fight." He pointed to the window. "We monitor them from that room up there."

"Why do you make them fight?"

Kovak looked out across the room. Trey waited a few seconds, and when the Agent still pretended not to have heard the question, he realized he wasn't going to get an answer and instead said, "You mentioned other experiments too, right?"

Agent Kovak turned on his heel and strode back into the hallway. Trey cast one look back at the Arena. His thoughts circled around gladiators fighting to the death. The drain in the middle of the floor made him wonder whose blood had been washed down it.

He followed Kovak to another room across the hall. When the doors slid open, Trey shivered, sensing this place held a lot of pain and suffering for the ghosts who entered. In the center of the room was a hinged metal table with restraints. A bright light was positioned above it, much like an operating room. From the ceiling hung many pieces of terrifying equipment—drills and lenses and sharp instruments—and scattered across the counter were syringes, drill bits, scalpels, and other lethal tools.

An open doorway led to another section of the room. Trey wandered past the table to peer inside. Large computer consoles faced a wall outfitted with more restraints. Trey walked over to examine the blank screens. He gazed up at the restraints on the wall.

Kovak's dark voice drifted from across the room: "Would you like to test this one?"

"I don't think so."

Kovak cocked an eyebrow. "I thought you wanted to know everything about the Alpha ghosts. This is where they came when they were first admitted to the program." He strolled to the restraints on the wall.

"And what exactly is 'this'?"

"Come here."

Trey gulped, suddenly clammy. "I'd rather not."

"Come here," the Agent repeated. Trey approached him meekly. Agent Kovak seized his wrist, pressed it to the wall, and attached it with the strap.

"I'm human. I have rights, you know," Trey said as his other wrist was cinched tight.

Kovak rolled his eyes, stealing the breath right out of Trey's lungs when he realized the Head Agent had probably heard those exact words before. "Just relax," Kovak said, restraining his ankles too.

Relax? Trey was now pinned to the wall in a crucified pose. His heart flew out of control. Kovak said, "This is only a demonstration."

Trey swallowed hard when the Agent stepped away and explained, "We hook the subject up here. Not an easy task, mind you—A7 kicked one of the handlers in the face and broke his nose." He gestured to the mass of wires and tubes that were connected to the consoles. "The subject is naked. We attach these electrodes to the skin."

Agent Kovak started to unzip Trey's jacket.

No! Trey thought, panic making his head buzz. "Wait," he croaked.

Kovak stopped, leaving the jacket half-zipped. "Just relax," he said again, to the opposite effect. He began placing the small electrodes on Trey's neck, his fingers creeping under the collar of Trey's T-shirt to attach electrodes to his chest. "The ones connected to the blue wires record heart rate, brain activity, body temperature, blood pressure, oxygen level—you get the idea. They send that information to those computer screens."

Trey couldn't speak. Kovak rolled up Trey's sleeve and placed electrodes on his arm, then held up a separate pair connected with red wires. "I won't hook these up to you. They're placed on the subject's temples. We type in a sequence, and the computer sends the information to this machine, which translates the code into an electrical shock of a specific voltage targeted at a certain part of the brain. Are you following me?"

"Um . . . barely."

"I'll simplify it. Depending on what sequence we type in, a particular shock will force the ghost to use one of its powers. We start off simple to make sure everything works. Usually the first powers we run through are the basics like intangibility and various ectoplasm forms. Then we start playing with the Divinity."

Trey stared at him. "So . . . you want a ghost to become invisible. You type a sequence, the ghost is electrocuted, and it turns invisible?"

"A crude interpretation, but yes. Then the blue wires record the body's response so we can learn how the powers work."

Kovak turned his back to Trey and strode over to the consoles. "Whoa, what are you doing?" Trey cried, squirming in the restraints when the Agent turned the computers on.

"You're not hooked up to the red wires," Kovak reminded him.

"Oh. Right. Does, um, does it hurt a ghost when you force it to use a power by electrocution?"

"Electrical stimulation, not *electrocution*," corrected Kovak.

"What's the difference?"

Kovak rolled his eyes with a sigh as he returned to Trey to pull the electrodes free. "This room, as well as most of the others, is soundproof."

"Were the twins present during these experiments?"

"Of course. They were present during almost all of our experiments."

"Do you think they're still alive?"

A genuinely concerned frown creased Kovak's brow. "I like to hope so. What's perplexing is the Alpha ghosts kidnapped them in the first place. They hate the twins."

"They do?" Trey asked in surprise.

Kovak removed the last electrode and bent down to undo the restraints around his ankles. "Sure. The twins are completely loyal to us. They assisted in the experiments and did whatever we told them to do. Dr. Anders theorizes the other Alpha ghosts took A1 and A2 so they could torture them to death, thereby seeking their revenge on them while at the same time putting the twins out of their misery, at least in their eyes."

"They would do something like that?"

"Like I said, they're cold-blooded killers, although their looks are deceiving. Remember that, Selman. Don't hesitate to pull that trigger."

Trey nodded. "Are you going to replace the twins with other kids from Project Gamma?"

Agent Kovak paused. "I suppose I could," he said, rubbing his forehead. "It would be so much work, though. Sifting through paperwork and medical records, matching a passive Divinity with a submissive personality, hours of conditioning . . . A1 and A2 were so well-trained. I can't emphasize how much of an investment they were. Funny thing is, they weren't even intended to become servants. We wanted their father for Project Alpha, not them."

"Really? Why?"

"He was a Telepath. We'd planned for him to be the first test subject in Alpha, but by the time we were ready to complete the transfer, he'd expired. He was the only Telepath we had in custody. His bastard sons were lucky we took them in his stead; they were slated to be dissected in Project Omega."

"But why did you need a Telepath?"

Kovak reached for the final restraint. "I can't tell you much about Project Alpha, Mr. Selman. You know we're studying the source of a ghost's power. The logical place to start is the brain. We wanted a kálos with mental abilities."

Once the last restraint was removed, Trey stepped away from the wall, rubbing his wrists. He zipped his jacket up as he followed Agent Kovak to the computer consoles. Most of the monitors showed jagged lines and graphs of incomplete data. Trey identified his heart rate on one of the charts. One screen was larger than the rest, and it showed the silhouette of a human body in different colors to indicate temperature. Only parts of the top half and the left arm were colored. Another screen was video feed showing Trey pinned to the wall, warily watching a point just beyond the camera.

Nostalgic, Kovak stroked the console. "You asked me why I make them fight."

"Yes." Trey wished he hadn't.

The Agent stared at the restraints on the wall. "A lot of our equipment is sensitive. It would short-circuit if exposed to even a small electrical surge. We need a way to, ah, *entice* our subjects to use their powers without the extra prod. We've found the best way to persuade them to cooperate is to outfit them with sensors and turn them loose in the Arena to fight."

"Each other?"

"Sometimes. We'd deprive them of food and water for a day or two in advance so they were competing for a meal. Other times we'd release an animal from Project Theta. I've found there is no better incentive than a wild beast trying to kill you."

He chuckled. Trey didn't. "Of course, it was all closely supervised. If it looked like the Alpha subjects weren't going to win, we pulled the plug on the fight."

Kovak studied the apprentice, then noted quietly, "You think I'm cruel."

Trey swallowed but didn't answer because yes, he did think Kovak was cruel. The Head Agent adjusted the knot in his tie. "Hmm. From an outsider's perspective, I can understand why you'd think that. I also used to have reservations when we first started this practice. It's just so barbaric. But their culture is barbaric. I find it disturbing, really, the lust they possess for fighting and killing. Once released, our subjects would turn on each other without a second thought. They actually *enjoyed* the fights. So," Kovak finished, "are you still interested in an internship?"

Trey felt like he was going to throw up. "I don't think this is the job for me. I'd rather hunt ghosts than torture them."

"Yes, well, just remember what I said about ghost hunting. Not a good business to be in," Agent Kovak warned, shutting the computers down. Trey started for the door, but he paused by the metal table. Metal cuffs for the wrists, ankles, thighs, arms, chest, and head were bolted to the surface.

He jumped when a hand grabbed his shoulder. "We run many experiments here."

Trey opened his mouth, but his voice was lost in his throat. Finally, he choked out, "Are . . . they . . . Were they conscious?"

Agent Kovak took his hand from Trey's shoulder and walked along the edge of the table, his fingers drifting across the cold metal surface. "You remember when we paid a visit to Phantom Heights and I told you we didn't vaccinate our ghosts?" Mute again, Trey just nodded. "We have a tight budget, Mr. Selman, and we're frugal about what we spend on conveniences for our test subjects. We can't afford to waste money on unnecessary vaccines, sedatives, or pain killers. It's rare for us to sedate a subject, plus we don't want the drugs to interfere with the test results. In Alpha, the only one we regularly sedated was A6, and that's just because he was too dangerous for us to handle otherwise."

Trey's stomach lurched. Without a word, he walked past Kovak and the metal table, and when he entered the hallway again, he didn't even glance behind to see if his host was following. He subtly touched his jacket, pressing a hard object against his hip to ensure it was still tucked safely away. He had what he came to get. He didn't want to know any more about Project Alpha.

Trey drummed his fingers against his folded arms as he impatiently waited by the elevator. Agent Kovak finally emerged through the sliding doors. He handed Trey a black case. "New toys," the Agent answered before Trey could even ask, "as a token of appreciation for your cooperation. These are just prototypes, mind you, but hopefully you'll find them useful. One for you, and I was even nice enough to give one to Maddie. We modified the design for her ectogun. Hers fire at Level 1D; ours Level 2C."

Trey stared blankly at Kovak, who added, "If you'll be so kind as to give Maddie a message from me—tell her we'd appreciate any progress she makes if she tinkers with our prototype. It's a shame she stopped doing business with us. We could have made a lot more progress if she'd continued sharing research."

Trey's mind was so numb with everything he'd learned that he could barely process the words coming out of Kovak's mouth. As soon as the elevator doors opened, he stepped inside. The Agent followed and pressed the ground-floor button. Trey closed his eyes. No wonder ghosts were so terrified of the AGC. He couldn't even imagine the torture the prisoners here had to endure.

As soon as the thought occurred, he froze, opening his eyes as a memory surfaced from the vault he'd locked it in, a vision of a green-and-blue-eyed teenager being thrown into the back of a truck. Trey cleared his throat. "Agent Kovak," he asked, his voice small, "just out of curiosity . . . which Project did you put Cato in?"

The Agent stared straight ahead. "I think it's best if you didn't know."

"Maybe . . . I mean, c-could I . . . ?"

"You know I can't do that."

Trey locked his jaw and closed his eyes, willing the nausea to pass. He listened for the elevator doors to open, prayed it would be soon. But they were deep underground, and the elevator crept up frustratingly slowly, and all he could hear now was Shannon's voice asking, "Do we? Really?" in response to his claim that they knew the truth.

Trey clutched the case tighter against his chest. Part of him didn't want to know the details. The other part always wondered, night and day, gnawing on every waking thought. Even if he could summon the courage to ask the truth of Kovak, he knew the Agent would lie. And besides, Trey wasn't sure he could handle the truth. After everything he'd seen today, he was afraid to know Cato's real fate if there was a chance it could be worse than what he'd been told. Now he feared he might be forever cursed to his own cruel imagination spinning dark scenarios. He'd come here to learn about the Alpha ghosts. Instead, he saw Cato locked in that cage, Cato strapped on the metal table, Cato being electrocuted . . .

"Tell me, how long have you been in your apprenticeship?"

Kovak's deep voice disrupted his thoughts. Trey almost didn't answer for fear that opening his mouth would release vomit instead of words. He took a few seconds to compose himself before responding, "Four years."

"Oh?" Kovak inspected his fingernails. "And how old are you?"

"Seventeen."

Though the Agent didn't make a big point of it, he was watching Trey from the corner of his eye, analyzing him. "Hmm, thirteen. Awfully young to start an apprenticeship in such a dangerous career."

Monotonic, Trey said, "I started with books and lessons. I progressed, I guess." As if it were that simple. What he didn't mention was the day Phantom made his first official appearance was the same day Trey had begged Madison to start teaching him how to fight.

You and me, Cay. One day the two of us are going to run this town.

Kovak flipped a switch. The lights dimmed, and the elevator shuddered to a stop.

Trey was too shocked to immediately process what had happened. His confusion shifted to unease when he glanced to the side and found Kovak glaring suspiciously at him. Did the Agent know he had the clamp in his jacket? Was he about to be interrogated? Or arrested and incarcerated for theft from a top-secret government agency? *Indefinitely*, Bridget had warned when he signed the paper. Trey tried and failed to swallow the lump in his throat.

"I'm not sure about your intentions here, Mr. Selman."

Beads of sweat welled on Trey's forehead. He met the Agent's gaze and said nothing. Kovak folded his arms, leaning back against the elevator wall. "There was a room I didn't show you. I told you Alpha is where we study how a ghost's powers work. We bring all our new subjects to Alpha to run tests on their powers before we send them to their assigned Projects. That room where we use electricity to stimulate power? Cato was strapped in the very restraints you were in."

Trey gulped and took a step back as Agent Kovak leaned forward. "One of the rooms down there is used to study the effects of a ghost's weakness. We can fill it with water, control the lighting, manipulate the temperature, or just about anything else. We put your friend in that room when he first came here. He's a Cryo. You know what we did to him? We muzzled him, stripped him naked, and increased the temperature until he couldn't take it anymore. You should have seen him, Selman. He was humiliated, and he was so busy trying to cover his genitals and pull the muzzle off that he didn't even realize the room was getting hotter at first. He pounded on the one-way glass, begging us to stop, until he became so disoriented he collapsed. We studied how his body reacted to the change in environment, and we timed how long he could last in extreme heat. The results were intriguing. Did you know he didn't sweat? His body cooled by an internal source until he became too dehydrated. He lasted longer than we expected."

Trey couldn't breathe. All he could do was stare at Kovak's face, the man's features distorted in the shadows. "After he recovered, we ran another test. We *lowered* the temperature. His body is naturally colder, so he can withstand freezing temps. He started shivering at negative 72.2 degrees, an impressive feat. Do you know what that is in Fahrenheit?"

Trey's eyes rolled to the ceiling in thought. "Um . . ."

Kovak gave him a few seconds, then sighed. "Ninety-eight. The room was at negative 153 degrees Fahrenheit before hypothermia finally set in. To put that into perspective for you, the lowest temperature ever recorded on Earth is negative 135.8 degrees Fahrenheit."

Agent Kovak's eyes bored into Trey. He leaned back against the wall again. "Disappointing. Earlier you said all ghosts belong in the lab. Based on your reaction, I'm afraid I don't believe that statement."

Trey clenched his jaw, struggling to regain his composure. "Cato and I weren't as close as you think."

"Oh? Weren't you his sidekick?"

Trey stiffened. "No."

"No?" Kovak repeated with a laugh. "You really believe that?"

"We would have been partners," Trey insisted. "Equals."

"*Really.* You actually think people would have seen you on the same level as a hero with superpowers? A human with some fancy toys standing next to the mighty Phantom." Kovak's lips peeled apart into a sinister smile. "Why don't you cut the crap and thank me already?"

"What?" Trey whispered, clutching the case tighter.

"I took Phantom out of the spotlight. It's all yours now whenever you're ready to step up and take it. Your turn to be the hero." He tapped the case. "This will be a good start. You're welcome."

"I wasn't competing against Cato. I . . . I never wanted . . ."

"Didn't you? If I check the logs, I bet I won't find a single phone call from you, will I? Admit it—you were secretly happy I removed Phantom from the picture."

"No."

"You didn't have to worry about being trapped in his shadow anymore."

"I was never going to be Phantom's sidekick!" Trey shouted, his voice ringing in the elevator.

Kovak straightened. "I think we both know why you're here."

Trey gulped. *Kovak knows . . . He has to know, all because I lost my damn composure. Mission fail.* Unable to meet Kovak's cold eyes anymore, Trey hung his head.

"It's not a bad idea, just unlikely to succeed. Catching my fugitives would certainly elevate your status in Phantom Heights. They might even call you a hero. Unfortunately, the odds aren't in your favor. I would have told you that in the beginning if you'd been straightforward from the get-go."

"Um . . . yeah," Trey whispered, so weak with relief he was certain his knees were about to give out. Agent Kovak flipped the switch, and the elevator shuddered and rose. Trey kept his gaze on his feet; he could still feel the Agent watching him with those black eyes.

"Main level," announced the disembodied woman.

Finally, the doors opened. Trey lurched toward freedom, only to find his way blocked.

Kovak leaned forward, his weight keeping the doors parted and his arm preventing Trey from passing without ducking. "Selman," he said, his voice low, "there are other ghost hunters out there. I'm sure you've seen some in Phantom Heights besides Maddie."

A molten bubble of rage clogged Trey's throat. "Sure," he seethed. "We've seen some. And you know what? They never help us. They catch or kill some ghosts on the outskirts, and then they're gone the same day. And besides, the name Tarrow is known throughout the entire ghost-hunting community. She's a legend. Everybody knows the names Madison and Jaxon. They . . ." Trey trailed off. He was getting carried away again, and Kovak's eerily passive expression made him swallow the next part of his rant.

"Jaxon Tarrow," Kovak murmured with a smile. "That's a name I haven't heard in a while. It still saddens me to think of how things might have unfolded differently if not for his untimely demise." And yet, his smile remained intact. Trey's eyes fell to the piece of paper Kovak extended to him. "You're right; Maddie is special. Most ghost hunters aren't interested in the scientific research like she is. I don't know if you've ever seen this before."

Trey cautiously took the paper and skimmed it while Kovak went on to explain, "It's a list of all kálos Divinities we know of. You can see the price we'll pay if you turn one in alive. Catch a Telepath," he said, indicating the highest reward at the bottom of the paper, "and you've got an easy 50k in your pocket."

Easy? Trey thought. *Yeah, right. Capturing a Telepath alive would be next to impossible.*

Agent Kovak slid the paper out of Trey's fingers and clicked a pen, then turned to press the paper against the side of the elevator and scribble a note at the bottom. He returned it to Trey and added, "Catch any of mine from Alpha, and I'll pay double that payout per head. You bring me A1 and A2 alive, and I'm willing to double *that*, 200k apiece. How does that sound?"

Trey stared at the barely legible handwriting, the bile building in his throat. "Money? What good would money do for me in a place like Phantom Heights? We're surviving on scraps between supply drops and fighting for our lives every day. I don't need *money*."

"You need an *out*. Phantom Heights has no future, and neither do you if you stay there. Leave. Go to college. I'm sure another ghost hunter would happily take you if you wanted to continue your apprenticeship."

Trey crumpled the paper into a ball. "There are no other ghost hunters like Madison. They're selfish thugs who are in it only for the money and the thrill. You know, the ones we've met in Phantom Heights don't care that there are kids in City Hall, or that those kids cry because they're hungry every single day, or that we're dying. All they care about is catching ghosts for this payout." He threw the paper ball at his feet for emphasis. "I won't abandon my friends and family. I won't leave Phantom Heights until every human is safely out."

Kovak rolled his eyes. "Please don't confuse stupidity with nobility. It's a shame you feel that way, but I don't suppose I can talk you out of your decision. My offer still stands. And I'm always willing to negotiate. It's your turn to be the hero now, Selman. Whatever your price is, you name it."

For one horrifyingly clear moment, Trey imagined what might happen if he told Agent Kovak he had A1 and A2. And his price? A military escort to guard the humans while they escaped, and enough rations to feed and clothe every single person currently in City Hall, and the reward money to be divided among the Phantom Heights survivors so they could start new lives. Yes, he could be the hero. The one who saved everybody.

"Name my price, huh?" Trey looked Kovak in the eye. "If I deliver an Alpha ghost, would you send the military to evacuate Phantom Heights?"

Kovak's brow twitched, but Trey couldn't tell if it was in amusement or annoyance. "Perhaps I misspoke."

"Why? Why won't you even consider sending the military in?"

"It's too complicated for a kid to understand."

"Try me."

Kovak exhaled, then spoke slowly, as if explaining to a five-year-old instead of a teenager: "The Ghost Realm has an active military. It's called the Shadow Guard. The riffraff you've been dealing with in Phantom Heights is not organized, and it's not military. The second I send in our army, they're going to send out theirs, and then it's all over. Do you understand? I can't risk starting an all-out war we have no chance of winning. This new weapon is going to make your ectogun look like a toy, but until it's ready, I'm not sending soldiers. Your two options are to either abandon Phantom Heights and continue your apprenticeship under a new ghost-hunting master, or stay and survive long enough for me to finish my weapon."

Trey clenched his fists. Kovak's answer made him sick, and yet, he was almost secretly relieved by it. *What would I have done if his answer was yes? Turned over the twins?*

Trey's final image of Cato blossomed in his mind—the panicked, petrified look on his friend's bloody face just before the doors closed. The small cages, the restraints on the wall, the drills and blades over the metal table, the electricity, the screams inside soundproof rooms . . .

His stomach threatened to empty itself all over Kovak's shiny black shoes. How could Trey consider, even for a second, condemning those poor kids back to hell? He wouldn't be a hero. He wouldn't be able to live with the guilt.

In Trey's silence, Agent Kovak bent over, picked up the ball of paper, smoothed the creases, and printed two words on the back. He offered it again. Trey didn't want it, but he accepted it. Agent Kovak pointed at the name he'd written—*Jules Pilecki*. "That, Mr. Selman, is one of our top ghost hunters. She's cashed out on that list more than anyone else. If you should ever change your mind, I'll put in a good word with her. She might even prove to be a better ghost-hunting master than Maddie."

"I doubt that."

"You were right when you said the name Tarrow is known throughout the ghost-hunting community. She *is* a legend. But her success is constrained to her scientific advancements and weapon development. In the field, she's earned the nickname 'Merciful Madison.' And in the ghost-hunting business, mercy is weakness. That lesson has proven to be true in Phantom Heights, wouldn't you say?"

Trey shoved the paper into his pocket. "Thank you for your time," he said, striding toward the sterilization chamber without a look back.

"You don't have to go through there again," Agent Kovak called. "You can go out that door there; it leads straight to the lobby."

Trey altered his course and pushed open the door. He jerked the visitor's badge from his jacket and tossed it onto the counter as he strode past the receptionist. He snatched his weapon belt but didn't waste the few seconds to stop and buckle it around his waist.

"Have a nice day!" Bridget called sweetly.

— Chapter Thirty-Eight —

Family

Once back in the tunnel, Trey needed every ounce of willpower to restrain himself from sprinting.

There are cameras on me, he reminded himself. *Agent Kovak himself is probably watching me right now.* When he finally reached the car, he threw the case onto the floor and slid into the passenger seat.

"Let's go," he said, dropping his belt at his feet and staring straight ahead. Wes studied him, hands draped over the wheel.

"What happened?"

"Just go," Trey snapped. "I wanna get out of here."

"You got what you went in for?"

"Yes!"

Wes raised his eyebrows but turned the key. The engine roared in his haste to drive away from the AGC. Trey stared out the window at the slate-gray smoothness of the tunnel walls in the intervals of light between shadow, not really seeing. Wes said something about a seat belt, but Trey ignored him.

The Alpha ghosts may be ruthless, but the Agents were the ones who had molded them into killers. The thought of being shocked repeatedly, forced to use their powers while the twins—those innocent kids—watched and listened to their tortured screams . . . and living in those cages where there wasn't enough room to shift or stretch . . . Days, even hours trapped in there would have been torture in and of itself . . .

"Pull over."

"What? Why?"

"I'm gonna be sick!"

"Not in this car you're not!" Wes slammed the brakes. Trey threw open the door and leapt out before the vehicle had even stopped. He doubled over, retching violently. Wes stepped out and observed him over the roof of the car. "You sure you're okay?"

Trey swiped the back of his hand across his mouth and slid into the front seat. "Just take me back," he whispered hoarsely as he buckled the seatbelt.

The labyrinth of tunnels spanned on and on, but finally, the light started to change, and soon after, the car was tilted upward. The ramp opened onto the dirt path in the woods. Trey eyed the trees as the car bounced along the trail, wondering if they were out of the cameras' sights yet. Probably not.

The dirt path intersected with a gravel road, which finally brought them to asphalt. Wes, Trey had noticed, never bothered with a turn signal. He hit the gas and whipped to the left, already accelerating. But ninety miles per hour on the open highway wasn't fast enough. Trey wasn't in the mood to talk to Wes, hated the silence, and couldn't stand listening to the radio. He sat with his forehead against the cool glass, swallowing bile while his stomach churned. Farm fields rolled by, broken occasionally by small towns and pockets of woods. His fingers crept to his pocket. "Hey, Wes?"

"Yeah?"

Trey pulled the crumpled piece of paper out. "Did you know Agent Kovak buys ghosts and other creatures from ghost hunters?"

"I did." Wes glanced at the list in Trey's hand. "How much would I be worth?" he asked with a sly smile.

Trey skimmed the prices. "Werewolf . . . I don't see it on here."

"Try lunos."

"Nope."

"Huh. What about weir? Spelled w-e-i-r."

"Okay, yeah, here it is. Two hundred."

"What, that's it? I thought I'd be worth at least a grand." Trey glared at him sidelong. "So, how much is Kovak offering for his escaped lab rats?"

"Why? You planning to sell them out if the price is right?" Trey folded the paper in half so Wes couldn't see the handwritten numbers on the bottom.

"Just curious," Wes replied with an innocent shrug.

Trey stared at the name in his lap. "You ever hear of a ghost hunter named Jules Pilecki?"

"Changing the subject," Wes muttered. "Fine. Yeah, I've heard of her. Never met her face-to-face, but I can describe her in one word: ruthless. But then again, most ghost hunters are. Why do you ask?"

"Kovak thinks she'd be a better teacher than Madison."

Wes drummed his fingers on the steering wheel. "Maddie is one of the few honorable ghost hunters. If you want to learn how to be a heartless cutthroat in the game for the sport and the money, then yeah, Jules could teach you that. If you still think you can take up Phantom's mantle someday, you're right where you need to be."

"You actually think people would have seen you on the same level as a hero with superpowers?"

Sick again, Trey shoved the paper out of sight in his pocket and slumped deep into the seat with his arms folded across his stomach. He stared out the windshield at the shimmering surface of a mirage on the road ahead, then sat up straighter. "Wes, is that . . . ?"

"A Tear? Yes, a small one. It'll be gone by the time we reach it."

Sure enough, it was already vanishing as they zoomed toward it. "Do you know what they are? Madison told me 'portal' isn't really the right word."

"It's not. 'Tear' couldn't be more accurate. Don't think of the barrier between Realms as a wall; it's more of a curtain. And curtains wear thin in places. Tears come and go because the curtain seems to be able to mend itself. Moonlight has an adverse effect on the curtain; it's thinner when the moon is full. It also seems to consistently demonstrate an annual cycle, thickest in the spring and almost veil-like come fall. Combine that with a full October moon? There's a reason that's such a spooky month. Lots of Tears, and lots of weirdness in this Realm."

They drove over the spot where the mirage had been. Trey looked in the rearview mirror to peer back at where the "curtain" had temporarily been torn. "Hey, Wes, what—"

Something landed on the front of the car.

Wes slammed the brakes. The car pitched, and yet somehow the cloaked figure crouched on the hood remained perfectly balanced as the tires burned streaks into the asphalt. Trey gritted his teeth as the seat belt cut into his chest, and then he was thrown back into the seat when the vehicle lurched to a dead stop.

The humanoid creature, dressed in black with a hood covering the top half of his face, bore the unmistakable white Greek letter α on his chest. "You betray us?"

"What? No, of course not," Wes said.

Trey bobbed his head and fumbled with the zipper on his jacket. "See?" He produced the device. "We got it, and I swear, I didn't—"

"Get out."

Trey squinted at him, trying to see beneath the cloak's hood. Something about him was . . . off. His eyes were dull in the shadows, but they pinned him in place with their otherworldly intensity, and Trey couldn't breathe in the rubber-choked air.

Wes grumbled, "So, this is your 'diplomacy'? I thought we had a deal."

"Shut up and get out."

"Wes?" Trey whispered.

The werewolf studied the Alpha ghost perched on the hood. Grudgingly, he yielded. "Do what he says."

Trey's hands shook as he fumbled with the seat belt. He tried to make eye contact with Wes for a cue. Did the werewolf have a plan? Were they going to fight? That would make sense, getting out of the car to have room for Wes to transform and Trey to access his weapons. But Wes gave no indication as he calmly opened the door.

The Alpha ghost leapt off the hood and landed nimbly on both feet, waiting for them. As Trey slid out of the car, he grabbed the handle on Kovak's case and brought it with him, already calculating how many seconds it would take for him to open it and retrieve one of the modified guns. Too bad Kovak hadn't given a demonstration on how to shoot them. Hopefully they operated like the earlier models Trey had sheathed in his weapon belt.

Wes slung his thumbs through the belt loops of his jeans, oddly at ease and showing no indication of changing to his wolf form. "This is—"

"I told you to shut up." The Alpha ghost pointed a gloved finger at Trey. "Open it."

Trey blinked. He turned, set the case on the hood of the car, and popped the lid, then took a step back to let the Alpha ghost approach and peer inside.

The air was so thick. Was it the humidity? Trey couldn't breathe. He tugged at his shirt collar and realized his hands were shaking.

The fugitive studied the interior of the case for a moment, then reached in and peeled back a corner of the fabric. He pinched something tiny between his thumb and forefinger, lifted it up, then dropped it on the asphalt and ground it in with his heel.

Trey's jaw dropped. "We were bugged?"

No answer. The Alpha ghost was gone.

Trey spun in a circle. "Where'd he go?"

"Don't know," Wes said weakly.

Trey twisted to look in every direction, but they were alone between soybean fields on an empty road. "How'd he do that without his powers?"

"I *don't know*," Wes repeated, still shaken.

Kovak leaned against the hard edge of the doorframe. Byrn was sitting at his desk, fingers flying over a keyboard, probably filing another report. How dull. "Had a visit from Tarrow's apprentice. Just sent him on his way."

"Any pertinent news from Phantom Heights?" Byrn asked without pause.

"No, not really. He didn't have any useful information. Just asked questions." A frown settled deep in his brow. "A lot of questions. And, no surprise, he asked about A7. Easy enough to redirect, but if—"

"Agent Byrn, Mr. Jeong is on line three," a woman's voice interrupted.

Byrn slammed his pudgy finger on the intercom button and snarled, "If it's about Project Alpha, I'm not taking it, Bridget."

"Understood, sir."

He shook his head and resumed typing without another word.

Kovak looked away and scratched his neck. Calls from impatient investors were only going to increase with progress in Alpha screeching to a sudden halt. At least he wasn't the one who had to deal with those unpleasant conversations.

He cleared his throat. "Anyway, as I was saying, if Selman didn't know we put his friend in Project Alpha, it's safe to assume they aren't in Phantom Heights after all."

"You're sure A7 didn't make contact with him?"

"Positive. Selman asked the wrong questions. Believe me, if he knew anything about A7, our conversation would have gone a lot differently."

"Hmm."

"But get this, he inquired about an internship of all things."

That was enough to temporarily still Byrn's fingers. "*Really.*"

Kovak nibbled at a hangnail. "Yes, that surprised me too. I know Maddie hates me for that little mess a few years ago, and I can't imagine her apprentice doesn't harbor the same resentment, although he denied it."

"I suppose you spoon-fed the usual bullshit, then?"

"Bullshit?" Kovak cried, insulted. "It's a well-crafted tale!" He applied an expression of sorrow and laced his hands in professional mourning. "If only I'd intervened just a little sooner," he lamented, "maybe I could have saved him. But there was nothing I could do except take the poor boy in my arms and hold him for his last few breaths so he didn't die alone. Such a tragedy."

A smirk cracked his mask of well-rehearsed regret. "I never saw

Maddie so heartbroken."

Byrn glared at him over the top of the screen. He pushed his chair away from the desk. "If Tarrow ever learns the truth—"

"She won't," Kovak dismissed with a careless wave of his hand.

"*If* she does, there's going to be a lot of trouble, and *I'm* going to have to deal with it. Nobody cares when kálos blood is spilt, but human blood, now that's messy. Lawsuits, investigations, questions from the Board—"

"He had to die." Kovak was staring into nothing, his mind clear and resolved to the decision he'd made a couple of years ago. "Holly was right; it was the only way to break Maddie's spirit." A single chuckle jerked his body. "And it worked. Better than I could have hoped. I didn't expect Phantom Heights to suffer so much when she fell apart but, well, sacrifices have to be made."

"We lost our most valuable independent researcher."

Kovak shrugged and slipped his hands into the deep pockets of his lab coat. His fingers found a small, thin square at the bottom. "An unfortunate but necessary cost. I don't regret my decision." He pulled out the hard little square and held it up to study it.

"What's that?"

"Don't know yet," said Kovak. The gadget looked like a two-inch-by-two-inch microchip. "One of Maddie's inventions. I'm going to send it to the techs in Zeta to figure out what it does."

"She actually sent you a gift?"

Kovak chuckled. "Not exactly. But I was nice enough to give her some Zeta prototypes to play with, so it's a fair trade, don't you think?"

Byrn grunted and seized a glass from the corner of his desk, then drained the remaining water in two gulps. He slammed it down and cleared his throat expectantly.

A few uncomfortable seconds passed while Kovak waited for his partner to realize his mistake. "Goddamn it," Byrn grumbled when no one came to refill his glass.

"I can't count how many times a day I forget and do the same." Kovak dropped the mysterious device into his pocket and peeled away from the doorframe. "Someday, when the dust has settled and we've won our war, Maddie will appreciate what I did."

He snatched a clipboard off Byrn's desk. "She buried her boy, and despite the initial crippling effect, in the long run I think it will make her stronger. A clean cut, you know? We just have to make sure what really happened stays buried with him."

Byrn grumbled, "Yeah, well, now the truth is out there with the Alpha subjects."

Annoyed, Kovak flipped through the test results without looking up. "The truth is whatever I say it is."

Madison leaned over Doc's shoulder to watch her separate capsules into piles. "Are all of those for the twins?" she asked.

"No. I'm just reviewing my stock and deciding what they'll need."

Madison glanced at the brothers, who were watching silently. As soon as her eyes met theirs, they averted their gazes. "This will be enough to keep them healthy?"

"Hard to say," Doc replied, pushing one pile away from the others. "I'm hoping to give their immune systems a huge boost. I've got cough drops, painkillers, allergy pills, antibiotics, vitamins, and supplements." She pulled out a small bag and set the various bottles, capsules, and instructions inside. "I'll need to assess their condition after a week or two so I can adjust their regimen. I'm also sending a first-aid kit with extra gauze and a bottle of antiseptic."

Madison turned her attention to the silent twins again, but they just gazed down at their disk. She lowered her voice and said to Doc, "I'm not sure about this. I mean, of course I want Vivian back, and I want her safe. But the thought of giving the twins back to those terrorists makes me sick."

Doc replied, "It really doesn't make much sense. I can't understand what value the other Alpha ghosts see in these kids. They went through a lot of trouble to save them. Let's go through with the deal and see what happens. Maybe they'll realize the twins are too much of a burden. But Vivian is the one in immediate danger right now, so we have to focus on her first."

Madison nodded and looked up at the sound of a fist pounding on the door. "Finally!" She rose and strode down the aisle as Emerton pulled back the bar and opened the doors. Trey stormed in, his fists clenched and his head down. "Hey," Madison greeted. "How'd it go?"

Trey marched past her without a word and headed straight for A1 and A2. "What happened?" she asked Wes, who trailed in after.

The werewolf shrugged. "He won't tell me. We had to pull over three times because he kept throwing up." He held out a black case. "The Agents were nice enough to provide us with some weapons, though. And we stopped on the way back and bought the twins some clothes. I had to guess on the sizes. And Doc," he added, holding up a plastic bag, "you owe me."

Doc, as eager as a kid on Christmas, took the bag and rifled through Wes's drugstore purchases. "Oh good—I was almost out of ibuprofen," she muttered as she returned to sort the new stock into her supply.

Madison accepted the case and watched her apprentice kneel in front of the Agents' slaves. He studied them intently even though they wouldn't meet his gaze. "Agent Kovak told me the other Alpha ghosts hate you. But that's not true, is it?"

They blinked. Madison was silent as she approached, listening to Trey continue, "They're your family, aren't they?" The twins' brows furrowed. They glanced at one another, eyes glowing, then briefly back at Trey and away again. "That's what I thought." He sighed. "You guys saw some gruesome things in the lab, didn't you? The Agents made you torture your own family."

The twins turned their heads away from Trey and stared vacantly at the floor while A1 clutched his mysterious silver disk tighter and A2 began to gnaw on his fingernails.

Madison swallowed. *Family.* At least their odd actions made sense now. "It's no wonder they don't talk," she murmured.

Trey leaned back on his heels. "The things I saw in there . . . I'm not going to be able to sleep for weeks."

She placed a comforting hand on his shoulder. "Thank you for going. I know it wasn't easy." He nodded. "Did you get what we need?"

He reached into his jacket and pulled out the clamp. Madison took it in her hands. "Looks pretty low-tech," she muttered upon studying it.

Trey shivered. "It works."

"How do you know?"

"Because I tested it. I wore one of the neutralizer bands."

"What? He tested it on you? I am going to give Kovak such an earful—"

"Don't. I was willing."

Madison fell silent. "Are you sure you're all right?"

He rose. "Honestly, I didn't have much faith in this plan before," he admitted. "But now . . ." He raised his head to meet Madison's gaze. "The other Alpha ghosts do know how to fight. I saw where Kovak . . . where he forced them . . ." Trey had to pause and clear his throat. The twins' glowing blue eyes locked onto him. "I know they can fight. If they fight for us, we might stand a chance."

"And if they turn against us?" Madison quietly asked.

Trey shook his head. "I need to lie down."

Madison set the clamp on the podium, her attention diverted to the black case. As much as she despised the Agents, her curiosity was piqued. "Did Kovak say what kind of weapons these were?"

Trey shrugged one shoulder as he sank onto the middle step. "I dunno, some prototype something-or-other guns I think. I really wasn't paying much attention. He said if you were able to improve them, he wanted your notes."

"Yeah? I hope you told him to go to hell for me."

A faint smile twitched his lips. "Not in so many words."

Madison set the case down on the lowest step and undid the clasps. She opened the lid to discover two silver guns resting in a thick sheet of foam. She pulled one out. "It's heavy. But this looks a lot like the ecto-gun I invented."

"He said these fire in the Level 2C range."

"He doubled the output? How'd he stabilize the core?"

"I don't know." Trey paused, watching Madison aim the gun with a practiced hand. "How did they get your design?"

She remained frozen for a moment, focused on an imaginary target. Then she lowered the weapon. "Double barrel instead of a single," she muttered to herself. She checked the magazine, then let out a low whistle. "Genius. An ecto-based core for one barrel and bullets for the other. Nine mil. Looks like you can switch between barrels to control which ammo you use. It's bulkier than mine, but this would eliminate our need to carry two—"

"Madison. How did Agent Kovak get your design?"

She stared down at the gun in her lap to avoid her apprentice's eyes. "We used to work together."

"You worked for the AGC?" he repeated in disbelief.

"Of course not," she snapped. "I worked independently. They purchased my research, and that funded my other projects. But that's ancient history. If Kovak thinks he can send prototypes and continue our previous arrangement, he's sorely mistaken."

She replaced the weapon in the case. Her eyes alighted once more on the clamp. These prototypes from the AGC were intriguing, but they weren't what Trey had gone there for. She'd have plenty of time to study the guns after Vivian was back safe and sound. She picked up the clamp again and cradled it in both palms. This little device was going to save her daughter.

Wes touched her shoulder and confided, "Maddie, ah . . . you should know we were attacked by an Alpha ghost on our way back."

"*What*?"

"Jumped on the car in the middle of nowhere when we were going ninety. How he got there and where he went afterward, I have no idea. He could have stolen that from us, but he didn't. I guess that means they're willing to trade fairly. Still, it was . . . unnerving. Trey and I didn't stand a chance. I've never been caught off guard like that."

Doc was still preoccupied organizing pill bottles while Lily approached the twins with the new clothes. "Let's try these on, huh?" she said cheerily. "We can't send you back in the rags you were wearing."

She tugged the T-shirts—one gray, the other navy blue—over the twins' heads. The jeans were more of a problem because the boys were too skinny and Wes hadn't thought to buy belts. Madison suggested rope, which was strung through the belt loops and tied tight to hold the jeans up onto their thin hips. They even had comfortable new shoes to replace the old, worn pairs. When the boys didn't even attempt to tie the laces, Shay was the one to realize the shoes from the AGC were simple slip-ons; A1 and A2 didn't know how to tie shoelaces. Each nurse knelt at each twin's feet and showed him how to do it. They were fast learners, able to tie their shoes after a single demonstration.

Doc looked her patients up and down. "Well, they look much better than they did when they first arrived," she said, nodding in approval.

Madison gazed down at the device in her hand. The voices around her were washed away in the blood pounding through her ears in time with her heart. She tightened her fingers around the clamp and raised her head. "Let's get her back," she said fiercely.

— Chapter Thirty-Nine —

Reunited

The door opened.

Vivian immediately identified the silver whistle around her visitor's neck and knew it was Jay. But something was different about the Alpha leader.

She rose warily as he approached. Usually he closed the door behind him and then hesitated as he took stock of his surroundings before coming to her. Not this time. He strode across the room with much more confidence than usual, like he was on a mission. She swallowed hard, suddenly petrified. Jay wasn't here to feed her; that much was clear. He had his hand behind his back, hiding something. Had the twins died? Was he going to kill her?

"Jay?" she asked, retreating a step. "What's going on?"

He halted in front of her, and she gazed back at him in a silent staredown. Her heart pounded. *Maybe he'll let me write goodbye to Mom*, she thought, her mind surprisingly clear when facing the end.

"Ms. Tarrow." She shuddered. "Are you ready to go back?"

Did I hear him correctly? "Back?" she whispered. A nervous laugh escaped. "I can? The twins are okay?" Jay nodded, and she stepped forward eagerly. "Yeah, let's go."

But Jay held up one hand to signal her to halt, and then he brought his other out from behind his back. Clenched in his fist were rope and a blindfold. "I'm sorry."

Vivian stared at the rope, unease forming a pit that sank into her stomach again. "That's not necessary."

"If you want to go back, it has to be on our terms."

She bit her lip and gazed at the rope again. "Okay." She held her hands out, wrists together.

426

Jay inclined his head, stepped forward, and looped the rope around her wrists. Vivian stood perfectly still while her captor tied a secure knot and then circled behind. She closed her eyes as the blindfold was draped over her face, blanketing the world in blackness.

Vivian exhaled, feeling completely vulnerable as the knot was tied. *Jay won't let anything happen to me*, she told herself. He couldn't, not if he wanted the twins back, so she surrendered herself to him when the touch of a strong hand on her upper arm gently but firmly guided her forward.

"We have a long way to travel." His voice was close to her ear as he steered her. "There are a lot of obstacles between here and our destination. You need to do exactly as we say. Got it?"

She nodded. "Stairs," he warned, his grip tightening. She slid her right foot forward until her toes touched the riser, and then she lifted her foot and set it down on the first tread. Slowly, she ascended the stairs, Jay's hands holding her steady. "Last step," he told her when they reached the top.

A draft stirred her hair. She hadn't had time to get a good look at the ground level during her escape attempt, but she knew the room was big. The building, like so many others in Phantom Heights, probably had gaping holes in the walls and roof. Not exactly the best living conditions to set up camp.

But something was wrong. It was the air. Vivian had noticed it before when Jay fell to the ground screaming and another Alpha ghost had charged in, snarling, making terrifying sounds from his throat even Wes wasn't capable of imitating. The air had been so thick she couldn't force it down her esophagus, couldn't push it from her heavy lungs. It had made the hair rise on her arms and caused goose bumps to erupt across her skin. But she couldn't remember which had come first. Had the air changed, or had Jay started screaming?

She faltered, but Jay continued to steer her forward. When he squeezed her shoulder, she stopped obediently. "Ready?" he asked.

She was about to answer *yes* when another person snapped, "I'm *not* carrying her."

"Please?" Jay implored.

"Hell no. She reeks, and I don't want her stink all over me."

Vivian bowed her head. Yes, she did reek, and she was already self-conscious about her rancid breath and greasy hair and nauseating body odor, but what could she do about it? The heat of her blush deepened when she thought of Ash and realized these guys no doubt compared Vivian to their companion. Did Ash smell as bad as she did? *Probably not*, she thought bitterly.

Jay beseeched, "Ax, just once could you please cooperate? She's safest with you."

The other ghost released his breath in reluctant submission. "*Thank you*," Jay said in exasperation as he grabbed Vivian's wrist. "Okay," he said, now speaking to her, "Axel is going to take you to City Hall. I promise he'll take good care of you." He lifted her arms, pulling her forward, but Vivian resisted. She trusted Jay, not Axel, and Axel certainly didn't sound thrilled about this arrangement.

"I'd rather walk there with you," she said, jerking out of Jay's grip.

"See?" said Axel. "She *wants* to walk."

Vivian gulped; even shielded behind the blindfold, she could feel the force of the intense glare Jay leveled in Axel's direction. He exhaled before gently explaining, "It's a long walk, Ms. Tarrow. I can't protect you as well, and there are a lot of ghosts I bet would love to get their hands on a ghost hunter's daughter. You're safer with Axel than you are with me. I'll meet you there."

"How can I be safer with him? Aren't you the leader?"

"I told you, if you want to go back, it has to be on our terms. Do you trust me?"

She shouldn't. She had absolutely no reason to trust this man, an escaped fugitive, a killer who had kidnapped her and held her hostage. And yet . . . she did.

She nodded, and then he was pulling her again. Hair tickled her skin, and then a head rose up between her arms. The ghost continued to rise, his body pressed up against her front until she was on his back, her bound hands clasped around his neck.

She anticipated breathing in Axel's scent just so she could criticize him for smelling as bad as she did. But he didn't. He smelled of the outdoors . . . and something else. Death. Blood.

His body was a rock against her stomach. She could feel strength and energy radiating off him, as though his muscles were made of steel fibers and his skin was charged with a low current that made her hair stand on end. Her stomach leapt into her throat. For one horrifying, embarrassing moment, she wondered if she was aroused by the godlike body against hers, but no, it was different. It was a fear she didn't understand, as if Jay had just placed her on the back of a panther.

"You'll be fine," Jay promised. "Arena's Honor."

"Arena's . . . huh?" she croaked, feeling weak.

Rather than answer her, he warned Axel, "Nothing happens to her."

"Yeah, yeah," Axel responded airily.

"I mean it. Don't go too fast. She better not have a scratch on her, or the humans will hunt us down."

Axel's diaphragm contracted in a hard scoff beneath Vivian. "I would love to see them try."

And then there was wind, and his muscles were moving with effortless strength. Vivian gasped; she hadn't expected the abrupt takeoff. She thought Axel would be slowed down by her added weight, but he ran as if she weren't even there. His gait was so smooth she could have sworn they were flying.

"Do you have your powers?" Vivian asked, inhaling the stench of the burning, rotting town. They must be in the middle of Phantom Heights. Where they'd come from, even which direction, she couldn't guess, which explained why Jay insisted on the blindfold. He didn't want her to find her way back.

"Shut up," Axel hissed. He paused.

"But you—"

"No, I don't have my powers, which means I can't turn us invisible, which means *shut the hell up* before they hear you and look this way. I'd rather not get in a fight with you on my back."

He sank down into a crouch, the hard muscles in his body tense.

She held her breath and tightened her hold around his neck.

Slowly, carefully, Axel eased around a corner. Vivian almost cried out in shock when he gathered himself and leapt. The air *whoosh*ed around her, roaring in her ears as gravity tried to yank her from her host.

Axel seemed to be airborne for a long time—how high had he jumped? Perhaps it was the fact she was blind and unsecured to his back that made the leap seem so perilous.

He hit a vertical surface—perhaps a wall?—and used the leverage to push off again. Vivian clenched her teeth. They must be so high off the ground now. When Axel finally landed, there was no jarring impact. He was already running, silent as a shadow. Vivian couldn't hear his footfalls, his breathing, anything. "What are you, a ninja? I thought you didn't have your powers."

Axel didn't answer. The wind was stronger here, wherever *here* was . . . Or maybe Axel was just running faster? Vivian couldn't tell; his flawless gait left her perplexed as to how fast they were actually traveling. He leapt again, although this jump was horizontal rather than vertical. "Are we on the rooftops?"

"What's a'matter, princess? Scared of heights?"

"No," she claimed, though her heart stuttered and betrayed her by racing Axel. Surely he could feel it pounding on his back.

He snickered beneath her and muttered, "Liar."

He leapt again, and Vivian sucked in her breath. She wasn't sure if she appreciated or cursed the blindfold as her imagination pictured the drop below. She felt weak and boneless when he landed again.

"You . . . you don't sound very old," she said weakly, praying Axel would engage in a conversation to keep her mind off the long drop to the ground.

"Neither do you. And you know, I gotta say, Tarrow, you ain't at all what I expected."

"No?"

"Nope. You're pretty disappointing."

Vivian stiffened, suddenly so heated that the fall didn't scare her.

She felt as if her whole body were expanding and she might just lift right off Axel's back and float like a hot air balloon. "Oh, really. How so?"

"Whoa, easy there, gem. Your blood pressure's climbing so high you might explode, and I don't think Jay'll forgive me if I bring back nothing but bloody pieces. I'm just saying, I had higher expectations, that's all."

Well, you're an asshole, Vivian wanted to fire back, but she simmered in silence to think up a more mature response. She exhaled before politely inquiring, "Then tell me, in what qualities do I fall short?"

"Beauty. Intelligence. Charm. Basically, any attractive quality."

"Yeah? Well, you aren't exactly a charmer yourself."

His shoulders heaved beneath her arms in a casual shrug. "Never claimed to be."

She muttered under her breath, "Then you're one to judge. Not like I could measure up to Ash on her pedestal, anyway."

"Oh-ho, wow. You're jealous. Ha, that's hilarious!" She could hear the smirk in his voice and immediately regretted letting that last sentence slip. She opened her mouth to deny it just as Axel warned, "Don't scream."

And then they were falling.

The shock of it took her breath away and drove the wrath right out of her mind. She clenched her teeth together so hard her jaw ached, fighting to contain the shriek that built in her throat as gravity pulled the two down, whipping her hair. Axel's cloak flapped at her sides, but he didn't seem at all panicked about the long drop. On the contrary, he chuckled, enjoying the free fall. Or he simply found her absolute terror humorous.

This landing was slightly rougher than the first one, although it wasn't the painful splat Vivian anticipated. Axel met the asphalt feet-first, crouching down on all fours to absorb the impact. Her strength gone, Vivian practically melted on his back. The ground was finally beneath her feet again, and she nearly fainted with relief.

From the shadows, I watched Axel straighten with Vivian on his back. Ash and I approached, and I noticed how hard Vivian was trembling. She was deathly white. "Moron, why don't you give her a heart attack?" I chastised.

"Jay said not to scratch her," Axel said with his usual amount of obnoxious cockiness. "He didn't say anything about her heart."

"I'm okay," Vivian croaked.

Axel knelt so I could grab her wrists and pull her arms over his head. She sank to her knees. I stared at her, realizing this was the third time I'd touched her. And she had no idea who I was.

"I don't suppose the blindfold can come off now?" she asked.

"No," Axel snapped.

"But aren't we here?"

I grasped her elbow, assisting her to her feet. Four times now, but who was counting? She was still unsteady after Axel's nosedive off the roof of a five-story building. "Yes," I told her, "but the blindfold has to stay on."

Ash strode into the dark shop, the black-and-white kitten slinking between her feet while I steered our prisoner after them. Inside, RC was sitting with his back to the wall, dozing with his head bowed. He kept muttering what sounded like, "I met . . . no . . . wait, no, I met . . ." but he never finished the thought, so I had no idea whom his fevered mind kept meeting. I directed Vivian through the maze of clothing racks while naked mannequins watched us navigate the deserted boutique.

"Hey," Ash called, her back turned to us. She was staring out a broken window to the cobblestone plaza. "The door is opening." She gasped. "I see them!"

I left Vivian—*please forgive me*—in Axel's care so I could peer out the window. The kitten was perched on the sill, gazing intently at the Dome. She peered up at me and mewed, tail twitching.

Across the plaza, figures filtered out of City Hall and emerged into the late dusk.

Holly carried the boy toward the doors. He remained perfectly still in her arms, his muscles taut, brow furrowed, as if by playing statue he could pretend she wasn't holding him. Madison was carrying his twin a few strides ahead, flanked by Cooper and Trey and trailed by Doc.

Holly had purposely dropped behind the others. She had stunned everybody by volunteering to carry one of the boys outside, but this was her last chance. Barely moving her lips, she whispered, "Let's try this again."

A1 didn't respond, and their precious time together was too short. Holly hissed into his ear, "I command you to tell me the truth. Was Cato in Project Alpha? Is he here?"

His glowing eyes locked onto hers, and this time they didn't dance away. Holly couldn't breathe. Her panic at the thought of a ghost inside her head caused her thoughts to become disjointed, but she forced the circulation to continue. *The truth. Cato. Alpha. Was he in Project Alpha?*

His voice barely above a whisper, A1 replied, "All information regarding Project Alpha is classified."

His voice was monotonous, robotic, as if he'd been preprogrammed with that response. Holly had guessed that Kovak had trained him to respond to specific commands, which was why the twins hadn't replied to anyone's gentle pleas—Holly knew damn good and well Kovak would never make such polite requests—but despite her suspicion that he wasn't mute, she gasped and almost dropped him in surprise. "I *knew* you could talk."

Doc held the door open for her. She smiled coolly and inclined her head in thanks, and as soon as she was past, she snarled under her breath, "Answer my question."

He just blinked at her, and it was too late. She was out of time. The raid team was lined up across the portico, armed and ready. Madison had already set A2 on the ground next to the stone pillar, and Cooper was reaching out to claim A1. *Yes or no*, Holly thought desperately at the kid as she transferred him into the werewolf's arms. *Give me an answer! Yes or no!*

Cooper turned away, his back shielding A1. If the boy had nodded or shaken his head, Holly hadn't seen. She backed away, bumping into Doc, who said, "Oops, sorry. Are you staying out, or going back inside?"

Holly swallowed and forced a calm smile. "I'd like to observe the transaction," she answered.

Doc closed the door. She went to her patients, and Holly crept behind the column where she could observe without being noticed.

She leaned her cheek against the cool stone, her stomach churning as she watched Madison glare across the deserted plaza beyond the transparent green shield.

The twins were alert; they gazed eagerly into the same shadows Holly eyed distrustfully. They were looking for their family.

Doc handed a small bag containing the first day's medicine to A1. "You have to follow the instructions I've written exactly. Do you understand? And come back to me in a week or so because I'll need to make adjustments to your dosages. Also, you have to make sure you both drink plenty of water, or you'll end up dehydrated again. That's very important. If you can't get clean water, contact us."

He nodded that he understood.

Doc reached out to stroke his hair, but he leaned away from her touch. She sighed and told him, "If you're sick again, or you're scared, or the Alpha ghosts hurt you, please come find us. All right?"

She straightened and glanced at the ghost hunter. "Are you ready?"

Madison nodded curtly. "I want my daughter back."

Holly lingered behind the pillar, waiting to see what demons would emerge from the shadows.

I leaned against the windowsill. The line of armed raiders hindered my view of Finn and Reese, but between the humans' legs, I could make out their glowing blue eyes searching for us. Even from the other side of the plaza, I could see their desperation, and guilt gripped my conscience. They couldn't detect us because we were just outside of their range. Couldn't risk them leading the ghost hunter straight to us like they almost did the last time we made contact. They looked almost back to normal now. They were alive and alert and seemed to be unharmed. Not a second had passed since we left them that I hadn't worried about them.

But as relieved as I was, we hadn't traded yet. Finn and Reese were still in the custody of the armed raid team and a werewolf, and there were plenty of opportunities for the exchange to go wrong. Our lab-brothers were still on the wrong side of the Dome.

Jay entered from the back of the shop. "Ready?" he asked. We exchanged looks and nodded. I took a deep breath and exhaled to calm my nerves.

Jay turned to RC sitting on the floor. "It's time for you to get into position."

Ash knelt and threw RC's good arm over her shoulder. She helped him to his feet, but he was dangerously unsteady. He swayed and mumbled something incoherent. "Come on, RC," Ash said. "You have to move the marker."

RC hung his head, his words slurring: "I just wanna sleep."

"You can sleep after," Ash promised. RC's left eye was as dull as a human's. I wasn't even sure he had enough strength to lift the marker with telekinesis.

Axel stepped forward and took over, letting RC lean against him for support. Jay asked, "You know what to do if anyone comes around the side of the building and sees you?"

"Yeah," Axel replied.

"Good. You're in charge of communicating with RC." After a pause, he warned, "And don't you dare tell him to write anything I haven't said." Axel rolled his eyes but helped RC stumble out the back way.

"Jay," Vivian whispered breathlessly, "what's going on?"

He paused to glance at our bound, blindfolded prisoner. "We're getting ready to trade you back to your mom," he answered. "Now, we didn't gag you, and as long as you don't make any noise, it won't be

435

necessary. Understand?"

Vivian bobbed her head up and down. "No noise. Got it."

Jay approached the window. Axel and RC were positioned just outside the Dome on the side of the building where RC could see through the boarded window and control the marker. "Axel, have RC tell them we have Vivian, and ask where the device is."

There was a tense pause in which the events out of our sight unfolded. Axel relayed Jay's message to RC, who used his power to make the marker move inside City Hall. Jay's words were printed on the whiteboard. After a few moments, a woman walked out and spoke briefly to the group standing on the steps. Wes frowned and followed the human inside to see for himself. He returned to whisper something in Madison's ear.

The ghost hunter glared into the darkness. Wes lingered in the doorway of City Hall, but his back was to us now because his attention was turned to the whiteboard in anticipation of our answer. Madison took a step forward and held the clamp above her head. "Here it is, as promised! Now, where is she?"

My heart fluttered. She was holding the one thing that could save RC and return our powers. Everything was at stake for us; the trick was not letting her know that.

Jay's voice was barely above a whisper, but I knew Axel could clearly hear him say, "We get our powers first. Then we trade Vivian for the twins."

I hated waiting for the message to be relayed through Axel to RC, the marker, Wes, and then finally to Madison. This method of communication was inefficient, but it prevented us from having direct contact with the livid ghost hunter who would rather shoot us than negotiate.

"I demand to see her!" Madison replied. "You don't get anything until I know she's okay!"

Jay exhaled, calculating. He stepped away from the window and approached Vivian, then turned her in the direction of the window. He set a hand on her shoulder. "Tell your mother you're all right."

She choked on a sob and called, "Mom?"

Her voice rang through the room of the abandoned building and echoed faintly across the plaza.

Immediately, Madison stiffened. "Vivian!" she called, her voice rising in desperation. She and the raiders roved the cityscape before them, vainly trying to locate the source of the call.

Madison pulled a pair of glasses out of her weapon belt and lifted them to her face. "Jay," I warned, "we're in trouble."

His grip on Vivian's shoulder tightened. "Tell her to stop. Don't use the infrared."

"Mom! Stop! Don't do that!" Vivian cried.

Across the plaza, Madison froze.

"Again," Jay whispered.

"Mom, can you hear me? Please put the glasses away! I'm okay! I'm scared, but I'm not hurt. Please do what they say!"

"That's enough," Jay said softly, squeezing her shoulder warningly.

Madison, her whole body quivering with rage, obeyed Vivian's request and slipped her glasses back into her weapon belt. "Nobody use infrared," she told her raiders. "That's an order."

Jay whispered, "That was good. Keep quiet now, okay?"

Vivian sniffed and bobbed her head.

Madison shouted, "Okay! You have my daughter, and we have the twins and your device. Let's trade now."

I glanced at Jay, my hands shaking under the stress. This was our one and only chance for a smooth transaction. Jay ordered, "Axel, tell them to throw the device on the ground."

After a moment, Wes leaned in to deliver the message to Madison. Finn and Reese looked up at her, their eyes glowing. They cowered beneath the fury of her thoughts. She yelled in our direction, "No way! Here's how we do this—we meet in neutral territory in the middle of town square for the handoff."

"That's not what we planned," I muttered.

Jay shook his head. "We'd be completely vulnerable, and there's no place to hide if they open fire on us. Ax, have RC tell them it's by our rules, not theirs."

When Madison received the message, she clenched her fists. "You aren't getting your powers before the trade!"

Jay scowled and drummed his fingers thoughtfully on the windowsill. Kit gazed up at him with her big golden eyes, ears flicking back as her tail twitched in silent inquiry. I was admittedly disheartened. "What now?" I asked.

Jay narrowed his eyes. "Ms. Tarrow, I need you to do something for me."

"What?" Vivian whispered.

"Your mom isn't cooperating. I need you to scream like you're in a lot of pain. Now, we could make the screams real, but if you can be convincing enough on your own, I don't see any reason to harm you."

Vivian nodded, considering Jay's offer. "No, *please!*" she shrieked. Her sudden outcry made me jump. She let out an ear-splitting screech. Kit pinned her ears, and Ash contorted her face at the racket.

Madison pleaded, "No, stop! *Stop!* Okay, you win! Stop hurting her!"

Vivian lowered her scream to several whimpering moans before falling silent. "Good job," Jay praised. Madison threw the clamp down the steps. It clattered through the green curtain of the Dome and settled on the cobblestones.

We waited. After a moment, the device skidded into the shadows to our left. Ash asked in confusion, "Why did RC throw it away from us?"

Jay, however, seemed to approve. "So the humans don't know where we're hiding."

Kit leapt from the windowsill and darted away to retrieve the clamp. She reemerged a minute later in her skin, the clamp sitting like a sacred artifact in her open hands. She padded straight to Jay and held it up as an offering.

Jay rolled up his sleeve. He looked at us, smiled, took a deep, shaky breath, and then attached the clamp to the metal band encircling his biceps. He flipped the latch, which turned on a red light, and then he slid the latch down until with a quiet *click*, the light went out.

Jay's eyes sparked to life, glowing silver in the dark. He pulled the clamp, still attached to the neutralizer, down his arm and held it in his hand. "I feel *good*," he whispered. He beamed as he unlocked the neutralizer, refitted the latch into position, and then tossed the clamp to me.

This was it. This was the key to the shackle I'd worn ever since Lastday when *They* put it on my arm. I fastened the clamp and flipped the latch, just as Jay had done. The red light blinked on, and the metal became warm on my bare skin. I pushed the latch down into position. When I pulled on the handle, the band loosened its relentless grip and slid down my arm without resistance.

I flexed my biceps. Strange—I felt almost naked without the neutralizer that had been a part of me for so long. A surge of power tingled through my body and recharged me like a river rushing through a parched riverbed. I was whole now. Complete.

Free.

I gave it to Ash next, but she just stood there with it in her hands. Jay looked out across the plaza to where the humans still waited with our lab-brothers. "I'll be right back," he announced, and then he was gone. I rushed to the window just in time to see a cloaked figure appear inside the Dome behind Madison, touch a hand to each twin's shoulder, and disappear again with them.

They rematerialized a few feet away. Finn and Reese were bewildered; they hadn't expected Jay to swoop in like that and bring them back so quickly. When their eyes settled on the group of us standing there, they did something I'd never seen—they smiled.

Ash, her neutralizer still active, dropped the clamp as she fell to her knees and threw her arms around them, pulling them close in a tight embrace. The twins didn't hug her back, but they didn't resist, either. They closed their eyes and bowed their heads, content just to be in our presence again.

Ash released them. "We're so sorry we had to leave you. But you know we never really left, right?"

Finn held out his hand. I reached out and accepted RC's disk from him. *That's a yes,* I thought. "Thanks, Finn."

He frowned and held up his fist with his fingers facing me. I stared at him, confused, and then I focused on his Mark—A2. "Reese?" He tilted his head at me but didn't respond. I hesitantly reached out, pulled off the hat, and set it over his twin brother's head. They nodded, confirming that I'd corrected the problem.

Knowing RC wouldn't want to carry this one since he had the other three, I slid the disk back into my thigh pouch. Jay was gazing at Finn and Reese from the corner of his eye. You wouldn't have been able to guess how distressed he'd been since we gave them up. But when I looked at Finn and Reese, they were watching Jay, and their eyes were glowing. They were smirking. Our leader could physically mask his emotions, but he couldn't hide his thoughts.

And yet, Finn and Reese hadn't spoken a word. I frowned, wondering why. When my gaze returned to our captive, I understood—they wouldn't speak in the human's presence.

I peered out the window again as Madison turned around, realized the twins were gone, and let out a cry of anguish. She dashed through the Dome and stopped, pointing her gun erratically into the shadows.

"*Where is she?*" Madison screamed. Her face crumpled as tears spilled down her cheeks. "I want my daughter! *Vivian!*"

Her haunting wail echoed across town square as armed raiders spread out in formation across the plaza. "Jay," I said, "we're a little short on time now."

Vivian flinched when Jay's hands found her hips, but he was just clasping her weapon belt around her waist. He whispered into her ear, "You may walk forward now. There's nothing obstructing your path." He pressed a stuffed bear into her bound hands and added, "It's been an honor to meet you. I'm sorry we had to put you through this."

Vivian took a hesitant step. She was leaving, and this realization shot a bolt of panic through me. I didn't want to let her go.

But she wasn't a pet or a prisoner. She'd be miserable with us, separated from the people she loved. Even if she knew who I was, that wouldn't be enough to make her want to stay.

As she walked past me, I reached across the gap and brushed the backs of my fingers across her arm, just to touch her one last time. She didn't pause when my hand made contact. She didn't even turn toward me.

I let my arm fall back to my side as she reached the threshold of the doorway. We retreated, knowing as soon as Madison caught sight of her, she'd run in this direction. I found my center—how good that felt, how natural—and the power tingled through me. I became invisible, vanishing into the shadows.

Vivian stepped through the doorway, feeling each step with her front foot before committing to putting weight down. "Mom?" she called uncertainly.

As predicted, Madison sprinted toward her daughter as soon as her eyes detected movement. "I'm right here, sweetheart. You're all right," she choked out when she drew near. Vivian halted, waiting for her mom to come to her.

The raiders converged and surrounded them. Madison pulled the blindfold away from Vivian's face and threw her arms around her daughter, sobbing with relief. The ghost hunter held her close, gripping her with strong, safe arms, then retracted so she could draw a pocket-knife from her belt and cut through the rope. She held Vivian's face in her hands, and Vivian gripped her wrists. They embraced again.

"You're safe now," Madison soothed, stroking Viv's hair. "It's all over."

Vivian buried her face against her mom's shoulder and sobbed.

Invisible, I stood in the shadows and watched the reunion, suffering hot pangs of jealousy as Vivian experienced what I could never have again—warmth and security in the embrace of a mom. I sighed and turned away.

— Chapter Forty —

Mercenaries

Holly held the filthy teddy bear between her thumb and forefinger.

"Doesn't it worry you that they know so much? How did they know where you lived? Or which room was yours? It's unsettling."

Madison snatched the bear away. "I hadn't given it much thought," she admitted.

"Oh, please," Cooper mumbled drowsily from his cot, one arm draped over his face. "If you ask any kálos out there where the ghost hunter used to live, I bet they could tell you. It's not that hard to figure out which room in the house belonged to a teenage girl, and they probably saw the bear and brought it back without knowing it had any special value."

"He has a point," Vivian acknowledged, taking the bear from her mom. Doc shined a light into her pupils.

Holly snapped back, "Madison would have been their biggest threat, and they knew *exactly* how to incapacitate her. Either they've been watching us, or somebody had inside information."

Cooper propped himself up on his elbows. "What are you implying, Holly? That one of Kovak's lab rats has been in Phantom Heights before?"

She turned away. "I don't know."

She wanted to drop it, but Cooper was intrigued now, and he sat up. "You know, that's not a crazy theory. The Rip has been here for years. It's actually very likely one or more of them came here through—"

"I don't think you should have made that deal," Holly blurted.

He stared at her, resentful at first that she'd cut him off, but then his irritation transformed into a cocky smirk.

Holly rubbed her brow and turned away. If only she could have had a few more minutes alone with A1. She knew Kovak had one person in custody who would have known exactly how to execute such a successful scheme. But . . . *no, surely not*, she tried to convince herself. Kovak would have told her . . . wouldn't he?

Holly glanced at Vivian. It couldn't have been Cato. Vivian would have recognized him. Her ignorance was proof he wasn't here . . . right?

Doc was still giving Vivian a thorough check-up while Madison hovered over the pair like a hawk. "Does anything hurt?" the doctor asked.

"Nope," her patient replied.

"Nothing at all?"

"I have never felt better in my entire life."

Doc stepped away in satisfaction. "She seems fine, Madison. Sarcasm is certainly not lacking, and there's not a scratch on her."

"But they starved her, right? Here, baby, eat." Madison held out a bowl, but Vivian pushed it away.

"I'm not hungry, Mom, and no, they didn't starve me. I'm *fine*. Promise."

"No, you're not. They tortured you. I heard you screaming."

"They just wanted you to cooperate. It wasn't real. I'm sorry."

Madison wrapped her arms around her daughter. "I was so worried about you. All I could think about was you sitting in a dark room without any food or water."

"But that's not what happened. I think I was in the basement of one of the old warehouses. I had food, water, Tessie, my favorite book . . . I got lonely at times, but Jay was good to me."

"Jay?" Madison asked as she released her.

Vivian nodded, running her thumb along her teddy bear's furry ear. "Jay is the leader. He was . . . an unexpected gentleman. He always addressed me as Ms. Tarrow, and he never hurt me, not even when I tried to escape. I actually got him to talk to me a little bit. It's so strange, how such a dangerous ghost is so scared of humans. I actually feel a bit sorry for him."

"He kidnapped you!" Madison exclaimed in disbelief.

Vivian nodded again. "I know." She sucked in a deep breath and said, "If I were dying, and the only way to save me was to kidnap someone, would you do it?"

Madison's silence was a yes.

"Then how can you blame them for doing exactly what you'd do in their situation?"

Vivian continued to stroke Tessie as she stood in front of the whiteboard. Holly also read over the list for the hundredth time.

Beneath Shannon's words, scrawled in a tighter hand, was an extra note that read:

A4 is blind

3 can pass through shield

"I didn't know one of them was blind," Vivian said.

"Agent Kovak contacted us," Madison replied, glaring at the board. "He also said three of them can somehow pass through my shield, but we didn't get any specifics before we lost the connection." She pinched the bridge of her nose. "Although they just proved that's true. Took the twins right out from under my nose. Wes? Which Divinities could breach my entoplasm shield?"

Holly turned to watch Cooper ponder. "Hmm, good question. Not many, but a few. Amínytes, I would think. Waymakers create portals between doors, so they could bypass your shield altogether. Blinking, but that Divinity is extinct. And, let's see . . . not a Shifter, but an Astral-Projector could send his astral self through. A Jumper, a Switch, and . . ." He trailed off, eyes widening.

"What?" Madison demanded.

"Well . . . Phantom could pass through." Holly caught her breath. "It's possible another half-breed like A6 could do the same. I don't know."

Holly exhaled. Vivian was lost in thoughtful silence for a moment before she uncapped a marker and added the names *Jay*, *Axel*, and *Ash* to the list on the board. She thought for a moment, then wrote *Seph* too.

"What can you tell me about them?" Madison pried. "Jay specifically. What does he look like?"

Holly didn't even realize she was biting her fingernail until the sharp pain announced the moment her teeth ripped just a little too far. She slipped the nail file out of her pocket and set to work on the jagged edge.

"I don't know," said Vivian. "I never got a good look at him."

"What about his height? Weight? Build?"

"He's about . . . I don't know . . . this high?" She held out her hand to indicate.

"Is he old?"

Vivian let her hand fall. "I don't know," she repeated.

"Guess. My age? Younger? Older?"

"Younger, I think."

"How much?"

"Ugh, Mom, I *don't know*. Maybe in his twenties? I told you, I never got a good look."

Cooper rubbed his chin. "So, twenties, you think? Did he have a beard?"

"Um . . . no, I don't think so."

"Huh. I'd guess he's somewhere between his first and second coming of age then—less than a hundred years old."

"Where do you think they'll go now?" Vivian asked as she replaced the marker. The list on the board was updated with all the information they had on the Alpha ghosts, and Holly suspected they had barely scratched the surface of these mysterious fugitives.

"They better not go anywhere," Cooper growled.

Vivian frowned. "Why not?"

"Didn't Jay tell you?" Holly challenged coldly.

Vivian faced her, genuine confusion painted across her face. "Jay didn't talk much. Why? What happened?"

"We made a deal," her mom said solemnly. When Vivian shot her a dubious look, she muttered, "Believe me, it wasn't my idea."

"Nor mine," Holly grumbled.

Cooper puffed his chest like an arrogant rooster and proudly said, "We gave them their powers. In return for daily medical supplies and protection from the Agents, they've agreed to help us reclaim Phantom Heights."

Holly rolled her eyes while Madison shook her head. They made brief eye contact—how strange to align with Madison Tarrow on an issue—and looked away.

Vivian gazed at her stuffed bear. "They actually agreed?"

Madison said, "Wes seems to think so, but I bet they're long gone by now somewhere in the Ghost Realm."

Vivian stared at the boards covering the window. Holly scrutinized the girl's features. Vivian seemed empathetic, but was there more to it? Had she grown attached to her captors during her time away? Or worse . . . had she uncovered a secret that was supposed to stay buried?

Holly turned away. She was going to have to keep an eye on the ghost hunter's daughter.

— Chapter Forty-One —

Prophecy

The fog—a curtain of cloud that dampened every surface, every noise, and shrouded the silvery trees—was so absolute the mango sky had been completely erased.

A raven cried.

The murk swirled in intricate patterns as Azar's cloak drifted through it. The fog never cleared here in the land of Evermist where vapor from the nearby geyser field wafted beneath the canopy of the eastern edge of the Grey Forest. Rayven, perched on Azar's shoulder, swiveled his head from side to side, straining to see.

The mist was alive. It roiled and churned, figures taking shape and then dissipating back into waves, haunted faces there and gone in a blink. Hæthril—spirits of those who had been forgotten in the fog.

"Are you afraid of the fay?" Azar teased when Rayven shied from the figure of a bearded man that rolled back into the mist just as quickly as it had materialized. Rayven made a rather pitiful noise in the back of his throat and hunkered low, shuffling closer to Azar's neck.

Azar paused, skimming the foggy forest for a landmark. He was somewhere southeast of Delkoa, the Second City, in the midst of the wild where packs of weirbeasts and feral Amínytes ran unrestrained. It was even rumored that nydæa wandered Evermist, although that had yet to be proven. The presence of a nydæa clan could rarely be confirmed, as witnesses almost never survived to pass the warning on. Civilization was sparse out here, although one kálos preferred to live secluded in the fog away from the constant squabbles and petty wars of the Cities. Azar needed to find her.

He pressed onward. The trees were shadowy pillars, sentinels holding down the fog with their arms and claws arching overhead. There—ahead and to the right, a dark shape loomed in the mist. Azar's cautious stride lengthened with confidence as he altered his direction toward the dwelling. As he drew nearer, the smudge took shape.

A ramshackle stone cottage, decrepit with age and neglect, was balanced hazardously on the mossy rocks. He might have thought, with its rotted shingles and grimy windows, that it was abandoned. But smoke trickled up from the chimney to meld with the fog.

Azar paused just before the door. Already ajar, it creaked open with a single touch.

The fog billowed behind Azar and rolled into the house, curling in whispering tendrils along the floor. He ducked beneath the doorframe and stood in the entryway, his gaze settling on a figure seated in a chair in the corner. She was an ancient kálos, small and frail with pale skin and snow-white hair. Allegedly she was nearly a thousand years old.

The marquise garnet embedded in the middle of her lower brow twinkled, but her eyes were closed. Her wrinkled body was draped with layers of gossamer fabric that shrouded her like the very mist surrounding her home. Azar had the brief thought that if too much fog trailed in through the open door, she might very well fade away into it forever and join the hæthril.

He hesitated, debating whether he should wake her, but then her lips moved. "The Warden's left his Prison to wander where he should not. Tell me, Shadow Lord, have you found yet what you sought?"

Her pale violet eyes opened to meet Azar's red ones. He closed the door. "I find your riddles and lyrics cumbersome. And only you can answer the question you just asked me." He tossed a drawstring pouch at her feet.

She raised her chin from her chest at the sound of the heavy coins striking the floor. A clawlike hand emerged from the shawls. She bent forward so precariously Azar feared she might fall from the chair, although he didn't move from his place by the door. "I require your Gift of Foresight."

Slowly, she straightened, her joints stiff from disuse and arthritis.

Without waiting for her response, he continued, "I need to know about the weapon in Project Alpha."

The Seer hooked one gnarled finger through the drawstring to loosen the pouch. Her hand quivered as she poured copper coins into her palm. "Generous when it suits you, though ruthless you can be. But the question you've chosen is one I cannot See. Hmm. No, the details you beseech are beyond my Divinity's reach. The Present is not in my gaze; instead I See through Future's haze."

Rayven shifted nervously on his shoulder, but Azar kept his frustration in check. "Very well. What does the Future hold if this weapon is used?"

The Seer's eyes glowed as she gazed through Time. "Triumph of the humans will be the destruction of us all. Their salvation will undo them, and both worlds will fall."

"What do I need to win the war? What is the key?"

Her knuckles popped as she curled her fingers over the copper. "Purest of demons, child of beast, harbinger of light, blinded who sees, blood of the enemy, son without wings, slaves who will rise to one day be kings. Seven to bring the Seventh, but Eight are the key. They must decide what the fate of the Realms shall be."

Azar stared at her for a long moment. What other eight could have such a devastating influence over the outcome of the war? "The Alpha fugitives."

The Seer smiled her gap-toothed grin at him. "Why ask questions of me when you already know what the answers will be?"

"What do you mean by seven? Will I defeat the Agents or not?"

"A question you asked, an answer you sought. You should be satisfied, and yet you are not."

"Because your 'answer' is a useless riddle," Azar snarled. "I paid you for information, and you've given me next to nothing."

Her hand, laden with copper, subtly disappeared into her shawls. "Such is the case, as you will see. Prophecies are worthless 'til they come to be. I remind you, Dark One, what you asked of me—like it or not, the eight are the key. The fate of the Realms will lie in their hands

. . . but I know not on which side they will stand."

Rayven squawked. Azar turned away and threw open the door. "Thank you for your time," he snapped, feeling less than appreciative now that his head was spinning. She watched him in silence, offering neither acknowledgment nor farewell. Azar returned to the wall of fog, letting it absorb him while the hæthril reached out, their cold hands passing through him.

Agent Kovak stood alone in the middle of the Alpha holding room.

He looked down at his shoes inside the tape edges of a one-foot-by-one-foot square on the linoleum. Barely enough room for his feet—a little more space for a ten-year-old's. But not much.

Alpha was quiet now, quieter than it had ever been before. A month ago, it was filled with handlers and technicians, and this room, even when his test subjects were unconscious, was never so silent. At the very least, A6's cage would hum as the electric current flowed through it, and the kids' breathing would be slow and steady. If A6 was awake, which he almost always was, he would be growling at whoever walked through the doors.

Kovak smiled faintly at the memory. Yes, A6 was an animal at heart, but there was still enough intelligence in his eyes and hatred in his snarls that Kovak had no doubt the half-breed knew exactly who was responsible for his transformation, even if he couldn't speak an identifiable language. What a pity he'd failed in Delta. And what a pity Kovak hadn't had the sense to send A6 to Project Omega instead of transferring him to Alpha. He wouldn't be in half as much trouble if he hadn't set a monster loose.

Kovak tilted his head, studying the row of cages. Byrn wanted to start recruiting new test subjects for Alpha, but Kovak was still skeptical. A1, A2, A6, and A7 were irreplaceable. The others he could continue without, but not the twins and the half-breeds. He couldn't afford to stop looking for them.

So, for now while it awaited test subjects, Alpha was quiet. Anders and a few technicians were the only ones working. They were so busy poring over the research notes and trying to restore the Grid to full capacity that they wouldn't be ready to experiment on new test subjects even if Byrn did happen to find suitable candidates in a timely manner.

Agent Kovak stepped out of the tape square and traced his fingertip across the keypad on A2's cage. "Wherever you are," he whispered to the silent room, "wherever you're hiding . . . I'm coming for you. Whether you're in this world or the other, I'm going to find you."

— Epilogue —

The green light contained in my cupped hands cast strange shadows. I tore my gaze away from the ectoplasm orb that pulsed with my heartbeat. I'd been experimenting—no, scratch that; I hated that word—*playing* with it while I sat against the wall with my knees drawn to my chest.

Ectoplasm was measured in grades. I wasn't powerful enough to reach the extremes, but I could condense and expand it between Grades C and E. Grade C—I brought my hands closer together, making the orb denser, more like a solid. Grade D, the universal neutral state—I relaxed my fingers a little and loosened the energy so it was less organized. Grade E—I pulled my hands farther apart and watched the energy pull apart too, crackling in tendrils like green lightning swirling around a void.

I parted my hands a little more. The ectoplasm snapped at the air as if to escape its invisible confines and creep back up my arms. It was closer to raw energy now. I couldn't be sure, but this might be Grade F. I couldn't remember ever being able to manipulate it this far down the spectrum before.

I cupped my hands close together, thrilled when the ectoplasm condensed into a glowing ball so tight and bright I almost couldn't see the individual tendrils making it up. Was this Grade B? Had my power really grown that much while it was locked away out of reach inside me?

I felt whole, warm, powerful. *This* was who I was supposed to be, not the empty human I was when that damn neutralizer was latched like a parasite around my arm, leeching away my power. As if I'd been sleepwalking until now, I felt alive again.

To be honest, this newfound power frightened me a little, as it had grown while I was in that place, but I hadn't had the opportunity to

452

learn how to control it yet at this heightened level. It stirred inside me like a living creature, eager to be released, intervals of warmth and cold and *energy*—raw, undulating energy. It was an exhilarating fear that made my heart race.

Finn and Reese were sleeping in the corner beneath threadbare blankets. This time, we were going to keep them safe. This I silently vowed: the doctor would never again lay her hands on them, and that bitch Madison would never harm them.

RC hadn't acknowledged them with anything more than a critical look when he and Axel returned, although I attributed that degree of indifference to his fever. Axel had greeted Finn and Reese with nothing more than a casual, "Hey, Bot, long time no see," as if they hadn't almost died but simply returned from a vacation.

A pained groan heightened in volume and pitch. RC was lying on his back, pinned down by Jay while Ash struggled to fit the clamp around the ruined neutralizer.

"Ah, you're hurting me!" he cried as it slipped off.

"I'm sorry," Ash whispered. She fumbled with the clamp.

Jay said, "If we can deactivate it, we can pull it off you."

RC moaned again. Finally, Ash snapped the edges over the torn metal and frayed wires. The red light flickered to life with a flip of the latch, and then Ash slid it into position to kill the neutralizer. She tugged the handle downward to slide the band off. This time it didn't constrict, but the injury was swollen, and RC jerked when it caught on the inflamed skin.

"Sorry," Ash whispered again, giving it a hard yank. RC yelped, but the band came loose, allowing Ash to slide it over his wrist. She held up the ruined neutralizer for us to see.

I couldn't believe it had still been operational, considering the condition it was in. The circular band was contorted into a shape that looked nothing like its original form. The sharp corners and razor edges had cut RC with every movement. Wires were exposed in some places.

Jay released RC, who lay still, panting and staring up at the holes in the ceiling. After a long minute, he turned his head to stare at his arm.

Blood and pus were seeping from the exacerbated injury. Jay dabbed the bodily fluids with a towel so Ash could slosh brown liquid from the bottle the humans had sent us, then awkwardly dress the gruesome wound. She wrapped the gauze around his arm several times to keep the padding in place. I couldn't tell how deep the wound was—hopefully mostly superficial and not too deep into his muscle—but at least it would finally have a chance to heal now that it wasn't continually being rubbed raw with every movement.

The green light called my attention again.

I stared at the ectoplasm still flickering in my hands. Grade B, if I did actually achieve that feat, was the brightest I could make, but it was draining. The energy was easiest to maintain at neutral Grade D, so I let it expand back to the middle of the spectrum. I couldn't stop marveling at the beauty of the swirling energy. It was entrancing. It was *mine*. It came from inside me, from my Origin, from my soul, I believed. I wouldn't let anyone take it from me ever again.

Ash's voice broke the quiet: "I think ice might help the swelling."

I peered up, the light from my hands throwing sharp shadows on my face to give it what must have been a haunted, terrifying appearance. Ash glanced at me, and then her gaze fell back to her work.

I rotated my hands until my right palm was facing the ceiling, the left still cupped on the side as if to shield the ectoplasm like a flame from the wind. Slowly, I pulled my left hand away, leaving the glowing orb to hover over my right palm. I took a breath and searched for my center.

Two distinct currents circulated in my core when my powers were active. One was green and hot, the other blue and cold. The latter was the one I brought to the surface. It chilled the blood from my heart to my left hand, where I channeled its intensity. This Divinity was not like the hot one that was strong enough in rage to resist the neutralizer for a few seconds and make my eyes glow green. This Divinity was rigid precision, focused and purposeful. Even with the tamed ectoplasm still in my right hand, the balance of power tipped enough for me to feel the cold wave that signaled my green left eye turning blue to match my right while they both glowed bright.

I clenched my left hand into a tight fist, willing the coldness to become tangible. My fist was forced open as the water from the air hardened into ice in my hand. It grew until I deemed it large enough, and then I opened my fingers and levitated it to Ash, who plucked the ice from the air as casually as one might pick fruit off a tree.

As the warmth returned to my blood, I felt the equilibrium return, and I knew the pigmentation of my left eye had just reverted back to its normal green.

"Jay?" Ash called quietly as she worked on RC's wound. "Are we really going to go through with this deal?"

We faced our leader. Even RC took the extra effort to turn his head toward Jay, who looked away from us to watch the twins sleep. His quiet voice somehow carried across Home: "Finn and Reese will insist that any deal we made with humankind is binding. We did give our word."

He inhaled deeply, then exhaled before he faced us again. "Their vote will count as one, and we know what it will be."

Axel replied, "Then my vote cancels theirs, because I say fuck humankind. They're on their own. I vote we leave this hellhole and go through the Rip."

"I second Axel," I announced. "I vote we leave."

Jay nodded, keeping a silent tally. Kit's ears fell. "My master is in the Ghost Realm." She drew her knees up to her chest and enveloped them in her arms. "I wanna stay here."

Axel challenged, "You're more afraid of your old master than you are of *Them*?"

Jay held up his hand. "She cast her vote. Don't try to change her mind."

His silver eyes fell on Ash, but she determinedly kept her gaze down on RC's arm as she tied a gentle knot to keep the ice in place in his bandages. "I don't know anything about the Ghost Realm," she admitted. Her eyes flicked up to Jay. "Do you?"

He didn't answer, maybe because he didn't want to influence her vote, or maybe because he didn't know, either. Her head dropped to her task again. "We'll be hunted no matter where we go. If we have to choose which enemy to face, Azar or *Them* . . . I don't know. I think we—"

"Stay or leave," Axel interrupted impatiently.

"Stay." She shot me an apologetic look and added, "Sorry."

Jay nodded. "RC?"

RC's eyes were closed. I thought he was asleep until he frowned and mumbled, "Bloody Scout, Jay, I can't even think straight right now. Whatever your vote is, double it and count it as mine too. I trust you."

Jay didn't answer. The final decision was in his hands. Phantom Heights was the only town in this Realm where we could hide. Either we stayed here and became mercenaries for humans at the risk of being betrayed, or we took our chances in the Ghost Realm, which was Azar's domain.

Jay bowed his head. I closed my hands, extinguishing the light and sealing the room in darkness once more.

To be continued

Acknowledgments

Writing is a solitary craft, but it takes a network of supporters to bring a story to life and publish a book. My thanks to:

My talented editors, Nikki Mentges and Megan Manzano, for their hard work, insightful suggestions, and keen eyes for detail. A special thanks also goes to Megan, Justine, and Ismael of the Inkwell Council for their critique.

Jason Anderson for his time and attention to detail while formatting the ebook.

Bridget Chandler and David Brauer, my first beta readers who bravely tackled the massive rough draft and helped me chisel it into a story worthy of sharing.

My creative team of cover consultants—Jo Pilecki, Sue Spitler, Joan Spohrer, and Claudia Parish. To Melissa Rendlen, thank you for sharing your well of medical expertise. My gratitude is also extended to Greg Anderson for his knowledge and assistance with the final formatting and any computer-related curveball that came my way.

The incredible mentors I've had throughout the journey! Thank you, Roger J. Kuhns, Therese Luce, Jean Bell, Shaun Mackelprang, and Ed Charlton, for taking the time to share your wisdom and experiences with me as I ventured into uncharted waters. And my eternal gratitude to the teachers in the dedication who forged me into a wordsmith and guided me down the cobblestone road.

Robert Salek, for his talents behind the camera to capture the author photograph at the iconic Michigan City lighthouse.

My friends and family—everyone who found a place in these pages—who supported me every step of the way, who cheered when I was victorious and boosted my spirits when I was low.

My early fans who appreciated my writing before I was published, and the Sandcastle Writers who lifted me up with encouragement and challenged me to keep writing. Special thanks to the Lubeznik Center for the Arts for giving us a home and a sanctuary where we can write.

Sara A. Noë is an award-winning author, photographer, and artist. She lives in a little cottage in Indiana with her cat, Calypso. Sara's writings have appeared in various anthologies and literary journals since 2005, and her photography has been exhibited in galleries and featured on the cover of *Voices* literary journal. Sara designs and creates her own book covers, graphics, and artwork for her novels.

A Fallen Hero, Book I in the Chronicles of Avilésor: War of the Realms series, has been critically acclaimed by *The Prairies Book Review*, *Literary Titan*, *NAM Editorial*, and *Chronicle Focus Editorial*, among others, since its 2018 release. The debut novel made book reviewer Lauren Gantt's Top 10 Favorite Books of 2019 list and won *Literary Titan*'s Gold Book Award in 2020.

THE STORY WILL CONTINUE WITH
BOOK II:

Phantom's Mask

CPSIA information can be obtained
at www.ICGtesting.com
Printed in the USA
LVHW031805160522
718766LV00002B/5

9 781732 599833